THANK GOODNESS FOR CHICKENS

Alice Mae

Published by New Generation Publishing in 2021

Copyright © Alice Mae 2021

First Edition

The author asserts the moral right under the Copyright, Designs and Patents Act 1988 to be identified as the author of this work.

All Rights reserved. No part of this publication may be reproduced, stored in a retrieval system or transmitted, in any form or by any means without the prior consent of the author, nor be otherwise circulated in any form of binding or cover other than that which it is published and without a similar condition being imposed on the subsequent purchaser.

ISBN
        Paperback   978-1-80031-047-6
        Ebook   978-1-80031-046-9

www.newgeneration-publishing.com

 New Generation Publishing

'Religions may begin as vehicles of longing for mysteries beyond description but they end up claiming exclusive descriptive rights to them.'
Richard Holloway, *Leaving Alexandria.*[1]

(People are tortured) '…and only for the fact that they choose a different fashion of showing their reverence, a different way of making prayer or following a different guidance to salvation. I make no sense of this. My mind fairly reels into a faint when I endeavour to unravel the nonsense of it.'
'And all and everyone convinced of their own rightness and righteousness.'
Christine Middleton, *The Witch and her Soul.*[2]

'But it's true, religion has propelled good men into vile behaviour.'
Bernard Cornwell.[3]

[1] Extract from *Leaving Alexandria: A Memoir of Faith and Doubt,* reproduced with permission of the Licensor, Canongate Books Ltd, through PLSclear. Copyright © Richard Holloway 2012.

[2] Extract from *The Witch and her Soul* by Christine Middleton, 2012, with permission from Palantine Books.

[3] Bernard Cornwell 11/10/20, personal correspondence.

To my Family

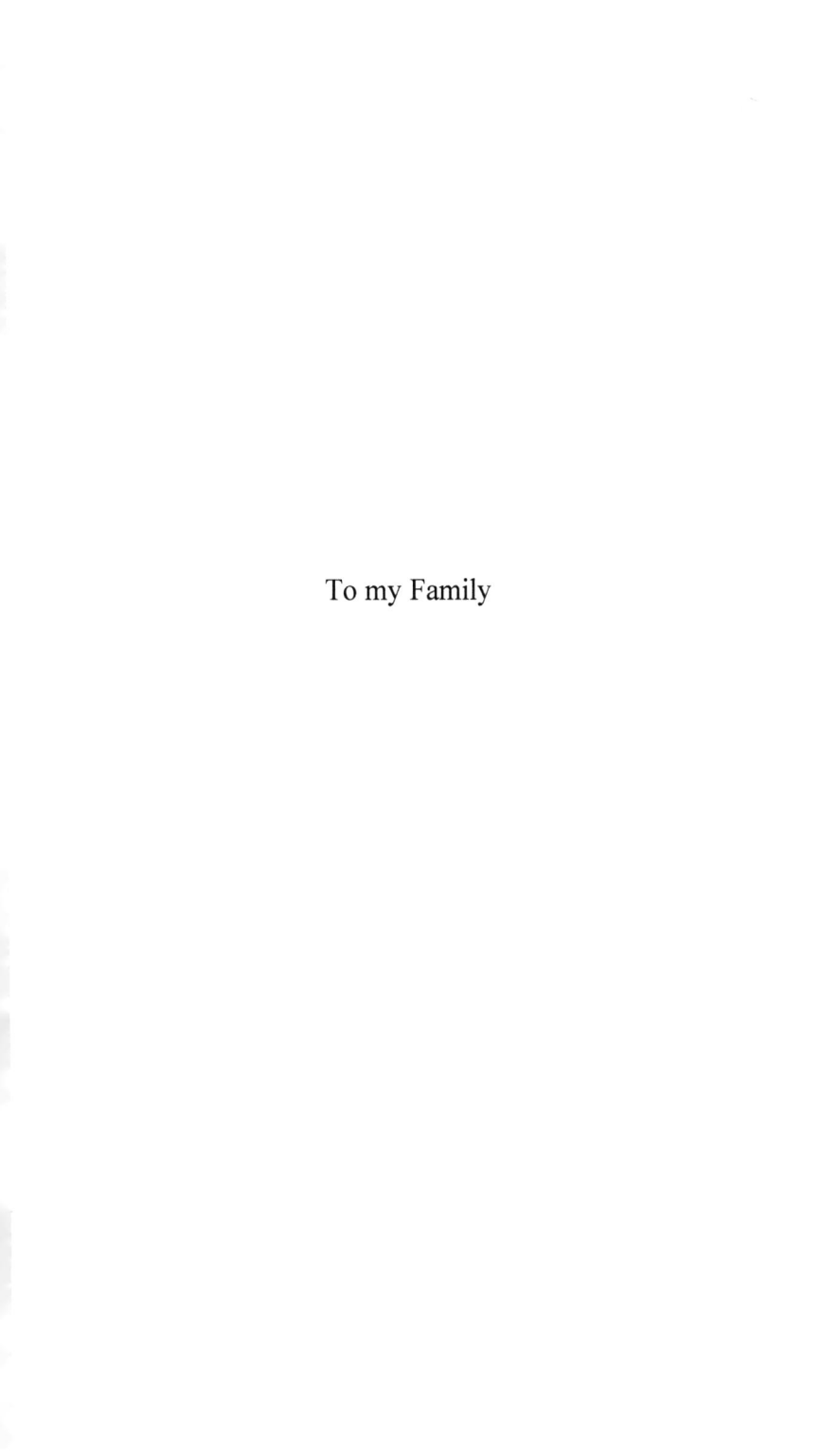

POLLY'S INTRODUCTION

My best friend's father was dying, but she said: 'It'll be alright because God loves us and Daddy is going to live with Him in a wonderful place called Heaven.' We were playing with our dolls. As I didn't have the faintest idea who or what God was, Beth invited me to her Sunday school where I could learn about Him and hear stories from the Bible.

One of the first stories I remember was about two men, one built his house on sand and the other on a rock. The sea washed away the house on the sand, but the house on the rock stood firm. Mrs Holland asked: 'Are you building your house on the rock or on sand?' I wanted to make sure my house wasn't going to be washed away, so went the following Sunday to find out more. One thing led to another.

At the same time my parents sent me to a Roman Catholic Convent School where I was taught by nuns. Their religious teaching contradicted my Sunday school lessons and there came a time when I had to choose between the two.

We lived next door to a Roman Catholic family, the Wheelers. They lived in 'The Elms' which we called the 'Big House' because ours was much smaller and uniform with the others in Elm Close. Mr Anthony Wheeler, son of (The Late Mr) and Mrs Wheeler, was probably about ten years older than I. He was unusual, I'd heard about his gruesome art, and felt a bit scared of him.

We were walking home after the funeral of Mr Wheeler's mother, Mrs Florence Wheeler…

CHAPTER 1

Late 1940s – 1950s

'So, is Mrs Wheeler's soul in Purgatory or not?'

'Oh, Polly *do* shut up.' The long Catholic funeral service had been torture for Victor and he felt stupid wearing his new black suit. The way Polly skipped every now and again annoyed him.

'What does it matter anyway?'

'But at school they say we should pray for Mrs Wheeler's soul so she doesn't suffer so long in Purgatory. Then at Sunday school Mrs Holland says Purgatory doesn't exist, and we're either saved and go to heaven, or not saved and go to hell forever and ever.' She shuddered. 'Imagine. Everlasting fire!'

'We're there now with you going on like this,' Vic whispered, scowling. Polly pushed him in the road.

'Stop it you two. Just *stop* arguing.'

'But is…'

'Polly! Keep quiet!'

'See…' said Vic in his I-told-you-so voice.

The truth was James and Vera had no idea how to answer Polly's questions. They'd been to weddings and funerals, had their children christened in the Church of England, and quite liked the vicar who visited occasionally. But they hadn't really thought much about what it all really meant. Now Polly kept asking questions about things she was learning it was awkward. James hoped she'd lose interest in religion before long.

Ever since the coffin arrived at the church, Vera had been sniffing and blowing her nose. She wiped her tears away with her best lacy handkerchief. 'I *do* miss Florence,' she whispered to James as they walked up to their gate. She stared sadly down the drive of The Elms. *Florence is not there anymore. Oh dear.* He put his hand on her elbow and guided her to their front door.

'But you hadn't known her that long, and you had virtually nothing in common.'

'I know, but we were friends, and shared how we felt about things.'

'You enjoyed the luxury, didn't you?'

'I suppose that as well, everything round there is so much nicer than at ours and she used to explain all about their beautiful pictures: the artists and so on. And I learnt about their church. They're very devout, you know.'

'Did she ever say anything about her son's painting?'

Vera looked worried and put her hand to her mouth, turning to see if the children could hear: 'She admitted she didn't like it, and that he wasn't the son she'd dreamt of having. And she didn't think he'd ever get married.'

'But round at the Broken Gate they say he paints really odd stuff. Repulsive, in fact. Dismembered bodies – and it's all rather grim.'

Vera took sharp breath in, 'No, she didn't exactly say that; only that she didn't like them.'

James shook his head wanting to close the subject.

'But… do you think we should start saying grace before meals, James?' He pursed his lips and screwed up his face.

'Not you *too*!'

*

At The Elms the following day, Anthony Wheeler and his Uncle Henry were breakfasting in the dining room. The white linen tablecloth had not been changed since the wake. Martha the housekeeper was tired. 'I'll bring coffee, sir,' she said looking around at all the discarded table napkins and glasses. 'Sorry things aren't quite ship-shape yet.'

'You should have a couple of days off,' said Henry, who had taken charge since he arrived. 'We'll manage, won't we Ant?' Anthony grunted. *Why doesn't he call me Tony? What would he think if we called him Hen?* Before his mother's death, he had decided to vent his annoyance by painting a triptych. The first panel would be a large chicken pecking around eating ants; the second, the chicken sliced in half so you could see what was going on inside: hundreds of live ants eating through the lining of the chicken's stomach; in the third, the chicken would have ants coming out of its eyes, beak, and all over its body. Every time he was called 'Ant' these images came to his mind. *As a sort of revenge, I suppose. But will I ever get round to painting it?* Henry, his late father's brother, was rather overbearing, bossy, and unrefined but Anthony needed his help. He looked around. *Mother would never have agreed to this mess even for two days. But she's… dead.* He stared out of the window and into the distance. *Oh Mother…* He rallied himself and looked at Martha.

'I'll t-take coffee upstairs please M-Martha.'. He looked at Uncle Henry, 'I-I…' but he padded into the hall and went upstairs to his studio. Henry watched the sad, round-shouldered figure until he disappeared. *So unassertive, no bloody get-up-and-go. Whatever will become of him?*

From his comfortable swivel-chair Anthony could see through the window down the garden. Archibald, his beloved cat, was prowling amongst the shrubs. Having drained his breakfast cup, he pushed himself round to face inside the room and study his paintings... *I see touches of Salvador Dali there. Yes, is it the same disorder of the brain... or... just that nothing really fits?* Recently he had spent hours on a large canvas with images that might puzzle a stranger but meant something deep in him: an opaque expression of desire. Dark figures entwined with each other, their action veiled by strategic materials and misshapen limbs. Anyone accusing him of depravity could in turn be accused of echoing their own thoughts. Their own *depraved* thoughts. One word would do: '*Abominamentum.' That's the title*. All his outrage and wretchedness could be poured into that one word: 'abomination.' The verse in Leviticus was one of the very few that described a man lying with a man rather than a woman. It was, unfortunately, the root of a belief held by millions: that man lying with man was a sin of grave depravity.

Why can't I be myself at home or church? He wanted to cry out, but remained silent. *I want to escape myself. MOTHER!* screamed his head. *Why did you insist I should behave like a man?* Then in a quieter voice he spoke aloud: 'Why wouldn't you even talk about it?' He was afraid to talk about his attraction to men... He lied to the priest in the confessional who absolved his sins. The guilt remained because he could not conquer his overwhelming desire.

He got down on his knees facing his painting, then lay face down on the floorboards. 'Holy Mary pray for me!' It was partly a prayer and partly a cry from the heart. A sharing of Christ's agony in the garden. 'Let this cup pass from me,' he prayed, then added 'Mary, Mother of God, hear my prayer.' He banged his head on the floorboards, and sobbed.

Henry called his name loudly up the stairs, 'Anthony!' There was a pause. 'Let's go into the garden and talk!'

Anthony did not reply. He remained prostrate.

Gone to sleep? Henry wondered. He made another coffee and sat down alone in the kitchen. Martha had jumped at the opportunity for time off. He studied his surroundings carefully, and for the first time since Florence died, started thinking. *I survived the war. Was lucky. Escaped injury and returned home fit. Can't forget those men I killed. Their bodies – faces, limbs, stomachs… ripped apart.* He shuddered and closed his eyes. He imagined his older brother, Ant's father, plummeting to the ground, his plane in flames… and now, his sister-in-law – gone too.

He was, however, a robust type. Stiff-upper lipped with no time for emotions… normally. He rejected his parents' Roman Catholicism in his early teens and made the best of life, enjoying its opportunities with the lads. He opened an antiques shop, about fifty miles from Halebridge, which was closed during the war but it had been thoroughly secured and was up and running again now. All good. Apart from Gus his only son. He was a tear-away.

His mind dwelt on his nephew. *I've always wondered what's wrong with him. Have to see if we can have a chat before I go home.'* He looked around and started to realise how much there was to do. They'd seen Florence's will, and he was surprised to learn that The Elms had been left equally to Anthony and himself. *Yes, after all, what would Ant want with a great big place like this? Surely he won't live here all by himself. Let him rest today – he obviously doesn't feel like talking. But cards must be laid on the table soon.* Just now though, he was pleased to have time to himself. He found a loaf in the larder, made a sandwich, picked up the telephone and phoned his wife at home.

She was understanding. 'Do what you have to do, honeybunch.'

He put the phone down and relaxed. Eating his sandwich, he started going round the house observing the furniture. *That crucifix! Wouldn't suit me. Gruesome!* It reminded him of his childhood revulsion when told that his first communion wine literally turned into blood. Everyone else in the family seemed to get a sort of comfort from it. *Ant can keep that.* He strolled into the garden where Archibald was lying stretched out in the sun. *Pity Bee and I can't enjoy the countryside together today.*

After taking his time admiring the fruit trees, he looked in the garden shed and his eye fell on his brother's gardening boots. Uncharacteristically, he suffered a sharp pang of sadness and tears welled up. *Riss's boots.* Standing there already to slip on when he go back from the war. Horace's love: the garden. He employed a gardener, but would still come out, put on his boots and dig. 'Good exercise', he said. Memories flooded back… not only of Riss in the garden, but all sorts of childhood experiences. There had been no goodbyes. *What a bloody awful death.* He grimaced and shook his head.

He closed the shed door with deliberation, lingering with his fingers on the handle for a while. *I can close the shed. But I can't close out Riss. You Wally!* He chastised himself. *I'm turning into a bloody wimp – like Ant.* He sat on a rotting wooden bench, which creaked with his weight, and put his head in his hands. Up to now Henry had been unable or unwilling to face up to the flames engulfing the diving plane that killed his brother. *Yes... I miss you, bruv! Flames? What did they do to you? How long did you hurt?* He was still brooding when he sensed movement. He opened his eyes and looked towards the shed. *Am I going mad?* The door had swung open. *Was that a hand on my shoulder? Is that comforting feeling real? Is it... is Riss telling me he's at peace?* Or was the breeze playing tricks with his imagination? He was close to weeping. He closed the door again and caught himself in time. He was not going to cry. But he felt comforted and knew Riss was alright now, and also he needn't worry about Anthony. At twenty-one his nephew was old enough to make his own way in the world. Henry sat down, head in hands, letting his thoughts wander.

*

Anthony got up from the floor. The release of emotion had removed the tension and he felt calmed. His thoughts were clear and he was determined: I'll never give in to the flesh. *No, NO, not ever.* He reversed his painting to the wall.

He dusted off his trousers and looked out of the window. Spring was in the air. The heaviness of his mother's death and his father's absence both weighed down on him, but he felt a freedom. The garden was full of promise and, beyond that, he would make his own choices.

Then he saw Henry, face covered in his hands. *Ohhh – so he is vulnerable...*

He went downstairs and walked outside. Archibald was sunning himself and he wandered over to pick him up, aware of disturbing him. But the cat rested happily on Anthony's left arm, with front paws over his shoulder. Purrrrrr. 'Come on my boy,' said Anthony gently, moving towards Henry's bench and absentmindedly testing it to see whether it would take his weight. He couldn't remember the last time it was used. He sat down setting Archibald on his lap, enjoying the feel of stroking the fur, the contented purring, the sun shining on his face.

Henry looked up and stared straight ahead. Anthony remained soothed by Archibald. One of the hens next door started squawking loudly and the cat pricked up his ears.

'Another egg,' said Henry.

'I'm going to j-j-join the Brotherhood of St Martin's.'

'You're WHAT?' Henry was staggered by his nephew's sudden declaration... so determined.

'I'm g-going to join the B-brotherhood when we've got all this s-sorted.'

You could have heard a pin drop.

Just the faint smell of blossom, occasional chicken-talk, purring, the rustle of the breeze in the leaves, birdsong.

Anthony had been contemplating this ever since his father was killed but it was only recently he had been accepted by Saint Martin's Monastery. Although not at ease living with his mother, he'd determined to stay at home while she was still alive. This was the first time he'd mentioned it to family, so no wonder his uncle was surprised.

Henry didn't take long to realise the idea suited his nephew more than anything else he could think of. Yes, he would fit nicely into those surroundings and that life. It was the last thing he would choose for himself, but Riss and Flo had both been devout and would approve. Yes. it would suit the family down to the ground.

He turned to his nephew who was still quietly engrossed in Archibald. Then he gave him an enormous slap on the shoulder and boomed out, 'Well said, my boy! I'm with you all the way!' His face was wreathed in smiles.

The sudden movement startled the cat who shot off into the shrubbery.

Anthony had a violent coughing fit and rubbed his knees where the claws had dug in.

The bench started creaking and then collapsed in the middle.

Anthony's wire-rimmed glasses hung off one ear and he fell towards Henry. They landed entangled, all arms and legs, with Henry underneath.

The cock next door crowed loudly and long, joining in the mayhem.

Henry's laughter was uncontrollable and infectious and Anthony struggled to free his limbs and get up. But suddenly his built-up tensions started to escape. Strangely, he allowed himself to laugh too. *So that's what it's like to laugh.*

It would be many years before he laughed, properly, again.

CHAPTER 2

The telephone rang in the West's house. 'Hello, Halebridge 2479, Vera West speaking.'

Anthony's hesitant voice was unmistakable: 'Oh, h-hello Mrs W-west, this is Anthony. I wonder if I c-could c-come and have a w-word with you?'

'Hello Anthony. Yes, yes, of course. When would you like to come? Is there anything we can do?'

'Umm, a-actually,' he hesitated. 'Yes, I have a f-favour to ask of you and P-Polly.'

Vera hadn't spoken to Anthony since the funeral, but Martha, the housekeeper, hinted she might be out of a job soon and Eli the milkman said he'd heard the place was being sold.

'You sound bothered. Is something wrong?'

'I-it's, um, Archibald. I don't w-want to leave him with a st-stranger.'

'*Archibald*? Why don't you come around for a drink? Bring your uncle if you like.'

'Thank you. He's g-gone now; is six, s-six o'clock a good time?'

'Six o'clock, Yes, yes.' It wasn't likely that James would be in, so she'd have to manage by herself. *But it's only Anthony. 'Do come.'*

Vera dashed to the best room, flicked a duster around, set the cushions straight, dived into the kitchen and tidied the dresser. *Perhaps James will be early tonight. You never know.*

Promptly at six o'clock there was a knock on the door. Polly got there first: 'MUM!' she shouted, not sure whether to smile, looking at Anthony wondering as usual what to make of him. He, unusually for him, smiled at her, before hastily lowering his gaze. Vera rushed from the kitchen. *How shall I tackle this without upsetting him? Step carefully now and think before you speak*: 'Anthony! Do come in.'

'Hello Mr Wheeler.' Polly, thin, active, curly brunette, was full of curiosity and determined to find out what was going on. She was unsure of her next-door neighbour after hearing about his paintings. He gave her another quick smile. *What does he want? He never normally looks at me.*

'What will you have to drink? Sherry? Wine?'

'C-c-cup of tea would be fine, p-please, Mrs West. I thought um…'

'Do sit down.' Vera indicated a chair. 'Polly! Make two cups of tea.'

Polly kept her eyes on Anthony. Vera stared hard, 'Now!' Polly scuttled into the kitchen.

'How are you getting on, Anthony? We hear the house is sold.'

'Urr-uuh, you know already?'

'Yes, Eli said that Martha said,' she put her hand to her mouth, feeling guilty realising she'd been gossiping, 'well, we were surprised. We didn't see a board or anything.'

Victor entered the kitchen just as the kettle boiled. Polly whispered urgently, 'Mr Wheeler's in the best room with Mum. Go and listen while the kettle makes a noise.'

'What's going on?'

'Just *do* it.'

'What does that wimp want?' Victor lingered. 'And don't be so *bossy*.'

'We'll never know if you don't go and listen, ass-head. Go on!'

She pushed him in the back, and looked for the biscuits. Victor crept upstairs and hung over the banister. Vera was asking all sorts of questions about the sale of the house and the new people coming in, and it took such a long time for Anthony to answer that Victor wasn't catching anything interesting. *Why doesn't Mum shut up?*

Polly carried the tray into the best room, and put it on the coffee table.

'Sugar cubes, Polly?' reminded Vera. 'And then feed the chickens.'

'Can't I...?' She peeked at Anthony but he was gazing at the floor.

'No!'

Eventually Anthony managed to tell Vera the reason for his visit.

'Urr... I know P-Polly loves Archibald and I can't t-take him where I'm going.'

This is it. Victor, two years older than Polly, strained to hear.

'Oh?' Vera hesitated, puzzled.

'Y-yes. We've s-sold the house, and I'm joining the B-Brotherhood of, umm, St Martin's – in the West Country.'

'Are you?' asked Vera, her mouth hanging open, eyes wide. *What a drastic step.* Nobody had hinted... 'You mean you're going to become a monk?' Forgetting her manners, she made a sort of whistling sound with her tongue curled behind her teeth. Victor had to restrain himself. His suspicions about young Mr Wheeler took on a different light. *Phew! Wait till I tell my mates.* His imagination ran wild with all sorts of scenarios, none of which had any basis in fact.

'Y-es. I was thinking about it before M-mother died, but I c-couldn't leave her. I can't take Archibald. Is there any ch-chance at all that P-Polly could look after him for me? I've seen them playing in your, garden, and they seem to like each other.'

This was a long speech for Anthony and he seemed relieved at the end. 'I hope you don't mind my asking. It's a big request I know but s-since you and Mother became friends, I thought you wouldn't m-mind.' He repeated himself a few times, feeling guilty asking. Everything else had been found a home except dear Archibald.

Thank goodness Polly isn't here. 'Ohhh...' Vera drew out the one word carefully, unsure how to reply. Not only was Anthony going to become a monk, which was enough to take in, but the Wests might find themselves looking after a cat. Polly would be insufferable if they refused. *I can't say yes, can I? Can I say 'no' though?* She couldn't think straight. Anthony was, as usual, studying a tiny speck on the carpet. But his face was flushed and he seemed to have a tremor in his right knee.

Victor weighed up how to tell Polly. *The weird lifestyle choice is OK. But the fur-ball?*

'Of course, we'll think about it, Anthony,' said Vera. 'She certainly does love him. I'm glad you felt you could ask. But, as you say, it's quite a big thing, so I'll ask James and see what he says. I really don't know what he'll think. But I'll ask him, yes. I won't say anything to Polly yet.'

'Of course, Mrs W-West, I quite understand.'

'So, when are you going? Soon?'

'Next week a-actually, Mrs West. Yes, it's next week.'

'Goodness me, so soon? So soon? We'll have to get our thinking caps on!'

Anthony hastily finished his tea and moved forward in his chair. 'Thank you so m-much, Mrs West. Thank you s-o much.' He stood up, looking disappointed. 'I'm s-sorry if I've burdened you. I expect M-Martha or Eli will help me out but I thought of P-Polly first.'

Victor quietly went to the kitchen door then belted down the garden to find his sister who'd be all ears.

'What d'you find out? What's happening?'

'Mr Oddbin's only going to become a *monk*!'

'Not ever get married?'

'Nope, s'pose not. Blimey, what a weirdo.'

'And what else?' she asked, willing her brother to say more.

'Here we go,' thought Victor. 'What's it worth?' Polly recognised her brother's bargaining game.

'Go *ON*, Pig!' She swallowed her annoyance. 'Tell me.'

Vic relented. 'He wants you to take on the precious Archi.'

Polly was wide-eyed. 'FLUFFY? Yipeee!' She took a running jump onto the rope hanging from their swing-tree, let it pendulum then jumped down and for once in her life gave Vic a big hug – much to his disgust.

He pushed her away. 'Wait, wait, *wait.*' The way she jumped to conclusions was so childish. 'WAIT!'

'What?' said Polly staring at him.

'Mum said she didn't know.'

'*What*?' Polly repeated, impatient. 'What do you mean?'

'Poor old Mum didn't know what to say. She was waiting for Dad to get home. He must have missed his train.'

*

Three days later Polly ran to answer the door to Anthony who was standing there with Archibald in his arms. Her eyes shone.

'MUMMMM!' called Polly, 'It's Mr Wheeler.' Vera threw her apron in the larder and came dashing out.

'Come in, come in! Do come in, Anthony.' He stepped over the threshold, restraining Archibald from escaping.

'Are all the doors closed, Polly?' Vera looked around nervously. 'We'll keep him in the kitchen to start with.' Anthony agreed with a grunt and let Archibald onto the floor. The cat slowly looked around hesitating with each step.

'Thank you so much, M-Mrs West.' Anthony explained about feeding and the vet. He gave them a bag of cat-food which would a few days. They watched Archibald investigate.

Anthony felt around in the bag and found a present. 'I'd l-like you to have this as a little reminder of our f-family.' He gave a rare smile then diverted his attention to the cat as Vera unwrapped a small picture.

'That's beautiful!' she said. Polly strained to look. *Not what I imagined.*

'Did you do that?' Polly asked. Anthony had framed a verse of decorated calligraphy for them. He was pleased Vera and Polly appreciated it.

'I did. *Gloria Patri et Filio et Spiritui Sancto*,' he said. Polly noticed he didn't stutter. '*Glory be to the Father and to the Son and to the Holy Ghost*,' Anthony translated reverently. He moved towards the door: 'I-I m… m-must get back.'

'Not even a cup of tea?'

'I'm… must go.'

Polly could see he was upset. Before he got to the front door she ran over and took hold of his hand for a moment.

'Don't worry, Mr Wheeler, he'll be really happy here!'

'Thank you so much!' said Vera, holding the picture up to the wall at the bottom of the stairs. 'I'll ask James if we can put it here.'

Anthony declined to look at the chosen spot and left as quickly as he could. His hands and arms felt empty as he walked up the drive of The Elms and opened the heavy front door. Inside, the sound of his footsteps echoed around the hall. He reminded himself that Archibald belonged next door, taking comfort from the feel of Polly's hand in his. *He'll be all right. God has called me to dedicate myself to Him.* But his trust in God didn't extend to his emotions. He was bereft. Another big hole in his life. Archibald gone. His paintings were of course also gone… still his but packed into crates, not likely to be seen again for years – if ever. Henry had reluctantly agreed to store them for him. He was leaving a few items for the Gristwoods so there was nothing left to do: kitchen equipment, wardrobes and curtains remained. Martha would keep a key and look after things until the new owners moved in. Henry would take him to the monastery in his Rolls Royce. *Not how I imagined starting my new life.* The arrangement was convenient, so Anthony considered it his last taste of luxury.

Doubts suddenly crowded into his mind. He closed the front door and reminisced. *I've always had everything I needed.* He hadn't even felt deprived during the war. On top of that he had no need to work. It was surprising what money could do if you knew people, and his parents had kept a wide circle of friends. *Will I manage? I'm used to comfort and now I've given nearly everything away.* He was donating his share of money from the house to the brotherhood. Henry had almost stripped The Elms bare when Anthony told him he wouldn't keep anything apart from his paintings and the *Canaletto* from over the dining-room fireplace.

'I've l-loved that all my l-life,' he told Henry as they were taking it down. His uncle, who only saw it in terms of value, responded with an exaggerated sigh.

'It can go in storage along with your baffling artwork.'

He peeped at his nephew to register his response, but Anthony missed the comment. *I'm sure God understands. Yes. God understands. Only these few things.* They closed the car boot, Henry got in and drove off.

'Holy Mary, Mother of God, pray for us sinners now and at the hour of our death, amen.' Anthony uttered the words without stutter as he walked back inside. He looked round the empty hall. Crucifix gone. Walls bare. Nothing left of 'home'. *Worldly goods will perish and pass away.* He took out his rosary, finding comfort in Mary's intercession.

He wandered around upstairs feeling only space, and recalling memories of his childhood and teens. He sighed, looked at his watch and realised Father Alphonsus would be expecting him for supper. Accommodation had been offered at the clergy house for the last evening. It was about a twenty-minute walk away from The Elms.

'Be sure the devil will tempt you,' Father Alphonsus warned as they conversed in the lounge after a communal meal. 'It is a life of self-denial and sacrifice and Satan takes every opportunity to prevent the devout from following Christ.' He crossed himself as if to protect from evil influence.

Anthony also crossed himself. His stomach tightened. After a time, he managed to say 'I-I-I know.' He could only study the ground. He looked up at his mentor, briefly, then said, 'Y-yes.'

The ensuing silence was interrupted by the telephone ringing. Alphonsus lifted the receiver. 'Henry? Yes. Anthony? Yes. He's right here.' Anthony stood, blushing, and accepted the telephone, clearing his throat.

'Still alright for tomorrow, my boy?' Henry's voice boomed down the line. He was in his usual ebullient mood which clashed both with Anthony's feelings and the atmosphere of the house. He felt bereft already and dreaded the drive to Devonshire. *I must be thankful.*

'Th-thank you, Uncle. Yes, thank you. I'll be ready early. No, nothing else, thank you. Yes, Ar... Archibald has gone. Yes, I miss him. No, I c-can't take him. Yes, he'll be all right. S-see you tomorrow.'

*

He had breakfast at six, said his goodbyes immediately afterwards, and walked back into The Elms. Inside, he looked for a map, but of course the shelf was empty. He reminded himself to leave Martha last minute details. In the dining room the bare space over the fireplace loomed large. The *Canaletto* had a special place in his heart. He had holidayed twice in Venice but more than that he'd always faced it while dining for as long as he could remember. In winter, with logs burning in the grate below, it was, to him, a symbol of comfort. He had no idea of its value nor was he interested.

He walked round the rest of the ground floor thankful much of the kitchen furniture and equipment was being left, so that room at least had a modicum of homeliness. Martha would continue using the saucepan, kettle, table, and a chair until the new people moved in. *I suppose it is like second home to her.* He checked the larder. *I wonder what she'll do. I must ask.*

He went outside into the garden and suddenly realised how lovely it was. Fruit trees, flower beds nicely laid out and tended by Sid. The smell of freshly mown grass. *Oh yes! Pay Sid. Ask Martha to give him his money.* He imagined them sitting in the kitchen talking about old times. He strolled down to the end of the path and noticed tree branches inter-tangled with branches from next door. *I've never noticed those before*. He passed the shed and collapsed bench. Thinking back, it came to him just how much of a surprise his news must have been to Henry. His lips curled up as he recalled the sudden drama brought about by Henry slapping his back. *That hurt!* He even chuckled. He picked up a piece of the rotten wood and examined it more closely. Riddled with woodworm, and crawling with ants and woodlice. *How did it stand our weight at all*?

Anthony dropped the wood and the replay began. Archibald was on his lap settling to a quiet snooze: *there was Uncle Henry sitting beside us in a morose mood. Why was he so glum? He must have closed the shed door because it had been open for years. I told him about going into the monastery and we were silent. Then came the booming voice and cheerful slap on the back! Archibald shot off my lap and hid; I started coughing and couldn't stop; the bench creaked and split in the middle. We found ourselves leaning towards each other until the bench broke completely. He went down first, and I fell on top of him. I couldn't get off him for a long time. He started to shake with laughter and that's what started me off. I couldn't seem to help it.* Looking back from this distance and seeing himself in such a ridiculous situation, he saw the funny side again. His mouth turned up at the corners.

True to word Henry arrived at the appointed time impatient to get going. Anthony didn't want to rush. *Good-bye dear home. I couldn't possibly stay here alone. I've got a completely different home waiting for me.* He slammed the door trying to drown Henry's, 'Come on. Come ON!'

The journey was uneventful. Fortunately, his uncle didn't chat all the way. He seemed occupied with his own thoughts. 'Gus worries me,' he said at one point.

'I haven't seen him since M-Mother's funeral,' said Anthony. 'I thought he l-looked all right then.'

'He was subdued, but he gambles and drinks... no holds barred.'

'I'll remember to pray for him.'

'That'll do him good,' said Henry sarcastically. A conversation-stopper.

Henry drove the Rolls to the front door of St Martin's and they both alighted. Anthony stumbled slightly and found his knees were wobbly. He lifted his small suitcase from the boot and focused his mind briefly, staring at the ground. Henry wasn't sure what to do – whether Anthony wanted him to go in or not – but before he made up his mind they heard the rattling of keys and a lively little man in old work clothes darted out of a side gate.

'Hello. You must be the new initiate? You're early. Father Brendon asked me to look out for you. This way.' He pointed to a large door, and spoke quickly as he led the way. 'I'm Tom, the odd-jobber. The brothers are spending today in prayer and fasting. I'll let you into the entrance hall.' He fished a key out of his pocket and opened large old wooden door. Anthony shifted his gaze from the ground to Tom to the door. His mood lifted when he realised it was a bigger and older version of the one at home.

'I'll leave you here, Ant. I don't think there's anything I can do. This place gives me the creeps. More driving now.' Henry turned towards the car. The thought of going inside that door, wondering what to talk about was totally out of the question. *Now! No fuss.* They shook hands.

'Th... th-tha—,' but before Anthony could finish, Henry butted in.

'So, this is it! Farewell, brother,' he said, tongue in cheek.

Typical, all bonhomie but doesn't know what to say really. Just go please. He tried again. 'Th-thank you for the l-lift. I'll be all right.' They shook hands again and, without further ado, his uncle got in the car as fast as he could while Anthony followed Tom into the building. When he looked around, the car was gone.

He found himself in a large wood-panelled entrance lobby, again similar to home, with three wooden upright chairs on each side against the wall. A statue of Saint Martin, patron saint of people of mixed race, was high on the left-hand wall, and the praying Virgin Mary knelt in an alcove on the right. Facing the entrance was an archway with a sizeable crucifix above. The stone floor led out through an archway into a quadrangle surrounded by cloisters. In the centre a fountain played. Tom indicated a chair. 'Sit down. Father Brendon will be here at five o'clock.' He turned to go. 'Must help Father Vincent with the chickens.' As Anthony nodded, a picture of Vera flashed into his mind, which briefly amused him *don't tell me, 'eggs!'* – something familiar. He looked at his watch, back at the floor, then thought of Polly and Archibald. Quarter to five. He looked around. *Austere.* He took a deep breath, shifted in his seat, looked at the fountain. *The soothing sound of water. Mary, Mother of God, pray for me.* He took out his rosary, another comfort. Feelings of uncertainty swirled through his mind instead of prayers. Mechanically he fingered the beads recalling the way Father Alphonsus smiled thoughtfully the first time he divulged his intentions. As they talked, yes, he had felt reassured. He loved serving his church; the ritual, being an altar boy, the depth of meaning in the catechism. He straightened his back, put his rosary away and took out his Missal, his most treasured possession since given to him at his first communion. *I can live amongst people who share the faith. I can live the life... although – God is all-important, isn't He?* He closed his mind on doubts. A bell tolled. Father Brendon walked slowly through the archway. 'Welcome Anthony! Keeping your mind occupied while you wait?'

Anthony stood. 'I-I only j-just…' It took him so long to get out his sentence that the monk anticipated what he was going to say.

'You'll need to contemplate these things in your new life, Anthony.'

Father Alphonsus had introduced Anthony to the Abbot soon after learning his intentions. They decided he would start a period of initiation, lasting as long as necessary for him to prepare to take his vows. Anthony visualised this might be two or three years, but his future superior made quite clear: 'Not everybody is suitable… first impressions can be misleading. We never advise haste.'

Father Brendon indicated the archway with a hand: 'Follow me.' They walked underneath and through to the cloister, turned left, passed through another arch leading to a separate block with leaded-light windows and a door with step which had been worn down over many years. This led to the Abbot's office.

'Come in. Sit. Brother Lucian will join us soon. He was about your age when he came many years ago. He'll show you round, help you get used to our routine, and be your teacher. Normally we live in silence. However, for one hour a day between six and seven o'clock, after the last meal of the day we allow ourselves to communicate. There are exceptions and your arrival is one such occasion.' He looked up in response to a knock on the door. 'Enter!'

Brother Lucian entered and greeted Anthony who briefly acknowledged him. He had not expected a foreign monk, but reminded himself that St Martin's brotherhood welcomed brothers from all over the world. After a few formalities, the Abbot ended his welcoming talk. 'Now. There is a letter for you Anthony, which I will give you. But in future you will need permission to conduct correspondence. Brother Lucian will explain. Surprised, Anthony put out his hand uncertainly and took it.

'Th-thank you.' Case in hand, he followed Brother Lucian, a bright, precise, upright man, to another block.

'This is your cell, Anthony,' he said in good English with Indian accent. 'It faces north but you'll get used to it.' It was basic: bed, table, bedside-box and chair. A small crucifix hung on the wall and there was a high window with bars. 'You can sort out your belongings after I've shown you round, and we'll visit the linen room first where you can pick up a cloak and robes.' They also visited the refectory, the chapel, then made a brisk tour of the whole site, including areas which Anthony would visit only infrequently after today. In the garden was an area devoted to vegetable-growing and the chickens. Again, Anthony felt a comfortable feeling of familiarity. A stream ran through the grounds and alongside was a path leading to a grotto. There were stone kneeling places at the grotto which featured several statues of the Virgin Mary, one of Saint Martin, and another of St Anthony. Candles flickered in the depth of the cave.

Back in Anthony's cell they opened the suitcase. He was to keep his own underwear, his Missal, writing equipment and toiletries. The rest would be taken away to store after he changed.

'As today is a day of prayer and fasting there is only bread and water for the evening meal,' said Brother

Lucian. 'We'll break silence when you can meet the others, then afterwards it's back to our cells until three-thirty in the morning when we celebrate mass in the side chapel.' Lucian closed the heavy door as he left. There was no key. Anthony had hardly uttered a word. He just stood listening to the silence. Alone. He was prepared for silence but the reality was different now, and made him anxious.

He sat on the hard bed and picked up his letter, recognising Father Alphonsus's handwriting. Thoughts of home came flooding back. He fought back the sinking feeling in his stomach. He opened the letter: an exhortation to accept the discipline of his new life and: '*remember our confidence is not in ourselves but in the Almighty*.' It concluded with a promise of prayers both from Father Alphonsus personally and from the church. Anthony contemplated his doubts. *But God's given me my body and brain for a purpose.* He wondered if this life of contemplation might have a positive influence on his nervous disposition. *Tonight, I'll specifically pray for courage.*

He put the initiate's grey habit over his underclothes and made his way to the refectory, wondering how he could put his confidence in God, instead of taking in his new surroundings. He ate his bread and water and soon permission was given to speak. Lucian was sitting next to him.

'It's rather a jolt to start with, isn't it?' Anthony nodded and looked at his empty plate.

'I-I-I'm…'

'Oh, don't worry, early days!' Lucian tried to put Anthony at ease. 'You seemed to like the garden, Anthony.'

'I d-did. Next door had ch-chickens.'

That night he didn't sleep at all before a bell sounded for mass. Brother Lucian knocked, guided him to the chapel and showed him his place.

Mass ended and he found his own way back to his cell. It was a clear night and a full moon lit his way. He was exhausted and went straight to sleep, but awoke later in the sweat, palpitations, and anxiety of a nightmare. The same hen/ant/egg scenario returned to plague his mind. The hen was enormous, standing over an egg with large, outstretched wings. The egg was covered in ants, this time wearing grey habits and wielding spoons with mediaeval spikes underneath. The egg was enlarging, changing shape, cracking – but only one ant remained, in its grey habit, bashing the egg with all its might when out crawled his dying father – unrecognisable – head and body broken and bleeding. Behind him was a plane. A plane in flames. The burnt figure of his father opened his eyes as he crawled towards Anthony. 'I don't understand, son,' he rasped. 'I don't understand…'

CHAPTER 3

'Can't you see who's there?' Vera was calling downstairs from the bathroom.

Polly rushed to the door to see a stranger on the step who instantly smiled, put a foot over the threshold and held out her hand to Polly. 'Hello, you must be Polly! Eli said your parents wouldn't mind if I knocked. I'm Mrs Gristwood from next door!' Then, seeing a figure hovering on the landing, pushed on the door, stepped inside, and called upstairs, 'Cooeee! I'm Barbara from next door. Just called on the spur of the moment!' She laughed.

Vera, towel over wet hair, panicked and rushed back into the bathroom rubbing her head frantically.

'I can see it's not a good time, dear,' said the visitor to Polly, backing out. 'But don't worry. I just thought I'd pop round to see if your parents would like to come around for a drink next week. We've taken over the Wheeler's telephone number, so you know it. We'd love to meet you! I've got two weeks off to sort things out – we'll be in a dreadful muddle, but you won't mind, will you?' She gave Polly a friendly, familiar look as though they'd know each other for years.

Polly was taken aback by the boldness of their new neighbour who waved as she went out the front gate, 'Bye!'

Vera came rushing downstairs with a headscarf on. 'She hasn't gone – you didn't let her go, did you? How could I come down with my hair all dripping… Oh, what an imposition!'

'Sorry Mum,' said Polly, 'I couldn't help it. She came, talked fast then went. I don't like her. She's nothing like Mrs Wheeler. But she wants you to go round for drinks and says you can ring her.'

'Oh, all right,' said Vera stomping upstairs. 'Suppose I'll have to.'

'Yes,' said Polly. She found Fluffy, sat beside him, and stroked him.

When Vera came back, hair in curlers, she glared at Polly, still grumpy. 'What did she look like, then?'

*

As James, Vera and Polly were walking down The Elms' drive, they stared at a pile of rubbish. Wooden crates were piled outside the front door along with a mixed assortment of discarded oddments. Vera gasped in horror. 'What a mess!'

'They've only just got here,' said Polly.

'Hmmm,' said James thoughtfully, 'I wonder what they do for a living.' They pulled the bell-rope. At least that was still working. A tall, well-built man opened the heavy oak door with a frown on his face.

'Oh, come in. I suppose you're from next door, I'm Noel – Noel Gristwood – do come in. He turned to the hallway: 'BABS!' he yelled. Then to the Wests: 'Just getting straight – not really ready for visitors, but you're only from next door, aren't you?'

What strange people. 'I'm James and this is Vera,' he ruffled Polly's hair, 'and Polly.' He offered a hand to Noel, returning it to his pocket when it was ignored and rattled his keys. Polly stared at the faded paint in the shape of a crucifix on the wall. The atmosphere in the hallway was totally different and took some getting used to. A hassled Barbara emerged from the kitchen. She tripped over some rolled up carpeting but steadied herself against the wall.

'We'll have to go in the kitchen, I'm afraid… no chairs anywhere else. Do come through.' In all the time Vera had visited Florence, she had never even glimpsed the kitchen.

Polly was getting into the habit of praying to God for help when she was unsure about anything. *Lord, help me to love these people.* She sniffed and followed her parents. *Smells musty and beery.* Vera was having problems adjusting to the extraordinary welcome from their new neighbours but James was pleasantly bemused. He liked the informal approach to life. *Why does Vera always have to be so hard to please? Some people feel more at ease when a place is untidy. Not sure about Noel though.*

'Sherry? Beer? Would you like lemonade, Polly? Noel! Find the glasses.' Barbara prepared some chairs for them to sit. One end of the table was covered with papers so they sat at the other. 'My work!' she said, pushing the papers further away. 'It's always all over the place!' James stole a glance at Noel and noticed the furrow in his brow deepen further as he continued searching for glassware in a crate.

'We're so impressed with Eli, aren't we, dear?'

'We are.'

'He certainly gave us a comprehensive introduction to the neighbourhood. Yes! Quite a character.'

'You can rely on Eli,' said James, 'He was hoping you'd give him an order.'

'Oh, yes,' said Barbara, 'from next week we'll both be going out to work – no children, you see,' she laughed self-consciously, 'and we don't really have much time for shopping.'

'So where do you work?' asked James.

'The *Shorewell News* in London, and Noel's an architect at the moment.' She rushed on without further explanation. 'But will you have sherry, both of you?'

Polly wanted to ask a lot of questions but knew her mother would object, so kept quiet. She sat surveying the muddle, and tried to get used to the change. *At least they're trying to be friendly. I wonder if they go to church. Better not ask yet. Get to know them first.*

The four adults sat drinking sherry and Polly sipped her lemonade thinking about the faded patch in the hall, the crucifix still powerful in its absence. The agony of Christ dying on the cross dominated the hall before. Apart from the beautiful sweeping staircase of course. *But that's one of the things Sunday school say the Catholics have got wrong. Christ isn't on the cross, He's risen!* Recently she had been questioning her enjoyment of the beauty of the statues and candles and all the trappings of the convent's way of worship. *Are these my idols? (Sorry, Mary!) What a dilemma. I love being in the school chapel though.*

'Thank you, thank you very much,' she heard her father saying eventually, 'you must come round to ours.'

Everyone stood and Vera tripped over a mat as she left the kitchen. She righted herself and asked, 'Would you like a few fresh eggs from our chickens? Florence enjoyed them.'

Polly piped up, 'Sometimes *our* chickens lay double-yolks!'

'Polly!' Vera scolded.

Nothing Polly said these days seemed right. *Mum's always cross with me.*

Barbara and Noel walked them to the door. 'It's going to take us ages to get sorted out, isn't it, Noel?' Noel frowned again. No reply.

The Wests walked down the drive. 'It's funny without the crucifix,' said Polly. James agreed.

'Trust you to notice *that,*' said her mother, 'I hope it doesn't take them too long to get straight. How did they manage to afford this place?' She wittered on. 'Can't see myself getting friendly with *her.*'

Later in the evening Vera decided to write to Anthony.

'Can I put a note in with yours – about Fluffy?' asked Polly.

'All right,' agreed Vera grudgingly. 'As long as I don't have to wait all week for it. But for goodness' sake *don't* call him Fluffy.'

Polly pouted as her mother settled at the bureau.

16 Elm Close.

Dear Anthony

As promised I'm writing to tell you that the new people have moved in and, although they are a long way from being sorted out, Mr Gristwood (Noel), said they understand the electricity and telephone, and will contact Henry with any questions.

So far they've kept the bell pull on the front door. It was strange to visit The Elms with everything being so different, but it will be more homely when their things are in place. We were surprised to be asked there so soon.

Polly wants to include a note with this. I hope that is allowed by your new institution.

We all hope you are settling in alright.
Yours sincerely,
Vera

Polly settled at her homework desk in the bedroom.

Dear Mr Wheeler,

I wanted to tell you Archibald seems quite happy when I call him "Fluffy", (I hope you don't mind) and is very comfortable in our house. The first time we let him outside he went back to your old house, but Martha let us collect him from the back door. Since the new people moved in he has stayed in our garden. He knows where to come for his food. I do love him.

We visited the Gristwoods and they were in a terrible muddle. I missed the crucifix in the hall, but my Sunday school teacher says I must choose between being a <u>real</u> Christian or a Roman Catholic, like you. She says that chapel statues are idols and it's a sin to pray to them. I'm torn because I love Mary and the saints, but when girls at Sunday school give their testimonies and talk about the difference Jesus makes when they ask him into their lives I feel I'm missing out.

> *Please let me know if you'd like me to write again, and if you'd rather I still called your fluffy cat 'Archibald' – I will if you like.*
> *Thank you for giving him to me.*
> *Yours sincerely,*
> *Polly*

She gave the letter to her mother who was rushed and enclosed it without checking. Victor was in the kitchen. 'Send him my love,' he said in a soppy voice.

'Victor! Go and tidy your bedroom. If you don't put your washing in the linen basket it'll go mouldy.'

Victor harrumphed and looking out of his bedroom window noticed his friend Darren beckoning from the path. He climbed down the drainpipe, and they ran down the road towards Nina and Dot.

Polly set out with the letter to buy a stamp. She noticed the four friends chatting at the end of the road and then going off together. *Probably going to the cinema... I wonder what's on.* She didn't want to go out with her brother, but wouldn't mind getting to know Darren better. She and Beth tended to be more serious than their peers, talking about ideas like where heaven was and how many people would fit in. On the other hand, she was beginning to feel a bit jealous that Darren was spending time with Dot. *Suppose that's just because he's Vic's friend and Dot is Nina's friend.* On the way back, as always, she studied the bombsite on the other side of The Elms, where Darren and Nina used to live. Only the chimney stack of number 14 was left standing. It held a morbid fascination, but sometimes triggered her recurrent nightmare: a bomber flying low towards her house. Stops on reaching it.

Climbs high into the clouds and rapidly dives towards her.

*

'We've had the furball for over a year now, and still stepping in his food. Why don't you put it on the shelf?' Victor never looked where he was treading.

'You mad?' retorted Polly. 'Mum would never agree – not even Dad. Get used to it.' Victor went into the garden to find his football. 'Your turn to feed the chickens tonight,' shouted Polly through the window.

'Not *tonight,* tomorrow,' came back Vic's voice as he kicked his ball against the wall. Vera came into the kitchen.

'What's going on? It's time you two were civil to each other.'

'We're just discussing,' said Polly.

'Vic*tor*!' Vera shouted from the kitchen, 'FEED the CHICKENS!' Polly smiled triumphantly but decided to go and help anyway. 'I'll get the water,' she said going towards the pen.

'For being a good girl, you can have a treat if you want!' Polly looked Victor up and down wondering if he was joking. 'Not jumping at the chance then?'

Polly was intrigued.

'This is a once in a lifetime opportunity,' he taunted.

'So, *what*?'

'Want to come to the cinema with us tomorrow, Pol?'

'Depends,' hedged Polly, judging the best way to play her hand.

'Meaning?'

'Depends what you're doing and who "us" is.'

'Right. We're going to *Singin' in the Rain* – nothing sinful!' He was getting used to his sister's self-imposed prohibitions. She was so touchy about things since she'd gone to hear that preacher who got them up to the front during the meeting. In his way Vic was trying to normalise her.

'*Singin' in the Rain.* Oh! Are you really going to see that? Beth says it's great. I've been dying to see it… Oh, I get it… You're just asking me because Nina wants to go!'

'So, you'll come? Darren will be pleased.'

'DARREN?'

'Why not Darren? You seem to notice each other quite a lot these days. I thought you'd jump at the chance.'

'What about Dot?'

'Dot's *history*. They split. She didn't like his sort of music or the way he was so soppy over animals.'

Polly's heart thumped.

They agreed on time and place.

On Friday evening the four of them set off for the *Odeon*. Polly and Darren were not strangers to each other, but it was odd for Polly to be on a sort of date with him rather than getting on with her own thing while he messed around with Vic. They liked talking about the same sorts of things, especially animals. Darren's dog had been killed when their house, number 14 on the opposite side of *The Elms*, was bombed and they couldn't have a puppy in their rented accommodation. Also, unlike Victor, Darren had a vague interest in church.

'What's it like to be bombed out?' she asked.

'People are afraid to talk about that, but I wish they would. They don't understand about missing Mum and

Mac, or why Dad can't do what he used to. We lost everything. It's left like a big hole in me, losing Mum especially. We've never got over it really. Living in a rented flat is horrible. No garden to start with.'

'But you can come to us.'

'Yes, I'm lucky to have Vic. And my other football mates but it's not the same.'

Polly was obsessed. She scratched his name in the lid of her school desk and the following spring sent him a Valentine's card declaring her undying love, anonymous of course. She, in turn, received an anonymous one. I know *he* sent it!

CHAPTER 4

Eli was cross when Vera opened the door to pay him. The rest of the family were out.

'Month after month and they're still not organised next door,' he said.

'What do you mean?' asked Vera, hand on mouth.

'Can't seem to catch them in, and bills not paid for weeks… Still in a mess if you look through the window.'

'Weeks?' Vera sympathised. 'Oh dear.'

'Should never have moved into that great big house if they can't afford it.'

'Not paying *any* bills?' she asked, fiddling nervously with her purse.

'Nope. Paper shop is giving up delivering, and the grocer only leaves stuff if they've already paid. They trust everyone else.'

'They're terribly disorganised, I know, but we hardly see them. How much do we owe?' She paid and Eli ambled back to the milk cart.

'Eli says he's having trouble with next door,' Vera told James when he came in laden with the Saturday shopping. She was increasingly agitated these days, and the running of the household was left to him so he too was hassled. Everything seemed wrong.

'Now what? There's always bother next door,' he said. 'First the Wheelers, now the Gristwoods. I suppose the Wheelers were alright though.' He was putting the shopping away. 'Give me a hand…'

Vera took the sugar and opened the cupboard. 'Not paying the bills… *any* of them.'

'And what are we meant to do about it?' James asked crossly.

'I suppose you could ask if they'd like us to pay Eli when he comes.'

'Me, me, me! Why can't *you* ask them?' Vera nervously put her hand to her mouth.

'Well…'

'All right. If I ask them, will you make sure Polly remembers to give it to Eli while I get the Saturday shopping?' Vera said 'yes', as though she wasn't certain.

'I'll go this evening,' said James.

'What will you say?' asked Polly, who had overheard.

'I don't know till I get there.'

'They don't even say thank you for the eggs,' Vera whined. 'And we've never asked them round here.'

'You're obsessed with eggs!'

Vera pouted and rearranged the shopping James had put in the larder. 'Why can't you put things in their proper place?'

*

As he walked up the drive towards the oak door James heard shouting. He hesitated before pulling the bell-rope, but decided to go ahead for Eli's sake. He tugged the rope.

'You go then!' Barbara's voice.

A fraught-looking Noel answered the door. 'Hello.' No invitation to go inside. James felt awkward. He smelt burning toast but put on a cheerful front.

'Noel! How are you? We don't see much of you and wondered—' James rattled the keys in his pocket.

Noel didn't show much interest. 'No, we're hardly ever in. What can I do for you?'

'As a matter of fact,' James started weakly but felt he needed to make the point. 'It's about the milk… Either Polly or Vera are always in our place Saturday mornings when Eli calls.' *What a cheek.*

'BARBARA!' Noel yelled back into the house.

Barbara didn't appear but called brightly from the kitchen. 'Yes?' she sang in reply.

'MILK? PAPERS? You said you'd pay.'

'I'm getting round to it. Don't worry.' Then a shout, not quite a scream, 'Ow!'

Noel rolled his eyes. 'Burnt herself.' He gave James a knowing look, sniffed, sighed, and rubbed the back of his hand over his forehead. 'She's… she's… oh!' He gave up and stopped shaking his head as he quelled his frustration. 'I'll sort it. Thanks. And don't bother about putting eggs on the doorstep. She…' jerking his head back referring to his wife in the kitchen, 'let the last ones go bad. Stuck them at the back of the safe and forgot.' He frowned.

'Everything all right?' came a voice from the kitchen.

'Yes.' Noel looked exasperated.

James winked at him and asked quietly, 'Have you tried the Broken Gate? They serve a good pint.' No response. Another crash from the kitchen.

'Have to go… Needs must.' Noel made a face as he closed the door. 'Not what I bargained for.'

James walked home slowly turning things over and wondering what to tell Vera. *His problems are worse than mine. Less said the better*.

'How did you get on?' Vera came to the door in her dressing-gown.

'They don't want any eggs.'

'Really?'

'That's what he said. No time to cook.' He went into the kitchen and opened a bottle of beer.

'So, what about the money?'

'Noel will sort it.'

Vera hesitated: 'But?'

'I'll see you upstairs.' James tasted his beer slowly, then gulped the rest. Fortunately, Polly was upstairs doing homework. He'd deal with her questions later.

The Wests had gone to bed apart from Victor who'd climbed out of his bedroom window. Noel slipped an envelope through the letterbox of the dark house.

*

Barbara set off for the station to catch the early train. She slept badly after another argument with Noel. But by the time she walked into the office she'd forgotten home and was concentrating on work. She dusted her desk and put things in their familiar places. Her workplace was as tidy and organised as home was a tip. A journalist at heart, work was her priority. 'We can really make a difference,' she said to Penny after bemoaning the sad post-war state of Shorewell. Penny Lower, who occupied the desk next to hers, had become a close friend. The paper, the *Shorewell News*, was run by a team of four who were respected locally for running campaigns – a different one every year. Their editor, Michael Foster, was friendly with the local MP who was a good listener and co-operated helpfully on occasion.

Michael called Barbara over to his desk. 'Barb, it's time we investigated the way council housing is allocated,' he said, looking through a pile of papers.

'Why?' she asked.

'Bert says there's a lot of talk in his pub about the wrong people being given precedence, many not really deserving it.'

'But,' said Barbara, who as Social Affairs Editor always wanted to suggest her own priorities, 'what about the bomb sites, constant reminders of the war? And what's more, the council might be able to use them for building.'

This was why Barbara and Michael were a good team. They could discuss issues without arguing. This time Michael agreed Barbara could do what she wanted. He gave her two months. 'We'll need to know who owns the land. See what you can find out.'

Barbara and Penny always had lunch together. They didn't go to The Anchor with Michael. Too boozy and dominated by loud men who liked their drink. Their boss said, 'That's where you find *life*... and news, when it happens.'

'Yes, *male* life. And you don't know what it's like to be leered at,' Barbara retorted, aggrieved by the stares if she but poked her head round the door. She knew Michael picked up useful information there, but the girls walked a bit further to Maisie's Cuppa, getting exercise at the same time.

'Any cottage pie today, Maisie?' Penny asked as they sat at their usual table near the counter. 'Cottage pie coming up, love! Two?'

'Definitely!' Barbara smiled. Maisie poured them both a free cup of tea. Her treat every now and again.

'How's life at The Elms, Barb?' Penny asked as the tea arrived. They both took sugar. Penny braced herself for more complaints about Noel.

'It was dreadful yesterday. He discovered… actually, the *neighbours* discovered… I hadn't got round to paying our local bills. How embarrassing is that? I knew we owed. It's just so difficult to get round to domestic stuff after a busy day.'

'It sounds as though you never do much housework!' Penny laughed. 'I must have my home tidy first. I feel terrible if I haven't paid my bills. Don't you?'

'Yes. But…' said Barbara, 'don't you think Noel should do the money side of things? Why always me?'

'Have you asked him?'

Barbara was about to say it was impossible to talk to him when the cottage pies arrived. They fell silent and quietly tucked in. 'What about you then, Pen?' She listened for a while about Penny's orderly life, then let slip, 'I don't know really what Noel is up to.'

'What do you mean?' Penny looked concerned.

'I just don't know. I'm a bit suspicious.' They chatted on forgetting the time.

When they reached the office, the sports reporter looked flustered and Michael was on the phone. He put his hand over the handset and looked straight at Barbara: 'Where the *hell* have you been? There's a break-in at the jewellers… Get round there, pronto. I'll man the phone.' At times like this they all worked together until Michael felt they had sufficient authentic material to publish. It might mean a late night. Never mind about Noel.

'Sorry.' Barbara grabbed her camera and rushed out.

*

Polly was the first to notice the envelope on the front door mat. She took it to her parents who were having breakfast.

> *'We would be grateful if you could give this to Eli next time you see him. I'll be in on Saturday fortnight if it isn't enough. Will call into paper shop soon. Noel.*
> *Enclosed £10'*

'I heard shouting coming from The Elms the other evening,' said Polly.

'Probably,' James answered casually, but was looking askance at Vera.

'Shouting?' queried Vera, putting her hand to her mouth again and looking worried. James noticed she was trembling.

'All husbands and wives shout at each other now and again, Pol,' he added. 'Nothing unusual.' *I need to get Vera to the doctor.* She was nothing like the confident woman he had married.

Polly went up to her bedroom where Fluff was asleep on the bed. 'Jesus, I can't get anything right with Mum and Dad.' Polly knelt by the bed, praying, and opening her Bible. 'Jesus, help them to love me, and help the Gristwoods to sort things out too.' She randomly opened her Bible and read, *God is our refuge and strength, a very present help in trouble*. 'Thank you, God.' *He's with me. At least He loves me*. She poured out all the thoughts and worries coursing through her mind, convincing herself at the same time she had faith. *Keep trusting, Polly, like they say in Sunday school.*

She went downstairs with a niggling feeling her faith wasn't 'quite there' yet. She hadn't had the dramatic experience Beth and Olive talked about. *They know the time and date Jesus entered their lives. I don't.* On the door mat there was a letter addressed to her. She opened it as she walked into the kitchen. 'What've you got there?' asked Vera. 'Who's that from?'

'Mr Wheeler.'

'What does he say?' asked Vera anxiously sipping her coffee.

'Give the girl time to look,' but James was curious. Polly dashed upstairs to read it.

> *~ Brotherhood of St. Martin's, Devon ~*
> *Dear Polly,*
>
> *I'm sorry it has taken this long for me to reply. My letter-writing is restricted and this is my first opportunity.*
>
> *I was delighted to hear from you. Although I was not a little concerned regarding your comments on the Roman Catholic Church.*
>
> *But first I must tell you I think 'Fluffy' is a good name. Mother would have objected, but I like it better than 'Archibald'.*
>
> *I am getting used to life in the monastery although it is a big change from The Elms. It is strange not having much to call my own. My cell is rather bare. Also, we live in silence most of the time.*

I work on preserving holy manuscripts, and we are all on a rota for housework. Also, you will be pleased to hear I help an older brother to look after the chickens and the kitchen garden. Apart from Tom, the handyman, and occasional workmen, we do everything ourselves.

But most importantly I'm concerned about your mention of 'proper Christians' and 'giving up our idols.' Maybe you misunderstand. Catholics do not <u>worship</u> the statues. We pray to the saints and the Virgin Mary asking them to intercede for us. I'm afraid your Sunday school teaching is quite contrary to the that of the true Church. I have been praying you will see the truth of the Catechism (read it again, carefully). It is important for you to receive the Holy Sacraments from an ordained priest and learn the truth. You may have heard Christ said to the apostle, Peter, 'I say unto you, you are Peter and upon this rock I will build my church.' (Peter means rock.) The Popes have continued in this tradition through the ages. We are the one and only true Church, and I pray you will come to understand this.

I hope you will write again.
Yours sincerely
Anthony
P.S. If you would like to speak to Father Alphonsus, I could write to him.
P.P.S. Please thank you mother for telling me the Gristwoods understood my

instructions and are getting used to The Elms.

'So, what does he say?' asked Vera when Polly came down, leaving the letter upstairs.

She waived it off lightly. 'He says thank your mother for her letter. He can't write often. Er... he's glad the Gristwoods are all right and thanks you for your help... and he's happy for me to call Fluffy "Fluffy".'

'You didn't tell him that, surely?'

'He doesn't mind, Mum... I knew he wouldn't.' Polly didn't want to prolong the conversation. She dashed upstairs again. *I must pray for him and tell Beth and the prayer group.* She added Anthony to her prayer list which included heathens in Africa and India, her parents, Victor, and Darren.

*

'Exciting news! Doctor Anderson is coming to Cotsford!' Announced Mrs Holland at the next Friday evening Bible Study. Polly, Beth, and the rest of the girls wondered why she was so excited. 'The Lord uses him to convert crowds of people,' she beamed. 'What a lovely Christmas present it would be for us if one of you asked Jesus into your heart. Write down: town hall, 19th of December. Pastor Ingrams is making arrangements.'

A fortnight later Polly entered the town hall to the sound of quiet singing from a large choir. She caught: *Are your garments spotless?* but it wasn't until the group's chatter and noise of seats quietened that she heard more: *Are they white as snow? Are you washed in the blood of the Lamb?* She was comfortable and relaxed. The choir looked angelic dressed in white. 'This is how Billy Graham does it in America,' Beth whispered, 'isn't it inspiring?'

But Polly was caught up in her own thoughts. *I'm not washed in the blood of the Lamb. Not properly.* As the evening progressed she became totally wrapped up in the message. *This message is for me!*

There were testimonies and solos for an hour until Doctor Anderson opened his sermon with prayer. 'Lord God,' he boomed slowly with great emphasis on every word, '*be* with us this evening. *Enter* our *hall* and our *hearts.* I *believe*, Lord Jesus... *You* want to enter someone's heart tonight.' He opened his Bible at Romans, chapter ten, verse ten: '*For it is with your heart that you believe and are justified, but it is with your mouth that you confess and are saved.*'

He eventually finished with: '*If you really believe you will confess and testify how Jesus has saved you. With your* mouth *you are saved.*'

The choir sang again as he lowered his voice: 'Now, if Jesus has saved you tonight, I want you to come up to the front and tell me. It won't be easy in front of all these people, but if you really believe...' and so he went on, inviting people to the front throughout the hymn.

Four people got up from their seats. Three of them in tears, including Polly. Each potential 'Convert*'* was accompanied by a badge-wearing 'Counsellor' as they were shepherded into a room back-stage where Doctor Anderson joined them.

'There is rejoicing in heaven tonight,' he said, beaming before he spoke to each individually. He looked into Polly's tearful eyes. 'And how long have you been a Christian, my dear?' he asked.

Polly's inner voice whispered: *Now is your chance. Confess.* She said, 'Since tonight!'

In days to come she would describe that moment as lightning striking her from top to toe. The relief and happiness were overwhelming and she knew *It* had happened. The preacher blessed her by placing his hand on her head and praying. He gave her a book to read, and sent her back to her friends.

'I've been saved!' she exclaimed joyfully.

'Praise the Lord,' responded Mrs Holland and Beth.

'Welcome to the fold,' said another person. But Polly was so happy she could think of nothing but how bright the world was. She was overflowing with love. *So, this is what it means to be born again.*

CHAPTER 5

Anthony was wearing his heavy cloak, running on the spot rubbing his hands together. Even after two years, early morning prayers were a shivering ordeal. No comfort of a fire to look forward to during daylight hours. *Years to go before I'll have a cell facing south...* 'You'll get hardened off after a while,' they'd said. *I'll never be like those who wear sandals without socks. Do they really not feel cold, or is it a form of penance? I can't go that far... yet.* To complain, he presumed, was a sign of disobedience.

He wondered about his vows. There were pros and cons. This life was all right in the summer. *Will I ever be able to commit myself completely?* Getting up in the middle of the night and unhesitating obedience to the rules was harder to practice than he imagined, and the old temptations would not go away. 'F-orgive me F-father, for I have sinned.' He entered the confessional making the sign of the cross, but knowing he would not be totally truthful… 'I…I-I complain b-itterly about the cold. It depresses me.'

'Is it simply the cold weather and lack of home comforts that you see as your suffering? Or do you have hidden thoughts eating away at your peace of mind? Examine your innermost being. Be honest about you guilt, Brother.'

Thankfully, the Abbot could not see the confessor's face burning despite the cold as he knelt on the stone step. Anthony's mind instantly flew to Sebastian who often signalled a willingness to meet in private. He felt guilt when his desires, from deep inside both mind and body, came to the surface. So far, he had held on to his integrity, but it was a struggle. *What if? No… not yet… not ever. I must continue to deny him.*

'Brother?' The voice of the Abbot was urging an answer to the dreaded probing question. But Anthony's ongoing burden of unease with himself could not be admitted.

'I have thought b-badly of my b-brothers who do not have p-patience with me.'

'Yes?' the questioner wanted a different answer. Recognising the voice, he waited for Anthony to acknowledge his underlying sin before it could be dealt with. He noticed the body language of Anthony and Brother Sebastian as they passed in the cloisters, rather more closely than necessary, and how their eyes strayed when they were meant to be engrossed in devotions. He let the matter rest and gave Anthony his penance for the week, which was light. Relationships must wait. It was part of the initiation process, and not the first time he had dealt with this problem. Indeed, sinful attraction towards a fellow friar was a temptation he had struggled with when he took his own vows of poverty, chastity, and obedience, so, in one way, he understood. But, now in his seventies, he did not recognise how denying the temptations of the flesh had evolved into bitterness. However, from his present position of power, he excused his occasional lapses remaining blind to his sins of avarice and manipulation.

Anthony left the confessional, went to a remote corner of the chapel, spent time on his knees completing the number of rosaries allotted for absolution, then rose preparing his mind for work. *My spirit should feel light and my soul refreshed.* But he sensed Sebastian was impatient with him. *What is this guilty feeling about Sebastian? Does every novice have this problem? Holy Mary, Mother of God pray for me. Yes, I love him.*

He escaped into working the colourful scrolling around his manuscript borders, becoming engrossed in the gold and red, purple, and green, and the pleasing rhythm of his hand marking the parchment.

But at night, as he dreamt, his pleasure became frustration. The wind blew as he walked in the woods, but the trees were upright and changing shape into young boys glancing at him like Sebastian did. He neither recognised nor got close to any of them. They were like soldier crabs waving red claws, temptingly within reach but moving just too far away when he approached. He floated above them but the sea started washing over them. He scrabbled around in the shallow water looking for signs of life, but became aware of an angry hooded figure towering above, his cloak about to trap him. He clawed at the mattress. Trying to find *what*? He woke up sweating and unsatisfied. *Pull yourself together*. He sat up sharply, then laid his head heavily against the stone wall. *How long would Sebastian's patience last? Holy Mary, HELP ME!* The early hours of the morning were always bad. *I'll be all right when I'm occupied.*

He joined the brothers in the cloister walk, reciting the rosary before processing into breakfast. 'Our Father who art in heaven, hallowed be thy name.' The beads passed through his fingers: small, cold, stones. The words tumbled out into space. They went nowhere. It was still dark. 'Father forgive me, show me a sign, help me.' He looked up, tears in his eyes, and looked at the sky. The face of the moon wore an ominous expression. He shuddered.

*

Tom handed a letter to Anthony surreptitiously with a wink. It was from Polly.

> *New Year's Day!*
> *Dear Mr Anthony,*
> *Fluffy and I are still great friends and he gave me a Christmas present – a dead mouse in my slipper! I couldn't tell him off on Christmas Day!*
> *Thank you for writing. It was a big surprise to get your letter and I'm glad you like his new name.*
> *My most important news is that I have —been saved! I am so happy. It happened on December 19th, a date I will remember forever. Jesus came into my heart when I confessed with my mouth that I believed, and I have great peace. I trust Him completely. He lives in me and I live in Him.*
> *There is absolutely no need for sacraments or saints. (I apologised to the Virgin Mary for ignoring her.) Jesus is all I need.*
> *Yours in Christ,*
> *Polly*

After supper Anthony told Lucian about the letter.

Lucian was attentive and thoughtful. 'They're not teaching her correctly? Does she think she can manage without the catechism and sacraments?'

Anthony frowned: 'The s-school teaches c-catechism but at the same time she is indoctrinated by her S-Sunday school. She s-seeks G-god earnestly, but leans towards an emotional experience with n-no historical or theological g-grounding. They s-seem to m-make it up as they g-go along. It is s-so beguiling.'

The bell rang for silence before Lucian responded. They parted and walked in the direction of their cells. There was no further opportunity to discuss Polly for a few days and, when the subject came up, Lucian didn't seem as open as usual, but agreed Polly should be taught her error.

Anthony felt he should reply urgently. Tom would post it.

~ Brotherhood of St. Martin's, Devon ~
Dear Polly,

I received your letter with news of what you call a conversion. It sounds as though this is real to you but I have doubts about the value of your experience.

I must emphasize that what you say has no foundation in the history or edicts of the church. I don't think you understand the significance of mortal sin. I urge you to talk to Father Alphonsus. He will teach you willingly. Do think seriously about this and the truths you learn the convent. Please do not reject the teaching of the one true church.

I will continue to pray for you.

I'm glad my Fluffy is happy. He used to bring me 'presents' from time to time, but Martha, thank God, dealt with them. There is a cat which wanders around the monastery. The cook for an unknown reason calls him 'Mouse'. He is short-haired. Nothing all like Archibald.

Yours sincerely,
Anthony

That evening the wind changed. It blew from the south, and the weather turned warm. Anthony climbed under his blankets and left his cloak on the chair. His mind was unusually at ease and he slept deeply until becoming aware of movement. He was suddenly alert. 'Is s-someone there?' he whispered. 'H-ello?' All was still, then another movement... he heard breathing.

'Shhh... don't make a noise.' Anthony swung his legs over the side of the bed and reached for his cloak, putting it round his shoulders. Adjusting to the darkness, he made out a figure only a few feet away. The door swung closed. Anthony's heart thumped loudly. His excitement mounted. He was aroused.

'No. N... n-no, Sebastian. You s-shouldn't be here.'

Sebastian reached out his hand to feel Anthony and moved closer to the small bed, breathing heavily.

'It's okay, Anthony. It's normal – goes on all the time,' he whispered gently. 'We need this – deserve it. Let's just spend time together. Don't fret. My love, you are the only one for me.'

'I c-can't. G-go away S-Sebastian! H-holy Mary. Pray f-f—' Anthony was panicking now.

'Everything really is all right… You mustn't worry, Brother.' Sebastian pushed his face against Anthony's. Anthony couldn't breathe.

'G-go away! This isn't right.' He turned his head away. His legs gave way and he fell back onto the bed. Sebastian was on top of him.

'I c-can't,' Anthony rasped. His strength did not match Sebastian's. His throat constricted.

'Of course you can!' the voice teased, then became threatening. 'Ohhh yes, you can! You're longing…'

Anthony was paralysed with fright. *Yes I am. No. No, I'm not. Not like this.* His mind somersaulted. Scared, longing, guilty, anxious, fearful. For a moment he weakened, *Shall we… I?* But his fear of sin took control. 'N… n-no! NOOO!'

'Shhh…' Alright then. The words were viciously quiet – hissing, and the movements changed.

How can I escape? Anthony's strength was returning, but there was no escape.

'If you won't give me what I want, then…' Sebastian dropped full weight onto Anthony's body and kissed him, his right hand searching wildly until a blade came from beneath his cloak and was thrust deep into Anthony's soft belly. 'DEVIL!' came the accusation with a mocking laugh, not so quiet now.

'Get behind me! Stop… stop… go AWAY.'

Sebastian's frenzied laughter echoed around the cloister and out into the night air as he fled.

Anthony fell, listening to himself screaming, '*MA–A–ARY!*' The stillness of the night was shattered. The whole fraternity was not only awake, but alert and vital. Rules were forgotten. Shouting figures came running towards Anthony's cell. Someone ran after the disappearing figure.

As he clutched his stomach, groaning, Anthony heard himself thinking, clearly, *Into your hands I commend my spirit.* Then he felt a familiar comforting presence. Yes! The crucifix, hanging there in the hall of The Elms.

CHAPTER 6

Eli knocked on number 16 and Polly answered the door. Fluffy was sitting on her arm, resting his paws on her shoulder.

'Happy, ain't he?' the milkman said, smiling and stroking him gently. Polly handed over next door's money envelope.

'Mrs Gristwood said they've put a note inside for you and make sure you see it.'

Eli opened the envelope. 'Right y'are. That's it then.' He gave Polly a knowing look. 'No more milk for number 15. Oh well. Dad there?'

'Dad's shopping, Mum's in bed – can I give him a message?'

Eli put the money in his old leather pouch, coins in the front pocket and silver in the back. 'Jis' say thanks for taking next door's money, and let me know if they change their mind.' He waved, climbed into his seat on the cart and picked up the reigns.

Polly saw Darren turning the corner, put the cat down and ran out to him.

'Don't let the door slam, scatter-brain!' he smiled. 'Ready for tonight?'

'Naturally!' Polly pulled him in, laughing. 'Come and see if you like my dress, it's upstairs. My *last* school dance!'

'I'm looking forward to dancing with a *live* band, Pol.'

'Me too!' They gave each other a quick hug.

'Heard from Vic then?'

'Just a postcard yesterday. Said life was great at University and that's about it. Mum was so cross. Dad said we had to be thankful he even thought of that and it'd soon be end of term anyway.'

'Wondering if I made the right decision now,' said Darren wistfully.

'*I* think you have!' Polly reached up and pecked him on the cheek. 'We'd've hardly seen anything of each other if you'd gone to university too, would we? Not wanting to be parted from Polly had played a big part in Darren's decision to do a local apprenticeship rather than go away. And the idea of waiting three or four years before his first pay-packet was a decider.

The discussion of Vic and Darren's life choices was soon forgotten, and Polly picked up her taffeta frock from the bed. 'Like it?' she put it up against her. It was very plain, obviously handmade with uneven stitching in places and mauve didn't really suit Polly's complexion.

'You'd look beautiful in anything!'

'Silly,' she giggled. 'Some things I make just hang on me. I'm a terrible dress-maker but I'm quite pleased with this.'

'Not kidding!' He smiled, not really caring much about details.

'Who is Beth going with?' he asked. Polly pursed her mouth, put the dress down and looked at him dubiously.

'She's not going at all... says it's too much of a temptation and Jesus wouldn't approve. She says I shouldn't go if I'm a *proper* Christian.'

'What does what's-his-name say about it?'

'Oh, Ian? He agrees with her. Dancing is worse than going to the pub.'

'Blimey! Is it that bad? Doesn't his dad go to the pub?'

'Huh it's not quite the same. Ian's dad isn't a…'

'So, her sanctimonious religion stops her dancing?'

'POLLY!' Vera was calling from her bedroom. 'Time for coffee – make sure it's hot, please.'

'Okay, Mum.' She and Darren ran down to the kitchen and put on the kettle.

'Polly put the kettle on,' sang Darren, teasing. 'Polly put the kettle on – we'll all have… *coffee*!'

'Shut up, stupid!' They giggled and tussled in a mock fight.

She stopped to put the biscuit tin on the tray. 'Don't know what's going on next door, but they don't want any more milk.'

'Didn't you hear?'

'What?'

'They're splitting up.'

'*Splitting up?* How d'you know?'

'My dad knows the woman Mr Gristwood's been going out with and she said he's going to divorce Barbara.'

'No! Next door's getting *divorced?*'

'Well, the people inside,' he grinned. A slap from the tea-towel lashed across his back, and again they burst into laughter.

'Polly!' Another shout from upstairs. Polly was used to Vera snapping at her, but her spirits sank into her boots every time. *If only I could please her*.

'They're getting divorced next door,' she said, thinking her mother should know.

'That's not the sort of thing to gossip about.'

'Okay, Mum,' she put the tray down, resigned to failing her mother, and left the room.

'Mum is so miserable all the time,' she told Darren, who'd made coffee for two and was sitting with his hands round his cup.

'Your dad's okay, isn't he?'

Polly screwed up her nose, 'He's all right but since Mum's—' James walked in with the shopping. Fortunately, the noise of getting the bags inside and brushing his feet had obscured the chatter.

'They're getting divorced next door, Dad.'

'Can I make your coffee, sir?' James liked the way Darren was so polite and was looking forward to having him as a son-in-law.

'Good man, Darren. Mum had hers?'

They sat around, shopping all over the floor, and talked about the Gristwoods, and how Mr was cheating on Mrs according to rumours at the pub.

'I thought that's what I heard but wasn't sure. Barbara's hardly ever in and her house is a mess. Her work is all she is interested in. If they'd had children…'

'You can't say *that*, Dad.' Polly was cross. Her parents had children and it hadn't solved their problems. Problems arose for all sorts of reasons.

'You back, James?' Vera was leaning over the banister again. 'Get all the shopping?'

James studied the ceiling sighing, then tried to conceal his annoyance from Polly. He sensed Darren knew how he felt. He just hoped Polly didn't take after her mother.

'Let's be off!' said Polly, looking at Darren. Beth's stand for the Lord still played on her mind. *Perhaps the Lord doesn't like me going dancing.* But she dismissed her doubts. They were off to meet friends in the village now. *I'm going to enjoy myself this evening.*

Darren called for Polly at eight o'clock and looked her up and down. He was tall, clean looking with fair hair and looked good wearing his best suit. Yes, it was obvious as she ran out to him that she had made her dress, but he was easy going and, unusually for a young chap, more interested in who Polly *was* than how she looked. At least she wasn't smothered in make-up like some of the girls. He understood dress material was still hard to come by and the Wests did have extra expenses. With Vera ill and Vic needing books for study, there wasn't much spare cash.

'Hello, darling. You look gorgeous!' He kissed her.

'Look at you, then!' Polly said. 'Bet you didn't make that.' She posed like a model on the catwalk, 'Like it then?'

He loved how she was delighted with herself instead of being fed up they couldn't afford anything better. He took her hand and hurried her along the Close, Polly stumbling in her high heels. She pulled him to a stop. 'How on earth am I going to dance in these?'

The evening was magical. 'Will you give me the pleasure of the last dance, madam?' asked Darren. Polly was relaxed and happy.

'Who else would I want to dance with?' He pressed her close. She gently rubbed her cheek against his. She knew, absolutely *knew* she was in love with him. They were meant for each other. She prayed more earnestly than usual for him before getting into bed. When he held her it felt fine, but now she was overwhelmed by guilt. Not only had she gone dancing but with a non-

Christian. A week ago, she'd persuaded him to attend an evangelistic rally where the preacher had explained the way of salvation and invited people to ask Jesus into their lives, while a choir sang, 'All to Jesus I surrender.' *How can he refuse after hearing that?* She rationalised by deciding he wasn't refusing but lacking conviction. He'd remained firmly in his seat. 'Not yet,' he whispered.

But thoughtful Darren felt Polly was going too far. When Vic was down from university and they were sauntering to the pub he admitted, 'Frankly, I'm scared for Polly and I can't bear the way she's rejecting so much stuff for God... giving up this, that and the other.'

'Daft ass,' put in her brother. 'She won't play cards with the family. She's sworn never to drink alcohol again. And it's all *the Bible says this and the Bible says that*. How can she be so taken in?'

'And she wants *me* to change too.'

'Ummm, she's leaving school and going out into the real world. That'll learn her.'

'But *will* it? Has she told you any plans?'

'We're all waiting for *God* to tell her – flash from the sky... *you know*. Dad says she's got to work at Woolworth's until she makes up her mind. Bloody hell, I could strangle that Mrs Holland.'

'Even Nina doesn't really like talking to her now. She says all their conversations land up the same way: Polly preaching at her.'

'Pol says she's *witnessing*. Even walking up the road carrying a Bible's being a witness. Witnessing *what* for God's sake?' He let out a long groan.

Darren looked at Vic as though he was hoping his friend could change things. 'Give me the fun Polly back,' he said, wistfully. 'Not sure how much longer I can put up with this.'

'Tried praying about it?' They sniggered ruefully, and picked up their step to the pub.

CHAPTER 7

Anthony lived. His wound turned septic and he took longer to recover than expected. He went to a convalescent home run by nuns. '…pray for us sinners now, and at the hour of our death…' The sound of rosary beads and the quiet whisper of a voice reciting the *Hail Mary* gradually woke him from his afternoon rest. He opened his eyes. Sister Amelia was standing by his bed eyes closed. He watched her as she eventually kissed the crucifix then let her rosary fall gently to hang from her waist. *Comforting*.

'Ah! So you're awake then, Anthony.' The soft voice was kindly and her smile gave him a secure feeling. She lifted her chin towards the window: 'Look at the sun shining out there! Would you like to try taking a walk outside?'

'I w-would,' Anthony stared outside, 'I w-would. Y-yes p-please.' The nun glided to the door and opened it.

'We must get you in a fit state to go back to the routine of the monastery, mustn't we? You can't stay here for ever.' Anthony smiled thinking he wouldn't mind at all.

'I'll—'

'See you at the back door in ten minutes.' He nodded then manoeuvred himself to sit on the edge of the bed. Every day he found movement easier and no longer needed to support his wound as he walked. At the allotted time he was by the back door. He took a deep breath of fresh air and enjoyed the feel of a light breeze on his cheeks. Sister Amelia pointed to a seat about twenty yards away.

'Let's go over there, shall we? No hurry.' Anthony nodded again. At last, he could see himself getting back to normal. He visualised Brother Vincent in the monastery garden. They moved forward together.

'D-do you g-grow your own vegetables?'

'We do. Sister Martha provides us with fresh food most of the year round. She is one of our older sisters, and an example to us all.'

'Our g-gardener is old and very w-wise. I enjoy h-helping him.'

'You'll soon be back to working in the fresh air. A great blessing from our loving Lord.' Once again he was encouraged by Sister Amelia. She was probably about ten years older than he – energetic and, how could he describe her…? Hardworking and creative. The other nuns rarely showed much imagination. She liked art, and they enjoyed thoughtful conversations. And it was good to converse in a 'normal' manner. Unlike St Martin's the nursing order had no rule of silence. On reaching the seat they sat down.

'I f-feel s-stronger today.'

'Well, your body is healing well now you are getting over your shock and the loss of blood. The sisterhood has been praying that our blessed Lord will heal your body and mind. There must have been turmoil going on in that head of yours. I think sometimes the mind is more difficult to heal than the body.'

'Y-yes? What m-makes you say that?' Amelia hesitated. She pursed her lips and frowned.

'Well, Anthony,' she hesitated. 'Ohh—'

Anthony looked at her. *I shouldn't have asked.* 'Sorry, sister, please don't... I-I mean... I m-mean...' He stopped. *Something is wrong.*

Looking back at the house she whispered, 'If you can walk a bit further tomorrow, perhaps I'll share something with you.' She was troubled in some way, but it was not his place to pry.

'I-I'm doing b-better every day.' Briefly they looked each other in the eye. A new and awkward situation for Anthony. So far they had only talked of physical needs. He noticed a beetle scuttling towards his left foot, but on coming up against it, it stopped, then went off in a different direction. He pointed to a rose rambling up the branches of a small tree and waterfalling to the ground.

'We had a rose like that at home. It reminds me of my parent's garden.' But his nurse was in her own world.

Very quietly she said, lips hardly moving, 'Can I tell you something, Anthony...? Tomorrow, when we're further from the house?' In the same breath she stood and said, 'We'll go back now. See if you can stand a little straighter.' He pulled back his shoulders, his mind thrown into a different sort of turmoil. A distraction from his own bewilderment and broiling emotions. *Share something with me? Holy Mary, ME?*

'S-sister, you've been so g-good to m-me. Yes, y-yes. Of c-course...' he nodded to the house. 'Would that be p-permissible?' They walked towards the door.

'You haven't taken your vows yet, have you, Anthony?'

'Not y-yet, n-no.' But he was afraid to say anything else. They reached the house and went inside.

She smiled and changed the subject, 'I'll bring your supper in a little while.' His mind ran wild.

*

Next morning the cook brought in his breakfast.

'Sister Amelia said she has to see the Reverend Mother first thing, but she'll take you for a walk in the garden later.' He put the tray on the table. 'Seems to me something isn't quite right.' Without further ado, he left before Anthony had time to respond.

'Thank you very m-much.' The door closed. He noted the milk was missing. A small inconvenience. *But what's wrong with Sister Amelia?* More bewilderment.

'I think you'll be ready for home in about two weeks.' A doctor jolted him out of his reverie. It was mid-morning. 'How do you feel about that?'

'Alright, alright, thank you, th-thank you.'

'Any questions?' Anthony had nothing to ask, and slowly shook his head, deep in thought. It would be strange after all this time to get back into the strict and silent routine.

'If you think of anything, just ask one of the sisters.' He smiled. 'You've done well. I expect you'll be glad to get on with the preparation for your vows.' The last few words made Anthony's stomach lurch. *I'll get back into the routine of the holy life and it will be alright. It is my calling.* He decided to spend the rest of the morning in prayer and fasting so rang the bell and told the orderly he would not be wanting lunch. His prayers were solely focused on preparing for the afternoon. *Holy Mary, Mother of God quieten my mind, take away all the impurities, give me peace. Forgive me, forgive me.*

Then came a visualisation of Brother Vincent – so clear – standing in the chicken run: 'No need to worry, chucks,' he was scattering feed, 'plenty for everyone. Seed for you, God's sunshine for me.' He radiated peace. And Anthony bathed in the same pool of peace.

When he met Sister Amelia in the garden, atypically, he was the first to speak greeting her with praying hands:

'The L-Lord be with you.'

'And with you.' They wandered slowly in silence. Peace.

Eventually Amelia spoke: 'How are you today, Anthony? Can we stroll as far as the herb garden?'

'I'm m-much improved, thank you S-sister. The d-doctor was pleased with me and this,' he swept his arm round as they viewed the garden, 'h-helps me h-heal.' He decided to take a risk.

'You mentioned my vows, y-yesterday?' Sister Amelia looked back at the house and urged him towards the walled herb garden. They sat down. Lavender was in bloom and they both inhaled deeply then relaxed.

'I just had a feeling you are unhappy about committing yourself for some... reason.' He frowned, stared at her and waited patiently for her to continue. 'Anthony,' she confided earnestly, 'be ab-so-lute-ly sure before you do.' She paused.

All he could say was a questioning 'Yes?'

'I took my vows about fifteen years ago when I was in my twenties. I thought when I became a bride of Christ,' she lifted her hand and studied her ring, 'I thought He would be...' Anthony felt himself going red and looked away but he was intrigued.

'You are m-married to Christ.'

Anthony could only just make out Amelia's words: 'It's not working out for me. I'm hoping you will understand... I want to confess something.'

'I'm n-not, not...'

'No, Anthony, but as a friend... will you hear me out?'

'A-as a f-friend?' She took his lack of refusal as agreement.

'I love one of the Sisterhood. I... I can't seem to help it. This morning Reverend Mother told me my struggle will only get worse. I have been trying to overcome... desperately... but I have to, well, break my vows.' She was struggling to keep control of her emotions. 'Mother told me it will only get worse. I wish I'd never taken them. There's no choice. I must leave the Order. I'll never be forgiven.'

Leaving the Order? She loves a woman! Does it happen to women?

'S-sister, I-I didn't know... I'm s-sorry. I'm so s-sorry.'

Speechless. He could find no comforting words. The silence fell heavily between them. Stunned, he could only shake his head.

'Anthony, forgive me. I'm telling you because I think you might understand.'

'Y-yes...'

'Anthony,' she was pleading. 'They condemn me. All of them except one. She must leave too. You don't condemn me, do you?'

Anthony had no idea how to answer, but out of sympathy and as a friend he whispered,

'I d-don't think s-so.'

CHAPTER 8

'I'm sure God doesn't want me at Woollies,' Polly told Eli as he did his rounds.

'Got religion, 'ave you love?'

Polly stared over the road at the beloved horses.

'Don't want too much of that – it can send you barmy.' Polly was about to defend herself as he walked away, but she remained silent. *Blessed are ye when men shall revile you… for my sake*. She called out: 'I'm being baptised by immersion on Sunday!'

'Enjoy yerself then,' he answered, making for number 17. 'I got me own problems.' He was preoccupied. Polly didn't ask about his problems, but he shouted back at her anyway, ''Orses are going! 'aving an electric float.'

But it was lost on her. 'Halebridge Baptist, three o'clock Sunday!' She was praying everyone she knew would come. After closing the door she recalled: 'The horses have got to go.' *Where? Poor Eli. I'll miss them too. I should have said something. Oh no. No, no, no.*

She went into the kitchen. Vera was up and sitting quietly at the table. Her antidepressants helped a little, but made her tired. She rarely wanted to talk and left James and Polly to do most of the cooking and housework. Dusting and making beds were her limit. 'The house is always in a mess, Pol.'

'I don't mind doing more cleaning, Mum.'

To Polly's consternation Vera came over to her, rested her head on her daughter's shoulder and sobbed. 'Don't ever leave me, will you, Pol? You know I couldn't do without you. I couldn't manage without you in the house.'

Mum's meant to be there for me. Polly was shocked. She patted her mother on the back.

'Mum, if only you'd put your trust in God. I mean properly, not just…' She stopped herself, but there was no reply. 'Mum! I'll have to wait and see what God tells me to do…' Vera didn't respond. 'Don't you see, Mum?'

'I suppose I have to,' Vera whimpered. She resumed her place at the table, stroking her mouth with her right hand.

'I'll make you a cup of tea, Mum. You'll be all right. Why don't you go back to bed for a little while?' *Why isn't she nice to me then?* Polly felt resentful and took her own drink into the garden. She needed reassurance from her mother.

That evening Polly and Beth were in Mrs Holland's home for the Friday meeting: seven girls present, all with Bibles on their laps. 'Olive, will you commit the evening for us?' They bowed their heads while Olive thanked God they had the opportunity to learn more about His Word.

'Amen. Thank you, Olive. *Now.*' She opened her Bible at a place marked with a slip of paper. 'Turn to Ephesians six, verse ten, and we'll continue to study the Armour of God. Tonight we've reached the Shield of Faith.' There was a rustle as they found their places. 'Does anyone remember verse twelve? Why do we need God's armour at all? Beth?'

Beth calculated on her fingers with her eyes closed. 'Our struggle—'

'*For* our struggle,' Mrs Holland corrected.

Beth shook her head quickly, as though shaking her brain cells into place, and acknowledged her mistake. '*For* our struggle is not against flesh and blood, but against the rulers, against the authorities, against the powers of this dark world and against the spiritual forces of evil in the heavenly realms.'

'So, what can you add, Polly?' Polly blushed, bit her lip, and looked at the ceiling. She panicked when jumped on to answer questions.

'Ummm...' Mrs Holland questioned one of the other girls.

The study on the shield of faith lasted half an hour, then it was time to share subjects for prayer. Polly asked Jesus for her baptismal testimony to be a good witness. 'I've asked the milkman to come, and my parents, and brother, and Darren. But Mum says I was christened as a baby and don't need to be done again.'

'So why do *you* think you need immersion?'

Polly knew this answer: 'We are immersed in the water to show we've been buried with Christ, then rise up a new person... born of the Spirit.'

'And?'

Polly hesitated. 'Oh yes, a baby can't ask Jesus to save him. Christening someone who doesn't know what's going on doesn't make the person a Christian.'

'And?'

Now Polly was getting flustered, so Beth jumped in. 'We are all sinners. A baby hasn't repented and asked Jesus to be his Saviour.' She finished with a flourish, quoting John, chapter three, verse three: 'Unless a man is born again, he cannot see the kingdom of God!'

'Yes!' Mrs Holland was smiling, 'That's why we have such a responsibility to tell the world – the *whole* world – that we must be born again – if we want to go to heaven. And...' she frowned, looking worried, 'we are all quite clear our baptism doesn't save us, aren't we?' The girls chorused their agreement.

After a pause Mrs Holland prayed for the unconverted girls before she looked straight in Polly's eyes. 'And are you *absolutely certain* you've been born again of the Spirit, Polly?'

Polly was sure. 'Yes, on the 19th of December.'

Her teacher smiled triumphantly. 'We'll commit Polly to the Lord for her special day, and make all our other requests.' She consulted her list. The girls knelt, eyes closed, elbows on chairs and faces in hands. They prayed 'as they were led,' waiting for the right time to express out loud whatever entered their minds. Beth usually felt inspired first, but it never happened to Polly until near the end. It wasn't so much the Spirit moving as plucking up courage.

*

Floorboards between the choir stalls had been lifted to reveal the baptismal pool, filled with water and heated. Three others besides Polly were going to testify about their salvation and be fully immersed by the pastor with the help of a deacon.

Several visitors arrived and the atmosphere was expectant as church members anticipated unsaved visitors responding to the Lord's message.

Predictably, Eli and his family did not turn up. Nor did Victor. Or James... Or DARREN. *Where is he?* But Vera was there with Doris, an old school-friend who supported her faithfully. Polly's mother was bewildered. 'Why does she have to do all this strange stuff?' she whispered to Doris, her hand shaking at her mouth. I don't like it.' James had flatly refused to come.

'I know,' said Doris 'It all feels weird to me.' They wondered what would happen next. At last, after hymns, long prayers and an explanation by the pastor, Polly stood in the pulpit wearing a special robe the church kept for these occasions.

'My christening as a baby didn't mean anything to me because...' Polly started but was interrupted by a disturbance in the congregation. She tried to think what to say next, but... *Oh no! Mum and Doris are leaving...* Vera was crying. Polly checked her notes and forced herself to read on.

As she emerged from the water crying, gown heavy and dripping, a bath towel was wrapped around her by the pastor's wife. In the vestry Mrs Holland helped her change. 'What's all this Dear? Such a wonderful testimony, but what a pity your mother went out.'

'I Kn-kn-know!' she sobbed, 'She doesn't understand. And – and... Darren wasn't there!'

'Dry your eyes and listen to what the guest speaker has to say. I'm sure the Lord has a message for you.' They returned to the front row of the congregation.

Pastor Ingrams' voice rose a few enthusiastic decibels. 'It is my privilege to introduce...'

The preacher climbed into the high pulpit overlooking the congregation. 'Revelation, chapter 3, and verse twenty,' he boomed: 'BEHOLD! I stand at the door and knock! If any may hear my voice and open the door, I will come in and sup with him, and HE with ME!' After thirty minutes he invited everybody to open the door of their heart to Jesus. 'Yes... I mean YOU.' He looked sternly at the crowd. He invited them to go out to the front and the organist played and the people sang quietly, 'All to Jesus, I surrender':

> *All to Jesus I surrender,*
> *All to Him I freely give;*
> *I will ever love and trust Him,*
> *In His presence daily live.*

The baptismal candidates and church members sang wholeheartedly, while the visitors sang doubtfully, or not at all. One person remained seated, unaware he would be targeted with special prayer at the meeting afterwards. Nobody approached the front, but the pastor urged them to have faith. 'The Lord will keep working in your heart,' he consoled as they left the church.

As they chatted at the corner of Elm Close before going their separate ways, Darren sprang into Polly's thoughts. 'I do wish Darren would contact me, Beth.'

'When did you last see him?'

'Well, he asked me to the pub on Friday, but he knows what I think about that now! I'll ring when I get in and ask why he didn't come today.'

But her call was delayed. As she walked into the kitchen she faced her mother, red-eyed and still being comforted by Doris sitting with an arm around her shoulders. Doris looked up and stared hard at Polly, who, not knowing what to say, felt a rising sense of indignation.

'You never agree with *anything* I do, Mum. Why did you walk out as soon as I started to speak…?'

'Damn and blast!' her mother yelled, thumping her fist on the table with a rare show of strength.

Polly flared up. 'You are so selfish,' she shouted, 'You never see things from my point of view.'

'That's not very Christian in my book,' exclaimed Doris accusingly.

Polly immediately felt a failure. She mumbled 'Sorry,' and left the kitchen closing the door behind her. *Why did I get angry? Jesus, if I am persecuted for your sake, then help me. Help me to control myself.* Then she remembered Darren and snuck down to the telephone in the hall. No reply. *Whatever is he doing? No football now...*

When Victor came in later, Polly flew to the front door. 'Where's Darren, Vic?'

'Ummmm,' he looked embarrassed.

'Go on. Where is he then?' Vic remained dumb.

'WHERE is he?' she demanded. Vic started upstairs and Polly followed him into his bedroom where he turned his back and rummaged in the wardrobe.

'It's no joke, all this religious stuff y'know, Pol.' For once he was serious.

'What?' The joy of her baptism, the comfort of the afternoon's congratulations were lost. Her emotions were raw.

He turned abruptly to face her: 'He's gone to Scotland for a week.'

'Scotland, *Scotland?* He didn't tell *me*.'

'No,' Vic replied, turning his back again and throwing out dirty clothes. Then, emerging for a second, he told her straight, 'You're too caught up in your own stuff!' He pulled out a drawer, crossly. 'You've really changed since I went to university ya'know. Damn, where are those shorts?'

'Victor! BEAST!'

'He asked me to give you a message...'

'And?'
'He'll send you a postcard.'

CHAPTER 9

'Oh look!' said Barbara, pointing out a digger and other signs of work on one of the bomb sites near Maisie's Cuppa, 'they've actually started.'

Penny examined the scene. 'They're not wasting their time, are they?'

'I must tell Michael.' Barbara focused her camera, clicked, then let it drop on the cord round her neck. 'It's going to be even more of a mess around here – for goodness knows how long.'

'*You* campaigned for it to start!' They settled at their normal table and ordered the usual.

Maisie was tidying the counter while her sister did the cooking. Barbara attracted her attention, 'Maisie, do you know anyone on the list for the new flats on the bomb site?'

'That couple at the window do, for sure, she hesitated... I think.' Maisie was biting her bottom lip. 'I think that's where they want a place.'

Barbara lost no time getting to the window table. Penny was embarrassed. *So crass at times. So eager to get her story. Too keen to please Michael.*

'Excuse me. I'm from the local newspaper. Have you noticed work has started on that bomb site?' She pointed to it. The couple were young, bright. She told Barbara she was pregnant and anxious to move... they chatted on...

Barbara returned to their table. 'Good picture. Might have to get this film developed before it's finished.' Their cottage pie arrived. She nodded her thanks to Maisie then looked back at Penny. 'Michael will be pleased.' She was all smiles.

'It's early to talk about people moving in before they've even cleared the site.'

'Oh no! You've got to think ahead. I mean, she's pregnant. Great story if they can be housed in time for the baby.'

'"News isn't news until it's happened." Michael's always saying that, especially to you, Barb. You're always getting ahead of yourself.' She lowered her voice to a whisper shielding her mouth with her hand, 'Suppose she has a miscarriage?'

Barbara stuck her fork into the potato and mince. It was better to have hot food midday than cooking in the evening. 'But Michael—'

'Michael, Michael, Michael… Don't get carried away, Barb. He's not as keen on you as you are on him, you know.'

'How do you know?'

'He's a married man. And you're still a married woman, in case you've forgotten.'

'Only just…'

Maisie was keeping an ear open behind the counter and didn't like their raised voices. 'What's got into you this afternoon, girls? Yer won't be 'avin' yer free cuppa if y'start up like this!' She was sometimes wary of the two journalists, but they were good customers and she liked them.

Penny lowered her voice. 'I only tell you what I think you need to know.' They looked each other straight in the face until Barbara's eyes welled up. She caught her breath and focused on attacking her dinner. Penny raised her eyebrows in Maisie's direction and pursed her lips. Maisie looked away.

'It's bloody difficult,' Barbara whispered. 'You don't know what it's like when you discover your husband's unfaithful.' They concentrated on lunch.

'What happens next at home then? Who's staying in the big house?'

'He is. He wanted it in the first place. I said it was too expensive. We never needed all that space. See what his new bit of fluff makes of it.'

'Can he afford it without your contribution?'

'You bet he'll try. Bigger mortgage – or maybe she's loaded.'

'And you?'

Penny's question brought Barbara up with a start. 'Rent a flat in London, I suppose,' she smiled. 'At least that cuts out the train journey. Big difference.'

The workmen wolf whistled as they passed the clearing work on the way back to the office. The girls ignored them, and walked in silence. Barbara stared at the pavement, preoccupied with Noel, and her anger came flooding back. *I hate going home these days – but what else can I do?* Penny silently planned her partner's evening meal.

It was a bright afternoon and the windows were open. Michael and Peter, sports reporter, were engrossed in typing. Barbara walked in the door and realised she'd forgotten to take her film for developing. 'Damn! Won't be a minute. Sorry!' She flew back out ignoring Michael's groan. Penny registered his disapproval and dialled a telephone number with her pen.

But Barbara didn't hurry. She sat in the warm sun for a few minutes and closed her eyes. The seat reminded her of the broken bench in The Elms' garden. *If I'd had that mended I could have enjoyed the sun out there… but the chickens would have driven me mad. And that wretched cockerel. The things I've left undone. Maybe Noel's got a point. I never made much effort to make it a home. Penny's right. If I were Noel, how would I see me?* She faced facts. *Shall I go back to my maiden name? … ughhh.* She made her way to the chemist. *Will he argue over the music… or at least my records?* She anticipated big rows and was deciding what she would fight for. After all, he was at fault. *I'm the injured party. Next week I'll sort all this out…* She checked her watch and started running. *Michael will not be impressed.*

*

'We've got to talk,' said Noel when Barbara arrived home. But she was tired. The train was delayed and more over-crowded than usual.

'What about?'

'Don't be bloody-minded. You know *what*.' She poured a brandy. '*I'll have a bath.'*

When she came downstairs, refreshed, Noel started again. 'This divorce business is jolly expensive.'

'And it takes a while, you know, unless we've lived apart for seven years.' They were both thinking that might be the best way: live apart.

'Someone should have moved out before… bloody hell!' He sat down with a thump and picked up his beer. 'We knew things weren't right as soon as we moved here.'

'I never really wanted this enormous place,' Barbara sulked, 'but we'll just have to start from where we are.' She said decisively.

'And?'

'I want this over. I'll be better off in London. At least I'll save the train fare and have more time for myself.'

'Right. Suits me.'

The evening rumbled on. They talked in fits and starts trying to keep civilised.

'Eggs on toast?'

'Fine.'

By next morning they had a plan. Barbara would ask her aunt who lived on a bus route if she could stay with her. Noel would remain in The Elms and put it on the market. He'd negotiate with solicitors and agents. They'd go separate ways and see how things worked out as time went by. Partly relieved, they left for work at the same time instead of one slamming the door in the other's face.

After a fraught morning, Barbara and Penny were waiting to order lunch at Maisie's. 'It's a big thing for you, after all these years with him, Barb.'

'Good riddance to bad rubbish.' She was morose.

Penny was thoughtful. 'So much to decide. Do you think he'll be reasonable?'

'That cockerel next door drives me insane.'

'That's nothing to do with it!'

Barbara conceded, her mind elsewhere. She didn't want to talk about it. She was sifting through the implications of her changed situation. They ate in silence.

*

All day Barbara worked in a hurry. Eventually she got home and left a note telling Noel her aunt in London was happy to have her, then plucked up courage to tell next door what was going on. Polly invited her in and offered a drink.

'Just a quickie then. I don't know what to do first.'

Vera was upstairs and the others were out. Fluffy was sleeping on a kitchen chair, and stretched his front paws in front of him, yawning.

'So, Polly's going to put the kettle on is she?' Asked Barbara looking a bit desperate. Polly was miffed. *It's one thing for Vic to joke about it... or Darren, but Mrs Gristwood?* Her stomach still lurched at the thought of *him*. She glanced at Barbara with a hint of a smile and changed the subject. Swallowing, she asked her if everything was all right.'

'Yes! Well, it will be when I've sorted out myself. I'm going to stay with my aunt in London. It's nearer work.'

Polly, not sorry, expressed surprise. 'You're moving!'

'I'm moving out... Neil's staying.' She studied the kitchen cupboards. 'Not easy, but as you get older you'll realise these things happen.' Polly put the tea in front of Barbara. *Treats me like a kid.*

'Shall I see if Mum will come downstairs?'

Barbara ignored Polly's offer: 'Is your mother disabled?'

'We don't know what's wrong with her. She's always fed-up and nervous.'

'I'm sorry to hear that. Maybe she should see a specialist.'

'They need to do a few tests.' Barbara wasn't really interested and the uneasy interchange ended.

'I only popped in to say goodbye.' She took a few polite sips of tea. 'I might not come back to Halebridge unless I visit the house for a few things. I'm sorry to miss your parents, but please pass my goodbyes to them, won't you, dear?' Polly cringed, and headed to the front door.

'It must be difficult. I'll pray for you.'

'And what good do you expect that to do?' Barbara smirked but then stopped near the front door and admired the picture on the wall. 'That's hand-written, isn't it?' She looked closer. *Gloria Patri et Filio et Spiritui Sancto*... Latin... beautiful.'

'We like it.'

Polly was impatient for her to go and just nodded. She opened the door and steeled herself to be civil. 'I'll pass on your message.' She offered to shake hands, but Barbara leant towards her and pecked her cheek.

'Nice knowing you,' she smiled, quickening her footsteps towards the gate where she waved. Polly half smiled and wiped the back of her hand against her cheek.

'I'll be praying, whether you believe in God or not.'
Goodbye, Mrs Gristwood.

CHAPTER 10

Anthony and Lucian were strolling in the garden after supper. 'I f-felt so close to G-god here this afternoon.'

What does Anthony really want to say? 'It's good that you are content in silence. Some brothers never adapt,' Lucian replied.

'B-brother, h-have you ever dug potatoes and f-felt them warm in the earth?'

'I've done garden duty, but no, I have never dug potatoes.'

'You dig the s-soil a little way from the withered plant and s-search for yield. When you p-put your hand into the earth and f-feel potatoes warm from the s-sun it is as though you are t-touching the fount of life. S-sowing and h-harvest; G-god and man working together. B-but there's s-something else when the s-sun sh-shines… a fulfilment. W-words can't explain, but I feel a gratifying peace.'

It was the longest speech Anthony had made since the stabbing.

Lucian felt no need to say anything for a while, then raised his eyebrows. 'You think you've given up earthly pleasures, and God rewards you in unexpected ways.' He gave the impression he himself was content.

But Anthony knew thoughts and feelings were as clouds passing over the sun. 'I didn't really want to come back here,' Lucian had confided in a moment of weakness after his mother's funeral. 'India is so different. Family is all-important. And it is vibrant and colourful.' He obviously missed his own culture, something which hadn't occurred to his mentee before.

'I know now why we are told it is best to remain in the monastery walls.' He said no more, and as Anthony had no concept of the nature of Indian culture he could only reflect on his own experience.

'In my m-mind I-I'm back h-home when I write to P-Polly. I must write again because she c-clearly loves G-God. But she ignores a-anything I say about the H-holy Church or the s-sacraments. I-it's difficult to express what I really want her to know.'

'Of course. These are reasons why Father restricts our letters. We are diverted from our purpose at St. Martins. Are you writing to your uncle too?'

'H-Henry? Well, I should write t-to him. His s-son, Gus, is a c-constant worry. H-he b-bullied me when we were children, and I-I find it difficult to l-like him. Now he's on drugs and will do anything to feed his h-habit, – never thinks about G-God or the afterlife. B-but perhaps I should be s-sorry for him. He's a lost s-soul. Uncle H-Henry: h-he means w-well, b-but we have nothing in c-common.' Anthony told Lucian the story of the bench incident and they shared a moment of restrained amusement.

'God bless him. We must say more prayers. All is not yet lost.'

Next day Anthony was helping Brother Vincent with the chickens. Vincent was the oldest working brother in the community and suffered from sporadic coughing fits … He sat on an upturned box and told Anthony what needed doing in the shed. 'I-I never thought I-I'd enjoy cleaning out the h-hen house!' Anthony said as he dusted himself off. Squawking issued forth from the nesting box and a hen strutted slowly through the doorway looking proud. Anthony collected the egg. The warmth reminded him of his potatoes and his thoughts about God, man, and nature. He placed it in Vincent's hand.

Vincent turned it in his palm. 'They don't know what they're missing, indoors, do they?'

As Anthony raked over the soil in the chicken-run, *missing, missing*, kept echoing in his mind and transported him to his garden back home. *Missing. Missing.* He stopped working and stood up. *That's IT! Uncle Henry was missing Father!* A piece of jigsaw fell into place. *Is that why the shed door was closed?* He knew what was going on. *Henry was missing Father; something in the shed reminded him – the garden tools – the boots.* He felt a rush of empathy with Henry, then a wave of sadness… for what? *For Father!* He put the rake down and pulled up a box near to Vincent. 'M-my f-father's p-plane was s-shot down in the w-war and w-went down in f-flames. He w-was never f-found.'

Vincent placed a grubby hand on his arm, squeezing it weakly. He confided, 'Things happened to me a long time ago. Not easy.' Anthony turned to study Vincent's face. He was watching the dark clouds looming in the west, but kept his hand on Anthony's arm, seemingly having forgotten it was there. Anthony's gaze turned to the chickens scratching contentedly away and pecking up the grit from time to time, not a care in the world. He managed a half smile.

'Thank goodness for the chickens!' Vincent turned from the clouds to the busy chickens and his eyes brightened. His hand dropped into his lap.

That evening Anthony wrote to his uncle. Then Polly came to his mind. He would ask Tom to post the letters again. *I mustn't continue breaking the rules. But just this once.*

~ St Martin's Brotherhood ~
Dear Polly

Peace be with you! I know I don't owe you a letter, but I've been reminded of The Elms and its surroundings this afternoon and wanted to write. Despite the lapse in our correspondence, I've been praying for you almost every day. Occasionally, I think of Fluffy too.

A painful and shocking incident happened which isn't easy to talk about, but I'm going to try to share it with you.

One of the brothers, who has since left, attacked me and I had to spend time in hospital with a wound in my stomach. I could have bled to death, but I reached hospital in time to be treated. It took me a long while to convalesce, and the memories still haunt me.

However, you'll be surprised to hear I enjoy helping with the chickens in the monastery garden. I used to wonder why you liked them, but now I understand; they take things as they come and just get on with life. My mother loved the eggs your family gave us after the war. I hope you knew how thankful we were. Now I have the pleasure of collecting them myself.

I wonder if you have had any second thoughts about speaking to Father Alphonsus? My offer to introduce you is always open.

Anthony.

P.S. If you reply, do please call me Anthony.

He read it through, admired his handwriting and felt pleased with himself.

*

Father Brendon called for him the following week.

'I've noticed you seem more peaceful these days. Let's see now, nearly four years have passed since that incident. *Are* you at peace brother?'

Anthony waited at the Abbot's desk staring at the wall. 'I feel better, m-much better, thank you Father. Yes, I'-m much better, thank you.'

'Can you talk about it, Anthony?'

'I-I don't know.'

'In what ways do you feel better?'

Anthony managed to say that he was happy in the garden.

'I do wish you would look at me, Anthony!' A touch of impatience. But Anthony persisted in staring at the floor. Father Brendon involuntarily stamped his foot. In a louder voice: 'And your vows?'

Anthony experienced the usual wave of anxiety when reminded of vows, although beneath the turmoil dwelt a knowledge that serenity would return. The Abbot was insistent. 'You won't be ready until you can confront the demons that have possessed your soul in the past. Your demons – and those of Brother Sebastian.'

It was the first time his name had been mentioned to him since that night.

He was silent.

'Have you forgiven him?'

Anthony didn't know what to say. This hurt. His love for Sebastian had been killed that night. 'F-f-forgive?' he managed to ask, feeling weak.

'Sit down.' Anthony walked to a chair by the wall. Father Brendon sat next to him. 'It is essential.' He said quietly.

'I d-don't understand why.'

'What do you think made Sebastian feel able to come to your cell?'

'Oh n-no!' Anthony's eyes brimmed with tears but the Abbot was unfazed and assessed Anthony steadily.

Gently: 'Tell me what you thought… I know this is hard, but I believe you are strong enough and the Holy Spirit will help you if you honestly seek to do His Will, and renounce all wrongful desires.' The seconds ticked by and Anthony blinked compulsively. He felt tears drip on his cheeks, and put a finger behind his glasses to wipe them away. Finally, a look of determination came over his face.

'I-I th-thought…'

'Yes, take it slowly,' said the Abbot, trying to soothe the moment.

'I thought he loved me.' It came out all at once.

The room was quiet.

'I know.'

Anthony risked a glimpse of the Abbot's eyes, but then looked down.

'Unfortunately, he did. That was the dreadful truth of the matter.' His words hung in the air. 'And did you love him, Anthony?'

Agonising – stop – please. 'I-I don't w-want to love m-men. I don't know why I do, I'm not normal and I-I don't know why.' This time the tears were unrestrained and there was nothing Anthony could do to stop them.

'At last. This is what I've been waiting for. Now I believe God will forgive you if you repent and can also forgive. Sebastian should have known better. He took his vows before God but was unfaithful to them. He did not overcome his desires, and you represented an overwhelming temptation. He was obsessed. He gave in to evil and, in doing so, become mentally deranged and violence became his master. I think in the outside world they call it the red mist.' The Abbot crossed himself. 'God have mercy on him. I fear for his soul.' Despite no further comment from Anthony, Father Brendon did not press him further. An uncharacteristic wave of sympathy flowed over him and he alerted himself to move away from his acolyte. 'I will return with you to your cell, Anthony. It is best you spend the evening in prayer and fasting. I'll send you water.'

They reached the cell. 'Think carefully about how Christ will judge us and remember that which is thought in secret will be brought into the light. The catechism teaches us how we will either be filled with life or damned for eternity. That is your choice.' They bowed towards each other with praying hands.

The Abbot prayed as he left Anthony alone for the night. He paused outside the closed cell door and mentally blanked out his own feelings. Taking out his rosary, he proceeded along the cloister. There were other matters to attend to.

Back in his cell, Anthony knelt and bombarded God with desperate pleas.

But in the morning the question was there again. *Why did God make me like this? I'm not attracted to women, and must not love a man. So, must I deny myself any physical closeness? Why does my flesh stir?* He closed his eyes. *Hail Mary, full of grace...* He remembered Sister Amelia. Her love for a nun had shocked him, but later he drew comfort from her confession. The more he thought about it, the more it meant to him and he wished he'd found words to comfort her.

The whole day seemed to be dominated by his battle against physical need. *Will my temptation never end?* Then at night he was digging potatoes. The deeper he dug the more potatoes he found. He started to gather lovely warm potatoes but they started burning his hands. He screamed but couldn't drop them. He shook his hands to get rid of them and awoke sweating, throwing off his bedclothes. *They're stuck, stuck to me.* He was shaking. *I can't rid myself...* He tried to prepare his mind for vigils, but knew deep inside himself, right deep down, there was a pleasurable desire he couldn't shake off.

When he walked out into the cloisters the moonshine was so bright he didn't need his candle. He yearned for his mind to be as clear as the moon.

CHAPTER 11

16 Elm Close, Halebridge.
Dear Anthony,

It was a lovely surprise to see your letter. Sorry I have been slow to reply.

So much has happened for both of us since I last wrote. I was shocked to hear about your frightful attack. I imagined monks living together in harmony. That was a surprise.

Sadly Mum only gets up for an hour in the afternoons these days. It's nervous trouble and doesn't get any better. Fluffy sleeps on her bed most of the time. He is still active and gets a lot of fuss.

I've been working at Woolworth's since I left school. I'm sure God doesn't want me to stay there long, but at least I can witness to people who don't know Jesus. I take my Bible to work in case anyone asks questions.

Soon after leaving school, I felt so close to God and full of the Holy Spirit that I was baptised properly by immersion. Mum was upset so her friend took her outside and when I got home, I was angry with her and then felt guilty. The day was totally ruined when Vic told me Darren, my boyfriend, had gone to Scotland without telling me.

We were together for four years, and I thought we'd get married one day, because I really loved him. Then he sent a postcard to say he loved me but couldn't live with how I go on about God, and so it was best to split. I've only shared this with my friend Beth, and we're praying for Darren to be converted.

I was absolutely devastated and never replied. Vic's still friendly with him and as I was the only reason he stayed in Halebridge, he's gone to university after all. Enough about that.

I'm pleased you enjoy looking after the chickens. At least we have that in common!

As for Father Alphonsus: Thank you, but I'm sure I don't need to speak to him as I am already SAVED and will go to heaven. I pray for you every day too because it's wrong to pray to idols. Jesus is our only mediator and we are cleansed of our sin when we accept Him as our Saviour.
In Christ,
Polly

She finished addressing the envelope and heard Vera calling from her bed. 'What are you doing in there? Isn't it supper time?' Polly went into her.

'Why don't we go down for supper, Mum? Get some exercise.'

'Pol, I can't face the stairs.'

'Just try. Doctor said you should. You'll feel better if you have a change of scenery.'

'You have no idea what it's like…' griped Vera, giving in to tears. Polly gave up trying to spur her into action and went down to lay a tray. She realised she was getting impatient, but no, how could she understand? *Is she trying to prove a point? Or is she really ill?*

As she walked to the post-box after supper, she mulled over Anthony's 'injury'. *Why would a monk stab him? He's certainly a bit strange until you get to know him but that's odd. Very odd.* She dropped the letter in the box.

*

'It is a God-given honour to share the platform with Doctor Franklin Hedges, who sacrificed his comfortable home in 1942 to live with natives in India. We can be sure God will speak through him.'

The baptist church was holding its October missionary rally all week, but Polly and the Johnsons chose to go Wednesday. Beth and her mother, Nessa, held the preacher in high regard. Almost worshipped him maybe. 'The Holy Spirit uses Dr Hedges in such wonderful ways,' Nessa told Polly. 'Miracles are happening in India.'

Pastor Ingrams swept out his right arm towards the missionary and announced, 'From the Mission to Unreached Tribes, Dr Franklin Hedges.' The congregation settled in quiet anticipation.

They listened to Hedges' description of his mission to Indian villages, running clinics and preaching the Gospel to the indigenous people. He'd learnt the language first; it was all far more complicated than Polly realised. He spoke continuously to the spellbound congregation for ninety minutes and wound up booming, 'Go into ALL the world! Not only around the corner, not simply in your town, or even just your country.' He paused as the organ faded in, 'But God calls us to go out into the whole *world!*' His message hovered before coming to rest in the minds of the earnest congregation.

The choir started singing quietly before he lent towards the microphone and asked in little more than a whisper, 'Are you willing to obey Jesus – or…' he paused a few moments for effect, '…holding back?' Another pause. 'I believe one of you is saying, "No, not me" to the Lord. So many excuses! You're saying, "I'm only a young girl, only a young boy, EXCUSES!"' He jabbed his finger pointing round at everyone. 'Just say, "Yes Lord. I'll go,"' he whispered. '"Send me, Lord. Wherever you want me."' Then with sombre reverence he gathered up his Bible, descended from the pulpit and sat in his seat, smiling at the pastor as he did so.

Pastor Ingrams announced in his 'dying angel' voice, 'Page number 30: *The millions living o'er the deep… Dare we heedless be?*' The organ thundered and the congregation rose.

> *Speed the light, the blessed Gospel light;*
> *To the lands which are in gloom and night,*
> *Souls are waiting and the fields are white,*
> *Speed the light, O speed the light.*

Polly was engrossed. She sang with all her might, finding as she sang that she was echoing those excuses the Doctor had voiced. *God couldn't possibly want me to do that. I'm no good at languages.* She compromised by deciding to pray earnestly for all the lost souls and give a donation towards the mission.

She walked to the corner of Elm Close with Beth's mother. 'Aha,' said Nessa, 'that service gave us all plenty to think about, didn't it?'

Polly agreed, 'It was breath-taking – full of the Holy Spirit. The Mission to Unreached Tribes does marvellous work.'

'Beth once asked me if I thought God might be calling her to the mission field, but it obviously wasn't the life for her!'

'Why ever not?' Polly was puzzled.

'Oh, can't you see, darling! If she has children, she couldn't possibly send them to boarding school. I don't agree with that at all. She could easily *do* the work. But…' She tailed off, contemplating.

'Wouldn't God help – if he'd *really* called her?'

'I suppose so,' Nessa hesitated, 'but I do pray about Elizabeth's future, and the Lord has told me I needn't worry about her doing anything like that.'

Polly was taken aback and didn't know what to say. 'I must get home.'

Nessa's expression changed from smug comfort to what Beth called her *confidential info look*. 'But I have a feeling He's calling you, Polly.'

'Really?' She dashed off. *Why is it right for me but not Beth? But is she right?*

*

'Ian is so immature,' Beth confided. 'I really have to move on with my life.'

'What do you mean?' asked Polly.

Beth blushed. 'Huh, I haven't told anyone else but,' she moved closer to impart her secret. 'There's this really nice boy – well, a *man* actually – at the bank. We're meeting for coffee!'

'Is he a Christian, then?'

'*Of course!* Irish, five years older than me. But don't say anything because I haven't told Mum yet. Honestly, he's got such better prospects. Ian takes the Bible so seriously, all the time. And gives nearly everything to the poor!'

Polly longed to be with Darren. *Darren – I can't have Darren. Get over him.*

As she stepped inside Vera called. 'Is that you, Polly? Where have you been?'

But Polly, knowing her father and mother were in bed, ignored Vera's question and went into her room and closed the door. She dropped into bed and fell asleep quickly. Around three in the morning Fluffy jumped up and nestled beside her. *So, it's my turn then!* She felt comforted stroking him, but when she tried to go back to sleep, she couldn't. She was unsettled. *I can't be a missionary. I've no idea how I'd start. If Nessa thinks it's not for Beth, why should I be different? There's plenty I could do at home for the Lord, anyway.* The words of the hymn sung so earnestly earlier in the evening repeatedly came back to her. 'Speed the light… before it's too late… before it's too late… late…' She fell into a fitful sleep. Fluffy's purring magnified and morphed into an array of sneering demon cats – all shapes and sizes – leering and hissing. She had to get down a hill to Beth, but there was no way through the ruins. The light was shining on top of the hill. *Maybe I don't want to go Beth's way.* Floating upwards she became totally engulfed by the light. She opened her eyes. The curtains were still open from the night before.

The next day, Thursday, daylight seemed to take on a different hue. As she waited behind the counter for customers to catch her attention, Polly found herself speculating. *Was my dream a message?* Interwoven with questions about the light were snippets of Dr Hedges' story. *Miracles happening! Not many converted. Need more workers.* 'It is such a privilege,' Hedges had said, 'to witness God working thousands of miles from home… so few missionaries spreading the light. The potential harvest is enormous,' then his voice softened, 'but the labourers are *few.*' After a lack-lustre day Polly was tired from standing behind the counter but had little diversion from her own thoughts. She spent longer in prayer and reading that evening.

All to Jesus I surrender. The words she sang after her baptism. *I'm not surrendering everything to Jesus at all. I'm* not *offering to be a missionary!* She punched the eiderdown in determination. *Where would I start?* After an hour on her knees, a time she came to think of later as her struggle with Satan as he tempted her away from God's will, she was overcome by the simplicity of surrendering. *Yes, Lord, I will.* With the bedroom door closed she said out loud: 'Yes, Lord I surrender. I surrender all.' She sobbed in relief. Her conscience was clear. When she finally stopped crying she fell into a dreamless slumber.

On Friday evening she waited to speak to Mrs Holland after Bible study. Her Sunday school teacher would be the first to know. Mrs Holland clapped her hands and called her husband to share the news. They prayed together and he laid his hands on Polly's head blessing her.

'But I don't know where to start. What do I do now?'

'I think you could train as a nurse,' said Mrs Holland, 'then go to a missionary training college to prepare for the Lord's work.'

That's it. I'll become a nurse.

CHAPTER 12

Anthony entered Father Brendon's office and stood before his desk eyes down as usual, silent. He was always apprehensive about these sessions. In fairness to the brotherhood, he should concentrate more on his spiritual progress and be more willing to commit himself. But he could not... quite.

The Abbot walked round to him. 'Peace be with you.'

'And with you.'

They bowed as was their custom and Father Brendon indicated the two chairs at the side of the room, they sat, facing each other.

'Now, Anthony, we've worked towards vows for a long while – too long.' He spoke in carefully measured tones willing Anthony to react. He directed his gaze towards his acolyte but wasn't expecting eye contact. 'Brother Lucian tells me you have made considerable progress.'

Anthony remained thoughtfully quiet and doubtful.

The Abbot had watched Anthony carefully and considered he had grown in obedience and usefulness to the monastery. But as for spiritual integrity he wondered. Anthony had to move on. 'Brother Lucian will start a more intensive period of training with you and then we will set a date.'

Anthony swiftly glanced up. 'Yes, Father.' *I suppose this life is the best I can expect.*

'There can be no higher calling than a life of discipline, self-denial and dedication to prayer for others, Anthony. The world would be far worse off were it not for our continual intercession on behalf of those who know no better.'

How patronising. He uttered, 'N-no, Father.'

'I have to discuss another matter.' Father Brendon took a deep breath in, as though adjusting to a less than ideal frame of mind. He chose his words carefully. 'I am obliged to pass on news our superiors have learnt from our main benefactors. We have been asked to do something not previously required.'

Anthony scanned his Superior. 'Ummm…'

'For four hundred years our monastery has been supported by several rich landowners, but these days, especially since the war, there is barely enough income to keep our good work going. Unfortunately, we have been asked to raise income ourselves.'

'Is that s-so?' Anthony was shocked. *And my previous enormous donation? What happened to that?* 'Visitors to our p-premises?' he voiced.

'We will open the grounds and selected rooms to the public. This is a large establishment for a few residents. It will be disruptive: that we must accept. We must all do as requested. Father Brendon consulted a list. 'We've noted your talent is calligraphy. I'm asking you make cards to be sold on open days.'

'I-I have a few p-pens, but only little ink.'

'Inks, pens and card will be provided for you to illustrate Scriptural verses in the service of the brotherhood.'

Anthony bowed slightly and smiled in anticipation of doing more of what he loved, although niggling doubts overshadowed his pleasure. 'Yes, Father. I-I will gladly design c-cards for the Glory of G-God.' He was frowning as the interview ended. But the Abbot was pleased Anthony responded in such positive terms.

He rang a tiny handbell. The door was opened from the outside by a brother who bowed. *Did he hear everything that was said?* The doors were thick and heavy but not fitted properly in the frames. Eavesdropping was expected.

Back in his cell he revised the discussion: *vows, money, calligraphy, cards, designs.* Then the order changed in his mind: *money first, that's wrong. Something is bothering me.* The rest of the list escaped him now, and he abandoned his attempted recall. The bell tolled for the Angelus. A triple stroke, three reverberating booms. Midday. He joined in procession with the brothers merging into single file in the cloister, mumbling prayers and fingering their rosaries, processing slowly into the garden and towards the grotto.

'*Angelus Domini nuntiavit Mariae*,' chanted the Abbot.

'*Et concepit de Spiritu Sancto*,' the brothers responded in lower pitch.

They knelt before the grotto murmuring, '*Pater Noster qui es in caelis…*' Anthony's lips moved in unison with the others, but his thoughts remained firmly planted on the need for funds. He was fighting suspicion. *What has he done with my inheritance?* The conflict made him feel guilty: *Am I falling into sin? Am I doubting; disobedient? Where has all that money gone, from me and from my brothers here?* He lifted his eyes to look around him. *What are they thinking?* he asked himself. His eyes caught those of the Abbot, who to his embarrassment was staring resolutely at him. The moment their eyes met they both hastily bowed their heads and closed their eyes. The recurrent image of Sebastian flashed before him, and he shook his head in disbelief. *No, no! Not Father Brendon!* But he felt no stirring for him – only revulsion.

After their sombre communal soup, bread and cheese, Anthony returned to his cell searching his feelings for balance. He made the sign of the cross, crying out to Mary and Saint Martin as he struggled to examine his inner self. He felt shame. *I'm unworthy. Forgive me, Mother. Guide me.* And finding comfort in these words and the patterns of his faith, he drifted into uneasy sleep.

'I have permission to talk with you,' whispered Brother Lucian after Litany in the afternoon the following day. He invited Anthony to follow him outside into the courtyard: a small empty space surrounded by thick stone walls sparsely furnished with two metal chairs and a statue of the Virgin Mary in a small alcove. A gate led through to the kitchen garden. They could feel the warmth of the sun.

'Concerning your vows. Father Brendon feels the delay is too long.'

'I know.'

'You would, naturally, be free to leave if you are not convinced this is the right path.'

'I-I do harbour… err, doubts.'

'It seems to me your devotion exceeds many others here. Of course, I mention no names.' He seemed lost in his thoughts. Anthony's habit of rarely making eye contact meant he occasionally wondered if he heard correctly. 'We start next week. In the garden room, on Monday, the hour before the Angelus.'

'Thank you,' acknowledged Anthony. 'Th-that is p-perhaps what I-I must do.'

Lucian wobbled his head, Indian fashion. Then changed the subject. 'Father Brendon asked me to do wood-carving to raise funds.' He sounded unconvinced as he shared the news.

Anthony's eyes opened wider. He was being given an opportunity to pose his question. 'Why are we short of m-money?' He was testing if Lucian shared his feelings about the fund-raising, but cautious for now.

'I am surprised, but if we are asked to do this for the brotherhood, then we must obey without questioning. But I sense an unsettled feeling amongst us. It feels at times as though we are being... what can I say?'

'I'm s-surprised by the challenges G-God sends me s-sometimes.'

'Yes.'

Next morning Anthony opened the cell door to find Tom outside, leaning on a table. Brother Vincent was helping him, puffing and panting having carried it from the work-shed. As was the custom, nothing was said. They all knew what was going on and it was heaved in. Vincent was holding his side and left immediately. Anthony watched him until he turned the corner then stared at the addition to his cell, assessing its size and height. 'Chair and cupboard later,' said Tom whispering in Anthony's ear. Although not subject to the monastery rules, he felt self-conscious speaking inside. Manoeuvring the table to a good position he whispered again: 'We'll order the rest.' He rolled his eyes as he left.

*

Two weeks later Anthony was mucking out the chicken pen with Vincent and mentioned Father Brendon had asked him to make changes to his schedule.

'The t-time I spend with you and the chickens h-has been reduced, B-Brother.'

'Why didn't Father tell me himself? I would have told him I get very tired these days…' He controlled his resentment. 'Oh, I should be counting me blessings. I thank God for the strength I still have in me old age.'

'I'll w-work harder in the t-time I do have,' said Anthony. He hurried away to shovel up the droppings and empty them into the compost. Vincent had a fit of coughing and sat on his box.

'Careful, son. No throwing eggs in that there bucket.' Vincent smiled a mischievous smile. His humour shone through unexpectedly and Anthony loved it. There were ways in which Vincent was like Uncle Henry. He could be unconventional at times. Most of the brothers seemed to wear the brotherhood as a mask, but Vincent displayed his true self. Maybe it was to do with feeling at one with nature, which was certainly not true of Henry.

Anthony let the chickens out to scratch in the garden and raked over the ground inside the pen. *I should reply to Polly.* How often the chickens reminded him of her. He anticipated writing with pleasure. Pleasure tinged with anxiety, figuring out how to deal with her convictions… *She is so sure she is right. Will she ever change?* He smiled to himself. *But I think I'm right too!*

Back in the cell, he sat on his new chair at his lovely large table and spread out his writing materials. He started by measuring out lines on the cards and practising decorative figures, and felt the warm glow of pleasure as he looked forward to spending more time creating patterns. *I'll write to Polly tomorrow.*

At bedtime as sleep came over him, he pondered her stubbornness but now he was beginning to see himself in the same light.

The chicken run was weirdly in his old garden at The Elms. The fowl were small and speckled and looked quite different from those he'd seen over the wall next door from his studio window. He became aware of a high brick wall between his garden and Polly's. From the other side he could hear Polly shouting, 'Eggs, eggs, EGGS!' He felt insecure as he stepped forwards, the ground moving beneath his feet with a scrunching sound. Shells breaking everywhere. Every step he took meant breaking more eggs. He was swimming in them, trying to make headway. As consciousness returned he was rubbing grit from his eyes. *I'm not getting anywhere. Floundering.*

The following day Polly was his priority. He wrote:

~Brotherhood of St Martin's ~ Devon ~
Dear Polly,

Thank you for your letter. I'm so sorry to hear of your mother's worrying behaviour but not knowing her full story I can't really understand what she's going through.

You have had many trials recently and must have been terribly upset when your boyfriend left you. But you didn't give up your faith for him, which I commend. However, it still puzzles me how you remain confident in a belief so contrary to the teaching of the Holy Church. It plays on my mind that you are choosing not to consult Father Alphonsus, because I'm sure he would be helpful. I pray for the eternal destiny of your soul because the sacrament of absolution and performance of penance truly are necessary for forgiveness.

Thank you for your sympathy regarding my attack. I have recovered from the wound caused by the apostate brother. It has taken longer to get over the shock. Certain things remind me and I relive the sudden stab. I go to the Blessed Virgin Mary for comfort.

My life is changing these days; indeed, monastery life seems to be taking a new course. The Abbot tells me, surprisingly, that we need to raise money for our upkeep. I have been asked to use my calligraphy skills to design cards for sale and my mentor has been asked to carve wooden statues.

You would imagine us free of financial concerns. We live so frugally. But no. It seems unspiritual to be raising money, but I have been provided with better pens, ink, and card, and enjoy the rhythm of forming beautiful letters and decorations.

I am also embarking on intense training to prepare for my final vows and pray to Saint Michael and Saint Theresa to guide me into the future. I may not write for a while.

I told Brother Vincent today I would have less time for the chickens, and he advised me not to throw the eggs into the bucket in my haste! Unfortunately he hasn't been well lately.

I send you prayers, in nomine Patris et Filii et Spiritus Sancti, Amen.
Anthony

As he put down his pen, words from his mother flashed into his mind. 'Anthony, you know, dear, you can't make an omelette without breaking eggs.' He'd never worked out why she'd said such a strange thing, especially as she never cooked. Nor did they spend time in the kitchen together. But there was no doubting her voice. *Is she trying to tell me something?*

CHAPTER 13

1960s

'So, you're off then?' Eli was standing on the doorstep of 16 Elm Close counting the West's milk money.

'Yes! At last, London, here I come! First day's training on Wednesday.' *Eli disapproves.* 'London isn't far. I'll get home on weekends from time to time.'

'Harrumph,' grunted Eli pointing over her shoulder. 'They ain't happy about it then?'

'Who?' Eli knew Polly was aware he meant her parents. He turned to go. Polly continued, 'You're probably right, but I *know* God wants me to do this and He will look after them. The Edwards have told Dad they'll take him shopping in their car. They might even persuade Mum to go.'

'You've made up yer mind then. Hope things work out. Won't need so much milk now, will they?'

'Dad'll leave the usual notes. See you soon.'

'Bye then.' Eli was over by his float. Life was miserable these days. No horses, no friendly Polly, not so much time to linger. The soft hum of the electric motor and the bottles rattling in the crates were his only the company. Monotonous; no personality.

Polly felt a sadness for Eli. His sparkle had gone with the horses. 'See you soon,' she called again, 'God bless!' Eli was down the road. He didn't want to hear anyway.

'Pol!' called Vera as she closed the door. 'Are you coming up or not?'

'Just paying, Eli. Wait a min!' She had been praying earnestly for her mother ever since the crying episode.

If only Mum could pull herself together and let everyone get on with life... 'Coming.'

'I'll miss you bringing my coffee, won't I?' Vera sniffed. 'Must you really go?'

Polly couldn't go through it all again. She put the tray down silently, kissed her mother quickly on the forehead then sat on the end of the S stroking Fluffy. 'Mum! Things are not as bad as you think. My friends have left home to train for different things and *their* parents manage one way or another.'

'But...'

'No, Mum! No ifs or buts. *Everything* will be all right. Here, let me show you a verse...' She went to find her Bible. 'Look what it says: "We know that in all things God works for good for those who love Him..." You love God, don't you?' Deep down she felt guilt at taking this tack, but ignored it. What else to say?

'Oh, oh, y...yes,' Vera stuttered, but Polly's obsessive Bible quoting did nothing to reassure her. She looked out of the window. It was raining. 'Never known God make much difference.' She sniffed again.

'I'll get your lunch then you might feel better.' Polly went downstairs.

CHAPTER 14

'Name?'

'Polly West.'

There were two Home Sisters, dressed in immaculate blue uniforms in the entrance hall of All Souls hospital nurses' home; one large and stern who remained firmly rooted to the spot ticking names off a list. The other small and twinkly darting here and there, chatting to everyone, dodging trunks and cases.

'Right, Nurse West, Room 623, sixth floor.' The large sister pointed at Polly's trunk: 'Sid and Ed will take that.' She ticked off Polly's name then looked her up and down. 'Follow the porters. Meet in there at five o'clock.' She pointed her pen towards a large room full of armchairs. 'Then we'll see you all together and introduce ourselves and you can tell us who you are. DON'T FORGET to bring your keys. The doors SELF-LOCK and you won't get BACK IN if you don't have your key.'

'I'd better go!' Polly turned to Beth and Flynn as the porters were disappearing into the lift leaving no time for proper goodbyes. 'Thank you so much, I don't know how I would have managed.'

'Bye then, Nurse West!' Beth grinned.

'That's me!' laughed Polly as she quickly blew kisses to the two lovebirds, standing with arms round each other, waving. The floors disappeared below the lift one by one and Polly tried to take in the strange surroundings. The porters' jokes were lost on her. She was bothered about how she was going to find her way around. *KEYS*!

'This where you want the bricks then, nurse?' Realising Sid was talking to her, Polly agreed.

'Bricks?' she managed, but they were off laughing. She surveyed her room. *Time? What time did that sister say?* The porters had left the door open with the key in the lock. She took it out, then put it back in. *Five o'clock.* The room opposite was still empty. She noted bed, cupboard, casement window with view onto a street, curtain to match bedspread, dressing table opposite bed, and hot Victorian radiator. As she looked in the mirror, she heard the clatter of the lift and voices. A new neighbour. *Thank you, Lord.* After the porters left, she wedged her door open and crossed the corridor. 'Hello,' she said brightly.

'Hullo,' the girl replied, with northern dialect.

'I'm Polly West, from opposite.'

'I'm Sally. Just call me Sal.' Sal looked as though she was about to burst into tears. 'This is so strange, I wasn't expecting to feel like this – leaving home, I mean.'

'I know, I don't know what to feel, but… I'm always happy to chat. Will you come down with me at five?'

By then Polly's Bible was on the bedside table, underclothes in a drawer, and paperwork on the dressing table. Downstairs they found the new students chatting in groups, while others were sitting alone looking nervous. The stout Home Sister bustled in and they all stood.

'You may sit.' After introducing herself, she described the home, the routine, and the schedule for the week. Many of the details escaped Polly completely. *What did she say? It's all a whirl, God help me!* She heard the sister saying: 'Nurses.

Whatever you do, always keep your door-key on you, even when you go the toilet. Otherwise, the door will close and you will *not* be able to get back in.' Some looked horrified. 'You will see your room number on the key, so to start with you'll find that number useful. If you find yourself on the wrong floor, look at the key, and you will be able to work it out.' She paused. 'Won't you?' The students stared at her stunned. 'WON'T you?' she commanded.

Having been measured on interview day their uniforms were ready to wear. They visited the sewing room in turn and collected two laundry boxes with dresses, aprons, hats, studs, collars, cuffs, and a cape. Among other things they were initiated into folding and fixing their hats, and the intricacies of the massive network of underground tunnels where they would find a bank, shop, and other amenities. By next afternoon, the fifty girls were all self-consciously standing in the practice room for a group photograph.

'You are now nurses,' the sister tutor told them when they sat at their desks afterwards. 'To the man in the street, you *know everything* and you *represent* the hospital.' Polly felt different; important and empowered, but she didn't question how or why. *I'm a nurse! I have to know everything!* The stiff collars, cuffs and buttons were already rubbing her upper arms and neck. *I'll get used to that.* Her hat was askew.

'I didn't realise it was going to be like being back at school,' said the girl at the next desk.

'Nor did I,' said Polly, horrified. 'Exams too?'

Sal had been prepared by her mother, who was a nurse. She'd even worked as nursing assistant at the local hospital.

'Oh no… we can't escape exams yet!' she told Polly when they went upstairs. 'And if we fail our prelims we'll be asked to leave.'

'Fail?' asked Polly, incredulous. The idea of *failure* had never entered her mind. Reality set in for the first time. She'd expected to wear the uniform and make patients comfortable but had given no thought to other aspects of the work. *But God will help me pass.*

CHAPTER 15

'Nurse West – night duty, male geriatrics.'

Polly groaned internally. The last pupil nurse to work nights in geriatrics had become so depressed she gave up training. 'Yes, thank you, Matron.' Polly's smile belied her feelings, but there was no disguising her dread when she announced her fate to the girls waiting outside. They hugged, sympathised, and encouraged her, all of them *sure* she'd be all right. One person even enjoyed gerries on day-duty.

'Second year here we come,' Sal said, happy with nights on maternity.

'It's all right for you!'

'You'll manage, you always do!' Sal replied. 'You thought you'd never get over the first long shifts but you did… and the exams.'

'You're right there.' Polly agreed she'd learnt enough to pass her first exams and wasn't so tired after shifts. 'I'm really enjoying myself! But there's an awful lot I don't take in—'

'Never mind, neither do I.' They laughed and went for coffee in the dining room where friends were joking at one of the long tables.

Polly had never been anywhere near geriatrics before. She'd heard of the smell, and stories of a multiple sclerosis patient who called out for help all night long. She rested for an hour before approaching the ward at 10 p.m. and reeled back from the stench as she approached. *God! Help. My first night without sleep too.* Taking in hand her negative thoughts she propelled herself into the ward. It was dark apart from a few bed lights covered with green material eerily illuminating faces below. Quietness was punctured by snores, occasional mutterings, and the soft voice of a man reaching through the cot bars of a bed situated in front of Sister's office.

'Give me the keys. Please give me the keys, Mavis. GIVE ME THE KEYS!'

The day sister and senior night staff nurse were discussing a problem with supplies. 'Ward Four has incontinence pads, and you'll need to sterilise the needles straight after report.' The other night nurses stood waiting, hands behind backs.

'Right. Nurse West?' The day sister addressed Polly directly. 'I hope you'll manage better than the last nurse we had from your set. We're here if you want to talk about anything, and please rest properly during the day, won't you?' Polly nodded.

'Thank you, Sister.' Sister spoke to the others.

'Show Nurse West the routine and start the back-round. No fluids for Bed Twelve, please. He's going to theatre tomorrow.' With her right index finger, she worked her way down the day's page in the report book with brief reminders of work to be done. 'Oh, yes. Bed Nine is diabetic, and please be more attentive to mouth care for Bed Seventeen.' She dismissed the junior nurses and handed over to the staff nurse in more detail.

Polly numbly followed the third-year nurse to the utility room and hoped she was friendly. Her first job was to help Nadine with the 'back-round'. She loaded the 'back-trolley' with a bowl of hot water, piles of brown straw-like stuff called *tow* for wiping bottoms, incontinence pads, clean sheets, spirit and creams, and pushed it onto the ward, wheels interacting noisily with floorboards. Nadine had a list of bed-bound patients who were incontinent and would need changing. 'A shock to start with, isn't it?'

Polly was trying to put on a brave face, but was glad of sympathy. 'I suppose you get used to it,' she said feigning cheerfulness.

'Some do, others don't.' She was trying to pull curtains around the bed, but the runners kept sticking on the rail. 'We mustn't forget the 'ins and outs' charts as we go around. If there is a board at the end of the bed, with the TPR charts, we must record how much urine is in the bottle or put + or ++ if they are wet.' Polly nodded. 'This man just needs turning and back care. There's no point in pulling the curtains all the way, it's dark.' Nadine pulled down the bedclothes, pushed her arms underneath his body and heaved him onto his side. Polly poured spirit onto her hands and rubbed his sacrum vigorously. *Shouldn't we speak to him?* It was an established routine: lift, turn, clean up, pressure care, mouth-care, move on – exhausting, hard work. Back in the sluice, soiled sheets were washed with bare hands in an enormous sink before being wrung out and transferred to the laundry-bags. There was a separate bag for patients who were barrier nursed due to infections.

The man in bed twenty-nine was awake. 'Can't I have a drink, nurse?'

'Yes, after we've finished the backs...' They rolled him onto his side.

'You got a boyfriend, nurse?' asked Bed Eleven, giving her a wink. *I can relate to this one!* It was a pleasant surprise to find that not all her patients were uncommunicative.

'Gerries is so heavy – so draining. I'm exhausted already,' Polly told Sal, sinking into an armchair when they met up for break.

'Poor you. I'm going to like my ward. The mums are lovely.'

'Three months!'

'You'll cope,' said Sal sympathetically, secretly thankful her stint was over. 'Lots of us complain when we start, but by the end we enjoy helping people who can't help themselves.' But after two months Polly was down in the dumps. *God is my strength and refuge and very present help in times of trouble* she told herself several times and asked him for patience and strength to keep going, however tired. *I can't tell anyone I dread going on duty and my sleep is suffering. It'd be like saying God wasn't sufficient. But...* Then one night, as she went round the ward to check everybody was still breathing and nobody had fallen out of bed, she noticed a single sprig of honeysuckle in a fish-paste jar on Bed Nine's table. She bent over, smelt it, and brightened up. A light shone in the darkness. *Thank you, Lord!* The fragrance of the scent lifted her spirit.

Geriatrics was the most difficult assignment she had. Every sister ran her ward with different attitudes and expectations.

'It makes so much difference what the sister is like,' she told Beth one afternoon when they met in Oxford Street.

'Oh, why's that?' Beth was not terribly interested in her friend's nursing, which sounded quite distasteful. 'Flynn and I are getting engaged soon,' she added excitedly. 'He's so good-looking too.'

'Some sisters are crotchety and bad-tempered, but others are really helpful and understanding.'

'Oh, I see,' replied Beth, absentmindedly. 'Have you seen the new jewellers in Cotsford?'

I can't share my work with her anymore. Polly felt blocked out. 'I haven't been to Cotsford since I started training. And I don't like the way we treat the patients sometimes, I mean…' Beth was clearly more interested in her future with Flynn.

'You *must* come with us one day and we'll show you the new shops.'

'Are you still walking closely with the Lord, Beth?'

'Oh *yes,* of *course!* Flynn and I will have a big house when we're married. We're agreed we can put you up when you visit England – and any other missionaries who need a bed when they're on furlough.'

'Oh thanks,' said Polly musing that furlough was a long, long way off.

'Our calling is to stay at home and *support* you… the Lord has made it quite clear.' She looked at Polly, put her arm around her shoulder, then triumphantly added 'What about *that* then?'

Polly was not impressed but smiled weakly. 'Thanks. It's hard to see that far ahead. I still miss Darren, you know, and none of the chaps I'm meeting seem that keen on doing the Lord's work …' But Beth wasn't listening.

Polly hadn't really kept in touch with home since she went to London. Family had gone out of focus. She decided she must pay a visit and caught the train to Halebridge. She let herself in No 16 and put her overnight bag on a kitchen chair feeling a stranger.

Things have been moved around. Footsteps sounded on the stairs. 'Hello Polly!'

'Oh, Doris!' Polly smiled uncertainly. She remembered her father had written to say her mother had to go away for a while.

'Your dad's out shopping. I come Wednesdays and Saturdays to help with the cleaning.' She paused for Polly's reaction. 'And I put some home cooking in the safe out the back. He's thinking of buying a refrigerator. Just a small one.'

'What about Mum then?' Polly was confused. 'Mum wanted a fridge years ago, but Dad wouldn't.'

'My dear,' said Doris in her motherly way. 'Things have changed you know since Vera went away. It isn't easy for him.'

'I'm sorry,' said Polly, mortified. 'I should have… I trusted Mum would be all right.'

'I'll put the kettle on, love. James'll be back for coffee soon.' Polly watched Doris take charge of the kitchen and felt out of place.

'So, how d'you like it? Milk and sugar?'

They heard James' footsteps. 'I'll take my bag upstairs.' Polly fled before James walked in, ran upstairs, and threw herself on what used to be her bed, feeling like an intruder. 'Jesus, I'm so sorry! Help me. I don't even know if this is still my bed! Help me face Dad. And help me sort myself out. And be with Mum…'

Fluffy jumped on the bed. 'Oh, Fluff, Fluff…' she gasped. 'My lovely Fluffy! What's been going on here?' She stroked his long fur and was shocked to feel his bones underneath. 'You're old!' she whispered. 'Fluff darling! You're so old.'

'You upstairs, Pol?' James was calling from the hall.

'Coming, Dad!' Fluffy's ageing had hit home hard. *But Mum? Why hasn't Mum come home?*

'Hello Dad!' She gave him a hug and the old familiarity came back. 'I'm so sorry, I realise that I sort of – lost touch.'

'We thought we'd lost you. It seems ages since you rang and you were always working when we tried. Did you get my letter?'

'Oh, Dad. I did see a couple of messages but… I've been so tired after my shifts…' She left her words hanging, hearing how hollow her excuses sounded. *I suppose I didn't think it was really important. I suppose I forgot about home. Completely.*

'Where's Mum? Why hasn't she come home?'

'Your poor mum was so upset after you left. She kept asking, *Where's Pol? Where's Pol*? And when we said *London* she burst into tears. She still can't move on and she's in Oakwood with depression; the antidepressants make her sleepy. I miss her so much. Victor visits me every three months or so, but this has grown into rather a sad house now. Doris is a bright spark though, and cheers the place up a bit, don't you Dorry?' They looked fondly at each other.

'It's only two days a week, isn't it, James? And I've got me own place to look after you know, and I'm not so young as I was.' She massaged her hip.

'Dad, I don't know what to say. Shall I go and see Mum?'

James' eyes lit up. 'We can go tomorrow. We'll see if your mum wakes up. Maybe, if she hears your voice…' His voice tailed off.

Polly bought some flowers and she and James found Vera in the sitting room staring into space, feeling along the edges of a handkerchief; one edge to the corner, then the next side and corner, fumbling round and round. Polly was appalled. She bent down in front of her mother's face. 'Hello Mum,' she said gently, trying to make eye contact, 'I thought you might like these.' She held out the flowers.

'Go away,' Vera mumbled, ignoring the offering. Polly looked at James for reassurance, but he was wide-eyed with shock. He was used to Vera's moods, but she'd never dismissed him. Polly stood back not knowing what to do with herself, and James put an arm round Vera.

'Come on now, love, it's our Pol. She's still the same ole' Pol.'

Vera stopped moving her fingers around the handkerchief and looked at James.

'Won't you say hello to Polly, dear? It's Polly, our Pol. At least look at the flowers.' He took them from Polly and put them on her lap to no avail.

'Pol's in London… gone to London.' And Vera started crying. Polly felt ashamed, and wretched. She reminded herself that her mum was bad before she went… *It's not my fault. And no matter how hard I tried, everything I did was wrong.*

When she got home she went to the bedroom, got on her knees. *'Lord, help me. I can only put my family in your hands and trust you. Surely You understand.'* She looked up Luke chapter fourteen, verse twenty-six: "If anyone comes to me and does not hate his father and mother, his wife and children, his brothers and sisters – yes, even his own life – he cannot be my disciple."

CHAPTER 16

'Get Tom to take two dozen eggs to the farmers' market today, will you?'

Anthony and Brother Vincent enjoyed their secret informality. Talking to Vincent was 'real life'. He collected the boxes for Tom and took them to the front lodge. Grinning in acknowledgement Tom handed Anthony a key.

'Letter for you in the post.' Anthony raised his hand in acknowledgement.

'Thank you.' He looked through the mail and hung the key back behind a crucifix in a shed nearby. (The theory was that if anyone with evil intent was tempted to take it for the wrong reason, he, or unlikely, she, would feel guilty seeing the suffering Messiah, and stop in their tracks). *Good. Polly.* He placed the remaining letters in Father Brendon's mailbox, outside his office, went to his cell, sat at his table, and opened his letter.

Nurses' Home, All Soul's Hospital, London

Dear Anthony, Happy New Year!

I'm at the end of my second year's training, working hard on the wards, and I've got to study. Exams loom! But there's so much I don't understand. I must do more study.

It is a relief to be almost finished night duty on geriatrics. It depresses me, seeing so many old people who've given up. And it's heavy work. I ask God to help me be cheerful. One marvellous thing though, is the dawn. However tired I feel when I see signs of light on the horizon, my spirits lift.

About midnight, Night Sister asks one of us the names, ages, and diagnoses of all thirty patients. Of course, we should know, but we're often too busy to memorise them, so it makes me nervous, but I wasn't too bad last time she asked me as I'd been on the ward a few weeks.

The senior nurse is reasonably kind, but two nurses don't seem to respect the patients at all. They are rough and only interested in getting through the work as quickly as possible.

As a second-year nurse I'm called a 'middle'! One of my new skills is giving injections. It can involve mixing different substances. I'm afraid of getting it wrong, but so far so good. Everything taken to patients must be on a tray (even hot-water-bottles). We sterilise syringes, needles, dishes and forceps in the big sterilisers and every time I open the steriliser my glasses steam up! Sister insists we stay on duty until everything's clean and ready for the following shift. Another grumble – sorry!

I go to Christian Union once a week with nurses and medics from other departments. We take it in turns to lead but have speakers from outside too. I've spoken about my call to the mission field. The Roman Catholics say they are not allowed to come which is sad. Do you understand why?

I haven't mentioned how my life was changed when I said 'yes' to God's call. Soon after I was baptised I realised I was rebelling by telling Him I couldn't possibly be a missionary. The thought kept returning until I submitted to His Will although I hadn't the faintest idea how I'd set about it. But He sent me the greatest peace, and it has stayed, so I feel sure I'm on the right path.

I witnessed to an older nurse the other day. She had met survivors of the German concentration camps. She told me I wouldn't believe in God if I had been there. Of course, I disagreed because nothing will shake my faith.

God tested me when I went home recently. Mum is completely withdrawn, and has been admitted to Oakwood. Dad took me to see her, but she told me to go away. Dad reckons it is partly my fault she is like this. I don't know how to deal with it. Meanwhile, Doris, Mum's best friend, is helping Dad at home.

I must get back to study. We're doing the nervous system, but I can't seem to relate the autonomic and somatic systems to the way the body works. I not sure I need that sort of information.

I've been full of my news and haven't replied to your letter properly. I'm glad you can do your artwork. I loved the picture you gave Mum and Dad, "In nomine Patris et Filii et Spiritus Sancti". I can't pronounce it, despite hearing it so often at school. I say it in

> *my own way, slowly, thinking about your beautiful picture.*
> *That seems a fitting way to finish, especially for the New Year.*
> *Yours sincerely,*
> *Polly*

Anthony put the letter onto his desk, closed his eyes for a while, then read again. *A Missionary! Poor Vera. Such a worry for her… and Oakwood. Oh no.*

In the name of the Father and of the Son, and of the Holy Ghost. Making the sign of the cross first, he worked through the beads, dedicating prayers to Polly and Vera until it was time for vigils.

'I-I've had another letter from P-Polly, B-brother,' he told Lucian the following day when they met for instruction. Lucian frowned, willing Anthony to look at him.

'What does she say?' Anthony handed it over.

'W-what would you do?' He studied Lucian's face.

'I can see Polly's beliefs are interfering with your spiritual preparations. Beware! This sort of literature will sow seeds of doubt. It is not sanctioned by the Holy Church and is of the devil, like the books banned by the Vatican.' He made the sign of the cross.

'B-but she s-seeks the truth, as I do, and is s-so honest. How could this be d-dangerous?'

Lucian was assertive. He looked up from the letter and reprimanded the novice. 'These letters must stop, Anthony.'

'*Stop*?' For once Anthony eyeballed Lucian.

'This is a matter for Father Brendon.' Lucian was gentle again. 'Originally these letters were harmless.

But this rigmarole has no foundation in truth, and it's disturbing you. The Abbot must counsel you.'

Anthony shook his head. 'I-I never thought…'

'No, neither did I,' Lucian interrupted. 'B-but P-Polly has a missionary quest. Don't you see?' He looked questioningly at Anthony who was plainly divided between his concern for Polly and the strict observance of monastic life.

'I-I don't understand.'

'Your friend Polly wants to convert you. Her views are heretical. She is distracting you from your devotions and study. You must divorce yourself entirely from the world. By now, after all your learning, I should not have to explain.'

Anthony felt chastised and turned away.

'I-I f-feel I s-should reply.'

'Not until you have seen Father. Meanwhile, put her out of your mind.'

Easy to say. They parted. *I'm losing a friend. This the hardest trial yet.* Anthony returned to his cell seeking the support of the Virgin Mary and forcing himself to trust Her.

'Father Brendon will see us together, Anthony,' Lucian announced a fortnight later. Anthony looked him in the eye briefly and bowed. *So, Lucian will be there too*.

Lucian read his thoughts. 'Father Brendon said it would be best if I was there, to help guide me with the future direction of our study.' He bowed and left.

The meeting with the Abbot was short. 'You must concentrate whole-heartedly on your vows now, Anthony, and worldly distractions divert your attention. Neither send nor receive these letters, nor indeed any others. I think you are naively unaware that this Polly woman is a heretic. A fanatical evangelist. She is not at all interested in what you say but trying to *convert you.* This is a test of your obedience. Please continue your study for the Glory of God. Go your way, and may God be with you.' Anthony bowed, and left the room. Lucian, who had been standing beside Anthony, said nothing. Although silent he clearly agreed with Father Brendon.

Vincent will understand. Anthony made for the chicken-house. Brother Vincent spent so much time alone he often spoke to himself.

'You know, don't you, Mrs Thoughtful?' Mrs Thoughtful's head was cocked to one side looking up at him. Yes, it was easy to imagine a chicken listening.

'W-what is she thinking, Brother?' Anthony gazed at him; a gaze preserved for Vincent alone. Vincent scattered the feed across the pen.

'When the rheumatics are stronger than your faith,' he said, 'it doesn't matter what people think.' Anthony's brow wrinkled. He took water to the trough thinking about the old monk. *He isn't himself.* Vincent continued. 'But I mumble away – and it gets it out of the system. *They* understand!' He chortled and coughed.

Anthony watched the birds pecking away. Simple. Vital. He relaxed, mulling over Vincent's utterance, then surprised himself by asking, 'Do you w-worry about keeping all the vows you have taken, B-brother Vincent?'

His friend took a rag off the old crate and sat down. He leant over to stroke Mrs Thoughtful, who ran off clucking. 'Son, I'm old and keep meself to meself. But I see you young-uns struggle. I've seen vows broken and it don't make that much difference overall. Unless the big boss notices, of course. But I do wonder what he gets up to when no-one's a-looking. There's always the outward show… and the brotherhood is a good system…' he coughed and tailed off into a calm silence. 'Just make sure there's enough of you young-uns to help us old-uns!' He gave another half-hearted chuckle and coughed again, rather alarmingly this time.

Is he all right? It's so unlike him to go on like this, thought Anthony. 'Have you s-seen the d-doctor about that cough, Brother?'

'You keep quiet about that… I'm *all right.*'

He doesn't like me interfering. I'll keep my thoughts to myself. But I'll keep watching him, nonetheless.

Anthony told him the story of Polly, her letters, and the meeting with the Abbot. Then he described his latest chicken dream. He turned the water bucket upside down and sat by Vincent. 'Brother, in my d-dream I was b-back home. I-I saw myself f-feeding chickens in our garden and I c-could hear P-Polly next-door talking to hers. The wall between us was higher than usual, but I c-could see through it: her chickens were q-quite different from mine. Then the wall and wire-netting s-started disintegrating – and the birds mingled. P-Polly and I f-fed them together but when I went to c-collect the eggs… it all f-faded.'

'Sounds to me,' said Vincent, after pondering a while, 'there's a barrier that stops you both seeing you are doing the same thing. You'll find the wall between you will gradually fade away.' He coughed and caught his breath. 'You wait. Do nothing. One day that wall will be missing, and you'll forget it was ever there. Things will be all right. All right.' He emphasised *all right* reassuringly, spluttered and rested his chin on his chest.

'Th-that isn't the t-teaching.'

After what seemed a long time, Vincent looked up: 'No, but it *feels* right. Who *really* knows what God ordains? Far as I see, Mother Church looks after us chicks, then soon we'll be under her wing and safe.' He cleared his throat. 'S'pose I reckon it won't be long 'fore I'm under that wing; right where I belong.' He leant against the hen house and closed his eyes. 'Tell them I'll be giving prayers a miss this evening.'

Anthony felt a surge of affection for the old gardener. He took his hand and kissed it. Vincent pursed his lips, tears in his eyes: 'You'd make a good son.' As he looked up at Anthony, two tears ran down his cheeks.

Anthony rose, looking away. He collected the eggs for the kitchen, and turned one over and over in his hand, deep in thought. *The churches have built this wall.* His thinking broadened as he considered the vast number of different churches. *Many, many walls! No. Churches don't build walls – the people build the walls. It's up to us to find cracks in the walls. And break them down. We can't all be 'right'.*

The moon was full as Anthony returned to his cell after matins. He had been considering Vincent's explanation of his dream alongside Father Brendon's words about Polly and their correspondence. The dream seemed highly significant now. *That's another brick in the wall.* He thought of the Abbot's veto on writing. He remembered Joseph's interpretation of the Pharaoh's dreams, and how they came to pass. As he got into bed his thoughts were wrapped up in Joseph: one minute a shackled prisoner, then suddenly called to help a troubled leader, and finally a powerful leader himself. *Extraordinary story! Joseph was faithful to God and became…* but he fell asleep, prophetic thoughts mingled with realising that the cold winter air affected him less than when he joined the brotherhood – and how much he would miss Polly's letters.

He woke, abruptly, dream thoughts mixed with physical sensations. *Cold. Joseph. Polly's letters. I'll miss them. Missing, what's missing? VINCENT.* His mind cleared and he remembered Vincent sitting in the chicken run. Not only had he been absent from evening prayers, but also at matins. *Brother Vincent was not at matins! Oh, no.* For the second time since entering the monastery, his voice shattered the stillness of the dark night cloisters. Grabbing his cloak and scrabbling for sandals, he ran out into the night.

The only sounds from the hen house were questioning clucks as the gate scraped: rusty steel on rusty steel. He gasped: Brother Vincent, his one real friend, still there, sitting on the crate, body slumped against the shed and the lifeless old head fallen forward onto his chest. Freezing cold. Dead.

CHAPTER 17

Northern Missionary Training College.
Edinburgh
Dear Beth and Flynn,
Greetings in the Precious Name of Jesus.

I've finished my nursing and midwifery training and came straight up to Bible college about a month ago. I'll soon be ready for proper missionary work!

Of course, we are all Christians here, which is exciting. Every student wants to learn about serving the Lord, and our tutors are united in preparing us to spread the gospel. We have single rooms; the boys are housed on the opposite side of the building, but we meet for meals and lectures. If a boy and a girl want to meet for a chat, there's a room by the front lodge with absolutely no privacy! It isn't as bad as another Bible college up here where boys and girls are separated by a wall down the middle of the lecture theatre! One couple, though, was reprimanded for mentioning they were engaged. Something to do with being bad for the morale of we singletons.

In Systematic Theology, which is my favourite subject, we are shown how the New Testament confirms or fulfils the predictions made in Old Testament prophecies. My faith has already been strengthened.

Field missionaries will come from different missionary societies to tell us about their work and the challenges. I will be interested in those who do medical work, and I think God is calling me to India.

For practice we're going to different places in the city to preach the gospel. I've been assigned a place that used to be the Workhouse, which is grim; the residents have no homes or family – nothing – and are really hardened against the Gospel. Second year students say that after years of college visiting, it seems only one person has shown any interest. But prayer changes things! At least seeds have been planted.

They set up a microphone off the High Street every Saturday to sing hymns, preach a sermon and call on the passers-by to heed God's word before it's too late. I might try joining with them sometime.

I didn't realise Christians have such a variety of ideas about interpreting the Bible. Especially the book of Revelation. I disagree with some of them on things like whether we should wear expensive new clothes, or which songs it's OK to sing. One chap won't sing anything else but psalms. I'm surprised. I thought it was straightforward until I came here. Now I see there are different ways of interpreting what the Bible says.

Now I'm in Scotland I have, for the first time, become aware of my race! The Scots are very hospitable, but they make quite sure we non-Scots know we're different. It seems to mean more to them than it does to us.

I've made good friends in our prayer group. But one poor girl plays on my mind. She asked for prayer because her uncle raped her when she was thirteen and she was worried she could never get married because she was now one flesh with him. We looked up Mark chapter ten, verse eight. We decided, Jesus was definitely talking about sexual intercourse when he said 'When two are joined together they became one flesh, the two are no longer two but one. We agreed, that can never change. I am so sorry for her. Do you think God really intended that? It doesn't feel right to me.

Now I must do half an hour on Greek verbs. It's interesting, but is it useful?

I'll be seeing you before too long, so will tell more then.

In Christ's love,
Polly

*

It was almost the end of Polly's two years in Scotland and at last she believed God was speaking to her through one of the missionary speakers. Croften Vetray, of the Mission to Unreached Tribes (MUT), came to talk about work in India. It involved medical work in the clinics and distributing recorded Gospel messages. Polly introduced herself.

'We need people who are totally dedicated to their calling. It's not easy, you know.'

'I'm not looking for an easy life, and God will give me the strength for whatever he wants me to do. Ever since Dr Hedges came to speak at Halebridge I've been convinced God has called me to India.'

Croften pursed his lips as though doubtful. 'Right, Polly, we'll see. We'll arrange for you to have an interview and go from there, shall we?' He wrote her details in a small notebook.

The process was more involved than Polly anticipated: 'Two interviews a medical and a talk with a psychologist!' she exclaimed to the girl in the room next to hers. 'The more questions they ask, and the more they explain, the more complicated it gets.'

'There's only one thing to do,' said her neighbour. 'Trust the Lord. Let's pray.'

A week before term ended a letter with the MUT logo arrived. She tore it open and jumped up and down: 'They've accepted me! I'm in!'

The caretaker, the only person around, looked up and smiled knowingly.

CHAPTER 18

1970s

'Not much going on here,' mumbled Polly, putting the key in the front door of number 16 for the first time in – how long? *No Mum no Fluffy – of course.* 'Dad!' she called. The kitchen was neat and tidy; more new things she didn't recognise – dishwasher, microwave… *Mum would never have had that.* She took the backdoor key from its old place on the shelf. *At least that's still there.* Taking a few deep breaths of the fresh spring air was revitalising. Buds on the fruit trees – *soon be blossom-time.* The bike shed was gone and a smaller new one was in its place. In the hen run… only two chickens... Everything felt strange. *This really isn't my home anymore.* She waited, hands on hips, watching the birds. It was reassuring – grounding – seeing them scratch in the dusty soil and hearing them talk in their own language. Something normal. Back in the house she opened the fridge. *Supermarket milk! What about Eli and his float? Maybe Dad doesn't need much milk now. Where is he?*

She took a glass of water upstairs, but her bedroom had signs of recent use. *Mine but not mine. Comb… and perfume? Doris?* The bed was tidy but 'slept in'.

With nothing else to do Anthony came to mind. *Why hasn't he written? Has God spoken to him? I'll write to the Abbot and try and find out.*

16 Elm Close, Halebridge

Dear Father,

I am writing to enquire about my ex-neighbour, Anthony Wheeler, who joined your monastery in the 1950s. He has not written recently, so is it possible for you to let me know if he is all right? I used to write to tell him about his cat. If he is unable to write please could you tell him, sadly, Fluffy died a long time ago.

But I have other news for him so, if he has left, please could you send a forwarding address.

I'm at the address above for a few months now.

With greetings in the precious name of the Lord Jesus Christ,

Yours faithfully,
Polly West SRN SCM
P.S. I enclose a stamped addressed envelope.

She studied the letter and prayed. *Jesus, please send me news of Anthony.* She sealed the envelope. *I miss knowing he is there.* She sat in a comfy armchair downstairs tucking her feet beneath her and settled down to wait for somebody to come home. *I suppose I need to decide what to do: unpack; contact churches to inform them of my calling and the work; Beth; find temporary job… of course, yes, I should try the hospital. Is it too late to ring?*

At last, a key turned in the lock. She jumped up and ran to meet whoever it was. 'Dad! Where have you been? Oh Dad, it's so good to see you!'

James put a bag down on the floor and hugged his daughter. 'My Lord, stranger! So, it's you!' They laughed and kissed each other. 'Where have *I* been? Cheeky devil! You, of all people, asking me where *I've* been.'

'But I thought I told you when I was coming, and it's so quiet here with no-one around, not even Fluffy.'

James took in a deep, tired, breath and studied his daughter: full of life and expectation. *So enthusiastic, full of purpose – but so way out.*

'It's just us two for dinner this evening, so I'll tell you where I've been and you can tell me what you've been up to.'

'Is Mum still in Oaklands? And what about Vic?'

'Tea please, girl! I'm tired and need a rest.' He hung up his coat and went into the front room where he sank heavily into a chair and put his feet up. 'Make use of yourself now you're here and bring a biscuit while you're at it.'

They talked all evening. Polly found a few things to cook and they had a quick meal in easy chairs. It dawned on her for the first time that everything had been falling on Dad's shoulders. He was still working part-time, going to visit Vera at every opportunity, running the house... garden. No wonder he was tired. By nine thirty he started talking about bed.

'I'll have an early night tonight and we'll talk more tomorrow. G'night, darling.' He bent over, gave her a kiss, went upstairs and then called down: 'Doris is staying at her place tonight but we haven't changed the bed. You're in Vic's room.'

'G'night, Dad!' And Polly was alone again. *Vic's room, how odd.*

She climbed the stairs slowly and wandered out of habit into 'her' room. She lifted the lid of her old desk. There were the remains of a pad of Basildon Bond and her geometry set plus a few exercise books. Her eye fell on scratched irregular letters on the inner lid. The name, *Darren,* followed by a heart pierced with an arrow. She stared at it for a few seconds then softly closed the lid. 'Goodbye,' she whispered. Lifting it again, briefly, she took out the writing paper and walked into Vic's room, still festooned with football heroes. *What did Beth say about Ian? Past history, Pol!*

Sitting on the bed she rummaged in her handbag and found a pen to make a list.

<u>Before India</u>
Visit Crofton (head office) to agree schedule
Raise funds/enlist supporters
Prepare talks about missionary work (slides?)
Ring round churches (or visit)
Get work
Collect things Crofton wants me to send ahead
Buy trunk (or advertise for oil drums??)
Learn to drive
See friends
Get inoculations
Book flight (later)
Contact the Fotheringills
Mum?
The Pastor
Mrs Holland?

She was surprised by the number of jobs. *Will there be time to work?* A sense of urgency focused her mind. Time was clearly limited. *But,* she thought, *God will help me fit everything in, I needn't worry.* Opening her Bible, she found herself at Proverbs, chapter three, verse five: "Trust in the Lord with all your heart and lean not on your own understanding: in all your ways acknowledge him and he will make your paths straight." *Yes, I do trust You. Thank you, Lord.*

It was ten thirty and, although not late, the activities of the day had taken their toll. Bed. Vic's bed.

*

'Let's have a word of prayer before we start.' Polly was visiting the headquarters of the Mission to Unreached Tribes, to discuss her plans with Croften. They bent their heads.

When they looked up he cast his eye over some papers, then put them back on the desk, making sure they were straight.

'It'll take two or even three years to prepare for this work, so don't feel you've got to be ready yesterday.' He laughed at his own joke, which Polly didn't find funny.

'Two years seems a long time, but three…?'

'In the Fotheringills' case, even though they were sure of God's will, the support was slow to come in… you'll need enough finance promised to cover five years.'

'But the Fotheringills had family to sort out, and no idea what would be needed in India.' Then, as an afterthought, Polly added, 'And anyway, Beth and

Flynn will take care of the financial side of things for me.'

'Polly, you only really know your home church. Even if Pastor Ingrams recommends you to other fellowships, they'll want to get to know you and decide whether the work in India is a priority for funding. India is not the only country they will be considering, you know. Don't forget China, Africa... the Jews: all unsaved. Others think we should start at home. They'll need convincing'

'MUT cares for the body too though.'

Crofton gave another annoying laugh. 'My dear, some people disagree with that. They think all their money should go towards saving people. I've helped the Fotheringills raise funds for seven years *and* worked with missionaries in Peru and Chile. I *know* what it is like – even for singles.'

Polly didn't warm to Crofton. *He's so patronising.* 'What about just *trusting*? My faith—' but she was interrupted.

'And are you sure your friends won't let you down? Can they keep records accurately and mediate between you, myself, and your supporters? Will they work really *hard* for you?' Hardly taking a breath, he asked, 'Have you got a job lined up for now?'

'I'm thinking about that.' But Polly was clearly keener to take practical steps towards India. 'Flynn's a banker and keeping records all the time. Anyway, I'll contact churches in Cotsford that might be sympathetic. Do you know other churches nearby?'

They talked business.

'Send me contact details for your friends, please?' Polly was glad the meeting was finished. They shook hands in the doorway and parted.

When she arrived home, it was nearly supper time. After seeing her father so exhausted the day before she decided to cook for him. She recapped on the day's events as she grated some cheese. *Why was I so annoyed by Croften? Phew. And this is only the start.*

She rang the local hospital and was offered a part-time staff-nurse's post straight away. A pattern gradually developed: nursing, visiting churches, family, friends, equipment/luggage preparation, headquarters. They all took longer than anticipated and she struggled to make time for personal prayer.

After a busy morning shift, Polly came home to a note on the mat from Beth: 'POLLY! Exciting news! Meet at 5 p.m. in café?'

Beth and Flynn were already sitting in the window seat when she arrived. 'We've ordered coffee and cake for you.'

Flynn greeted Polly warmly and reached over to give Beth a kiss. 'We have an announcement to make!'

Beth took over: 'We've set a date for our wedding,' and in the same breath, 'God's told us you're to be my bridesmaid.'

'Really?' asked Polly, not sure whether she could drum up much enthusiasm. 'When?'

'Christmas!' they chorused. 'The best time of the year!'

They were so keen to tell all their plans her own news was marginalised. She updated them just as they were saying goodbye.

'We're right behind you,' said Flynn in his smooth Irish accent. Then in his preaching voice he added, 'It will be the *real thing,* praying in detail, knowing we are working together to spread the Word of the Lord in India. We *love* the people of India.'

'*Do* you?' asked Polly, dubiously, supressing her cynicism.

Two hundred people came to the wedding, mostly from Northern Ireland; Beth was in her element but surprised how much she had wished her late father could have given her away. Polly was also surprised – at the pleasure she found in supporting her best friend.

After the honeymoon in the Bahamas, the happy couple came back to a new four-bedroomed detached house with garden. It was a convenient distance from both Church and work. Well set up for the years to come. Or so Polly thought.

CHAPTER 19

Polly's departure for India was looming. Two months to go. She was shopping in Cotsford when she bumped into Beth:

'I've got so much to tell you,' Beth was bursting with news and Polly with questions, 'but can't stop now… you know…' Polly didn't know but resigned herself to wait. They kissed and turned to go their separate ways. But then Beth turned back and grabbed Polly's arm: 'We're moving to Northern Ireland… when can we talk?'

*

'Exactly what date are you leaving?' asked Beth with a twinkle in her eye. Flynn was buying tea and cake.

'New Year's Eve. Why…? Spill!' she ordered.

'Oh good. We'll just fit it in!'

'Fit what in?' Polly's favourite coffee and walnut cake was placed before her.

'Plans are fixed for our move to Ireland. My home!' Flynn said. Beth continued: 'and we want you to be our special missionary guest at our Christmas house-warming party.'

'But aren't you happy here?' Polly's eyes darted back and forth between them. 'And my flight is on New Year's Eve.' She wondered if they'd heard her first time and forced a laugh. 'That's the last thing I expected to have to fit in my preparations!' She felt weak. The cake no longer appealed to her. She smiled uncertainly at her friend. 'Why do you always have to do these things at Christmas?'

Beth didn't give Polly's misgivings much thought: 'Well, you know… new country, new house, and visit from a new missionary all in one… AND,' she lowered her voice… 'then we can start a family.'

Polly winced. 'But I'll be spending time with my family over Christmas.'

Beth seemed unaware of her friend's conflict of interests. 'Flynn can't wait to be closer to his family… and you *must* come because we've persuaded so many of Flynn's folk to contribute to your support and they want to meet you. You're the first proper missionary we know personally! And Mum said she'll come over with us and stay for a few weeks.'

'But I haven't agreed yet.' *What a cheek. I wasn't expecting…*

'God is on the throne! I'm sure it's alright. When we asked Him if it was His will, He made it quite clear to us. Our promise from the promise box said, "This is the way, walk ye in it."'

'But that was for you, not *me*.' Polly was cross and couldn't hide it.

'So? We're working for you, isn't it only fair you return the favour? There are so many more of my family than Elizabeth's. There's only her mother.'

'But my family? It could be my last Christmas at home for years. And Vic's got a new baby.' Polly was stumped for words.

'Are *they* supporting you?' Flynn asked in a deprecatory tone.

Polly felt a twinge of anger. *I'm being taken over.* Did their supporting her mean she was indebted to them? She could only think about Christmas and her family. *Beth will have her Mum at Christmas. But it's different for her. Does God really want it this way?* Polly felt a surge of sympathy for her mother which surprised her. Then she felt guilty again…

'Yes, think of it! Several of my family will be faithfully giving to you.' Flynn's eyes pierced through to Polly's scull: 'It's only reasonable.'

She was shocked. 'It's kind of them…'

'Yes, they've prayed for MUT since the Fotheringills did a deputation meeting at our church. They're Irish you know!'

'No, I didn't know.'

'Anyway, God told us you should come, so you *MUST.*'

Polly sucked her bottom lip. 'Mum and Dad….'

'Are your family even Christian? We can work around it… On second thoughts, invite them too!'

'*Flynn!* Have you even thought about *that*?' They drank their tea in silence.

'We'll commit it all to the Lord,' Flynn and Beth looked lovingly at each other.

'Thanks, Flynn.' Then with a touch of sarcasm, Polly added: 'Nice tea.' She left them wrapped up in their excitement and wandered home. *I'll have to let somebody down.*

Back in her bedroom she deliberated. *It seems I should go to Northern Ireland, but it doesn't feel right. Would God really tell them He wants me there? What will Dad do? Visit Mum in Oakwood? I want to see Vic and my new niece. I should stay at home and lead my own family to the Lord. But I'm relying on my supporters!*

What did missionaries say so often? *The devil prowls around seeking whom he may devour. He'll do everything he can to stop us doing God's will.* She visualised putting on the breastplate of righteousness. Its brightness deflected Satan's arrows. *I'll have to let family down.*

Faced with an unexpected trip to Ireland in her last few days in England needed careful planning. She blinked back the tears. *This will be hard, but the Lord has helped me before.* She wrote a heading down: 'Information for supporters in Northern Ireland.' She took a ruler and underlined it twice, then gathered the latest publicity material.

*

James was exasperated.

'Listen! It'll soon be Christmas and then January – and you'll be gone. Come and see your mother soon, Pol.' His daughter's lack of enthusiasm to visit Vera seriously bothered James. 'Will you come Friday?'

'But last time…'

'I know. But she's still your *mother* and I'm sure underneath she longs for you. Don't your patients tell them how much they miss their children visiting?'

Polly argued that God's work had priority over family. She side-stepped her father's question.

'Have Vic and Nina been lately?'

'Why don't you ask him yourself? Before Nicola was born he was in Scotland, and now they're busy and tired.'

James was weary. *What is going on with my lovely daughter? She's not the girl she used to be… so helpful and loving… She's…* He gave up and looked at Polly. She'd picked up a magazine.

'Well?'

'Everything I do is wrong. She doesn't want to see me.' Then crossly, 'Alright, I'll go.' She brightened up. 'I'd love to see little Nicola again though. I'll ring them.' A look of relief passed over James' face, but he said nothing.

A couple of days later Polly visited Oakwood by herself. She had a packet of her mother's favourite biscuits in her bag. Vera was in the lounge with several other residents. She was staring into space, an untouched drink in a mug by her side. Polly did her best:

'Hello Mum, It's your Polly!' She opened the biscuits and put one in her hand. 'Your favourite custard cream!' She picked up the mug and put it to Vera's lips, but no. She nibbled the biscuit, still vacant. Not a word. Polly was at a loss. She sat by her mother's side and went to hold her hand but Vera pulled it away. *I just can't get it right.* She sat a bit longer then got up to go.

'Bye then, Mum. Bye!'

That evening she and James walked round to Vic and Nina's place. They were welcomed into a downstairs flat in a quiet tree-lined road.

'Crickey, if it isn't my sister granting us a visit!' said Vic. 'And Dad! Hello again!' Polly thought how Vic had changed over the last few years: *married, rented home, job with good engineering firm, baby Nicola. More responsible, but still teases me.*

'Where's Nicola?' asked James making himself at home.

'Asleep in the bedroom and should wake up any time now.'

They piled into the small kitchen. *Home from home*, thought Polly noting utensils and items James had passed on to them. Nina made tea while Vic finished the washing up. Quiet crying triggered an enthusiastic response. He wiped his hands on his trousers, half-way through the door.

'I'll go. It's my turn!' he grinned at Polly as he dashed out. *He can't wait to pick her up!*

'She screamed last time she saw me.'

'No!' said Nina. She'll get used to her Aunty Polly.'

'Aunty Polly!' Vic repeated to Nicola in his arms. 'Look at Aunty Polly.'

'What about Grandpa then?' James grinned. Vic handed her over and James went soft and gooey.

Polly had worked with babies during her midwifery training, and thought of them in practical terms without emotional attachment. Having a family of her own didn't fit into her plan to dedicate her whole life to the Lord.

'Oh you little darling!' She stared at the sleepy bundle and felt warm inside when it was her turn to hold her. 'Please don't cry now,' she cooed, jogging her gently up and down.

'See, she's settling with you,' said Nina. 'I can see Mum in her, can't you?' Polly looked at Vic but he changed the subject.

'I'll go for fish and chips: 'Okay with everyone?' A man of few words when hungry, he left for the chippy.

Time flashed by. Everyone was happy and the evening was a great success. That was until Polly's bombshell landed.

'We're doing Christmas dinner this year, aren't we, Vic?' Nina announced. 'It's going to be exciting having you both here. It'll be a squash because my mum and dad are coming too; and Darren and Dot will pop in for tea!'

'Really look forward to that,' said James eagerly. 'I'll visit Mum in morning and then relax with you for rest of the day.' Polly's face betrayed her heart dropping to her stomach.

'I'm going to have to be a party pooper,' she hesitated.

'You're *what*?' asked James. 'Don't say you can't—'

Polly put her hand on top of her dad's.

'Dad, I'm really sorry… but I've got to go to Northern Ireland.'

And so, it all came out… Beth and Flynn, their new house, her duty to reciprocate the support, the lack of time…

'After all this time preparing, I'm suddenly left with just three days for final packing, my valedictory church service, and that's it – I'm off!' She kept repeating her apology. Family ties pulled hard for the first time.

'But perhaps you'll come to my valedictory on the 29th of December?' She was trying to lighten the mood that had changed from excited anticipation to dejected disappointment.

'Valedictory?' said Nina flatly, looking from Vic to James.

'Did you say the twenty-ninth? I don't know.' James shook his head slowly and Vic just stared at Polly.

'Ireland,' he said, ignoring her invitation… 'Hear that, Nicola?' he lifted his baby and held her before his face. 'That's it then,' he said to her.

'That's it then?' He addressed Polly.

James broke the silence, seemingly resigned to Polly's latest obstinacy.

'I suppose we'll get used to it.'

'But we did hope,' said Nina, offering room for Polly to change her mind.

'End of subject, Nina. It's no good.' Vic said glumly.

'Yes, we did just *hope,*' said James.

'Dad!' said Vic abruptly. 'Subject closed.' Polly was shocked. She'd never heard Vic talk to their father so sharply. Nicola whimpered.

'When are you going to see Mum?' asked James. Polly blushed.

'I went this afternoon. I took her biscuits which she nibbled but...'

Vic interrupted. 'She brightens up when she sees, our little one, doesn't she, Nina?' Nina smiled and James grinned but neither looked back at Polly who was still thinking of her mother:

'...she just stared into space. Wouldn't hold my hand... drink her tea. Nothing.' *But I love little Nicola. And family is where I belong.*

*

Polly's eyes were agog when she first saw Beth and Flynn's new home in Ireland. Detached, five-bedroomed, architect designed – all very modern. It was not far from the beautiful Mourne Mountains surrounded by trees and near the village where Flynn's parents lived.

'We didn't want to live too close to Belfast,' Flynn confided. 'Not these days – IRA and all that.' Polly nodded. *They're living under the shadow of the threat of violence.*

Some of Polly's new supporters invited the threesome to Christmas dinner. Far more luxurious than Polly ever imagined. She was almost afraid to touch the fine china, and felt nervous and out of place… 'I can't really eat this much,' she whispered to Beth, looking at the pile of food set before her.

'Oh, don't worry, just leave it. They won't mind.' And Beth started a conversation with her other neighbour.

Christ's disciples left all their possessions and followed Him in poverty. Our riches are in heaven, not on earth. The lavishness threw Polly who had given away her best coat to shed her guilt about keeping two. *But I can't do God's work without these people. I must compromise.* Other students at Bible College trusted God for everything and believed raising funds for support showed lack of faith. Their needs were usually met, although on occasion their faith was tested and they had hard times waiting for the Lord to supply. But MUT were more practical. They argued the job couldn't be done properly if you were hungry or had financial worries.

Flynn and Beth defended luxurious Christian living:

'God gives us richly all things to enjoy,' Flynn said to Polly. 'You've got a lot to learn if you are going to work with people who have different outlooks on life… you can't expect everybody to change their way to *your* way.' Polly kept her peace. *You're a fine one to speak, Flynn.*

Polly's missionary talk was to take place at the church on the evening of St Stephen's Day. The projector was set up, and forty chairs arranged in rows for the congregation. She'd prayed the Lord would give her a special message. *Trust in the Lord with all your heart, and lean not unto your own understanding*: that was it! The lights dimmed for the 'deputation slides', and the projector beamed light onto the screen and the show started. They saw a clearing where workers had set up a compound. There was a clinic room with a queue of women in saris and kurta pyjama clad men waiting outside for treatment. Then there were children sitting on the ground listening to a tape-recorded Bible story, in their own language, and other pictures were of the surgical team and patients with bandaged eyes.

'Praise God!' said a man in the audience. One or two mumbled agreement but most listened quietly until after the challenge she posed at the end.

'God wants us to trust Him totally in everything, and he will supply our needs…' She didn't labour the point, just sowed a few seeds of deeper dependence on the Lord.

Polly had left a short time for questions afterwards. Flynn's father asked, 'What about language? How are you going to communicate with the tribes-people?'

'My main task will be to take tapes to the villages, carrying the Gospel in their language. And, as a nurse, I will support clinic teams who *have* learnt the language. There'll be interpreters if I need them.'

'Wonderful work!' They sat down again, as others murmured, 'Yes.'

Flynn announced a word of prayer.

'We'll commit Polly to the Lord and pray for the people of India.' Heads were bowed as he raised his voice and stretched an arm over the faithful and the prayer routine took over. The loud 'Amen!' echoed through the church, followed by several spontaneous hallelujahs.

With the lights up, Beth's mother helped Flynn's parents to hand round tea and biscuits. Polly heard people say how they had enjoyed the slides and commenting once or twice on how brave she was going out into the unknown. 'But the Lord is with her,' she overheard. A woman told her about her son who wanted to be a missionary but couldn't quite make up his mind; and another explained she couldn't afford to give to any extra missionary work, but would pray for her.

'Thank goodness you didn't mention the Roman Catholics,' Beth whispered as people drifted off.

'Why?' Polly was thinking of Anthony, and her jaw dropped when she heard Beth's reply.

'I forgot to pass on Mummy's message before you started.' She took Polly's elbow and guided her to face the wall. Leaning closer to Polly's ear and facing the wall herself she said,

'You have to be careful. Flynn's family *hate* Roman Catholics.'

*

Polly scanned the gathering at her valedictory meeting in Halebridge Baptist Church, on December 29th, and did a double take when she spied Darren and Dot in the back row. *Fancy them coming!* A church deacon was speaking with them, but no sign of her family. It was a complete contrast to the Irish event when all Flynn's family came. Polly spoke about her calling to the mission field and her conviction that God wanted her in India. The pastor and elders laid their hands on her head and blessed her. Members of the congregation prayed 'as they were led' and it ended with a hymn laden with meaning for missionaries and their sympathisers. It was sung in 1956 by five missionaries before they ventured into an Ecuadorian jungle to meet the Auca Indians, tribespeople unused to strangers. The five men had been shot and killed – with arrows. Wives and children were left to fend for themselves. Polly determined, in that moment, how she must be ready to die for the Gospel.

As she boarded her plane to the unknown, the words of the hymn came back to her:

> '*We rest on Thee, our Shield and our Defender…*
> *…We rest on Thee, and in Thy name we go.*

Crofton and another MUT director waved her goodbye. None of the family came. Beth and Flynn sent a message through Croften to say they were with her in prayer…

CHAPTER 20

'Now let us consider the facts.'

Anthony was standing before the Abbot's desk again. But this time it was unexpected. *What's wrong?*

'I'll get straight to the point, Anthony.'

'Yes, F-father.'

'I've had a letter from your solicitor…' He sorted through a pile of papers and found the one he wanted. 'Please sit.' Anthony sat on a chair near the desk. A woodlouse was crawling on the floor.

'I have to tell you about this letter. But first and foremost, you've been here two decades and *still* not taken your vows. According to Brother Lucian you were developing well until the unfortunate discovery of the late Brother Vincent.' A cloud passed over Anthony's face. They both bowed and made the sign of the cross. That unforgettable evening came into focus. The guilt of failing to check on Vincent earlier balanced by the comfort of those last words he uttered: 'The wall will go. It'll be *all right.* Who *really* knows what God has ordained?' Anthony had mulled over these words every day, and they sparked off one chain of thought after another. Brother Vincent was never happier than with the chickens and remained resolutely silent at business meetings. But Anthony glimpsed his wisdom and had grown to respect his opinion. He'd said those things… then gone. He appeared to have accepted the monastic lifestyle, but knowing Anthony had not, yet, he must have had a reason for what his pronouncement. *Was it a warning…? Don't be taken in?*

'Please speak, Anthony,' the Abbot was still waiting for a reaction.

'He m-made me th-think…'

'Yes, I can see that but I want you to *share* what you think.' The Abbot wished he could just fathom Anthony's mind.

Anthony would never share Vincent's dying thoughts with any of the brotherhood. He circumvented the question.

'I-I think he was incredibly w-wise. I-I miss him. I-I d-did not expect—'

'Our future lies in the hands of God whether we live or die.' The Abbot was annoyed with himself for cutting Anthony off before he had finished. 'We must not question His divine will.' He willed Anthony to return his gaze. 'However, we have to make decisions from time to time.' He picked up the letter and took a deep breath. 'One of those times is *now*, Anthony.'

Anthony waited with a burning curiosity, 'Y-yes, F-Father?'

'Before I read this aloud, please answer me. Do you really want to take your vows or not?'

What does it say then? 'I-I don't know. I'm sorry – I-I've prayed so hard and for so long.'

'Very well. I'll read this letter and suggest a course of action. It's from the solicitor who looked after your father's business and helped you sell the house.' Acutely alert, Anthony's eyes pierced the back of the paper.

The Abbot read: 'I am instructed to inform you that following the death of Simon Bloom, your mother's brother, and in the absence of other relatives, you stand to inherit his property and money in Guernsey.'

'Why m-me?' Realising at once he was questioning the ways of God, he felt faint and dropped his head to his chest.

'Please remember your posture when we are speaking.' Anthony slowly sat up and placed his hands, clasped, in his lap. Father Brendon continued, 'It is not for me to answer that question. I can only guide you how to proceed. Firstly, you will recall the brotherhood is in urgent need of funds. Secondly, something I shouldn't need to remind you: "The love of money is the root of all evil."' Anthony was stunned. Doubts flooded back about the use of his previous donation. He tried to read his superior's body-language. *Abashed? Guilty? Hiding something?*

'As usual, no response,' noted the Abbot. 'I'll give you a binary choice, Anthony: accept or reject. Take two years sabbatical. Go out into the world and see if you feel more at home there than here. Look for your place in the world. Ask why you've procrastinated for so long. Then think of our community, which could be *your* community, and ask if you are letting us down. The brotherhood rejoices in younger members joining, but there is no place here for those whose heart and soul are not engaged.'

Anthony understood the choice, but questions tumbled around without answers. *No-one really knows what God has ordained.* He was overwhelmed by his new inheritance but had a feeling this was the way forward.

'How long do I-I… before I-I must d-decide?' he asked, surprised at his growing boldness and mistrust.

'I consider one week to be enough. Spend time in the chapel. Brother Lucian will counsel you tomorrow. I pray you will be guided by the right motives.' He dismissed Anthony: 'Go in peace. The Lord be with you.'

'And w-with your s-spirit.'

Anthony opened the door and Father Brendon approached behind him. Shock waves spread through Anthony as he felt a light touch on his arm. The Abbot was close to his ear, too close, whispering, 'Remember Anthony, the love of money is the root of evil... *all* evil.' And softly as though almost not wanting to be heard, 'Stay with us. It may be possible to reach an arrangement.' Anthony faced Brendon and, for once certain of his conviction, looked him full in the face and stared into his eyes for a full five seconds. *You are repulsive.* This time it was the Abbot who shifted his gaze, pulled up his hood, folded his hands into his sleeves and stared at the floor waiting for Anthony to exit. *There's a woodlouse down there somewhere.*

Making the sign of the cross Anthony entered the chapel and knelt before the altar. His mind reeled from the Abbot's intimations, but then with a surge of excitement his thoughts turned to his Uncle Simon's property. *Is this really my chance? Guernsey... house... Is God sending me a sign. Would God really expect me to spurn another gift and hand it over to a place in which I'm losing faith?* He shuddered at the thought of his suspicions.

He lifted his rosary. *In the name of the Father...* there was no longer a prayer inside him. There was plenty to pray about, but the beads slipped through his fingers while plans tumbled through his mind. The brothers filed into the chapel for five o'clock prayers. Father Brendon's empty gaze was turned onto Anthony, who returned a look and took his place in the back row. He already had a hunch of his answer, but wisely considered it for the full week before facing the Abbot. This time his face was bright and full of purpose.

'What have you to tell me?' There was a sense, today, that the two men were on equal footing.

'Th-thank you,' he said with confidence. 'I-I accept the two-year s-sabbatical to c-consider my position.'

'It doesn't surprise me in the least! God be with you. Please finish your quota of cards for open day. And write out the verse I gave you: 1Timothy, chapter six, verse ten: "The love of money is the root of all evil." Write it in both English and Latin, *Pecunia est radix omnis mali caritas.* It's Wednesday today. You may leave a week on Monday. Tom will return your suitcase on Saturday.' They bowed to each other.

Simultaneously they said, 'Peace be with you.' Anthony smiled as he left. He was looking straight ahead.

Lucian was party to the proceedings, but Anthony hardly spoke to anyone else. The cards, plus normal prayers and duties occupied his time. He returned to his cell after supper rather than talk with the others. His whole week filled with the unexpected future before him. The demands of monastic living contrasted starkly with the promise of two years freedom. *The root of all evil.* As he scribed the words carefully and decorated them with his signature script, he dwelt on the meaning of the verse. The more he thought on the words, the stronger he questioned: *Is the love of money really the root of all evil?* He allowed the question to remain. *Analyse and decide this for myself!* He thought of Sebastian's possible motives for his attack. *Was that evil?* Then for the first time allowed himself to dwell on the evil of his father's plane plummeting to the ground in flames. *But Brendon! Could he, just possibly, be speaking to himself?*

When the week was up, he changed into the suit he wore when he entered the brotherhood. It was hardly wearable – far too big. He packed the modest objects he had been allowed to own and made for the main door where Tom had called a taxi. Father Brendon came to wish him a formal farewell.

'Anthony, you've contributed much to our brotherhood. I hope you will come back and take your vows. You will be missed.' He held out an A4 envelope. 'Your passport, medical card and one or two other documents. Also enclosed is a letter I received from your apostate friend, Polly. I have not seen fit to reply. It was not appropriate.' He proffered another envelope. 'Here you will find a card you have inscribed: *Pecunia est radix omnis mali caritas.*' Anthony frowned. This time his silence reflected a confident judgement of the man to whom he had been subjected for too long. The man was talking to himself. But the Abbot had not finished.

'Put this card in your Missal and contemplate the meaning every day. Ask yourself: is my money more important than serving God and praying for the sick? Examine yourself: your motives, desires, your relationship with the Almighty.'

Anthony knew the Abbot was reluctant for him to leave; the more he said, the more he condemned himself.

'Th-thank you, Father, I-I will c-carry it with me.' He couldn't wait to get away. The taxi came and Brother Lucian materialised from inside the building.

'Farewell, my brother.' Anthony smiled sincerely. 'G-goodbye, and thank you for your f-faithfulness to me.' He bowed to the self-conscious Abbot then climbed into the taxi. *Pathetic*.

'Where to, sir?'

'P-Portsmouth please.' He turned to take a last look as the heavy front door swung closed. Tom waved from outside the gate, grinning from ear to ear.

CHAPTER 21

Bombay airport was the gate to a different world. Polly's thoughts were disconnected from her body. Sights, sounds, smells, people all unfamiliar. *Strange. Is there anything I recognise, understand?* The atmosphere was muggy and close, and having come from a cold England and air-conditioned plane, she was dressed in completely the wrong clothes. *Thank goodness someone is meeting me.* She managed to find her luggage then looked through Crofton's lengthy instructions. Scanning the crowd at arrivals she saw a placard saying POLLY. *Ah, there! Luke Fotheringill.* She waved and made her way towards one of the few men wearing western clothes.

Eventually they reached the train station and found their reserved seats.

'Ignore hands coming through the windows!' he shouted. 'We'll go straight home because we can't hear ourselves speak here. Talk later.' It was a relief not to have to make herself heard, and she sat quietly, sweating, and fanning herself with the instructions.

When they arrived at Luke and Elaine's flat Polly was introduced properly. She found a cooler dress and they sat in a living room. Pleasant, apart from an open drainage channel running the length of the wall from the kitchen to outside. Her home for the first week.

'I can't wait to start!' she exclaimed as they drank tea.

'Take your time! You'll need to adjust first,' said Elaine. They had been in Mangalam for long enough to see mistakes made by over-enthusiastic newcomers.

'We'll show you the cassette machines we take to the villages soon, but we won't expect you to travel in week one.'

Polly knew translators had produced cassettes explaining salvation for tribes without a Bible in their language. One society reckoned there were 'two thousand more languages to go' before the whole world could hear their message. They were counting them off as they were 'reached'. Years later Polly realised the catchphrase raised funds, but revealed shocking ignorance.

'It's painstaking work... terribly, terribly slow,' said Luke.

But Polly was bothered about the beggars. 'Why did we ignore them?'

Elaine looked at Luke and said, 'We struggled when we first came, but after a while you get used to them... if you give to one, they'll never leave you alone. There are so many. They can get quite aggressive and the money we have is not ours to give. It's donated for the Lord's work, so our duty to be good stewards.'

'Some of them are employed by gang-leaders who live lives of luxury. It's a complicated business. But when they know you're not going to give, they stop asking...' Luke added.

'Oh.' Polly was doubtful but she kept further thoughts to herself.

'We've been looking forward to your coming,' said Elaine in her strong Irish accent. 'Did your family mind your coming?' Polly felt the old tension in her solar plexus as the three missionaries shared details of their background. 'We'll show you around tomorrow, then maybe by Thursday you can start learning the routine.' Polly was full of unanswered questions.

Elaine continued, 'You'll find it bitty, but one thing at a time. Everything will gradually fall into place.' Polly thought of days when she had started on a new ward. They never seemed to have the equipment she was used to, but after a few days she learnt how the new set-up worked.

But this time the task was formidable. She'd have to use her initiative travelling around this extraordinary country with its bizarre customs, languages, culture, food, weather. To support clinics with medicines and equipment, at the same time as keeping fit physically, mentally, and spiritually, was going to be tricky. She was bound to make mistakes. At Bible school they had described the change from home country to mission field. 'Culture shock,' they said, 'can finish you before you've even started. You're keen to do the Lord's work, but nothing is familiar and your body is not used to the conditions. Beware of neglecting yourself and your needs. Keep close to the Lord. Do not forsake prayer. Feed the soul. Remember Jesus said *I am the bread of life. I am the living water*. Eat and drink of Him. Nobody else is going to do that for you.'

In the next few days Elaine and Luke did all they could to make Polly comfortable. They introduced her to friends from Church and workers with other Missionary societies and explained they needed a girl to do housework and cooking so that they could concentrate on the Lord's work.

'I've found a servant for you, dear,' said Elaine as they were buying provisions for Polly's flat.

'A servant? For me? I'm not sure...' Polly had not prepared for this but Elaine persuaded her by arguing the local people expected missionaries to employ somebody.

'It works both ways. The only alternative for some is begging. We don't treat them like servants, you know. They usually enjoy the work and are very good cooks.' Polly gave in. Veena did not look at all strong. She was small and very thin, but proved to be helpful and cheerful. She spoke good English and was a mine of information. The two girls got on well together.

*

Luke had collected mail from the post box and handed two letters and a postcard to Polly. She tore the first open. *I never thought I'd hear from Anthony again!*

~ Belle Vue, 21, Rue de la Mer, Guernsey ~

Dear Polly,

I expect you are surprised to hear from me, and I will explain my silence and my new address. The Abbot forbade me to write as letters from home disturbed my meditations and study. It's true, they caused me to dwell on home.

I was only given your letters when I left the monastery for a two-year Sabbatical. One was addressed to the Abbot. He said he hadn't replied.

I was warmed to hear you liked my gift to your parents. I thought they might store it but the thought of it hanging in your hallway is gratifying. Although we might rush the words when we pray, they signify the mystery of the Blessed Holy Trinity, which is indeed miraculous. As we commit ourselves in the name of the Father and of the Son and of the Holy Spirit, in communion with the Church worldwide, it signifies our unity with God and men.

I'm spending my two years based in Guernsey because an unexpected solicitor's letter arrived informing me Simon, my mother's brother (a Guernsey businessman), died and I was his only beneficiary. So, for the second time, I've a big decision to make about money. Father Brendon realised I was torn about committing myself to the brotherhood and gave me the opportunity to examine my thoughts, motives, and relationship with God. So here I am, in 'my' house to think and pray. He asked me to consider the verse 'the love of money is the root of all evil.'

Piers looked after the house after Uncle Simon's death. He was Uncle's 'nurse' for several years and they were extremely fond of each other. I must take after Uncle because Piers (younger than my uncle but older than me) says I remind him of Simon in many ways. As soon as we met I felt I'd come home, for the first time in my life.

I hope it won't shock you when I say we're now partners. Knowing Piers has helped put my life into perspective and the change is so great I can't yet fathom it. I confess I have never been happier.

I was sad, though not surprised to learn that Fluffy died. Giving him up was a sacrifice but I made friends with 'Mouse'! (I think I told you about him.)

> *I wonder where you are now. I'll address this to Elm Close and hope it finds you.*
>
> *I hope we will meet one day and discuss our faith in person.*
>
> *Piers has a black Labrador called Tiffany, who is very friendly and such good company.*
>
> *Yours very sincerely, and God be with you,*
> *Anthony*

Her pleasure at hearing from Anthony was mixed with discomfort about the nature of his partnership. But that was forgotten when she read Beth and Flynn's postcard, sent from another holiday destination.

> *The Giant's Causeway!*
> *Dearest Polly,*
>
> *Expecting our first baby in six months! Sick – but isn't it exciting? God is SO good to us with our lovely house, then this blessing. (Don't tell anyone, it's early days.)*
>
> *Your supporters are all donating as promised. Aren't they good?*
>
> > *Praying for you every day!*
> > *Love, Beth and Flynn*

Around the edge, in tiny writing, she had written, '*You must come to the Giant's Causeway when you are over! It's extraordinary.*'

Polly was annoyed. *Yes, they certainly enjoy themselves. That's all they seem interested in.*

The other letter was from her father, dealing another emotional blow.

16 Elm Close
Halebridge

Polly,
Words cannot express how bereft we are you have chosen to turn your back on us. Darren came to your valedictory meeting and said you told everybody your parents never understood Christianity and didn't realise serving God had to come before family needs.

We hoped we'd done our best for you from the day you were born. But your rejections have so deeply affected your mother that I begin to feel she may never recover. The whole business has made me extremely sad.

I keep asking myself why you chose to go to complete strangers at Christmas. We were all so disappointed.

You needn't bother to come home anymore. Vic and Nina are good to me, and I love little Nicola. She is the light of my life.

I've forwarded a letter from Guernsey. No idea who it is from.

I hope you are happy in your new life and things work out for you.

Your utterly disappointed,
Father (Dad)

What have I done to deserve that? He doesn't want me back home. He's written me off. What sort of witness have I been to family? As was her habit when things went wrong, she knelt by the bed. 'Oh, God,' she wept, 'I'm trying to do your will. Why have you forsaken me?' but realising she was echoing Christ's words on the cross, she felt comforted thinking she shared

Christ's pain: *This is what it means to be suffering like Christ*. 'Thank you, Lord, thank you. Help me to bear this cross.'

Elaine sensed something was up when Polly went into the office: 'What's wrong, dear?'

'My father has written to say I might as well not go home. They think I've turned my back on them. But I haven't, really! I love them.' She started to cry.

'Come here!' Elaine put her arm round Polly's shoulder. 'We'll pop in the house and have a little prayer together, shall we? The Lord knows all about it. The old devil doesn't give us any rest, does he?'

Polly was reassured. But it wasn't until the evening she was able to look at things clearly. She picked up Anthony's letter. *So, Anthony* is *homosexual. I did wonder, but what do I know about it*? Nurses she worked with in London sometimes discussed same-sex relationships and, imagining she knew nobody in that position, her only point of reference was a Bible verse condemning the act of man lying with man. *It feels odd to me, but what is so evil about it?* It was more important to her that she could confide in Anthony as a friend. So, she took up her pen.

> *C/o Mission to Unreached Tribes*
> *Box 384, Mangalam, Tamil Nadu, India*
> *Dear Anthony,*
>
> *I was so pleased to get your letter. Dad forwarded it to India for me. I'd given up hope of hearing from you again when the Abbot didn't answer my letter.*
>
> *Your news is so unexpected. Fancy your Uncle Simon leaving you his house, and in such a delightful place! I thought you would*

have taken your vows by now! But I'm glad you didn't if you were uncertain.

Having mentioned Dad, I must share a heavy burden. He's gathered the impression that home means nothing to me simply because I am following the Lord's will. It has made me realise how I rather ignored the feelings of my parents, being so obsessed with coming out here and raising support. He's told me I needn't 'bother to go home'. I couldn't stop crying, but now I realise it's all part of doing the Lord's will. Roman Catholics – nuns and priests - give up home to fulfil their calling, don't they? I thought their parents felt proud of them.

Life is SO different in this country. I can't tell you everything but, for example, people set up stalls on the pavements and fill them with strange gods or flower garlands. I've never seen so many gods, although I understand there are shops in Lourdes with hundreds of Roman Catholic idols and so-called holy water. It's a somewhat similar situation.

There is so much we could talk about. I hope you don't mind my telling you about Dad's letter, but it helps me to share it with you.

You sound happy for the first time. Did you feel at all fulfilled at the monastery, or at peace in any way?

I'd like to meet you again some time, although I have no idea when.

> *I know we've different beliefs, but also I feel we have much in common.*
> *Very sincerely,*
> *Polly*

Beth and Flynn hadn't said much, so she replied on a post-card. A picture of Ganesh, the Hindu elephant god, seemed appropriate. It would give them an idea of the culture:

> *Glad to hear the support is coming in. Some missionaries feel the power of evil when they see Hindu gods like this one. I don't. More about that later. Love Polly. P.S. Congrats re. baby.*

She placed it on top of Anthony's letter, ready to post, and considered replying to her father. She didn't know what to say so left it for another day. *If my trust were stronger I wouldn't be so upset. Think about your armour, Polly. Which piece is missing?*

CHAPTER 22

~ Belle Vue, 21, Rue de La Mer, Guernsey. ~

Dear Polly,
Thank you for writing. I think we would enjoy meeting after corresponding for so long. I always remember Archibald when I write to you! I'm glad you wrote to me about him.

I've been sorting out Simon's house and continue to pray about leaving the monastery. I spent hours learning the tenets of the Roman Catholic Church, every one of which contains sub-sections ad infinitum, branching out into elaborate detail. I studied long hours often doubting if it was significant to everyday life. On reflection, I see how getting away from home helped me to <u>know myself</u> and getting away from the monastery helps me to <u>be myself</u>. And that includes having my dear partner, Piers. I cannot see myself putting those robes back on but the future remains unclear. I will not leave the Church entirely. I will decide by November.

Did I feel fulfilled at St Martin's? Not really. Talking to Vincent, God rest his soul, and being surrounded by the contented chickens bought me greater peace than singing in chapel.

Now I have a second chance. I think I will be more help in the outside world doing something like helping the homeless, hopefully relieving their need, if only a little. I'll try spending three months with Father Dominic in London and see how that transpires. I feel I'm taking a risk. I fear the reaction of homophobes who will recognise my 'type'. But I can't keep hiding. Piers says we can only do what our fear allows us to. Some people are beginning to realise our sexuality is genetic, so I hope and pray the future will bring us more freedom.

I've had disturbing news from my Uncle Henry. He tells me my artwork and treasured Canaletto are missing from his storehouse along with a few of his valuable antiques. The police said they will keep an eye on the market. But they don't hold out much hope of finding the thief. This news is hard to assimilate, but I felt guilty about treasuring them and accept this as a reprimand from God.

Apparently my cousin Gustavus has been charged with grievous bodily harm and the court case comes up in March. I'm unable to speak to him. He has no respect for me.

I'm sorry your father is reacting as you say, but I suspect he will change his mind. I will say a daily rosary on your behalf. I can't help feeling going to the confessional would help you examine what went wrong, I remain saddened at the way you make up your own mind about following God. But I had a dream, not long ago, which showed me the different paths we follow will eventually merge.

Despite differences in our faith, Polly, I value your prayers.

Yours most sincerely
Anthony

> *P.S. My beautiful new home is spacious. Piers will look after it when I'm in London. You are welcome to come and stay for as long as you like. God be with you. A*

*

A few weeks later, Anthony and Piers were on the beach in the spring sunshine. The tide was out and Tiffany was splashing in and out of the waves as she fetched her ball from the sea.

'That's fine. Tiffany and I are used to being by ourselves, aren't we, Tiff?' She wagged her tail but her mind was on the ball being thrown back in the sea, and she bounded away following the direction of his hand. 'Funny how dogs love to fetch!'

'So, you don't m-mind if I stay in London for two or three m-months? I-I want to see how things w-work out for me,' said Anthony, looking fondly into his partner's eyes.

'You know I'll miss you. But this,' he said, spreading his arm across the beach then sweeping around the cliffs, 'will keep me going!' They sat on the rocks beneath the cliffs, staring out to the horizon. Piers scanned the beach for other walkers before putting his arm around Anthony's shoulder, wary of showing affection in public.

'I hate how people c-constantly judge each other. Because, if G-God is Love why would he b-bring us together and s-still want us celibate? There's absolutely no s-sanctioning of our s-situation in Church doctrine or the Bible. J-Jesus teaches Love as His highest value, yet c-communicants are so ready to c-condemn us. B-but I'm learning so m-much from your w-way of looking at things!'

Piers just grinned. Born a Roman Catholic he rarely went to confession or mass. Anthony welcomed his common-sense approach to religion and wished he could free himself of the rules and regulations that had been drilled into him for as long as he could remember.

'TIFF! Home, girl!' Piers called, and she bounded up shaking sand and seawater over them. They laughed at her. *Sand, sea, and silence. Here, we are free.*

The following Monday Piers waved Anthony off. His anticipation of a lonely few weeks was not as keen as his concern for Anthony who was nervous but compelled to press on. London certainly did not welcome gay men, especially those with anxious mannerisms.

Peering over the ferry rail, Anthony shuddered, his new-found determination deserting him. He looked forward to meeting Father Dominic who led the homelessness outreach team in his church near the Shorewell arches. *With Piers I'm fine. But London…? Will I meet bullies… or worse? And Father Dominic?*

He stepped off the train at Victoria and saw a someone wearing a clerical collar behind the turnstile. He checked his pockets, straightened glasses, picked up suitcase and went through the turnstile fazed by the frantic activity.

'How nice to see you, Brother,' said Dominic as they shook hands.' He put his hand under Anthony's elbow. 'Welcome!'

'Y-yes, yes. *Y-yes*!' Anthony beamed.

'And this is my helper, Tim.'

A taxi took them to the Presbytery where Father Dominic had tea prepared. 'After tea Tim will show you your room. That suit you?' He looked Anthony up and down, cocked his head to one side and after a few moments realised the new arrival would probably like a wash and brush-up.

Anthony returned and stood behind a chair at the tea table. Dominic said grace then they sat down.

His room upstairs was simple but comfortable. He unpacked his Missal and put it on a box by the bed. The Abbot's decorated card was tucked between the leaves. *Pecunia est radix omnis mali caritas.* The love of money – *evil*? He sat on the chair and closed his eyes. *London's so busy, all these high buildings, traffic… the monastery… Guernsey… I must get used to this!* As his mind flitted between different locations, sleep took over.

'We do the soup kitchen at 10 p.m. every evening. Want to join us tomorrow?' asked Tim at breakfast.

'Y-yes, y-es,' said Anthony. 'I-I've never l-lived in a busy place l-like this before. We don't h-have the h-homeless in Guernsey and there's hardly any c-crime. There w-wasn't much *real* life in the m-monastery so this is a ch-challenge.' He saw Piers in his mind and thought of something he said. He smiled. 'S-ink or s-swim!'

'Real life? Phew! You'll find that in bucket-loads here. You watch your back all the time. You can only trust those you know well. Keep an eye open for anyone acting suspiciously and remember the professional pickpockets. They easily deceive, work in gangs, and you don't notice until it's too late. Best not carry much and make sure cash is safe. Always lock your door. Strangers are in and out of the building, and I know it sounds untrusting and even unchristian but be-*ware*. Be very careful!'

'I… I-I'm not used to anything like this at all.' Anthony was nodding his head as he plucked up the courage to adjust.

'You'll soon learn. Why don't you take a walk and get your bearings during the day – then we'll set out at eight-thirty this evening. It takes a while to get set up before opening at ten.'

Real life! Anthony's hands were shaking and his knees felt wobbly. *I must get out there.*

CHAPTER 23

C/o Mission to Unreached Tribes
Box 384
Mangalam

Dear Anthony

It was good to have your news and thank you for the offer of accommodation if I need it.

How devastating to lose your artwork and the precious Canaletto. I'm so sorry. The Lord tests us sorely at times. I don't think dealers have anything to do with recognisable pictures though. Maybe someone will reveal its hiding place.

I hope you like my typing! I learnt at missionary college but didn't have a typewriter before. I type information to give out with cassettes. I'm speeding up and although it's still slower than writing by hand, at least you can read it!

I don't find it easy trying to do God's will. It was awful saying goodbye to family, especially Victor and Nina's new baby! I told the family I couldn't be with them for my last

Christmas at home. No one understood, but I had to be in Ireland because Beth and her husband have enlisted a group of Irish people to support me. The wealth and lavish behaviour of Beth's in-laws clashed with my concept of serving Christ. I know it was Christmas, but I gave up my worldly goods to serve the Lord and found it hard to accept their plenty. I thought of Jesus saying it is easier for a camel to pass through the eye of a needle than for a rich man to go to heaven. I won't elaborate!

It sounds bad but I am a bit resentful. Beth, my friend who helped lead me to Christ, is married, expecting her first baby and lives in a wonderful house. My boyfriend gave me up because I was going to be a missionary, and I'm not sure if I'll ever love anyone else or have children now.

I'm hoping I won't need to learn an Indian language, although I begin to wish I could speak at least a little Hindi. I was told my role wouldn't need language skills, but I visit different language groups with gospel cassettes for their MUT machines. I also deliver extra supplies of medicines and might replace an eye-clinic nurse on leave. (We specialise in eye care.) I could never learn all the languages spoken in the villages, but I do find it frustrating when the locals don't understand me. I'm convinced the committee don't realise what it's like. They exasperate me, to be truthful. Some of the information they gave me before I came was quite wrong.

I can see that we both have a struggle with riches. It's hard to get our priorities right. No one can predict how they'll react in different situations can they? Sometimes I am quite bewildered.

Please tell me how you get on in London with the homeless. And I'm sorry to hear about your cousin. I will pray for him.

Sincerely,
Polly
P.S. Some of the Irish supporters are flying out here to see our work.
P.P.S. I confess everything directly to Jesus, and the heart of my belief is that I don't need a confessional between me and Christ. (I suppose I've sort of confessed to you because I need to. But there's a difference!)
Polly

She put the letter in an envelope then immediately started another:

```
C/o Mission to Unreached Tribes
Box 384, Mangalam, Tamil Nadu

Dear Beth and Flynn,
  Thank you as always for your
work at the 'home end'. I've
enclosed a list of address
changes etc.
  It's my fourth month in India
and I have a fairly good idea of
my role though it will take a full
year to learn the whole routine;
remote villages, special
festivals and so on. I'm used to
filtering the water and not
taking risks with food, but it's
difficult when we travel, and I
live in fear and dread of getting
'Delhi Belly'!
  There are so many Christian
churches in Mangalam. They've
been started by missionaries from
a variety of denominations a
handful of which I didn't even
know existed! The really strict
congregations are exclusive and
have stringent rules for
converts. They call themselves
Christian but they teach a
variety of doctrines. They all
have converts. Strange, isn't it?
```

The Fotheringills say they've met evangelical missionaries who are friendly with Roman Catholics and even work together occasionally! (They don't break bread together of course.)

We're off to a far-flung village tomorrow where they are working with a travelling eye clinic. I'm dying to see how it works and might even get a chance to assist the surgeon. I'm sure you've heard how awful the trains are in India. I don't like them at all. They tell me I will be collected at the station by a bullock cart.

I'm told there are at least five other languages spoken locally including Tamil, Telugu, Malayalam, and Bengali. I think they have commonalities, but the amazing thing is that so many people speak English too. Young children come up to me in the street and say: 'The river Thames is in London,' or 'London is the capital of England.' They are so bright and keen to learn!

Prayer requests:

For health and safety especially while travelling.

For guidance at the eye clinic. Wisdom to know how to help and when to witness.

Vivaan (our general helper): for wisdom to see the error of Hinduism and recognise Jesus is the way, the truth, and the light.

Yours in the love of Christ,
Polly

CHAPTER 24

Polly was preparing for a trip to a village in the north the following day, not a great distance from Delhi. Vivaan would help with the luggage. They had packed the equipment required and she was working through her personal list when Luke returned from collecting the mail. A letter from Anthony and a hastily written post-card of the Tower of London from Flynn. She read the card first:

> *On quick London visit. We'll be touring India 5 weeks starting in 8 weeks: Agra, Delhi, then drop down to you. More details later. In Christ, Flynn.*

She put it in her case and left Anthony's letter to read later:

> *~ Belle Vue, Guernsey ~*
> *Dear Polly,*
> *I like your typing. But I doubt I'll ever want to type as I love the rhythm of writing.*
> *Your work sounds interesting, but do be careful as you travel and eat in strange places. The medical work obviously fulfils a great need in places with no other eye care. I've heard thousands of Indian people are blind but have no treatment.*
> *I have finally left the monastery. I had no doubts when I visited Father Brendon. As he requested, I considered the money question.*

I'd donated my first inheritance to the monastery and was never satisfied it was used for God's glory. Rather the opposite. I became suspicious of Father Brendon and his activities but have no proof. Piers thinks the poor are pressured to given money to the Church and I fear it goes towards extravagant living for those higher in the hierarchy. I wonder if some of our leaders have lost sight of their spiritual motivation.

And many use the concept of their 'normality' (what is 'normal'?) to abuse gay people judging us abnormal. Piers has taught me so much about what it means to recognise one's homosexuality. We are how God made us.

I've been questioning whether the love of money is the root of all evil, and think homophobia is a root of evil and nothing to do with money. It is as Hamlet said: 'There is nothing either good or bad, but thinking makes it so.' I wonder who first thought same partner relationships should be illegal?

The Abbot said I was in danger of committing mortal sin thus condemning myself to hell. Thankfully, I now have the strength to reject dogma which is at variance with a God of Love. I'll remain in the Church but be my own master. Celibacy is not for me. Thank God I didn't take my vows. I know your church also condemns our sexual activity. But how many appalling sins are committed in secret by priests because they have no outlet for their desires?

I spent three months at St Mark's helping Father Dominic in his ministry to the homeless but am home again now. I witnessed awful conditions, quite outside my experience. In Devon we prayed and gave alms (insignificant really) but St Mark's is involved <u>in a practical way</u> and people are so thankful for its ministry. The crypt doors are open for some to sleep overnight. Father Dominic leads our team by walking humbly in God's love.

You write about the 'evil' of riches from a different viewpoint. Your fellow Christians seem to be living double lives: preaching holiness but living lavishly. Maybe your friends exemplify people who love their money. Perhaps I am now counted among the rich. But I will help the needy and restrict treating myself.

You are right, it takes time and soul searching to discover the truth about ourselves and our motives.

But sometimes we need to relax a little! Do you have any fun? I think I have started to learn what fun is.

Please tell me how you view my thoughts above. I hope you will still feel you can stay in my house when you visit England.

Sincerely,
Anthony
P.S. Happy Christmas!
P.P.S. This year I am sending cards for the first time. I will stay in Guernsey for Christmas with Piers and Tiffany. I learnt so

much in London and want to return in the New Year. A.

The journey, the work, and the aftermath were demanding. Polly had no time to reply to either, although she did plenty of thinking. A month later she settled down to the typewriter:

```
MUT, Mangalam

Dear Anthony,
   I enjoyed your Christmas
card. A Guernsey cow. That's a
first for me!
   Your letter gave me so much
to think about. I am not
surprised you have left the
monastery. I understand your
reasoning. More of my thoughts
on your lifestyle later.
   Be assured I am doing my best
to take care of myself. I put
purification tablets in the
drinking water and chlorine
tablets in the water for
washing salad and vegetables.
I've learnt to eat with my
fingers (right hand only)! I
still rest on Sundays and try
not to get overtired.
   I wish you could visit the
eye clinics. There's hardly any
paperwork, and although people
queue for days, they get
treatment in turn. It is
```

rewarding to help the surgeons, and see dramatic results. Other times it can be very sad, especially for some young children. The girls don't stand much chance of getting married if they have bad eyes, but on the positive side, a lot of them listen to our tapes as they wait for or recover after their operations. A few ask questions, and the linguists can sit and talk with them about the Lord. St John's gospel is the only book of the Bible translated into a selection of languages so far. But that contains John chapter three verse sixteen which is central to our message. Such an important verse.

The work at St Mark's must be a big encouragement to those you help. Helping the poor is out of the question here because we haven't the resources for the tremendous numbers in need. It's tricky enough just shopping, and being surrounded by beggars. One man approaches us as we go down the steps from the general store and moves the stumps of his arms back and forth in front of our faces. It turns my stomach to think of his suffering. Apparently some babies are deliberately disfigured to beg for the family.

The Kavanaughs (Flynn's friends), have visited to see our work. They witnessed patients listening to tapes, and saw a few people who are really interested in being saved. They met Vivaan too, and are praying especially for him. But they asked a lot of questions about our use of the Revised Standard Version of the Bible. They are going to discuss concerns about this with their fellowship. It seems their congregation believe the Authorised Version is the only inspired Bible. So many versions were written before and after 1611, why decide only that one is inspired? They visited another church in Mangalam who agreed with them, so they compared us unfavourably. I didn't anticipate this sort of problem.

I too am challenged by the attitude of the Church (yours and mine) to homosexuality. To be honest, when we first met I sensed there was a difference about you that I couldn't pinpoint. I can't describe it exactly, but I was a bit afraid of you. But I saw how upset you were when your mother died, and began to change my mind, then you asked us to look after Fluffy. I was delighted!

I learnt a lot about different sexual orientations when I lived in London, and the penny dropped. I see God has created people this way and can't condemn your relationship with Piers. As a friend I am happy that you have found him, but the problem is reconciliation with Church teaching. Many members are adamant it is wrong, because the Bible says man lying with man is an 'abomination' in God's eyes. I have to take that seriously, and need to search the scriptures when I have more time. It isn't the only aspect of my faith I have problems with. I've got to find out what God is saying in the whole Bible, not just in a few chosen verses. I've realised when people quote the Bible, they pick out verses that suit their viewpoint, and ignore parts which don't fit in. What about

Deuteronomy twenty-three, verses one and two? 'No one who has been emasculated by crushing or cutting and no one who has been born of a forbidden marriage to the tenth generation may enter the assembly of the Lord'! How many people bother about that? Or even read the whole Bible?

I have not.

Regarding celibacy, that is my way of life because I'd feel guilty marrying a non-Christian. I find it desperately hard and bang my head against a wall at times to rid myself of frustration. I have to plead with God to take temptation from me. I daydream about the boy I loved, Darren. He's married and has a child now, but I can't be yoked with an unbeliever, anyway.

You can see I doubt my teaching and weaken at times. Guilt forces me to creep back to Him for forgiveness.

Writing of riches after the above, seems frivolous. You can't escape from sexuality but you can from wealth.

I'm not sure that I have 'fun' as such. I hadn't thought about it until you asked. Maybe the most fun I had was with my brother as a child. Am I still allowed fun? I'll have to think!

Flynn and Beth are visiting in a few weeks. I'm longing to see Beth but not sure about her husband.

Yours, with love in the Lord.
Polly.

P.S. I'd love to meet Piers.

MUT, Mangalam

Dear Beth and Flynn,

Greeting in Jesus' name. I'll make this fairly brief as you are visiting so soon. We can talk then. It will be good for you to see the work for yourselves. So much easier than trying to describe it to you!

Dad wrote and said I needn't go back home. He was badly hurt after I spent my last Christmas before India in Ireland. I was terribly upset at the time, but the Lord is watching over me and will provide for the future.

Anthony (used to live in the big house next door, do you remember him, Beth?) has inherited a large property on Guernsey and said I could stay there if I need to. He has left the monastery and is wondering about dividing his time between helping the homeless in London and his house in Guernsey, which he shares with a friend called Piers. They have invited me to stay with them.

Give baby Judith a hug from me! I'm sorry she won't be coming with you. I'm longing to meet her.

Not long until your visit! May the Lord keep you safe.

With love in Him,

Polly.

CHAPTER 25

Article in *Shorewell News*, March 29th 1979:
COMMUTERS ANGRY WITH ARCHES PEOPLE
Walk to work intolerable due to beggars.

Complaints have been made to Shorewell District Council about increasing numbers sleeping rough under the arches.

"I can't walk through the arches without a smelly person accosting me for money," said Audrey Burton, cashier, 36.

"The walk to work is blighted by people who haven't had a bath for weeks," added Peter Noon, customs officer, 45.

These comments highlight a growing problem for the council who admit that the situation is out of control. The police have recorded several robberies lately, but have insufficient evidence against anyone to make an arrest. It is reported the beggars approach passers-by under the arches, but thefts more usually take place in the market close by, largely when customers are distracted talking to stallholders who also report missing items of food. The thieves lose themselves in the crowd before they are identified.

Our social affairs editor, Barbara Gristwood, has been commissioned by the council to write a report on the Arches People but we will investigate the reasons behind their circumstances: Why they are here? Are there prospects for moving on?

*

'Usual Monday pie, then?' Maisie smiled at Barbara and Penny as they settled at their regular table in front of the counter.

'Of course!' they chuckled at Maisie, surprised she had even asked. 'Could we survive without your cottage pie, Maisie?'

'Well, girls, I've got news for you.' She passed the order through to the kitchen, then came and rested her hands on the back of the spare chair.

'Another grandchild?' Barbara asked.

'I've got enough of those for the time being!' They laughed. 'No! How can I put this?' She bent over in conspiratorial manner and whispered, 'I'm retiring.' Penny gasped. 'Next week might be your last cottage pie... err, *Maisie's cottage pie*, anyways.'

The friends were taken aback, and Barbara, sensing a story, motioned to Maisie to sit down. The threesome leant forward in a huddle.

'Now I don't want no headlines in the *Shorewell News* or nowt, no headlines: 'No More Cottage Pie at Maisie's! Promise?'

Barbara feigned disappointment and mocked: 'You're deserting us!'

'Hurrr, I'm seventy-five you know, and Nora's no spring chicken. I can't ask her to keep helping me, so

I'm goin' a 'joy the grandchildren. 'Ave a good time.' She looked up triumphantly. 'See London! Lived 'ere all these years and never 'ad time to 'splore proply. Buck Palace 'n all that, you know!'

'Oh Maisie, we'll miss you!' Barbara squeezed Maisie's arm.

'Aww,' Maisie smiled, 'that's nice!'

'But will Maisie's Cuppa close… become a dry cleaner's or a betting shop?' asked Penny.

'Oh *NO!* I'm get'in a nice young man to run the place, and he'll plan the menus and so on. It might change 'cos I bet 'is gran never made cottage pie. Max is from the Caribbean…'

Barbara and Penny tossed the news over in their minds while Maisie dashed off to serve another table.

'All change then,' said Penny, wondering what Max's grandma *did* make. 'I wonder if we'll want find another place.'

Nora bought their food and put it before them smiling, 'There y'are loves.' Barbara went to thank her, but she rushed back to the kitchen.

Penny changed the subject. 'You know you said you found it tough to "just be a reporter" when you researched the arches for your report, Babs?'

'Ye-es?'

'What did you actually mean?'

'The thing is, I can't do a report properly without interviewing the Arches People to find out why they're homeless – and it's really hard to keep my distance.'

'*You* finding it *hard*! Tell me another!' Barbara had a *seriously-hard-nosed-reporter* reputation in the office.

'I *am*,' Barbara remonstrated. 'S'pose I'm getting softer in my old age! Whatever. I mean, while I gather my information I have to keep my wits about me and make sure they don't take advantage, but one or two of them are beginning to pull at the heart strings.'

'I'm shocked,' Penny responded. 'That's a first!'

Barbara pursed her lips. 'Shhh, don't pass this on, but if I tell you one or two of their stories, just see what you make of them…'

They were running late, so they finished their food, paid, and dashed back to the office.

*

The following week Barbara and Penny said goodbye and thanks to Maisie, giving her a box of chocolates. They immediately spied the new face behind the counter, Caribbean, young-looking, short curly hair, all smiles. Maisie brought him to the front of the counter.

'These are the ladies we call "The Press", Max.' He burst out laughing and Penny and Barbara warmed to him immediately. 'So, meet Max,' said Maisie. 'I hope you'll keep turning up for his new menu.'

'Caribbean food is very tasty!' They looked up at Max.

'It'll have to be pretty good to beat Maisie's cottage pie!' said Barbara.

'Oh, you wait till you've tried my lamb jerk! Not *too* hot, especially designed for Londoners!'

'Some Londoners like it hot!' she replied, teasing.

'Same as usual? For the last time?' asked Maisie, blinking more than usual and hastily ushering Max back behind the counter.

*

A mile away, at the homeless centre, Anthony picked up his pen.

> *~ St Mark's Centre, London ~*
> *Dear Polly,*
> *It's taken a while to answer your last letter because my dodging back and forth between London and Guernsey, and the occasional weekend away requires a different routine which, so far, I've failed to accommodate.*
>
> *I hope you noticed that I didn't send a Christmas card with a cow on this year (even though the milk marketing board likes to promote Guernsey milk!).*
>
> *Thank you for keeping an open mind about Piers and me. I used to fear people's reactions until I got to know Piers better, and he has shown me how to deal with 'ignorance' as he puts it, and be more confident. We mustn't think of ourselves as victims, but quietly assert ourselves in the way of life we find most fulfilling. This is not the whole answer or even always helpful. The Church teaching complicates our situation and I'll be interested in your conclusions after your research.*
>
> *I still examine myself regarding riches. If I am a good steward they should not lead to evil. I'm making some interest-bearing investments to provide a pension for my later years. I've also put aside money for travel and the purchase of a few special oils including one or two of Salvador Dali's symbolic works (not featuring dismembered or disfigured*

animals now); and it allows me to make ongoing donations towards the centre. While I see even one person without a home, I could never be extravagant. No, I don't feel guilty about keeping my inheritance.

I am interested in the clinics you speak of, not only the medical work but the spiritual help they offer. It can feel hollow talking about God to homeless people because I ask myself what He has done for them. They may, understandably, scorn religion and swear robustly. Some of them are grateful and give lip-service at least to admitting the Church has its good points.

I have good intentions to encourage people to attend services, and mention the importance of belief, but when the opportunity arises I'm tongue-tied.

I was shopping in the market early morning three weeks ago, and bumped into a rough young girl who I can't forget. Her clothes were ill-fitting and shoes falling apart. When we collided, my heavy crucifix hit her in the face. I wanted to tell her about the importance of faith but all I said was 'Pardon me.' She looked up, stunned. For a moment our eyes met and I said, 'God bless you, my child'. That was a big mistake. Her profanities shocked me and I froze. I felt a pull on my arm and she'd gone. I looked round but she'd disappeared with my bag.

I'm usually so careful. They say you need eyes in the back of your head, but I was completely distracted. I lost my breakfast bread and milk, and, more importantly, my beloved Missal given to me on my first communion when I was seven. Mother called it my 'comfort blanket'. I smiled later when I realised the calligraphy card about money and evil was inside. If she can find out its meaning she'll tear it up. I've never seen her before, so I wonder where she comes from. (Father D thinks it's better for me to concentrate on people who come into the church now, rather go on the streets.)

I telephoned Piers and he said it was time I stopped using my Missal as a prop! He wants me to 'cut loose' as he put it. Father D, though, thinks if we pray to Saint Anthony it will be found. He's put a notice up in the crypt, with a description of the girl. I'm sceptical. I don't think people read the notices.

I'm afraid the longer I work here the trickier it becomes. As I get to know people better, I feel more involved in their stories and it isn't easy to draw a line between my feelings and Church policies. It gets rough, but I have home to enjoy and am back there in two weeks' time. Then, in a month, Piers and I are off to Spain to visit a few galleries!

With warm greetings,
Anthony

CHAPTER 26

'The lamb jerk was *scrumptious*!' Barbara was licking her lips and Max smiled as he collected the plates.

'Ah, so I've won you over, have I?' he smiled.

'After all these years, the change is good for us,' Barbara agreed.

'It's tasty with the spinach salad and rice, isn't it?' Max was delighted by his success.

'I hope we'll still be able to find a table when the crowds start pouring in,' Penny said with a grin.

'There'll always be a table at Maisie's for The Press!' said Max, adding 'So what about mango cheesecake, then?'

'You'll make us fat!'

'No, very slimming…'

The girls ordered.

'What's the latest with the arches, then?' Penny asked Barbara. 'I'll show you the progress report when we get back to the office if you like.'

'Any personal stories in your report?'

'Not much detail of personal histories, more the facts of the current situation and not terribly hopeful prospects. I can tell *you* a couple of stories though… they're going public anyway but without names.' The friends leant towards each other. 'There's an elderly man from…'

'That was quick!' said Barbara as the mango cheesecakes arrived. Max smiled turning towards the kitchen.

'See what you think of that!' he called over his shoulder.

Barbara continued, '...this elderly chap from Jamaica. I think he's called Nick. He's good mates with a young woman, and they stick out from the rest because they are such an unlikely couple – they work together. He needs a walking stick and she's completely agile. Vulnerable but feisty.'

Penny frowned. 'He's not… they're not *together,* are they?'

'Oh, no, I don't think so. I wondered. But I noticed them first when I followed the police after an argument broke out near them. As the police sorted things, the girl was giving, I think, food, from a plastic bag to the man. She ignored the fracas, but the Jamaican guy was checking out the patch carefully, without drawing attention to himself. It's almost like he was a substitute father. She speaks English – well, I couldn't place her dialect but it includes a lot of swearing! – and he's got a strong accent so it was quite hard to make them out. I haven't heard him swear at all.'

'Do you think they feel safe?' asked Penny.

'No! They know they take risks but what else can they do? I was talking to a Salvation Army woman who said Nick and the girl never seem to get in any trouble, although she wonders where the girl gets the food. She discovered Nick used to go to church in Jamaica and might be happy to talk. The Sally Army's been there for years you know. They do a lot to help.'

'So why are this couple there?'

'You can't just go up to these people and start asking questions!'

'Why not? I suppose it needs a certain talent.' *Not exactly Babs' forté!*

'I decided to ask if I could sit with them. I explained the report and asked if they'd help. Nick gave her a light prod, but she was fast asleep under her dirty covers. He patted a space the other side of him for me to sit.'

'Great. And…?'

'He said she was "up all night till morn", so we left her. He was injured in the British army in World War Two. He recuperated here and the army cared for him until he was considered fit for work, then he was on his own. No money to go back home, and no home here. Couldn't get a job because he had no fixed address and his leg was still painful. The fit white men got work, but most black people were turned away. He did try being a postman, but they said he wasn't efficient and gave him the sack. There's apparently a network of army friends in the arches area who watch for signals all the time and know how to keep safe. He uses his old army whistle when he's worried. Also,' Barbara rolled her eyes scorning, 'he trusts the Lord!'

Penny wondered what she would do in their situation: 'And the girl?'

'…was the oldest of nine children born to travellers who told her to get out of their van when she wouldn't help with the kids. She wanted some freedom. She went out one evening and they'd gone when she got back. Moved on and left her, poor girl. She made her way to London and had to manage alone. Talk about freedom.'

'Phew! What must she have felt like?' Again, Penny puffed out her cheeks trying to imagine how she would feel.

'Lord knows! She goes out at night and early morning to find food, and, in return for the protection of Nick and his contacts, shares the food she can scavenge, steal or beg with him. So that's how they manage. It's easy in the market with crates of stuff all over the place.'

'But will she ever get *anywhere?* I mean, what chance does she have of doing anything worthwhile – getting a job or a place to live?'

'That's why I can't ignore their plight… and they're only two of many. But what a *hopeless* life. It wasn't their fault they landed up homeless. Just circumstances. The police say they've got to clear the place of beggars and need to move them on. So, it's desperate.'

'Where will they go?'

'Where?' They both stared out of the far window.

They paid Max and left.

'After I've given in the report, I'll have another think.'

'Why don't you join the Sally Army?' Penny was grinning.

'Yes, what a *good* idea.' Barbara was frowning.

*

The following Monday Barbara and Penny were back at 'their table'. They could hear Max in the kitchen with the chef.

After commenting on the delicious aroma. Barbara said, 'I've told Nick and the girl… she's a bit suspicious… but I've told them… um, *asked* if they'd like me to do research into who might help.'

'Yes? What did they say?'

'She piped up that she wants to learn how to read and write.'

'Is that the first thing she said?' Penny was astounded. 'When you think of her – homeless, hungry, no clothes – and she wants to be educated?' Barbara had her head in her hands and talked down at the table.

'Her right! But astonishing. It was the last thing I expected. Nick went to school in Jamaica, and…' They hadn't noticed Max waiting to take their order.

'Excuse me, did you say *Jamaica*?'

'Oh, hello Max, Jamaica, yes.' Barbara gave him a questioning smile.

'That's my home! My beautiful home.' Max dashed to the kitchen with their order. Penny and Barbara heard a burst of laughter from the back.

'He's telling the chef!' said Barbara.

When their steaming aromatic lamb jerks arrived, Barbara asked Max, 'So what made you come from the lovely Caribbean to this rainy, cold country?' Penny raised her eyebrows, pleasantly surprised to hear Barbara add, 'If you don't mind my asking.' *She's learning!*

'Pleasure's mine.' He was delighted to chat. Putting a spotless tea-towel over his shoulder he gazed out of the window: 'Jamaica's a wonderful island. I love my home. But my father never came home after the war. I'm still searching for him. He joined the army when I was a kid; I wouldn't recognise him.'

The women were wide-eyed.

Max laughed, a nervous laugh. 'But your jerk will spoil… I chat, chat, chat too much!' he imitated the movement of his lips with his fingers and thumb.

'Ask him his father's name when we pay the bill.' They did.

'It's Reginald. Reginald Leroy Reid,' said Max wistfully, 'all I know is he came to London after his army service, and must be about… um, in his sixties.'

'Like Nick, but it can't be him,' said Barbara. 'No harm in asking, though.'

'I've contacted the army,' said Max but they lost track after hospital.'

After Barbara delivered her report she made a few phone calls to the council, the local MP, the *Evening Standard*, and a few personal friends who might be able to shed light on available help and accommodation.

'I'm setting a few wheels in motion,' she told Nick as she crouched beside him. The girl slept on although Barbara guessed she was listening.

'What's her name?'

'Mags,' he smiled. 'She's a good girl, but she's lost and lonely. This is no life for a young-un.'

'No. Far from it.'

'I've tried helping her read, but I'm no good either,' he said. He fumbled clumsily in a plastic bag tucked down by Mags, and bought out a nice quality but dirty card. At the top of the card was printed, 'ST MARTIN'S MONASTERY' Beneath was a meticulous calligraphy inscription: *Pecunia est radix omnis mali caritas*.

'Can you help?' he asked. 'That's no English, is it?'

'No. It looks like Latin, but I don't know what it means.'

Glancing at the sleeping Mags, Nick pointed at the reference underneath the Latin. 'Can you find out? She thinks it message for her. I say it's Holy Scripture.'

'Can I have it copied?'

'You certainly can.' He nodded at Mags. She'd be happy if you can work it out.'

'Pec-u-nia est ra-dix om-nis mali car-itas. Can't she read at all?' she whispered.

'She knows her two times two four, and c – a – t is cat, like that. Small things, only small things. She saw to the kids and hardly had school. No proper clothes and the school children, horrid to her. She stick up for herself. She strong, but likes I got friends.'

Barbara was even more motivated to get these people off the street. 'I'm going to meet the MP for this area, Nick, and see what help he suggests. Meanwhile, I'm going to write a short article in the *Shorewell News*. Is that all right?'

'No names, no names! We don't want no trouble. They sees me a-talking to you an' don't like it.'

'I'll be careful.' She copied the card in the office. A distant memory stirred in the back of her mind. Max was forgotten.

*

Article in *Shorewell News* April 13th 1979
THE ARCHES PEOPLE
New Campaign

Those of you who complain about beggars as you walk to work underneath the railway arches, will be pleased to hear Shorewell Council has accepted the *Shorewell News'* report by Barbara Gristwood, which will be published in six weeks.

Gristwood interviewed a small number of these homeless people, and obtained valuable information from the Captain Diana Rodgers, of the Salvation Army, on top of hearing from volunteers who nightly donate food and clothing.

We want to bring to your notice that these desperate people are homeless through no fault of their own. There are those with mental problems: others have escaped a violent family situation. Orphans escape from foster care. All are scarred and scared for genuine reasons.

Following the ongoing success of our campaign to clear and rebuild the bomb sites, we are today launching the plight of the homeless as our current appeal.

Several possible sources of aid have been identified, and as a voice for local residents we want to work together with you to improve the lot of these despairing people.

The *Shorewell News* will now prioritise the plight of the Arches People. We will keep you informed of progress.

Michael Foster, Editor

CHAPTER 27

1980s

'There's a telephone call for you in the office, Polly.' Vivaan was out of breath after finding Polly at lunch in her flat. She hurriedly wiped her mouth and fingers and ran after him. Fortunately, she got there in time. It was Flynn. The line was bad but she managed to make out the message. He was arriving in two days. Alone. Beth was in hospital, dehydrated after a severe attack of *Delhi Belly*. He rang off without more detail leaving Polly in a whirl. She found Elaine and explained the position.

'Hasn't he given you any more detail, dear? Is he expecting us to put him up?'

'I don't think so. He usually books expensive hotels. But I'm worried about Beth. Fancy leaving her in hospital in Delhi. I can't believe he'd do that.'

'Well, we'll have to wait and see if we've got the right end of the stick. I'm prepared for feeding extra as usual. He, or they, will be welcome to eat here.'

'That's so kind, Elaine. Thank you so much. But…'

'Yes…? Oh! of course.' Elaine always thought of details. Polly needed to say 'no' more often. 'You'll need some time off. We'll manage. You need a break anyway.' Polly gave Elaine a quick kiss on the cheek. 'There's nothing we can do about your friend from this distance except pray. Try and leave her in the Lord's hands.'

Polly wandered slowly back to her flat. *Easier said than done. Spending my precious holiday with Flynn of all people. God, please help me.* She lectured herself to stop worrying.

*

A tuk-tuk drove into the compound early on Tuesday afternoon. The scruffy chickens scattered and dust settled as Flynn paid the driver, climbed out and surveyed his surroundings. Despite the heat, he looked fresh and well-dressed. Polly and Vivaan went over to meet him.

'Welcome to Mangalore!' She smiled.

'Is this it?' He looked Vivaan up and down nodded then stared at Polly. It was difficult to know what he was thinking. *He hasn't learnt that nodding means no, yet.*

'Come and meet Elaine!' They made their way in silence into the shade of the house. Polly turned to Vivaan, 'Thanks,' she smiled and wobbled her head side to side. He went back to the office.

Elaine was resting with a glass of water.

'Hello, Flynn.'

He responded to the sound of the Irish accent and seemed to come alive, 'Hello, Elaine, well met.'

'Yes, it's not often we hear an Irish accent around here! Lovely reminder of home. What can I get you? Fresh lemonade? Tea? Sit.' She gestured a cane chair. He sat.

'Beth? Is she alright?' asked Polly.

'Elizabeth? Oh yes, she'll be alright. She's in a good hospital. But so annoying to get something like that at a time like this.' Elaine put some fresh iced lemon juice by his chair. He ignored it.

'I'm well looked after in my hotel.' Polly felt awkward. He wasn't easy to interact with. She tried to think of something to say: 'And…'

'This is just a flying visit.' He looked directly at Polly: 'We need to talk a few things over. I'd like to take a quick look around tomorrow, then I'll relax at the hotel and leave the next day. I hope that fits in with your work.'

'I've got a couple of days off to show you round.' Polly ventured.

'Oh good.' He actually smiled, but then added rather critically: 'Do you have *much* time off?'

'It's definitely not a continuous holiday, here, Flynn.' Elaine showed a side of herself previously unseen by Polly. Disapproval fluttered over her face. 'So how many meals would you like us to provide?'

Flynn recognised the reproof and blushed. He raised his palms upwards signalling acknowledgement. Quietly he said: 'Will you excuse us?' He looked round at Polly, took a quick drink, raised his glass in acknowledgement to Elaine, and turned back to Polly. 'Is there somewhere quiet we can go?'

Polly led him over to her flat in silence. By now she realised he was not enjoying the trip. At all. They sat in easy chairs.

'That's better.' He had the air of a man on a mission. He drew in his breath: 'Business today, play tomorrow?'

'I thought you were going to look around the mission tomorrow.'

'Only briefly. I might never have a chance to come to Mangalore again, and I must shop for something nice for my poor wife.' Polly raised her eyebrows and waited for a sermon. She wasn't far wrong.

'Firstly, I'm glad to say the support side is working out for you. We hope and pray that it continues. You probably noticed the Kavanaughs were unhappy to see you using the RSV. The congregation is split about how important this is. I'm not keen on changing to new versions when they come out but they are easier to understand and apply to life. I still have my treasured AV and use it when I preach to our congregation. I do not take sides in the fellowship argument, but there will be a meeting about this next month, and I will let you know how it goes. We need to pray that a majority will vote to continue supporting you. We need 60% in favour to carry the vote.'

'That's a—'

But Flynn continued more earnestly: 'But there is absolutely no disagreement about homosexuality, Polly. Are we correct in thinking you might accept accommodation from your ex-next-door neighbour who Elizabeth strongly suspects is queer?'

'Errrr…'

'As I thought. Do you think you ought to check before accepting this offer? Especially if he is indulging with the 'friend' who lives with him. Don't you know what the scripture says about this? 1 Corinthians six, verses nine – eighteen makes it perfectly clear.'

Polly was finding it difficult to control her indignation. 'Yes, but——'

Flynn wouldn't let her get a word in edgeways. 'Our bodies are temples of the Holy Ghost and these people defile their bodies.' He was emphasising each noun. 'To accept their hospitality is to condone their practice. Need I say more?' He put his head in his hands in despair: 'There are times, Polly,' he said wiping his brow, 'when you need a husband to keep you on the straight and narrow!' Polly stood, hyperventilating and red-faced, but he inched forward in his chair and continued. 'I'll just say one more thing: your support will plummet if Anthony is indeed doing what I think he is, and they know you've accepted hospitality from him.' Polly ran a hand through her hair.

'Beth—'

'Elizabeth thinks I am being harsh, but she is with me in conviction.' He changed his tone. 'Sermon over.' In softer voice but still formally: 'Let us commit all this to our Heavenly Father.' Polly forced herself to sit. *The more I comply with him, the sooner this will be over.*

'Father, we come to you through Jesus, our Saviour. We thank you for Polly and the valuable work she is doing for you. We know you led her here, and you know all about the disputes which need resolving. We commit the fellowship meeting to you. Touch their hearts with your love as they think about the inspiration of your holy word. Draw us together and help us to agree. May it be possible for Polly to continue here. AND...' He took a deep breath, 'Speak to Polly about man lying with man. Show her the error of their ways, and provide her with somewhere to stay on furlough. Thank you.' He looked up. Polly kept her eyes closed and hands clasped tightly. She neither thanked the Lord nor said Amen.

Flynn eventually stood: 'I'll go back to the hotel and have a swim now. I'll come back tomorrow at about ten. I'd appreciate Luke putting in an appearance, OK?' Polly pursed her mouth.

'Luke's—' She was going to say 'away,' But Flynn cut her off again. He could see she was upset.

'Sometimes we need to be cruel to be kind.'

He moved towards her and put an arm round her shoulder. She winced. *How can I be civil to this man?*

'We both trust the Lord. He understands.' He walked towards the door. Polly led the way outside. 'I'll hail a tuk-tuk out on the street. Basic,' he cast an eye around the compound, 'like many things I've seen in this country, but,' he tapped his wallet, 'no strain on the pocket.' He turned back towards the road and laughed loudly. His first expression of humour. Polly stared. He got to the entrance but remembered something and turned back. 'I forgot Croften's message. Tomorrow. Don't let me forget.' Polly didn't bother to reply. He was out of earshot. She went back to find Elaine and told her the whole story.

'It was great to hear his voice when he arrived,' Elaine said wistfully, 'a reminder of our beloved homeland. But oh deary, deary me, as soon as we started to talk red lights started flashing. Chauvinistic pig!' Despite being shocked and wound up by her friend's husband, Polly, taken aback by Elaine's uncharacteristic judgement, was amused. But her mirth was short-lived:

'How on earth am I going to get through tomorrow? I wanted to strangle him. I've never felt—'

'My dear,' Elaine took hold of Polly's hand and stroked it, 'have a headache tomorrow and be indisposed. I can deal with that self-opinionated spoilt little rich boy.' Polly couldn't believe her ears.

'I couldn't possibly expect...'

'I *insist.*' Elaine was adamant and sounded more Irish than ever. 'After all, I haven't got the personal involvement. It won't take so much out of me. You've been put through the wringer quite enough already, precious.'

'You are just so kind.' Polly kissed Elaine. 'Come and have a thank-you supper with me tomorrow evening.'

'I will. Luke won't be back until Thursday late, so I'd have been by myself.'

Polly went back to her flat, sat down with a drink and put her feet up. For a while, stunned, she could only mull over the day's events. After a long time, she made her way slowly over to the typewriter.

```
Mangalam, India
Dear Anthony,
   I'm so thankful I can
'offload' to someone outside
the mission who understands.
I've just had a dreadful visit
from Flynn. I can't really put
my feelings into words. Apart
from everything else, he left
Beth in hospital in Delhi with
dehydration due to diarrhoea,
poor thing. And he seemed more
cross about his spoilt holiday
than sympathetic with her. I
spent a tense afternoon with
him and Elaine, an angel in
disguise, is going to look
after him tomorrow.
   But furlough is coming up and
I'd love to accept your offer
of accommodation please. Flynn
is adamant it is wrong for me
stay with you, and vehemently
```

condemns the practice of homosexuality. But when I discussed it with Elaine she said I take everything too seriously. She's got a lovely sense of humour which helps.

After the Kavanaughs talked about Biblical translations, I discussed the topic with the Fotheringales and have started to change the way I think about the Bible. I've seen our missionary work cannot possibly be 'strictly accurate.' We've got to accept compromise especially as Indian languages do not have the exact equivalents of English or Greek words. After all the English language does not always have exactly the right words to represent Greek and Hebrew meanings.

Some missionaries here are relaxed about things like allowing women to preach with men in the congregation. Anyway, quite often out here there are only women teachers available! It feels right and I'm sure the Lord understands. But I'll be out of step with both the home office and certain supporters if I'm not careful. I feel conflicted one way and another.

My thinking is so narrow! I try to obey God in everything. But it's like walking a tight rope.

If I live in Belle Vue I will have peace and quiet to get down to real study. I urgently need to understand the message of the whole Bible, not just one or two selected passages. I've started going through Genesis prayerfully. I will keep going until I can reconcile my inner discord.

As for riches and evil, I've trusted God to provide my needs and have so far scraped by. Flynn and Beth spend liberally on holidays and an easy life, but I don't think you'd call that 'evil'. Although their faith seems to be going out of focus.

Adam and Eve were tempted by with the knowledge of good and evil. Money wasn't invented then!

I understand what you mean by speaking to poor people about the Goodness of the Lord. I wonder occasionally if our converts' interest in the gospel springs from a glimpse

> of, what must seem to them, our wealth. Do they think they might benefit financially if they join us?
>
> A popular film being shown in the bigger churches now is about a paralysed girl from a rich American family who is helped enormously by her rich parents. The message is to trust the Lord and He will provide. But some of the viewers here feel a failure when it doesn't work for them.
>
> I'm so sorry to hear about the loss of your Missal. 'The Lord works in mysterious ways.' This might sound trite, but maybe He is using you to work out a purpose for the girl.
>
> Enjoy Spain. It must be exciting to have a holiday after all these years! I'll be interested to hear about it when you come back.

She removed the paper from the typewriter and signed off by hand:

Greetings in the Lord's name,
Polly.
P.S. Do you keep chickens in Guernsey? We have them here – completely free range – but rather scruffy. Polly.

The following evening Elaine came round. The flat was filled with the tempting smell of Veena's chicken curry.

'Has he gone?' asked Polly.

'Yes, he has. I think he was feeling a bit guilty about leaving Beth in Delhi so we only spent about three hours together.' Polly raised her eyebrows. Elaine needed no further prompt.

'He almost as good as said he'd *make do* with my company rather than Luke's, but when I explained some of the technical side of our work I think he realised I wasn't just here to support my husband. He did say he hoped you'd soon be better.'

Polly nodded. 'And then you took him into town to find something for Beth?'

'Yes, he paid an enormous sum for an elegant sari. Of the type the super-rich would wear to a wedding. I offered to barter for him, but he just paid the first demand much to the surprise of the shopkeeper. It was a good one, but too expensive.'

'And did he give you a message from Croften for me?'

'He did. I'm sorry to say it's rather impersonal. Flynn rang HQ about your potential support problems and the Kavanaugh's worries and Croften gave him a list of four things to pass on to you.' Elaine counted them off on her fingers. 'Thank you for valuable work you're doing; it's essential to raise enough support for next term; an HQ rep will visit A.S.A.P, and lastly, remember we are baptised into His suffering.'

'Is that all? They have to fit a sermon in somehow, don't they?'

'Tell me about it! Then just as he was going he whispered they'd keep the second business quiet for the time being, and you'd know what he meant by that.'

'I expect you guessed.'

'Yes, Anthony…'

'Yes.'

CHAPTER 28

The representative from MUT HQ turned up on New Year's day, three weeks before Polly was due to leave for England. She hadn't met Baz before and they only exchanged a few words because she went for another trip half-way through his visit, and was busy with preparations to leave when she returned. Luke took him to several of their centres, and he spoke to a group who were hoping to build a new church:

'Oh, that's good. Lovely, yes, lovely. I like that.' He asked Luke a few questions, not probing deeply, but they spent long hours in the office thrashing out administrative problems. As he left he thanked them all and said he'd enjoyed his stay.

Polly had no chance to debate the HQ visit until Elaine was helping with final packing.

'Was he terribly critical?'

'You concentrate on the journey now, dear, it's all a bit complicated. Croften will update you when you meet up. I'll just find my bag and jolly Luke along then we'll leave.'

At the airport they stopped at the barrier.

'We'll be praying for your future. Give our love to them all, Polly dear.'

'England, here I come! I wish I knew the Lord's will now,' said Polly, as Luke handed over her bag. 'I've felt so right here and have learnt *so* much. Thank you!' She kissed them both and they hugged.

'Come back! You've fitted in beautifully,' Luke said, 'it would be hard to replace you. Safe journey!'

'Yes, and enjoy Guernsey,' added Elaine. 'Don't *worry!*' And as an afterthought she called, 'Let us know how your study turns out!' Polly walked off then swung back and blew Elaine a kiss, realising with a sudden pang of regret she might never see her again.

Once she was settled in her window seat, the sadness of leaving colleagues was replaced by the anticipation of meeting Anthony again. Staring down at the clouds she wondered what he would be like... the 'odd' neighbour she used to try and avoid. Scared because she didn't understand him. A wave of anxiety swept through her. *He's practically a stranger. Living with him? But the Lord is in control.* The stewardess was offering her a meal and she hastily pulled down the table.

As the man next to her was served he asked, 'Enjoyed India then?' From snippets of conversation she'd overheard with his companion, she gathered they were tourists.

'I suppose so!' she said uncertainly. 'I was working.' They all started to eat.

'Good for you,' said the second man said, in an American drawl. 'Not everyone's got the stomach for it!' His joke. Polly gulped.

Her neighbour agreed: 'So how did you find it?'

Polly, just about to put rice in her mouth, put it back on the plate. 'I can't generalise. I've enjoyed a few places.' She hesitated. 'Enjoy isn't exactly the word I'd use though.' She tried her food again. *That was a mistake, I don't want to talk about it.* Thankfully, the Americans fell back into reminiscing about the places they'd been. Continuing to eat she remembered how eager she was as a young missionary starting out to win souls. *I'd have jumped at the chance to witness to strangers. Now I don't want to talk about my work. If they start again, the medical side will do.* But there were no further questions. They ordered alcohol, downed it in one go, and went to sleep.

Polly closed her eyes, but her brain was too active to rest. *Anthony will have changed. And I was so young... was I even a teenager? He won't recognise me!*

Hours later, and boarding the light aircraft to Guernsey, she was still doubtful. The plane was noisy and slightly shaky. *Whatever have I let myself in for? And what next with Flynn and Beth? How does she cope with him? And what about the church?*

Alighting onto the tarmac in Guernsey the peace and quiet took her by surprise. *Hardly anything going on.* She spotted two men and a dog through the window of arrivals and guessed who they were... Anthony, still wearing round wire-framed glasses, round shouldered, and his older, taller friend who looked a cheerful type.

Anthony looked straight at her as they came to greet her. 'Polly!'

But an excited dog was sniffing by her feet and, instead of greeting the men, she bent down to stroke her. 'What a beautiful dog *you* are!'

Piers beamed. 'We think so, don't we, Tiff? Wait till we take her to the beach... you'll love that, won't she, Tony?'

There was no formality and Polly felt immediately comfortable. They collected the luggage then walked through the terminal building where everyone seemed to know each other. Polly wondered if she was dreaming. 'Bit different from Heathrow!' She liked the unhurried atmosphere.

'Guernsey's l-like this!' said Anthony. 'Quiet and f-friendly.'

'You can't be long back from your travels.'

'No! We m-made certain to be here. We w-wanted to sh-show you round from the s-start and make sure you f-feel at home.' Polly was happy. Anxiety immediately forgotten. Contentment rubbed off onto her. All traces of Anthony's nervousness, apart from the occasional stutter, had disappeared. His gaze was steady as they spoke. She felt she really did know him, although he had changed. And it was so wonderful to have the company of a dog!

'Can we go to the beach this evening?' she asked.

'Aren't you tired? What time did you start?'

'Suppose I am tired, yes, but I've been sitting nearly all day. Maybe just a quick stretch!'

By the time Polly had unpacked a few essentials and tasted a casserole Piers had left to slow cook, tiredness overtook her. She was too tired for a walk but went to bed confident she would be happy.

*

As soon as she opened the bedroom door next morning, Tiffany came bounding in and escorted her downstairs. Anthony was right, the house *was* large – huge – and she made her way to the kitchen trying to remember which staircase led to what. She heard voices and a kettle boiling.

'Good morning!' she beamed. Piers and Anthony responded together.

'Tiffany found you first then.' Piers fondled the dog's ears.

'Oh yes.' Polly anticipated an interesting day. 'She's just adorable!'

'Help yourself to whatever you l-like,' said Anthony.

'No formalities before midday,' Piers announced.

Polly opened the cereal packet. 'Grace?' she smiled.

'What's that?' Piers and Anthony played ignorance. The milk jug was on the dresser. Apart from the sound of panting and the fridge motor humming away, it was quiet. She picked up a spoon.

'This takes some getting used to!'

'You've changed,' said Anthony.

'You have too!'

'M-much water has f-flowed under many b-bridges since we last met.'

Piers and Polly sized each other up quietly.

'This is perfect: your lovely house, Guernsey, Tiffany, I love it already. All I want to do is relax.' She noticed the toaster and picked up a slice of bread.

'Just take a couple of days off,' said Piers. 'Guernsey does that to you. You start to realise things aren't as important as you thought they were!'

'Really?' asked Polly. 'I can't see that happening to me! Not yet anyway. I've got to… ohh, maybe…'

'Shhh!' interrupted Anthony. 'Piers knows what he's t-talking about. Just w-wait a couple of days and settle down. Then s-start thinking of all those other things.'

'I must tell HQ my address, and the Matthews… and Vic.'

'Right, a couple of phone calls and unpacking. Have you got washing? Need shopping?'

The calls to Croften, Vic and Beth took longer than Polly anticipated but she couldn't stop short when it had been so long since she'd spoken to them. Flynn annoyed her again when he insisted on taking over from Beth and continuing his diatribe against same sex relationships.

231

'This isn't going to be so easy,' she said to Piers and Anthony on returning to the kitchen much later. 'So much has changed, and Flynn's so dogmatic.' She was tense.

'We're used to people who don't understand our position,' said Piers. 'We've put up with it all our lives. Old hat!' He was totally relaxed, and smiling, nudged Anthony. 'Thank the Lord our love has been legally recognised now even here, in Guernsey. It's good to know we can't be charged any more, isn't it?'

Polly was astonished by his casual attitude. She stared at him, feeling a growing sense of respect. He was emanating a calm which rubbed off on her.

'B-but I'm afraid the ch-churches t-take time to change their views,' said Anthony frowning. 'S-stuck in a m-muddy rut.'

''Fraid so,' continued Piers. 'But Polly, what do you want to do?'

'I must pay you for my calls.' Despite Piers' influence, Polly's mind was darting from one thing to another. 'I didn't know my father had moved in with Doris so Vic and family have number 16 to themselves. Something else for me to get used to. So many changes… and Flynn…'

Piers changed the subject: 'You haven't seen the chickens yet!'

Polly's glum face brightened up immediately. 'Ohhh! First things first!' They traipsed out into the enormous back garden, where she could hear familiar clucking as the birds came into view. Scratching, pecking. 'They're so happy and healthy,' she said, 'Ours in India are so bedraggled.' *Ours? I don't know. I don't know.*

'Yep, we let them out most days. Free range.'

'And eggs?' asked Polly dragging her thoughts back from MUT, 'This is definitely home!' *Maybe.*

'Eggs of c-course!' said Anthony. 'S-several eggs a day. If we g-get more than we need we p-put them on the front wall with a t-tin for donations and the locals h-help themselves. We'd give them away, but p-people like to give in return. W-we attach a note saying, 'D-donations towards h-helping the homeless in London.'

'But one lovely lady makes us cake!' added Piers.

By early afternoon Polly was beginning to enjoy her new surroundings and her problems were receding into the background. But then came the telephone call from Crofton.

'Hello?' There were no formalities.

'Polly! Flynn and I would like to meet you at HQ next Wednesday at 10.30.'

'Oh?'

'There are a few matters to discuss. You'll probably guess what this is about, but we won't start now.'

'Is Flynn coming from Ireland?'

'Yes.'

'And Beth?'

'No, just Flynn.'

'Oh. Can you tell me…?'

'Wait until we meet, Polly. Leave it for the time being.'

Silence.

'Goodbye.'

'God be with you too,' said Polly after putting the phone down. *Ever heard of good manners?* Instead of flinging herself on her knees by the bed, Polly found herself sitting at her bedroom window with a view out to sea. *Lord! How beautiful!*

CHAPTER 29

'Can I try ringing St Martin's, the number on this card?' Barbara showed Michael the copy of Mags' card.

'How do you think that will help?'

'I want to follow up Mags' hunch that there's a message in this for her. I know it isn't the way we usually work, but, for once, can we do '*mystical*?'

Michael smiled. After working with Barbara for several years he recognised 'a Barbara hunch potential'. At times, s*ometimes*, it could lead to good sales.

'If I can find out who really owns this card, I'll be able to trace the person who had the heart to bless her. I mean, most people get angry with beggars.'

'Do your own thing… but no longer than a week,' he winked. Barbara was chuffed. She lifted the phone.

'Hello, St Martin's Monastery?'

The Abbot was not cooperative. He admitted it was one of their cards but flatly refused to name the artist.

'He left months ago, and I have no idea where he is. I can't help you at all.' Call ended.

'Umm.' Barbara studied the calligraphy thoughtfully. *'What does this remind me of?'* She laid it on the desk.

Michael was keeping an eye on her. Late afternoon he said 'Forget it! Let it go!' Barbara glared.

'It'll come to you in the middle of the night.'

'You don't know what happens to me in the middle of the night!' And she gave him a seductive grin.

'One day I might have to find out!'

'Oho!' Barbara blushed.

'Get on with your work!' He teased, picking up the papers he was working on without glancing at them. 'Looks as if you might need more than a week.'

Distracted though she was, Barbara knew he was right. She needed to get copy out for tomorrow's edition, so rang the Salvation Army for news.

As she went to sleep that night, fantasising about Michael, she was back at The Elms. Michael was approaching her. But there were crowds everywhere. Noel was behind her and she ran in the garden to escape. *I must get back to Michael. Impossible.* She floated to the end of the garden. The shed and broken bench. Chickens clucking over the wall. *Does Michael like eggs?*

She was in next door's garden. The mother of the serious little girl was saying, 'Would you like some eggs?' They were in the hallway, and the decorated calligraphy shone out like a neon sign. *That's it*!: colourful border, scrolls, Latin verse. She sat up in bed, heart pounding, excited. *Elm Close! I'm on my way*.

Next day Barbara burst in the office.

'I know what it is!' she shouted. Michael's lips curled up in amusement, despite being annoyed at the rude interruption of his morning.

'Pull yourself together, girl.' She rattled off the significant part of the dream, deciding to tell him the story later. Despite her enthusiasm he put his foot down. 'If you want to visit Elm Close, you'll have to go after work…'

Undeterred she set off for Halebridge at five o'clock prompt and headed straight for the doorknocker on number 16. Vic answered and they were both surprised. 'I thought Mr West lived here. Is he around?' Despite a confusing interchange of information, Barbara was straining to see if *that picture* was still at the bottom of the stairs. She declined a drink. 'Vic, I've got to get back to London this evening, so you must think me awfully rude, but I just need a little information about that calligraphy if you don't mind.'

Vic, somewhat bemused, compared the picture with Mags' card. There was no doubt. Capital letters with thinner double lines, the diamond shaped full stops. The colours were slightly different but the border decoration was the same. 'Not my field at all, but I can see what you mean,' he said, wondering whatever was going on. 'Mum said the man who used to live next door before you gave it to us when we had his cat. I'm not keen on having God-stuff in the hall but I just haven't got round to taking it down.'

Barbara laughed at his description. 'Thank you so much, Vic. Thank you *so* much!' She pumped his hand and left a bewildered man standing in the doorway contemplating the whirlwind, and staring at the bomb site opposite as was his habit before closing the front door.

Next day Barbara reported back to Michael:

'Surprise, surprise. The artist is the guy who sold us the big house so I know him slightly. Strange person, very quiet. Anthony Wheeler. And believe it or not, I've learnt Polly, Vic's sister, is staying with him. She must be forty or so by now! So da de dah,' she flung her arms into the air waving a piece of paper. 'Address!'

Michael was laughing at her antics: 'You're mad! But yes, I'm impressed.'

Excitedly, Barbara picked up the telephone and rang Anthony's number, forgetting his nervousness. As soon as he answered, she was telling her story in detail. Too much detail.

'You've f-ound the c-c-calligraphy card that was s-stolen in the m-m-market?' And m-my M-m-missal?'

'I'm ninety-nine percent sure it's your calligraphy; I've compared it to the verse you gave the Wests. But what's a Missal?'

'H-how d-do you know the W-W-Wests?' Anthony couldn't marshal the facts.

'Noel and I bought The Elms from you.'

'You're not Mrs G-G-Gristwood?'

'Err, yes, I was. But we're no longer together.'

'I'm s-sorry…'

'Is there any chance of talking about your calligraphy and, perhaps, meeting to catch up? I thought you'd joined a monastery!'

Anthony was shaking. The card in question had been in his Missal. His head span. Out of the blue so many memories flooding back.

'I-I-I…' Piers came to his side when he heard the stutter and noticed the shake. He offered his hand.

The shy, stuttering man she remembered came crashing into Barbara's mind. *When will I ever learn?* 'Shall I ring you back later? Or would you like my number?'

'Y-yes p-please.' Piers helped him jot down the number and he put the phone down. Anthony was overwhelmed by a host of memory flashes. His old reluctance to talk about himself paralysed him.

'Tiffany!' called Piers. 'Here, here!' Lovely, affectionate Tiffany came bounding towards them and jumped up for Anthony to stroke her.

'Come on. BEACH!' The dog ran to get her lead.

Piers nudged Anthony gently in the direction of the cloakroom.

'Hat and sunglasses. We need sea and fresh air. It's not going to rain.'

*

Barbara was haunted by the phone going dead, and by Anthony's stuttering.

'I think I need a stronger curry for a change, today.' Barbara gave Max her Monday order. 'The whole works.'

'I'll join you!' said Penny. 'But... not *too* hot!'

'I always take the delicate English taste-buds into consideration!' They were used to Max's teasing about their reactions to spicy food. 'No chillies on the side for The Press!'

'I'd forgotten what that monk-to-be was like. Or maybe I didn't take much interest. So much was happening. Buying that colossal house, which I *knew* was too much, then rows with Noel – anger. I forgot about his nervousness. I've blundered in as usual. Started straight in with everything, his calligraphy, his old home, the monastery – even my divorce. Oh God! I'm such a chump.'

'Why's that so awful then?'

'It triggered his stutter... I didn't notice it when he answered the phone.'

'Oh, you can never stop to put thoughts before actions, can you? What do I keep telling you? Engage brain before mouth?'

Max put the food in front of them. Barbara breathed in deeply. 'This smells delicious, thanks.' She needed the diversion. Max studied them quizzically but kept his peace.

Penny jabbed at the meal with her fork to let the steam out. She looked at the dishevelled Barbara.

'Food.' Penny ordered Barbara, surveying her plate. But her friend was too agitated.

'If I'd visited Anthony instead, I'd have remembered what a sensitive person he was – awkward and stuttering. But the person who picked up the phone sounded so confident… even bright and happy. I should have thought of the person I was speaking to instead of enjoying my-excitement.' She planted her elbows either side of her plate, putting her hands over her ears as though drowning out the sound of her own voice.

'At least you're aware of your problem now.'

'He sort of agreed to my ringing back, but I'll have to wait a few days. Damn.'

'You've never said much about that house – or Noel come to that.'

'I didn't think about it much at the time. Blanked it out. Put it to the back of my mind and suppose it's still simmering. Even during the divorce, it was as though it was happening to someone else. Work kept me going. Don't get me wrong, it still does, but…'

Now she'd started, Barbara couldn't stop. 'The funny little girl with the nervy mother seemed to think *eggs* were the answer to everything. Then the eye-catching calligraphy in the hall, at the bottom of the stairs.' She started eating then smiled and decided to tell Penny where Michael came into the puzzle. 'It was dreaming about Michael that brought back the memory of that picture.'

Penny's plate was nearly empty. She was a good listener 'This project may take more out of you on a personal level, so you *must* watch out for yourself… I think you need to talk more… Noel and all that.'

'I could be a bit stressed.' She'd had enough to eat, pushed the rest of the food to the side of the plate and put down her fork. They ordered coffee. 'But I've got to talk to Anthony. I'll be careful. Gentle.'

Penny sighed.

CHAPTER 30

Polly swallowed involuntarily as she walked into HQ. *Nerves*. Crofton and Flynn were visible through a glass partition. They were behind a desk leaning towards each other talking in a conspiratorial manner. As she approached their expressions changed and they acknowledged her. Then, all smiles, Crofton extended his hand.

'Welcome back, Polly! It is so good to see you.'

Flynn walked up to her and holding her by the shoulders, gave her the once over. He kissed her. 'You're fit!'

Polly smiled. *A different Flynn to the visitor in India*. 'I'm still getting used to England: not so dusty, no bullocks in the road, no gods for sale on the pavement!' Crofton frowned.

Flynn was thinking about his own plans. 'Elizabeth and I plan to visit India again. Total flop last time. We'd still love to see the Taj Mahal, and the beaches. Stupendous!' Crofton's frown deepened.

'Wouldn't you visit the work first, and see our few converts? They need all the encouragement we can offer.'

'This will be *holiday*,' Flynn laughed, but Polly noticed a shadow of confusion cross over his face.

'Sounds like you're thriving in the bank.' Polly smiled weakly, but her words and thoughts conflicted.

'Another promotion coming up at the end of the year! The Lord is so good to us!'

Polly's suspicions were confirmed. 'The Lord's work' was a cover for living an interesting and comfortable lifestyle. Crofton offered her a drink.

'Tea please, little milk, no sugar.'

'Coffee for me, please. Milk and sugar. Sweet tooth!'

'In India they serve tea in small cups with condensed milk.'

Crofton grimaced in disgust. 'Couldn't face that! I do like a large mug of builder's tea with proper milk.'

'They don't hang about drinking tea like we do either,' said Polly. 'They down it quickly and keep working.'

But Crofton, Flynn and Polly drank English fashion. After second cups with biscuits, Crofton put his mug on the desk and stretched. 'Now. Shall we get down to business?' He seemed reluctant. Polly felt more relaxed.

'Unfortunately, yes,' said Flynn.

Hard-nosed businessman. Nerves gone; Polly took control. 'So, let's get straight down to the money question, then.' Both men shifted uncomfortably.

'And it's a pity the AV Bible question is turning out to be divisive.'

They were taken aback.

'You know I'm flexible on that question, Pol,' said Flynn, 'But...

'But the supporters are not so flexible, Flynn?' She studied Crofton who was making and remaking steeples with his fingers.

Then Flynn leant forward: 'That's still the subject of a church meeting. BUT Croften and I are agreed on the homosexual problem.'

Crofton. startled out of his reverie, addressed Polly directly. 'Do I understand the person you are staying with in Guernsey… what's his name?'

'Anthony… and Piers.'

'…is gay?'

Flynn had obviously put Croften in the picture and decided he needed to take over. 'You know their behaviour is abhorrent to God.' Flynn was forceful, loud, and segued into the wound-up preacher. 'The Bible says in no uncertain terms that man sleeping with man is an abomination.'

'But there are so many other…'

'No ifs and buts, Polly,' said Flynn. 'Elizabeth totally agrees with me. And the Church is adamant on this point. Remember Sodom and Gomorrah? People simply will *not give* towards your support unless you give up this friendship, will they?' His last question addressed to Croften in bold self-righteousness.

'And we have to ask you,' said Crofton, 'urrrhhh, is the Lord still calling you to save souls in India?' Polly was surprised at Crofton's hesitation and change of subject.

Polly was firm: 'Yes, I think so, but He has also shown me…'

'Yes, *but, but, but…*' Flynn looked at Croften for support.

She continued: 'I'm going to take time to study the Bible thoroughly; to pray and seek the Lord in all things. Doing God's will is not so black and white as I used to think. I need to research my beliefs carefully.'

'I think that settles it!' said Crofton.

'Settles what?'

'The question of whether you can return to India with us next term.'

'Why?'

'You've lost your conviction that the Bible is the truth; you are doubting the scripture.'

Flynn stuck to his own line of argument: 'Non-Christians will see you staying with those...' he hesitated, '...*men*... and think you are condoning their behaviour.' He relaxed. 'So, for the time being, you won't need anyone to help raise your financial support.'

Crofton had already picked up a pile of papers. '...That's *that* problem solved then.'

Polly looked out of the window upset, and surprised at what seemed to be such a rapid conclusion. 'Wait a minute. Don't you think...'

Crofton ignored her and continued in a softer tone. 'I've received a pile of letters saying how much the clinics appreciate your help. Especially when you've taken equipment and helped them set it up. And the Fotheringills strongly recommend you return for another term of service.'

Polly needed to have her say: 'My point is I simply can't be untrue to myself. I am open to whatever the Lord will teach me. I believe, if I study His word prayerfully, He will reveal His Way. Nobody else knows what is right or wrong for me! I want to know the *truth*.' She noticed Flynn clench his fists, and the anger in his eyes made her fear for Beth. Her own anger flared up but a picture of Pontius Pilate washing his hands and asking, 'what is truth?' flashed through her mind and her thoughts turned inwards. *Calm down, Polly*.

Crofton had become more contemplative. He leaned back. 'This is a new one for me, Polly. I will keep your name on our books, and we'll consider the position in a year or so.'

'I doubt I will be available for support work in future, then,' said Flynn, looking pleased.

Crofton was surprised by Flynn's attitude. 'If the Lord wishes Polly to return to the field, He will show us too. We must keep an open mind. I must confess, I've never actually read the whole Bible, have you?'

'Well, no… but the position on homosexuals is quite clear.'

'I can only find one or two references to homosexuality in the whole Bible… and didn't Jesus condemn the Pharisees for being such sticklers to the law?' asked Polly, her hackles rising again. 'If you *knew* any gay people personally, and realised the struggle they have…'

Crofton raised his eyebrows: 'John eight, verse seven. *If anyone of you is without sin…*' He expected Flynn and Polly to know what he was talking about and waited for a response.

Flynn played his trump card triumphantly: 'The Lord can *heal* them. In fact, He wants to *heal* them of this iniquity. Have you even thought of suggesting Anthony seeks healing from the Lord?'

'Then why did the Lord create people like that in the first place? The discrimination they suffer is the abomination.'

'What, people offended when they are preyed on in public toilets?'

Polly shot back: 'You can't generalise!'

Flynn was growing impatient. 'We could go on all night like this.'

His accent is attractive, but how does Beth…?

Crofton decided they were getting nowhere but was lost for a decisive statement. 'Let us pray for guidance,' he said, bowing and clasping his hands.

They prayed in turns. Flynn told God what he knew to be the truth and asked Him to reveal it to Polly. Crofton, more humbly, sought forgiveness for all human weakness, and Polly asked for help to know His will.

They opened their eyes and seemed calmer.

'Lunch down the road. Just a quick one, on the firm?' asked Crofton. One thing Flynn and Polly could agree about, they were hungry.

Flynn consulted his watch immediately after they'd eaten. 'Must dash back to the airport then, and catch up with the Mrs! Expecting the second. Not as easy as the first. Nanny has more hours with Judith so Elizabeth can rest. I insist...'

Polly couldn't bear to hear what Flynn insisted on: 'Yes, and I have things to do before I go back to Guernsey.' She watched their expressions defiantly. 'Is Beth managing, Flynn?'

'Not too bad but we've asked the nurse to—'

'Yes, you have explained.' Crofton stopped him, irritated. 'Will you see anything of your family Polly?'

'I've had a chat with my brother. His family live in the old family home now, and I don't think Dad wants to see me.'

'Then why don't you ask your brother if you can stay?' asked Flynn.

'Because I upset them all horribly going to Ireland the Christmas before I left. I can't suddenly expect to be welcomed with open arms.'

'But you put the Lord's work first,' said Crofton. 'You did the right thing there.'

Flynn seemed to suddenly realise the consequences of their move for Polly. 'Of course, you were going to come to us. Well, it's a bit awkward now, isn't it? Didn't your brother have a baby?'

'Yes, Nicola. She was lovely. And I want to see her, but...'

Flynn was checking the time and didn't respond. 'Sorry, must dash!'

Croften looked sympathetic and smiled at Polly: 'You'll work things out, I'm sure.' Turning to Flynn he said, 'I'll give you a lift to the plane.' They dashed towards a parked car, jumped in, slammed the doors and were off.

Polly was left, feeling strangely empty, on the pavement. 'Another couple of days in England,' she said, as if to herself, then acted on impulse, went in a phone box and dialled Vic's number. Her heart danced for joy when Nina answered.

'Hello Pol, surprise, surprise!'

'Nina! I'm in London.'

'Whereabouts?'

'About forty-five-minutes by train.'

'Come and see us! You dad is desperate to see you.'

Polly's heart missed a beat. 'Nina… I've only spoken to Vic since—'

'*Can* you come?'

'I'd love to come but I feel so bad about—'

'Come!'

'Is there still a bus from the station?'

Polly put the phone on the hook and made for the mainline station.

By six o'clock she was walking over the doorstep of her childhood home. Nina held back a brown

Labrador puppy who was trying to jump up at her. 'Coco!' Nina scolded.

'Oh, Nina,' Polly sighed as she wiped her shoes and helped close the door. 'And who's this?' she said, bending down to the little girl half hidden behind her mother.

'Nicola!' whispered a little voice before she hid her face from view.

'Do you know who this is, Nicola?' asked Nina, letting the dog bound off and hugging her sister-in-law. 'It's so great to see you!'

Polly felt guilty and was tongue-tied. 'I'm – actually – well… I feel terrible—'

'Never mind, you've come. Vic will be happy! Come through. We'll ring Dad in a minute…'

'Does he *really* want to see me?'

'Don't be silly. Of course, he does. He and Doris play Bridge at the club and visit Mum, but live a quiet life these days. He remembers what he wrote to you and keep talking about writing again, but hasn't quite gathered the…'

'I don't blame him. Poor Dad. I don't know how to face him.'

'Help us feed the chickens, then you can keep an eye on supper while I take Nicola upstairs.'

With Nicola tucked up in bed, Polly, James, Vic and Nina sat at the kitchen table talking furiously. Their conversation was animated, though Polly was quieter than the others. She felt an outsider. But this was her family. *I belong here.*

'Will you deign to stay the night then, sis?' asked Vic.

'Ohhh…' Polly didn't know how to answer. The more welcoming they were, the worse she felt. But she was so happy to be at their table.

'I've a return ticket for the ferry the day after tomorrow, and have a couple of errands before I go back to Guernsey.'

'All right then.' James was obviously tired. 'We could fit in a visit to Mum. She's been asking for you…'

'She didn't want to see me before. Or has she changed?'

'Yes, a little. She's on new tablets, which have helped to stabilise her, but she's not enjoying life as she should. She just sits in her chair all day long.'

*

Polly gazed at the sunny horizon as the ferry sailed for Guernsey, mulling over events of the last two days. *I'm 'Aunty Pol' to a sweet little girl. 'Polly dear' to Dad who I've neglected for the Lord's work. 'Dear Sis' to Vic, who doesn't really seem to have missed me, and… just a naughty girl to my mother, it seems. That never has, and never will, change.*

She held on to the rail staring at the calm sea and breathed the ozone. *So many thoughts to sort out. But Anthony… the change, the colossal change in him. He's certainly content… happy with Piers. Does he need healing? Healing? As a friend I feel No. It's only people in the church saying Yes because they think the bible says so. I must learn. Study and learn.*

CHAPTER 31

Sitting quietly on their favourite rocks at the bottom of the cliff, Piers and Anthony were throwing sticks for Tiffany and calling her from time to time.

'So,' Piers eventually said, 'take a deep breath, pardner.' He was perched on a higher boulder in a good position to reach Anthony and massage the back of his neck. 'It's only me... talk slowly.' Anthony turned. He gathered strength gazing into Piers' eyes. 'Everything's fine. Love me chook?' Piers asked.

'Yes, of c-course.'

'And Tiff?' Anthony managed to smile, 'Of course!'

'Good lad! So how far back did she throw you? Take it slowly,' he said softly.

'R-right b-back. R-right back... everything c-came b-b-back. E-every-th... all m-m-muddled...'

'Look at me, Tony,' Piers said, patiently waiting for Anthony's gaze to focus back on him. '*Every*thing?' he questioned. Then with a glint in his eyes he sang teasingly, 'Chook, chook, chook, chook chicken! Lay a little egg for me!' Anthony sniggered, joining in the next line without a hitch: 'I haven't had an egg since Easter!' They wandered down to the sea, quietly singing a Beatles song recently learnt by Anthony, 'Love Me Do'. Tiffany bounded towards them and shook herself drenching them.

'Tiffany!' scolded Piers in a loud voice. They strolled along the shore. Then he said: 'Let's take one thing at a time.' *He carries so much baggage – his mother's dislike of him; his father's plunge to death in*

250

a flaming plane, the strain of keeping everything in the closet, Sebastian's advances and the stabbing –
'What's on top of your list?' he asked.

'I-I-I'm so l-lucky to h-have you, Piers.' Anthony stopped and rested his head on Piers' shoulder.

'Shushhh,' said Piers. They were silent again.

'The s-s-stabbing. That night! N-no I s-s-s…' Anthony blurted and jumbled up his next words.

'Never mind now, watch the sea… coming and going.' He spoke with rhythm. They enjoyed the waves. 'The s-sea, the sea, the sh-shining sea…' Anthony focused on the different ways the waves broke and rushed towards them. Constant but irregular. Sameness but variety. The vast expanse, the wonder, the healing power of nature. They said no more.

They dashed to bed early that night, then lay satisfied on their backs with the window open and a gentle night breeze cooling their skin. Anthony woke up after an hour and needed to talk. They spoke of their lives before they met, about Simon, and about their love for each other till almost dawn. Piers needed to clarify his mind too. Although his parents had accepted him eventually for who he was, other people on the island, especially churchgoers, bothered him. He'd always had problems trying to obey the demands of the Roman Catholic faith.

'I'll phone B-barbara Gristwood b-back,' Anthony suddenly announced when they eventually woke up in the morning.

Piers turned and rested on his elbow looking intently at his partner: 'Wait till you're ready, till you're absolutely sure.'

'In two or three days…'

*

Polly turned the key in the door of *Belle Vue* and Tiffany greeted her. 'Hello. Tiff!' she said, stooping to fondle her. 'Piers! Anthony!' Tiffany found her favourite squeaky toy and dropped it at Polly's feet. She picked it up and threw it down the corridor. 'Silly old Tiff! Find Anthony. Hello!' In such a large house her call went unheard into space. They could be anywhere, but they were, of course, in the garden. She blew them both a kiss from the window. 'Coo-eee!'

'It's getting chilly out here. We'll just do the necessary, then come to the kitchen. Five minutes. Put the kettle on!'

'I'll get sorted.'

'Stress-free zone!' said Polly as the men walked in the door.

'Not always,' said Anthony. Piers noticed no stutter and realised Polly's presence gave him a sense of security.

As they drank tea, Piers threw together a vegetable curry. They weren't strict vegetarians, but hardly ever ate meat. When Anthony went to the bathroom Piers gave Polly the thumbs up.

'Be gentle with Anthony. I think he'll be alright, but he had a phone call and it brought things back…'

'Oh?'

'Reminders of Elm Close and just about everything.' Piers continued cooking.

'Funny, I've just visited there. Didn't plan to, but I did!' Anthony walked in with a questioning face so Polly told him where she'd been.

'That's a c-coincidence,' said Anthony. 'After all this t-time we've both h-had a c-connection with Elm Close the same week! T-tell me…'

'Flynn and Crofton suggested I rang home, although I was really embarrassed. I didn't know what Dad would think. But Nina answered and said he couldn't wait to see me. She invited me over, then when I got there they were so enthusiastic that I stayed the night! It was wonderful to be reunited with them all, and Nicola is so, so cute! I've missed all her early years. She's almost six!'

'S-so you w-went to number 16. Did you look over the w-wall?'

'You may not want to know this, but The Elms is not a family house anymore, it's a nursing home.'

'Oh n-no!'

'But the outside is much the same, and they've kept the garden nice.' Piers was alarmed unnecessarily.

'B-Belle Vue is m-my real home now.' Anthony was positive. 'The Elms was not a happy place.' In a weird way knowing his old home had totally changed shut a firm door on his early years. *Progress.* Piers kept his thoughts to himself.

'I-it was other things – that upset m-me – you know, thinking about the p-past.'

'Let Polly tell us her story,' Piers called from the sink.

Polly picked up a tea-towel. 'In a nutshell…' Polly summarised her visits to MUT Headquarters and the family. 'And now I've got to consider my future,' she said. 'So much is changing. Not least the way I'm thinking; what I believe. My faith. I hardly know where to start.'

'Another one!' said Piers wishing he could take his words back.

Anthony grimaced. 'Piers says no hurry. One thing at a time... s-space m-myself out. S-space ourselves out. There's more to s-space than m-meets the eye.'

'There, Pol,' Piers said. 'Worth thinking about. What comes to the top of the pile?'

'Bible study... and hope that helps to answer my question about whether the Lord actually *wants* me back in India!'

'That really it?'

Polly pursed her lips. 'Top of the pile?' She coloured. 'Well, to be frank, I must decide if I can stay here with a clear conscience.'

'That t-tells us.' Piers looked at Anthony who was frowning. He threw a warning look in Polly's direction.

Polly stood up and put her arm round Anthony's shoulders. 'I desperately want to. I've just got to convince others it's OK.' She screwed up her mouth. 'And myself I suppose. It's things like my fear of hell and so on. I'm dithering all over the place!' She made light of it. Piers dished up and the curry made the perfect diversion as Piers had put in a few more chilli flakes than usual.

During dessert she told them more about the meeting with Flynn and Crofton. The three shared their thoughts calmly, discussing Polly's calling, training and work, and she expressed what it really meant to her to follow the Lord. When it became tricky with different points of view Piers announced, 'Time for a drink!' He poured wine for Anthony and himself and encouraged Polly to have one too.

'You know I don't drink,' she said.

'It will help you relax,' said Piers.

'But I made a vow never to touch alcohol.'

'Jesus t-turned water into wine,' Anthony reminded her.

'Partners in crime?' Piers encouraged, raising the bottle towards her. 'Rules and regulations?' he grinned.

Polly was confused. 'What do you mean exactly?'

'POLLY! You take things so *literally.*'

Polly deliberated but relented: 'Just a tiny drop, then.'

Piers poured just over half a glass for her and topped up his and Anthony's glasses. Anthony was uncertain but raised his glass to her. 'To all our searchings.'

Polly tasted a sip, liked it and then another sip… but she needed to order her mind: 'The other points are,' she counted on her fingers, 'one, my supporters are dropping off, two does God want me back in India? Three, family. I love them, but where do they fit in? Four: I need a job!'

'We've b-both got th-things to deal with,' said Anthony, more relaxed now. 'More wine?'

'Not tonight!' Polly giggled. 'Mustn't overdo it.' She felt satisfied, yawned, and studied Piers. *He always seems calm.*

'See how things map out in a few months' time,' said Piers.

'But what about you and The Elms?' she asked Anthony. 'What reminded you of it?'

He was more relaxed now and with the help of Piers explained the telephone call from Barbara Gristwood.

'Barbara was too demanding,' said Piers. 'She spoke quickly bombarding Tony with questions, all with different implications. He got flashes of the business with that monk and the stabbing – he relived so many things in a few moments. We're trying to get back to our happy relaxed selves, aren't we, Tony?'

'Oh, my goodness.' Despite the wine, Polly's voice was quietly sympathetic and soothing and Anthony was comforted by her concern for him.

'But the p-picture I gave your p-parents s-started it off! A c-curious thing.' He squinted at Polly, bemused, as though trying to fathom how the world works.

'The decorated writing?'

'I must g-go back to my c-calligraphy. I miss it.' Anthony was thrown into reverie. Piers was doing his best to be light-hearted.

'Tony will ring Barbara back when he's ready,' said Piers.

'Y-yes,' murmured Anthony putting his head on Piers' shoulder. 'I will. In m-my own t-time.'

Polly took the hint. 'I'm turning in now. All this talking's given me food for thought.' *Yesssss, I feel happy. Now I come to think of it, nothing is really that important. How nice!*

*

Polly reported back on her visit to town: 'I got on the bus to the hospital and they offered me bank work as a staff nurse. No holidays or sick pay, but I can pick and choose my shifts.'

'When are you starting?'

'Have to have a medical, but fairly soon I hope. But I can study while I wait.'

She found old notes she'd taken on Genesis while in India. *I finished that.* She reminded herself, *I've noted significant things I thought God said.* She read the margin notes, *Doubts, mainly it seems… Creation: seven days – really?* She skipped through them, anxious to break new ground. *I'll do alternate Old and New Testament books.* She found St Matthew's Gospel.

There was so much to note, so many different topics. *It's going to take years!* She asked the Holy Spirit to guide her but dozed off until she heard a voice filtering through her dreams, 'Supper! SUPPER!'

She went downstairs and sat at the table, they were both well into the wine and poured one for her. Anthony looked relaxed. 'Why does the Bible say such awful things? I still can't understand. Flynn and his church believing the worst. I want to justify my position. I used to accept other extreme statements… still do, to a certain extent.' She paused to think. 'Do you ever pray about it?'

'We go to mass, but live a lie,' said Piers, as they tucked into spicy beans and couscous with green vegetables and carrots.

Polly scanned the two of them.

'Haven't they guessed?'

'We tell them we're friends. We don't talk about it.'

'Piers has taught me to take life more, you could say, with a pinch of salt, Polly,' Anthony said.

'On the odd occasion when I take mass I just believe God in His love understands,' said Piers.

'It's simpler,' said Anthony.

They continued their meal deep their own thoughts, until Anthony suddenly announced: 'I'm going to ring Mrs Gristwood… B-Barbara.'

'Remember how pushy she is? Steady as you go, chook,' said Piers.

'Y-yes, I know.'

'Why don't *I* ring her?' asked Piers.

'I'm r-ready, thank you. I-I g-go to London in a f-fortnight and I thought I'd t-tell her we c-could meet then.'

'I'll come with you then!' said Piers. 'Can you manage the livestock for us, Pol?'

'Of course! Tiff will be good company while I study. I'll manage!'

'That would be a h-help,' said Anthony, looking at Piers.'

'I could see the work with the homeless for myself.'

'Y-yes, you c-could. Y-you could.'

*

Polly was seeing Anthony and Piers off with an excited Tiffany by her side.

'You sure you trust me?' She laughed.

'It's Tiff we're trusting!' called back Piers.

'Study hard,' said Anthony as he waved goodbye.

'We'll want to hear all the answers when we come back,' called Piers. But she was out of earshot.

Polly opened the car-door, but Tiff whined and stared after them. 'It's alright, Tiff,' she said and a forlorn Tiff reluctantly jumped in. 'Don't worry, they're coming back, and I'll be here.' She drove off with the dog breathing down her neck from the back seat.

'I've got to get serious now,' she said as they reached home, 'but let's go to the beach first.' Tiffany perked up. 'Beach', to her, was 'walk' to the rest of the dog community. 'You don't do *serious*, do you, Tiff? How am I going to get myself sorted out? I'll do what Piers says, take one thing at a time.' She looked back at the panting dog thankful she could chat freely to her. 'Space, Tiff, space. We'll have *fun*, won't we? The sea, the sea, the sparkling sea!' she sang. They walked towards the cliffs. Tiff understood. Polly was laughing.

CHAPTER 32

Barbara and Penny were preparing to leave Maisie's.

'It'll be so interesting meeting Anthony Wheeler this afternoon… this is the opening I've been *waiting* for.'

Red lights flashed. 'Opening to what?' Penny asked. 'Slowly, softly, blunderbuss!' she warned as Barbara took stock.

'Yes, yes… I must remember he's fragile – and the stutter. He's bringing his "friend". I expect Piers is coming to protect him from me.'

'Lioness!' Penny growled at Barbara.

They giggled.

They walked through the door which had been opened by Max. He never missed an opportunity to remind them about his long-lost father.

'Don't forget – Reginald LeRoy Reid.' He whispered, grinning, as they said good-bye.

'Get the prayer meeting going!' Barbara teased. She knew Max had joined the local Pentecostal Church. She was an atheist, but there was a vibrant quality about that crowd, noticeable when she watched as they left their building one Sunday. *What goes on at their meetings?* She'd been strongly tempted towards writing a feature on them. *They seem so cheerful – and such colourful, meticulous dress.*

'Bye, Babs!' Penny waved as they went in opposite directions. 'Be gentle!'

'I'll try,' she sang back. She boarded a bus for the arches and eagerly dismounted, but then paused and shivered involuntarily as she pondered what living in a place like this must be for Mags and Nick.

'Nick!'

'Hello Barbara.'

'Just checking you're in!' *That's so crass…* 'Will Mags be awake soon?' She detected an eye-lid flicker from the pile of coverings. 'I'll find Anthony and Piers.' Nick smiled a rare smile and Barbara thought she imagined a fleeting likeness to Max! Gone in a flash.

Anthony and Piers were on a bench by the river. She parked herself, self-consciously, alongside Anthony who vaguely remembered her. They shook hands and he introduced Piers.

'Steady as you go.' Piers directed Anthony, instead of acknowledging Barbara. She heeded the warning. *Don't say sorry for the phone call.* She asked no questions but admired the view and made an unsuccessful effort to relax.

'Please don't worry about this meeting.' *Is that a silly thing to say? Help!*

'I'll make sure things go smoothly,' said Piers.

'D-do you think M-Mags will be w-willing to return my M-Missal?' Anthony asked.

'It's not much good to her, is it? She can't read. But she does seem to treasure it. I've thought about that… I mean, why would she want to keep it? I can only think that perhaps it's the only book she's ever had, and I gather she's desperate to read and write.'

'The p-paper has a lovely f-feel,' said Anthony, rubbing his fingers and thumb as though fingering the pages, 'India p-paper.'

They walked to the arch and stopped a distance from Nick and Mags.

'It m-must be d-dirty by now,' he said absentmindedly as they absorbed the dank conditions under the arch: rubbish, smells, ram-shackled make-do shelters: sleeping bodies, one or two with a makeshift begging bowl.

'This p-place is like other places I-I visit with the ch-church. I've never b-been here though.'

'You have to watch out this end of the arches. Nick always keeps an eye on what's happening. They know his friends watch his back. I think you'll find Mags is asleep,' said Barbara. 'Nick says she chooses her time to wake up. She's not stupid.'

Mags looked asleep. Barbara went over alone to Nick.

'Anthony and his friend are over there.' She pointed them out. Nick nodded, casting a glance at Mags.

'She'll come to in a while.'

Barbara beckoned the men over and Nick sensed their awkwardness. Then a beautiful smile spread across his face. 'Who goes first then?' he said, in the singing voice Barbara had come to enjoy.

'You decide!' *Oh god, what happens now?*

Nick eyed them slowly, 'Three of you?' he asked, skewing his mouth in doubt.

Barbara picked up the hint. 'Shall we go and buy a few bits and pieces in the market, Piers? Nick, fancy a few apples?'

Anthony crouched by Nick and shook his hand.

'P-pleased to m-meet you,' he said. Piers recognised reassuring signs and relaxed. He gave Barbara the thumbs up and they walked away towards the market.

'No easy armchair!' Nick joked, quietly watching Anthony clumsily lowering himself to the ground.

There was that crucifix hanging round his neck. *Yes, that's it!*

'You ain't used to sitting on the floor!'

'The m-monastery beds were b-bad. They were alright when I-I was used to them – b-but I should have been m-more thankful.'

'Yep. You get used to things,' said Nick, groaning as he moved a leg, 'But as you gets older...' His voice tailed off. He had a peaceful way about him. Anthony felt at ease.

'How long have you b-been here, Nick?'

Nick hesitated, wondering how much to confide. 'Name's Reggie, actually... it's only our Mags and the journalist woman calls me Nick.'

'Sorry, *Reggie*.'

'Yes, Reggie,' he repeated, as though pleased to hear his rightful name. 'Always Nick to Mags but... huh.' He didn't finish his sentence as he became thoughtful.

Anthony weighed up his words and let them hang a while, before asking, 'Do you think she w-will ever w-want to give me my b-book back? I've had it since I was s-seven.'

'She loves de paper and closes it and strokes the cover. I try reading her, but not much good.'

'I could find her another one, just like it... a new one.'

'Try when she wakes up.' Reggie prodded her gently. 'Time to talk to the man, babe...'

Mags stretched and rubbed her face. Anthony felt awkward and wished Piers were back.

'Fuck, fuck, fuck!' Mags announced. 'Time?'

'Come on Magsy... jis few minutes. Creeper's here.' He threw a sideways glace to check Anthony's reaction, but he was watching Mags. Hair ruffled and dirty, clothes small and ill-fitting. He waited for Mags to look at him. But she addressed Reggie.

'Creeper?' she asked. 'Fuck! He mad at me?' Then she saw the crucifix.

'What d'you want?' she barked, still eyeing the crucifix, but Reggie answered.

'You wanted to know 'bout de posh card – an' he'll know.' He fished out the calligraphed card. 'It don't make sense,' insisted Reggie.

Anthony's face lit up, then quickly clouded over. *How can I possibly quote Latin in these circumstances?* He searched for words.

'You goin' a speak, mister?' asked Mags, boldly studying his face.

'You know what this means?' Reggie rested his hand on Anthony's shoulder. 'These words? That's no English, not that we knows.'

Anthony plucked up the courage to pronounce the significant words in front of them: slowly and carefully, without hesitation: '*pecunia est radix omnis mali caritas.*'

Mags was blank. Reggie saw a funny side, 'Hah, ha, hoo!'

Anthony couldn't see the joke. 'It's L-latin for *The l-love of m-money is the root of all evil.*' Then hastily, 'But I don't think it's m-meant for you. Not at all. N-no, no, no.'

Mags screwed up her nose, 'That all – that *all*?'

Anthony recognised her disappointment. Utterly lost, and hopeless.

Reggie seemed to recognise the phrase. 'No problem here then!' he chuckled, self-mockingly. But Mags, disgusted, buried herself back in her rags firmly closing her eyes and letting out a string of obscenities. Anthony blinked. By now he was used to foul language and could ignore it.

'N-no, I-I know. That v-verse was not m-my choice,' stammered Anthony, abashed. 'The Abbot instructed me to do it… to p-pray about it.' He felt out of his depth as he realised they'd have no idea who the Abbot was.

'That's from de Word!' said Reggie. 'They said it in church, back home.'

'God's Word,' mumbled Anthony quietly, without picking up on Reggie's observation. Then he spied a familiar shape amongst the rags that were Mags's bed – just rags. He couldn't stop himself: 'My Missal!' he said aloud.

Mags recognised the tone of ownership, grabbed it, and hugged it to herself. 'Mine!'

Anthony's mind, swimming alternatively in disgust at the squalor and the conflict of knowing his newly found treasured property was out of reach, went into overdrive. *For her my book is everything. I have more than enough. Pecunia est radix omnis…! My chance to live the life rather than pray about it.* He welled up. He stood up with difficulty, leaning on Reggie's arm and feeling he had to leave. He shook hands with the friendly Jamaican, thinking that in some abstruse way they had something in common.

'I'll l-leave it with her.'

Reggie, overcome by Anthony's reaction, silently acknowledged his gesture.

Barbara and Piers were ambling over with two plastic bags of shopping. Piers studied Anthony: 'You alright, chook?'

'Thank you. Yes, y-yes, Thank you.' His eyes were twinkling. He seemed different somehow. Piers was fascinated.

'Enjoy,' said Barbara offering the bags to Reggie without second thought.

'Ta, lady.'

Piers smiled, 'It's nothing. Nothing. See you again soon, Nick!'

Mags had gone back to sleep. 'God bless you friends,' Reggie called after them.

'Success?' asked Barbara as they walked away.

'The L-Latin well, w-was so… w-well, completely out of place.'

'You can't exactly pontificate, in a place like that, can you?' agreed Piers, 'But...'

'I saw my M-missal and M-mags hugged it to herself. I-I h-had to leave it behind. That c-card was rubbish to her. But it s-spoke to m-me.'

'So what's next?' Barbara knew better than to question Anthony's meaning.

'Tell me later, Tony.' Piers understood. Anthony turned to Barbara.

'I'll use my new one.'

'OK then, let's have an ice-cream by the river.' Piers went to buy them at a kiosk while the other two found an empty bench and sat down.

'When I recognised the calligraphy and realised I had met you before, Anthony, I had a strong feeling something significant was going to happen. But you didn't get your property back, and the writing Mags was so desperate to understand turned out to be just rubbish to her when it came to it. *How can I make a story out of this?*'

'Y-yes, but I will not f-forget Mags. I'll t-tell F-father Dominic what happened.'

'You feel there is more to it too, then? I can watch this space!' Anthony agreed.

'But don't push your way into it.' said Piers, slightly annoyed.

Barbara was puzzled, 'But…'

'We'll let you know,' said Piers, sure Antony had had enough for now. The two men said 'Good-bye', making it clear they wanted to move on, and headed for St Mark's. Barbara, rather disappointed, sat down to think.

'I f-felt such a hypocrite sitting with them. A r-rotten hypocrite. They have nothing,' Anthony mused. But a new light was shining in his eyes: 'I h-had a s-sort of epiphany about living the C-Christian life. S-somehow wanting to have my p-property back from a destitute young girl was selfish and linked to that verse. My M-missal doesn't matter any m-more.' He wanted to take Piers' hand, but a London street was far removed from an isolated Guernsey beach.

'Hearty congratulations, dear fellow. You've come a long way, chook.' Piers felt like hugging Anthony but smiled, repressed the urge and slapped him gently on the back.

'Reggie recognised the v-verse was f-from the W-word of God, as he p-put it. That's interesting. I'll go and s-see him again. And I'm so p-pleased I enjoyed a c-conversation with a s-stranger. He didn't j-judge me.'

Piers said:

'Urr… Reggie, did you say?'

CHAPTER 33

Polly got on famously with Tiffany. She put the surplus eggs on the wall, and chatted to neighbours when they helped themselves. She was happy, felt she belonged, and enjoyed the peace of an empty house. A valuable opportunity to study although rather surreal. Yolanda updated Polly on local news when she visited to help with cleaning and minded Tiffany when Polly went to work.

When Piers returned leaving Anthony in London for his three months stint, he asked Polly what she'd been up to.

'It was a bit odd having this great big place to myself, but I had plenty of chance to study and think… I've made notes on every chapter, then, when I'm on the beach or relaxing I ponder asking how it fits in with the rest of Scripture and what I know of God's character.'

'Isn't that rather much, Pol?' asked Piers, diplomatically, thinking she'd never get to grips with the whole thing. Polly was quiet.

'Anyway, how's Anthony and what happened in London?'

'It was interesting. Tony was pleased. We met up with Barbara, Nick – apparently his real name is Reginald – and Mags. Briefly, he felt such a hypocrite when he saw how much Mags loved his book, he left it with her. There's more to it. We'll have to wait till he can tell us the detail himself. I'm proud of him because he's speaking to strangers and managing his stutter… In the end he was happy to let Mags keep his security blanket. Such good progress.'

Polly was fascinated by the story but obsessed with her own project. She nodded her head sadly:

'That's something I've got to deal with: hypocrisy. It's not just a feeling, but a *reality*. I must get to the root of it somehow.'

Piers saw his opinion wasn't going to curb her determination to keep digging.

'You mentioned translation before…' He tailed off, having started to brainstorm but gave up.

'People go to war over this sort of thing! I've got to find out as much as I possibly can. I've been to the Christian bookshop to find something on how the Bible was compiled. I mean, who decided this collection of books are "His inspired words" and others are not? But nobody in the shops seems bothered. They talk about history *in* the Bible. Not *of* the Bible.'

Piers was moving towards the door.

'Imagine this group of men debating, arguing, all with their own preconceptions, deciding…' Polly couldn't let go.

Dog with bone. Thought Piers with his hand on the doorknob. 'I bet they never agreed. Committees never do.'

'Exactly!'

'And our Bible has more books in it than yours!'

'Yes!' Polly's eyes were alight with fascination: 'Why have *we* decided those books are *not* inspired?' She was exasperated. 'Must have a drink!' Piers frowned. Had introducing Polly to alcohol been a mistake?

*

A few days afterwards Polly showed Piers an advertisement in a Christian newspaper. 'I must go to this exhibition in London!'

The Nation's Biblical Heritage – collection of out-of-print Bibles.

'They claim to have items of antiquity from BC 2040! Can you believe that?'

'That certainly is your cup of tea!' Piers responded.

'Just what I need, and I could call in on home, visit a few friends, and even see Anthony if he's free.'

The following week she tracked down the same advertisement outside a chapel in South London. The door was wide open and a man with a serious face and wearing a clerical collar was welcoming visitors. *So informal? The chapel is tiny… insignificant even. How strange.* She pored over a range of Bibles and texts carved on ancient tablets, many of them thousands of years old. *These are priceless and no security obvious. Utterly priceless.*

She wandered about the display mesmerised. *Astounding*! *What an extraordinary collection, I had no idea these old versions even existed. Versions with only one or two copies made. Unique tablets…!* She was particularly attracted to one side of the chapel displaying ornate decorative writing like Anthony's calligraphy but varied, richer and even more elaborate. *Exquisite*! She was staggered at the beauty and wondered how much the texts differed. And two or three were only short texts, a few verses long, but she couldn't see much helpful information.

She followed the trail to the last exhibit, near the exit. It was the King James Version 1611. She stopped, dumbfounded.

'Why do they stop at 1611?' she asked the pastor in charge.

'Oh yes, the King James Version. This…' he said authoritatively and walking over to confirm what they were talking about '… is the *only* one really inspired by God.'

Reminded of Flynn, and too shocked and stunned to ask more, Polly smiled and walked away.

*

Anthony was free for an early evening meal.

'How's T-tiff?'

'Tail's wagging as fast as ever!'

'I m-miss her… and Piers of c-course.'

'How much longer before you come home?'

'About seven weeks, P-Polly.'

'I came to see a remarkable collection of Bibles.' And she told him about her experience.

'H-how unusual is that?'

'*Most* unusual, I think. But my hopes were dashed, when the pastor at the door told me the AV was the only true word of God! Several more versions have been published since then.'

'And it doesn't even include the Ap-pocrypha!'

'It's partly because I read the RSV my support's dropping off!'

'It reminds me of the Pharisees and S-Sadducees who Jesus accused of being t-too scrupulous about details of the law.'

As they walked to a small café for coffee near Anthony's base, the noise of the traffic rendered them silent. But they were both wondering if they were still being too legalistic: too literal? They sat for a coffee and Anthony asked:

'Did P-Piers tell you I've met the g-girl who stole my Missal?'

'Yes, but he didn't give me much detail. I was pleased you'd found it.'

'I p-prayed to St Anthony! But I felt d-different when I saw how the girl – Mags – treasured it. You should have seen her.'

'So, do you think St Anthony helped you find it?'

'I d-don't know about that. B-but I do know I-I… as I s-sat there with R-Reggie and M-Mags in a flash I-I had a D-Damascene m-moment and got my wealth into p-perspective.'

'So, she can keep it?'

'G-gladly. But, P-Polly, I wish you c-could meet them. I saw their s-squalor and how much that one b-book meant to her. And I s-saw my wealth, and it meant nothing. Loving my belongings is the s-same as loving money.' Anthony appeared to have remembered something. He drew his chair closer to the table.

'Nick, umm, Reginald, the Jamaican who protects her, s-said she has women's p-problems at certain times, you know.' He was embarrassed but carried on. 'S-spends hours in the underground t-toilet. P-perhaps half the night.'

Polly inferred he was talking about menstruation. She was frank. 'You mean she has no sanitary protection?' Anthony went pink.

'I n-never thought of th-th-that.' He avoided her gaze.

She didn't want to set him off stuttering again and sought safer territory.

'So, what *has* she got?'

'A few b-bits of blanket – rags – p-plastic bags, the clothes on her back… and my Missal. Polly, I want to help her.'

'She may not want your help you know.'

'I'll ask Father Dominic. He's worked with these people for years. He's wary of helping individuals.'

'What about her friend, the Jamaican? Did you say Reginald?'

'Yes, N-nick is only Mags' name for him. He told m-me his real name.'

'Right… Reginald.'

'B-Barbara p-picked "Nick" up from Mags. He used to g-go to ch-church in Jamaica. He doesn't have much in c-common with the others.'

'Their lives are so alien to ours.'

'It's humbling. W-well, you c-can't compare them.'

'No, Polly agreed and mulled over Anthony's experience. So where does the journalist fit in?' she asked. 'When I last saw her, I was perhaps eleven or twelve? I didn't take to her.'

Anthony ignored the personal opinion.

'B-Barbara works for *The Sh-Shorewell News* and is doing a report for the c-council on the homeless. She was introduced to M-mags and Reginald by the Salvation Army. She c-contacted me because she thought the c-card in my Missal was like the one hanging in your hallway. Reginald said M-mags wanted to know what the words were. That's why she visited your family house and eventually t-traced me.'

'She's been to number 16?' Polly spied a clock on the wall.

'Look at the time! Five more minutes!'

Anthony hadn't finished and spoke faster than usual. 'Mags wants to l-learn to *read!* As though her other needs are ins-significant! I think G-god p-planned for me to meet her. I have a link now with her and Nick… R-Reggie, I really do.'

'You can't stop calling him Nick, can you!' Polly laughed. 'Maybe if you made a point of telling the journalist his real name, it might stick in your mind.'

'I will. Would you like to meet F-father Dominic and see how he works?' Anthony stood up at last.

'Definitely. Next time I'll see more. When I was in India I felt I was helping people in need but what you've just said makes me think. I'm not so humble as you. And I didn't realise there was such need in my own country.'

They parted to go their own ways. 'Look after yourself,' said Polly as they kissed goodbye. 'I'm sure I will meet Mags one day.'

'You w-will! Safe journey!'

They were both content and parted with plenty to think about. Anthony slowly made his way to the church, head bowed, reminding himself to tell Barbara Nick's proper name. Reginald… Reggie. S*uits him much better*!

On the train to the ferry Polly flicked through a magazine. Her eye caught the word 'Biblical' and she reread the advertisement: *Biblical Archaeology Review* an American magazine, *I had no idea…* She noted the details on a tissue and went to sleep.

'Hi Polly. See Tony?' Piers wanted news as soon as they met.

'Yes! I did... He's so earnest about helping the poor and I think he feels fulfilled at last. He sets such an example in humility.'

'Does he miss me?'

'Of course, he does! He sends his love. Heaps. But the work keeps him focussed. When I've finished...'

'Your exhibition – was it helpful?'

'Helpful? No!' But it was breath-taking! Unique; the covers, presentation, ancient tablets. Old Bible versions I'd never heard of. But they ended at the King James version! She almost shouted the information she so wanted to Piers to understand how shocked she was. 'But I know my next step.' And she told him about coming across the advertisement.

'I'll order a few copies and see what I can learn from the Dead Sea Scrolls research. I suppose the exhibition was impressive and if I'd studied the exhibits for hours, I could have learnt a lot. But not the sort of information I want. It was an extraordinary collection of antiquity; nothing to do with researching the TRUTH!'

Piers was non-committal. He couldn't understand why Polly was going to such extremes and doubted the magazines would help. It was good to have news of Piers though. 'Good luck with that,' he said thinking of dinner.

Polly ordered BAR, signed up for a couple of night shifts at the hospital, then settled down to a few days serious slog at Isaiah. *Old Testament turn*. She closed her eyes in prayer: 'Lord...' The intention was to ask for guidance as to what God was saying in the first chapter, but her mind was full of the last two days and she had a lot to say to God before starting again twenty minutes later: 'Lord...' but her mind swung back to the exhibition and the finality of the beautiful Bibles ending at 1611. 'Lord!' she exclaimed, what is wrong with these people?' She picked up her Biro for a moment then decided to go and see how the chickens were getting on. *They help me think.*

*

As Anthony was chopping vegetables for the soup kitchen. Polly's words flew back to him: 'Tell the journalist Nick's real name is Reginald'. He repeated the name to himself. *I must tell Barbara.*

After his shift he found the telephone number of the *Shorewell News*. 'Hello, Anthony Wheeler speaking. Is Barbara Gristwood available please?'

CHAPTER 34

Three o'clock in the afternoon. Reg sat bolt upright, startling Mags, immediately alert. He was straining to see into the distance: 'Mags, Mags!' He shouted excitedly.

'Wha's wrong?' She was agitated. 'What?'

'Listen!' He shook her shoulder. 'Hear th*at*?' He was pointing to the other end of the arch and cupping his ear with the other hand. 'I knows that! I *knows* it!' Mags heard a guitar and singing. It meant nothing to her.

'Some bugger singing?' she grumbled. But Reg struggled to get up and fumbled for his stick.

'*No, NO! Listen!*' He joined in the words... '*Ah Wen Yu Ben De*,' he croaked. Mags strained to listen, attracted to the lilting voice.

'Music,' she said. 'Yeah good music!' But she was wary. 'Snoopy's there.' Barbara was with a young black man. A young black guitarist singing a Caribbean folk tune. 'Snoopy? You *knew* she was coming?'

'No, babe, No. But now I...' Mags saw tears in the old man's eyes as he made urgently towards the musician. The young man passed the guitar to Barbara to free his arms and lurched towards Reg. The men fell on each other. 'Sonny! Sonny! Maxwell, is that you, my son?'

'Dad!' They were locked in embrace, swaying from side to side, Reggie's stick now redundant, abandoned.

Barbara was taken unawares by her own tears. But she felt wary and vulnerable standing alone now, holding the guitar. She edged towards Mags, watching the scene unfold. Mags was wide-eyed and confused. *Hey! Nick, Nick? Wha's goin on? Who?* Barbara, unthinking, crept too close to Mags who was bewildered by Nick and Max being totally wrapped up in each other. She spied the guitar and grabbed it. Barbara gasped but was open-mouthed, stunned by the scene playing out before her. She turned to Mags, and was astonished to see she was in a world of her own, plucking the strings tentatively leaning back against the damp bricks of the arch. Barbara went up to Reg and Max, all semblance of a professional reporter lost, as Max gave her a heartfelt hug, crying into her neck.

'It *is* Dad! It's my *dad*!' He grasped Barbara's shoulders and looked warmly into her eyes at arm's length, with Reg behind him grinning from ear to ear. Max couldn't voice his words of thanks. He linked arms tightly with his dad, 'What can I say?' he said, to everyone in general. 'Praise the Lord!'

Soft guitar sounds interrupted the drama. Mags was humming Max's song, and picking out the notes on his guitar: 'You've got it, babe!' Reginald said amazed, and Mags, eyes gleaming, smiled.

'Dad used to play!' Her face was radiant. He'd never seen her so happy.

*

Barbara sat at her desk the following morning. 'Barbara!' called Michael, sharply. 'Penny for thoughts!' They were the only two in the office.

'You made me jump!'

'That's what I meant to do! Dreaming of me again?' She blushed.

'Shut up, Casanova!' She shook herself and piled up the papers scattered around her. 'I've got to sort myself out. I'm too involved.'

'That's never you!'

'Must be my age!' she joked. Then, seriously, 'But what's next? *What* next?'

'Pub lunch? My treat.'

Penny was out, so Barbara agreed despite her dislike of Michael's pub. 'Right. Long as there's no football talk and no chauvinist remarks.'

'I'll devote myself to you! We'll find a corner, have a beer, and the gaffer'll take our order at the table.'

They pushed through the noisy crowd at The Anchor bar and made for a window. 'We'll open this and get some fresh air!' Michael was more than usually solicitous.

They ordered and were served drinks.

'Right,' said Michael, sipping his beer, 'tell me all about it.'

'It was so emotional! If only I'd got pictures. I didn't get pictures! I had the camera, but was holding the guitar! It was such a private moment really, for Nick and Max. Despite the place they were the only people in the world. Reggie, I mean.' She made a mental note to call him by his given name. 'I couldn't see for tears. I don't know what came over me.' She stretched out for her glass, guiltily glancing at Michael. 'Then Mags grabbed the guitar and started playing the song she'd heard Max sing! Remarkable.' She was shaking her head slowly as she recounted a story unlike any in her experience.

Michael was more practical. 'Max found his dad, then – and you got involved with your story. You were instrumental in the outcome.'

'I was. But I could kick myself. Why didn't I discover Reginald's real name before? I wasted so much time. Why did he choose to tell Anthony, of all people, and not *me*?'

Michael didn't want to say it aloud. *She thinks the world revolves around her*.

Barbara answered her own question. 'I only heard Mags call him "Nick" and I guess to him I was just a journalist fishing for a story.'

'These people sense attitude, don't they?'

'I *must* check my facts. I'm always too rushed.'

'Was Anthony at the reunion?'

Barbara clocked that Anthony hadn't been updated. 'No, he wasn't. I must ring him. He wasn't feeling himself. He's off home soon, but he'll be at the church now. First job after lunch.'

'You really are caught up in this, aren't you? You'll be taking up social work next!'

'God forbid!' But she couldn't stop thinking about them.

'Max won't let him stay on the streets.'

'What will happen to Mags?'

Barbara churned over different lines her story could take, still emotional as she relived the moment father and son met. The food arrived.

'My stable journalist, publicist through and through – until this. I must ask you though, what do we get out of our investment? This is a one off – nothing to do with the council, that work is complete. After they've accepted the report, we'll get permission to produce copy for the paper, but this human-interest story stands alone.'

Barbara turned to Michael: 'Max confided in me. I can't betray him.'

'But he knew who you worked for and needed your contacts.'

'I suppose so.'

'And it would be great to publish good news for a change. You're on to a popular line here. Keep in touch at the café.' He patted Barbara's arm. 'This is sort of thing is just what we want.'

Back at work, Barbara felt happier – but her ethical boundaries were wavering.

'See what turns up tomorrow,' said Michael turning to the muddle of papers on his desk. Barbara continued to daydream.

*

Max was back at the arch as soon as he was free.

'Dad, you've got to come home with me,' he said. He saw Mags gaping at him, and smiled at her from time to time. Eventually he addressed her,

'How would Dad have managed without *you*?' Instead of hiding herself in her rags, she looked him straight in the face.

'What will I do? Wha' about me?'

'Yes, son. What can Mags do?' Max frowned. 'If I leave here,' said Reginald. 'She comes with me – we need each other.'

Max considered the practicalities of taking them both home… how to even get them there in the first place. He couldn't really take them on the bus in this state. *The smell!* Waves of sympathy flowed over him, towards them both. *She's lovely though.*

After a long moment Reg spoke:

'Think about it, son. You knows where we are. It'll work out.' He raised his eyes. 'De Lord aboves a good 'un.'

'You're right. He'll find a way. I'll come back!' They regarded each other fondly. 'Don't you worry, friend,' he addressed Mags, 'God works in mysterious ways!'

'Mags, she is,' said Reg 'an' she don't know 'bout God!'

'Mags,' said Max warmly. 'The Lord has blessed us all!'

Mags said nothing, but the Creeper's words came back to her. *I took advantage of him, and he said, "God bless you, my Child."* She had a funny feeling inside, remembering how she effed and blinded at the time.

After Max had gone she said to Reggie: 'I asked Creeper what God had to do with me. I never thought He'd notice me – but maybe He has…' Her voice tailed off. She settled down for sleep but it deserted her. She felt strangely happy.

*

'I can't wait to hear what Max has to say, Pen,' said Barbara as they walked to lunch.

'Let's see!' said Penny, deep breathing the tempting smells wafting from Maisie's. Max raced to meet them and shook Barbara's hand, pumping it hard.

'How can I thank you? How can I? I'm so, so happy! God worked through you to bring me my dad!'

That was the last reaction Barbara expected to hear. And Penny was taken aback. They took off their coats and sat. Barbara ignored the God comment.

'You *do* look happy! No thanks needed. I was only doing my job and the most unexpected coincidence happened!'

'Coincidence? It's a wonderful answer to prayer! God is great!'

Again, Barbara was bemused. Penny sniggered, her handkerchief hiding her mouth. She was tickled to see Barbara, over-confidence gone and lost for words.

'God?' she questioned seriously.

'Meeting my father is the best thing that's ever happened to me!' said Max. 'And for my family back home. Now, your usual?'

'Please. If you can concentrate!' Penny went along with the flow.

'Okay–AY, coming up!' Max sang in the lilting voice that reminded Barbara of his song. He disappeared into the kitchen.

'God's going to find you very useful!' Penny teased Barbara.

'Heavens, no! Dare I say, God forbid?'

'He's never hinted at religion before, has he?'

'Yes. I knew he'd joined a Pentecostal church and noticed they're a happy group. But that's all. Maybe they've all been praying he would find his father.'

'And you were the one! The one chosen to make the prayer come true!'

'Michael will laugh!'

'Michael,' Penny warned, 'is still a married man – remember?'

'I *know*! But he likes me. I know he does.'

'You'll have to settle for mistress if that's what you want.'

'He says he'll leave his family…'

'You should be giving up on him after all this time.'

Barbara shook her head.

'Here you are. Only the best!' Max came out beaming.

'So? What happened after I left then?'

'Thank you,' said Penny. Max perched at the neighbouring table.

'We talked and talked. I want Dad to come home with me, but he won't be separated from Mags. So – I say she can come too, but Dad says she certainly won't go on public transport in the state she's in.' I don't know what she thinks, except she don't want him to go. Another thing to pray about!'

'You'll have to explain all that God stuff!' Barbara heard herself saying.

Penny opened her eyes wide in astonishment.

'I will, I most de-fin-ite-ly will,' Max was beaming.

'But…' his face clouded, 'how to get them home in that state… and it's a big, big change to make.'

It dawned on Barbara that resolving the matter was far from a straightforward. She scratched her head.

'I'll see them again after work!' said Max, animated. 'See what they think today.'

Back at the office Barbara talked out loud to herself. 'What to do next? Just *what?*'

'Pray, obviously!'

'Pen!'

'Wait for the trumpets to sound and the clouds to open up…' They both collapsed into laughter.

Michael was trying to make a phone call. 'Settle down, children! Are we at work or not?' But it was he who came up with a suggestion later: 'Why don't you ring the monk and ask what he thinks, Barbara?'

Without hesitation Barbara picked up the phone, signalling 'thumbs up'.

'Hello Anthony s-speaking… Oh g-good… Oh dear, I see… We might be able t-to… It's p-possible that our funds could c-cover that purpose… I'll speak to F-father Dominic… very t-tricky.' Not only did the Church arrange for Reginald and Mags to stay in the crypt, but they provided decent clothes. Reginald only had a walking stick, his plate, and a few pieces of bedding fabric. Mags had a similar collection, with the addition of Anthony's special book. After a week Max picked them up in a taxi. He hardly recognised them. He was struck by the change in Mags. She, remembering his singing, smiled shyly, and Max smiled back. Reginald noticed but said nothing. *It's not real all dis! Praise the Lord!*

'You've no idea of the difference,' Max said to Barbara and Penny the following week, 'you should see Mags. She scrubs up real nice. No kidding!'

Was that a twinkle in Max's eye?

'I've got to pick my moment to ask if I can write their story up.' Barbara said to her aunt when she got home. It was possible she'd never see Reginald and Mags again. But her dilemma was solved on her next visit to Maisie's. Max invited her along with Penny and Anthony to tea at his flat.

Before the door opened, Anthony had joined the girls. He was happy but drained. It was a cold day. He was sweating.

'You alright?' asked Barbara.

'I h-hope so.' He seemed evasive.

'Do you think you should see a doctor?'

'Oh… Not yet.' He rubbed his forehead 'B-but let's forget about m-me now.' He smiled when he saw Reginald in the passage.

'WELCOME!' sang Max as he greeted them, 'Welcome to our happy family!'

*

Max, Reginald, and Mags agreed Barbara could write up their story on condition that God received credit, which Barbara agreed to in a bemused fashion. Michael was doubtful, but she explained it was that or nothing, so they came up with a compromise: God would share the credit with the *Shorewell News*:

December 3rd 1981
WAR HERO REUNITED WITH SON – FIRST CONTACT SINCE WWII
***Shorewell News* reports on their successful venture**
Two homeless find permanent home
Exclusive from Barbara Gristwood

Whilst working on a council report concerning homelessness, I had the privilege of reuniting the missing father of Max Reid, manager of Maisie's Cuppa, with lame Reginald Leroy Reid, resident under the arches. Jamaican born, Reid senior left his wife and toddler son at home to fight in the British Army and had no means to return after being injured. Reid junior came to England to seek his father and our research led to his discovery.

Mags, abandoned by her traveller family, made her home under the Shorewell Arches near Reid senior who refused to abandon her when offered a home by his son. Reginald and Mags are, after considerable adjustment, happily living with Reid junior.

This happy reunion would not have come about without our help and that of Mr Anthony Wheeler and St Mark's Church outreach team.

Max Reid is keen to share how he prayed for help to find his father. He believes God has used the *Shorewell News* and *St Mark's* in the process, and insists all glory must go to Him.

Barbara put two copies of the edition containing the article in her bag and made her way to Anthony's church. She found him sorting clothes and very tired.

'I've brought you a copy of the paper with a short report of our success story!' she said as soon as he noticed her. He sat down before taking it. Barbara felt concerned.

'I wish you'd have a word with the doctor, Anthony.'

'I don't really w-want t-to. B-but, yes. I s-should.' He waved the paper at Barbara and smiled. 'Thank you. G-good news for a ch-change.' His fatigue was banished for a short time.

'I'm so p-pleased I left the m-monastery.' Barbara studied him carefully, wondering why he'd told her.

'Ohhh.' She watched him reading the article, unsure how to respond.

'I'll l-leave you then.' Anthony was in a different world.

'Y-yes, good-bye,' he said, still studying the paper.

CHAPTER 35

'Aunty Polly!' When the eleven-year-old girl opened the door, Polly was stunned by the likeness to her younger self: She'd paid quick visits since coming back from India, but this time she wasn't in such a rush.

'Nicola! Oh Nicola!' They hugged.

'Sis!' A shout from upstairs. Polly always expected Vic to come sliding down the banister, but instead he was running downstairs two at a time, jumping the bottom four: '…don't stand there gawping.'

Polly flung herself into her brother's arms.

'Where've you been all my life? NINA!' Vic bellowed towards the garden. 'I'll tell Mum that Auntie's here,' said Nicola, and ran outside.

'Yes, I'm here!' said Polly, almost crying. It was so good being welcomed by her family. 'I feel…'

'Oh, never mind all that now. Come and sit in the kitchen. Or do you want to go straight down the garden?

'Let's do chickens.' Middle-aged Polly was giggling again like a teenager. 'Are there eggs?'

'We never know, do we – until we open the mystery box,' Victor teased. He'd never fallen in love with the birds as had Polly. 'Funny old Pol's back!'

'Shut up.' They walked into the garden enjoying being together.

Nina and Nicola were inside the chicken run talking away and scattering grit. Coco bounded from the bushes to Vic and jumped up. Polly watched amused. *Vic and Coco?* She spied a garden seat and pulled her brother towards it. 'Sit down a min.'

'What's all this?' Vic asked, reluctantly sitting down.

'I don't know how to start.'

'You sure?' Polly slapped him on the shoulder. 'You can't take me seriously can you?'

'Life's too short,' said Vic, 'enjoy it.'

'I've had a sort of Pilgrim's Progress experience in reverse!'

'You still talk gobble de gook then!'

'I'm sorting myself out.' She said crossly. 'You know when Pilgrim's burden fell…?'

'Polly! NO!'

'The main thing is, I suppose, I've left MUT. I rang Croften and he wasn't surprised.'

'Well, that's a relief anyway! Great!' He jumped up.

She gave up trying to explain the massive change in her outlook since her study, but her carefully prepared speech was not going to work. She saw things from Vic's point of view. *He thinks I'm still trying to convert him.*

She realised she wasn't really making sense to him and he would never grasp her meaning, but she still wanted to try.

'Come on, Sis, come on.'

Polly could see Nina knew she needed time with Vic, and pulled him back:

'I've got to tell you I've changed.' Vic was embarrassed. God was a mystery to him belonging in that fairy-tale box somewhere deep in his brain. He said in a flat, questioning sort of way:

'God's voice… where exactly did it come from?' He was trying hard but impatience was his middle name.

'Oh, I don't know.' Polly couldn't think.

Vic cheered up. 'I see, see, see!' He hastily moved on. 'Eggs?' Polly felt a failure. *Nina will listen.*

They crossed the grass.

Nicola looked up: 'Guess what's in the nesting box!' she called, '*CHICKS!*' Polly was transported back to old times. 'Come and see Aunty Polly,' said Nicola delighted with her new discovery.

*

Polly had one of the best evenings ever because it was unrushed and she managed to talk properly to Nina when they were washing-up. Vic and Nicola were watching a film.

'Enjoy your chat with Vic?' Nina threw Polly an amused look. Polly was wiping up.

'He's hopeless unless he's teasing me or discussing things like mending the car or… well… football, of course.'

'No, he doesn't do personal, whether it's me, him, or other.' She paused. 'Although he is concerned about Nicola on occasion. But I've realised since I married Vic, we two have hardly talked properly.'

'No, I suppose not. All this time I've been wanting to ask you if Darren and Dot told you anything about my valedictory service before I went to India?'

'Not much. They said it was odd. Nothing like a normal church service.'

'Not at all. I was a bit taken back seeing them there, you know. But Darren already had an idea of what was going on. That's why he gave me up.'

'Yes, I know that much. But he could never understand why you took it all so seriously.'

Polly sighed. 'I was devastated to lose him.'

'But you couldn't possibly expect him to go to your extremes.'

'I thought I could persuade him.'

Nina shook her head. 'Polly!'

'I know.' She paused. 'I was wrong. I see that now and don't blame him. Thinking back, I must have been such a killjoy and of course I couldn't change his views. But I… I've changed.'

'How?'

'From the first day Beth introduced me to—'

'Oh! Beth! What's happened to her?' It was impossible to keep to the task with so little news having passed between them for so long.

'She married Flynn Matthews, who worked his way up in the bank to a highly-paid position and…'

'She moved from Halebridge…'

'Yes, settled in Ireland and live a life of luxury.'

'Still religious?'

'Well, yes – in a way – although it's all "Flynn says this and that," and to be honest, I can't really go along with their… well… somehow it all seems superficial. Their whole approach to religion is at odds with mine. I thought Jesus taught that we should give away our riches, and trust Him to provide.'

'Do you still think that?'

'I suppose I don't.' Polly paused. 'I haven't really thought everything through since I've changed my view of the Bible. It's such a relief to lose the burden of hell waiting there to burn us all up. I can't think why…' She gave up trying to explain. 'Anyway, after all the support they gave me in the first place, they've more or less cut me off completely for staying with Anthony.'

'Because he's homo?'

'Unfortunately, yes. They can't get over the verse in the Bible that declares homosexuality an abomination.'

'They do get stuck on certain specific points, don't they?' Nina asked. 'It's strange to me how they can believe that sort of thing.'

'It sort of jars with... real life doesn't it? The other thing is they say they *love* the Indians, who they've never met... but they *hate* the Roman Catholics who are their neighbours. How does that make sense?'

'Easier of course. Easy to say you love people you don't know.'

'But delusional.' Polly realised she'd hardly started to explain her recent eureka moment. *Silly, it doesn't make sense when I try and talk about it.*

'I just want you to know – I've changed, Nina. And...'

Vic was calling from the sitting room: 'Come and sit down you two! We can do that in the morning.'

Nina gave Polly a resigned grin. 'Plenty of time to catch up properly now!' They chatted eagerly as they went to the sitting room.

'Shusssh!' uttered Nicola. They looked at her, laughed and obediently settled comfortably in front of the television.

Polly felt happy. *Patience. Let it go. At least I can go along with the way my family wants to do things now.*

Next morning, spurred on by Vic's singing at the top of his voice as he shaved, she got up early and joined Nina laying the table for breakfast.

'Anthony went home to see his doctor, and I think it might be serious so I'm getting worried. I'd rather go home fairly soon.'

'Any idea what's wrong?'

'I've got a horrible suspicion… but early days. I really don't know.' They had breakfast together. Nina asked no more questions.

'Take a couple of sandwiches for the journey,' she said after they'd cleared away.'

'Thanks.' Polly took the bread and butter out of the fridge and found a knife. 'I'll go after the rush hour and face up to things.'

'It's frustrating not knowing, but you're probably thinking the worst,' said Nina.

'I suppose so. I'm good at extremes!'

'Don't jump to conclusions. And promise us you'll stay longer next time.'

'Piers will be worried too. Not that I'll be very calm either.'

'Let us know, won't you?'

'I will.'

Nina touched Polly's arm. 'We're family,' she stressed. 'We're in it together.'

For the first time in years, Polly didn't feel she had to manage alone, and deeply appreciated unqualified support.

*

Piers carried Polly's case over to the car at Guernsey Airport. She stooped to rub Tiff whose tail was doing its usual exercise. 'You glad to see me back?' She addressed the dog avoiding Piers' face. He was unusually quiet. Polly dreaded the news. As soon as they got in the car she asked the dreaded question.

'What did the doctor say?'

Piers hesitated and sighed: 'He had the scan.'

'How long have we got to wait?'

Piers seemed to be in a vacuum. 'I was hoping it was a problem they could sort out…' Polly put her hand on his knee, heart in stomach.

'Piers,' said Polly quietly, 'what… is it?' He slapped the steering wheel hard.

'My – poor – Tony.' He shook his head in disbelief. 'It's the brain.'

'Cancer?' asked Polly incredulously.

'Tumour. But they'd said there was no need to worry.' Piers narrowly missed a cyclist. 'He knew he should have seen the doctor sooner but refused. Now it's too late. It's an *aggressive* – brain tumour.'

'Here, let me drive,' said Polly as he drew into the kerb weeping.

'That's the first time I've said it.' Piers didn't argue, but got out of the driver's seat.

'Let's go to the beach for a few minutes.' She sat at the steering wheel hardly aware of what she was doing herself, feeling devastated but needing to prepare herself to meet Anthony at home. Piers was in pieces. *How long is it since Simon died? Poor thing. What is in store for Anthony?*

Piers, not caring where they went, watched glumly as she drew up in a quiet spot with an expansive view of the sea. Feeling numb, she opened the windows. The only sounds were the breaking waves and Tiffany's panting. A seagull screamed. Another answered.

'I don't know what to do.' He bashed his head with the heel of his hand, and between sobs he floundered. 'Polly! Polly, what can we do? They say – not long.'

Polly knew that certain brain tumours could develop rapidly: 'Headaches?'

Piers nodded, 'Not all the time.'

They sat together, Polly fighting back her shock, and Piers taking deep breaths trying to control himself.

'Tony's waiting for us at home. We shouldn't be too long.'

'How's he taken it?'

'Stunned. But he's trying to focus on feeling better.' Tiffany wanted to get to beach and was making hints in her own inimitable way, nudging them and whining.

'Not now, girl,' said Piers absent-mindedly patting her head. 'She can't understand why we don't go for a walk.'

'Why don't you take Tiffany, and I'll drive back and see Anthony.' Piers brightened, 'Maybe I will.' He turned to the dog: 'You win.' To Polly he said, 'We'll walk home.'

Polly took her time preparing to face Anthony, and puffed out her cheeks. 'Phew.' *Just me and Anthony then*. Wrapped up in her bewilderment, she started the engine and drove off, fighting to concentrate.

Once home she sorted her things and took a while clearing up the kitchen before going down the garden. Anthony was sitting right next to the chicken run. He looked up as she approached and smiled weakly. 'I think Whitey is b-broody.'

'How long has she been sitting?'

'I d-don't know, but she's hardly c-come out of the box for three d-days.' The others were scratching away contentedly.

'D'you want a drink?' asked Polly, desperately. Conversation was not spontaneous.

'N-not really, thanks… You h-have one though.'

'I think I will.'

She made a mug of tea and carried it back into the garden, dragging a metal chair over close to Anthony.

She sniffed. *They need cleaning out*. They sat in silence. After a while Anthony said:

'D-do you think Whitey would s-sit on my lap?'

'She's very tame, so we could try,' she went to the nesting box and carefully lifted the resting hen controlling her wings. Anthony put out his arms to take her. The project was successful. Whitey settled and Anthony gently stroked her. Polly picked up her mug from the grass. The time passed.

'P-piers told you then?' Anthony still gazed at Whitey.

'Yes…'

They both kept their thoughts to themselves for several minutes. Then without warning, Tiffany came bounding down the garden. Whitey struggled, flapped her wings, and rushed off to hide in the shrubs dodging in and out to find the safest place. Anthony laughed remembering Uncle Henry and the bench: 'Last t-time it was Archibald. At least my ch-chair hasn't c-collapsed,' he managed to jest.

'Tiff!' Polly felt a little release in a weak laugh. 'Just see what you've done! Here girl!' She slapped her thigh to encourage the dog away from Whitey. *Dogs know their priorities.*

Piers came running from the back door surprised to hear laughter… 'What's she done now?'

'Grab hold of her!' Polly called and slowly walked towards the hen's refuge. Anthony went to the other side of a shrub with arms outstretched.

It was good to see Anthony could still move easily, and, as she said later, 'come back to life.' They were all aware that now was a time to treasure. Piers breathed a sigh of relief. *Anthony can still laugh then. Poor dear Tony.*

*

For the next two days Polly avoided the subject of Anthony's illness. She gauged Anthony would speak when he was ready. Then on the third day all three were sitting at breakfast.

'I expect you know s-something about the w-way things are likely t-to be for me, P-Pol. I've been t-told that after a while I might h-have mental problems… b-but I might not.'

'Everyone's different,' Polly said.

'I know. B-but I want to be prepared and for Piers.' He looked sadly at his soul mate.

'I want t-to do as much as I c-can while I c-can. I've decided who I want to s-see and what I want to d-do.'

Piers was following Anthony's lead and glad to be practical.

'What can we do?'

'Anything, just say,' added Polly.

'I want to see Uncle Henry. I feel g-guilty about almost ignoring him after entering the m-monastery… he and Gus, I've not even t-told them properly about this p-place. I m-must invite Henry over here. We used to be close. W-ell. H-he was good t-to me.' He grinned. 'That bench c-collapsing! It helped us for a m-moment after Mother died, and I knew he was m-missing F-father.

'I remember your Uncle Henry,' said Polly, 'he was quite jolly.'

'B-but he was always t-telling me to "be a m-man". He h-helped with practical things, but h-he made me f-feel inadequate, although I h-had no idea why. Maybe it was b-better that F-father…' Piers interrupted gently.

'No need to go into ifs and buts, Tony, chook. What can we do?'

'I want to t-talk to him about all that, now I understand myself.'

He addressed Piers: 'You've h-helped me understand hugely.' Turning to Polly he said, 'Writing to you all those years h-helped me too.'

'But would Henry listen?' asked Piers. 'There are people who never understand. They don't bloody well want to.' Polly was surprised. It was unlike Piers, who was usually respectful. *He's distraught*.

'Is there anyone else you'd like to talk to?' she asked.

'There's M-Mags! I can't forget the s-state she was in when we first met, and I want to h-help her learn to read and write! It's something I feel I really want to do.'

'Mags,' said Polly, 'I'd love to meet her one day.'

'And I wonder if Barbara would be willing to help? Even come and visit; or whether she would feel that's a step too far? Although we do have a personal link – through The Elms.'

A week later two letters arrived for Anthony. The first from Barbara.

c/o The Shorewell News *Office. August 18th 1985.*
Dear Anthony,
I can't tell you how sorry I am to hear your news. What a devastating blow for you.
Yes, I would be delighted to visit you next month.
Is there anything I can bring from England? Please let me know if there is anything at all I can do, and when is the best

time to come? A weekend would suit best, if possible.
   Yours very sincerely
        Barbara

The second was a complete contrast. It was not from Uncle Henry but from his wayward son, Gus.

Bromley, Sunday
  Hi Anthony!
  Dad's ill, so I'll come.
  See you next week.
  Gus

Anthony sat down with a slump. Polly was the other side of the kitchen table,

'Good news? Are they coming?'

'Yes – but...'

'Oh?'

'Barbara will come when c-convenient with us, next month. But H-Henry – Gus has written bluntly s-saying Uncle's ill. So, my c-cousin is c-coming next week. Typical. *H-his* agenda.'

Piers came downstairs and sat next to Anthony.

'G-Gus!' said Anthony. 'Gus.'

'Who's Gus?'

'My c-cousin. Older than me, H-henry's son. We were thrown together to play as boys. He t-taunted me about being an altar-boy and scared me with all sorts of stories. Then he joined a gang who terrified the elderly. I lost touch.'

'Perhaps he's changed by now,' Polly suggested.

'Henry heard he was into drugs and had fallen back on crime to feed his habit.'

'That's bad news. I wonder what he's doing now?'

'We'll soon find out.' They passed the letters round the table.

'I'll be working most of the week,' she said.

'I h-hope he's c-calmed down,' said Anthony, 'I'm not f-feeling like d-dealing with aggression – the s-scorning sort. I-I wish Uncle H-Henry could come. I can't f-face G-Gus.' The long speech tired him. He closed his eyes.

Piers put his arm round Anthony's shoulders. 'We'll cope. He'll be different from the character you knew. He could be seventy by now if he's older than you.'

*

'A-hoy there, Ant!'

Polly was at work. Anthony and Piers were in their favourite garden chairs. Jolted from contemplation by the loud voice, they saw the culprit using a stick to limp towards them. He halted at a bench half-way down the garden then eased himself down.

'Hello, old boy! Or is that a mistake?' He guffawed at his unfunny joke, then weighed up Piers. 'You must be the "partner",' he said with heavy emphasis. Anthony groaned inwardly, but uncowed, drew back his shoulders and was ready to defend himself:

'What d-do you mean by that, G-Gus?'

'Yer, yer, suppose we have to keep up with the times,' Gus retorted. 'Doesn't seem as though either of us are quite the energetic rebels we used to be.' His chuckle dropped a pitch.

'It was quiet until you t-turned up,' said Anthony. *I'm weak in body... but* He drew back his shoulders again *strong in spirit.* He assessed the intruder silently.

Piers disliked Gus more by the minute, but moved to sit beside him. Before he could open his mouth, Gus laughed again.

'It's not going to collapse, by any chance?' Anthony, moving to a chair opposite, threw Piers a wry smile. He tried again:

'Listen G-Gus, we didn't expect you t-today, but now you are h-here, please c-calm down.' Gus was surprised, but didn't change his tone.

'Still afraid of that thing called fun, Ant?' Anthony closed his eyes, visions of the tryptic he'd imagined with all the ants came flooding into his mind.

Piers was furious. He raised his voice: 'Gustavus. If you carry on like this you won't get as far as the kitchen.'

'Got a drink?' was the response. In a more subdued tone, he addressed his cousin.

'You seem a tad seedy, and there's no need to be afraid of me.' Anthony opened his eyes.

'Afraid?' He shook his head slowly. 'I-I might be s-seedy because I haven't long to live. But I'm h-happy and wouldn't c-change anything. Y-you're the unhappy one, G-Gus.' He stood up and beckoned Gus towards the house. 'C-come on.' Gus got up with effort and followed meekly through the back door.

'Nice place you've got here.' Anthony ignored the remark and sat at the table summing up his cousin: 'G-Gus, I'm ill, but c-content, and so is P-Piers. T-take us as we are or s-stay elsewhere. What will you d-do?' He stared Gus in the eyes and waited. Gus looked away and went quiet. Silence. Eventually Anthony, easily in charge, questioned, 'W-well?' Gus stared out of the window.

'You've changed.'

'S-so?' Anthony asked. He moved towards the telephone. 'Shall I ring a h-hotel for you?'

'At least give me a beer.'

'No, G-Gus.' He picked up the receiver.

'Dad's nurse asked me to come.'

'Unlike you, your f-father s-supported me.'

'Sorry, mate.' Gus shuffled uncomfortably. 'Where shall I put this damned awkward thing?' His stick wouldn't hook on the table.

Anthony put the receiver back and rested the stick in a corner: 'No alcohol before 6 p.m. in this house. Tea, c-coffee or water?'

It transpired that Uncle Henry was in his late eighties and had suffered a stroke which had affected both mind and body. He had no idea he was in a residential home.

'I did go rather wild,' Gus said. 'Gave the cops a run for their money!' He'd never held a job or marriage. Had three children by different partners but never been a dad to them. Now he had his failing body to live with. 'You never expect this to happen,' he said, examining himself.

They managed to have a reasonable conversation for a while.

'Nobody t-told me Uncle was c-confused. B-but I w-want him to know—'

'I don't do sentimental stuff,' interrupted Gus. Piers joined them.

'You rest,' he said to Tony. Then, with effort, to their visitor, 'I'll show you your room.' He picked up the tea and went to the door. Gus stood and as Anthony handed him his stick he said bitterly, 'You can want all you like, but Dad'll never get the hang.'

*

It was hard work hosting Gustavus. For Anthony because he was always aware of the way his cousin treated him in the past; for Piers who tried to ignore the quips and lapses into rudeness; and for Polly because of his suggestive attitude towards her. She hid their alcohol from Gus, but helped herself rather abundantly.

At last Gus's flight was due and Anthony, who had found it impossible to talk about anything serious with him, wrote a letter to Uncle Henry.

'P-please give this to your F-father's nurse. Put it in your j-jacket p-pocket so you don't forget.' He made a note of the address and phone number of the residential home. *I'll get through to him one way or another.*

'Thanks for the holiday... I'll recommend this place,' quipped Gus painfully edging towards departures.

'Don't f-forget my letter,' called Anthony with as much strength as he could muster.

Gus gestured towards his pocket, grinned, and waved. Then a sudden recollection. Shifting his weight to a baggage trolley he turned: 'Oh. Forgot to tell you your so-called art earnt me a pretty penny.' He reverted to his gloating-bully-face: 'The punters fair fell over themselves for the proper stuff. Thanks a bunch!' Turning his back on the threesome he let out a manic laugh.

Polly and Piers instantly supported Anthony as he paled and weakened. They ushered him to a seat. In not much more than a whisper he said:

'My Canaletto. My artwork.' And passed out.

CHAPTER 36

Piers spotted a business-like woman coming through Arrivals walking brusquely in his direction and went forward to meet her.

'No trouble spotting you with the dog!' she said. Introductions over, Barbara started asking questions:

'I *thought* there was something wrong. What's the situation with Anthony? Serious?' Piers caught his breath. *Must protect Tony.*

By the time they reached the house she knew almost as much as Piers about Anthony's condition.

'You never know how a brain tumour is going to affect a person, do you?'

'No…we're…'

'I'm just taken by surprise. So shocking. The Arches People and the church and everyone who knew him, especially Father Dominic and Reggie…' She spoke like a steam engine puffing out smoke. Piers opened the front door and interrupted the flow:

'Let's go upstairs first and then you can find your way to the kitchen. Take it slowly with him… if you can.' He tried to lighten the atmosphere. 'Anthony thought you might like a coastal walk if the weather holds. Make the most of Guernsey while you're here!' Piers made his way downstairs. 'No hurry!' he called out.

'I'll freshen up.' *I suppose I'm a bit wound up. Relax. Now Barbara, concentrate.* She sat on the bed and breathed in for a slow count of six then opened her mouth and exhaled for a count of eight. *Slow breath out: pheeeewwww… slacken jaw, slide shoulders blades down.*

By next day she felt more at home. 'You two are such good company,' she said as they sat on the patio outside the living room. 'I could do with a month of this. No dashing around. The beach, the island, your home, it's all quiet, unrushed.'

'It was for us, until Tony…' Piers broke off, sighed, and changed tack. 'But now we've got to make the most of every moment.' He threw Tony an encouraging grin.

'There are things I'd like to do and enjoy, but I doubt I'll achieve many now.' Anthony lapsed into a reverie.

'Such as?' asked Barbara.

'I'll get drinks,' suggested Piers. 'Iced homemade lemonade? Mint?' They all agreed.

Anthony was contemplating the sky. 'G-going back to S-Spain to look round the D-Dali exhibition again.'

'Let's think about that.' She became hesitant spacing her words more carefully: 'When you wrote, was there anything particular you… had in mind?'

'Y…yes,' said Anthony. 'Although I-I'll understand if it's t-too much to ask.'

'I won't know till you tell me.' She leaned forward but, remembering to take things slowly, sat back a little. 'Sorry. No hurry.'

'I k-keep thinking about M-Mags.'

'Yes?' Barbara waited. 'Extraordinary girl.'

'You know how she loved my M-missal just because it was a b-book; but she also appreciated the India p-paper.'

'And did you know she picked up the guitar and within five minutes was picking out the tune to Max's song?'

Anthony smiled. 'Yes, that g-girl has so much p-potential. It's wonderful she has a roof over her h-head now. That's a s-start.'

Barbara readily agreed, thinking overtime, but trying to hold back.

'I want to h-help her read and write. M-more than that, to have opportunities other young p-people have.'

'What can I do though?'

'I-I'm leaving her m-money and, if you don't m-mind my asking, p-please can you p-point her in the right d-direction, after I've gone?'

Barbara was stunned. 'Of course! I do know people, but I never had children – *we* had no children.' *What news can I get out of this? There's another story here. See what Michael thinks.*

'Yes! Yes, of course.'

'W-will you? C-could you?' They heard Polly come through the front door.

'Ah! That's Polly. Do you think you'll recognise her?' Piers asked Barbara as he put the drinks down.

'Hmmm. She was only a child.'

Barbara thought many years back to the West's home. 'I'm not sure she liked me much.'

Polly was in outdated mufti when she came to join them, but still had work on her mind. She raised her glass round the group.

'We were *so* busy. It's hard when you can't give the patients the time they need. Need fortification now!' She downed a whisky. 'Oooh, that's better!' Then in the same breath, 'Hello, Barbara, you made it then.' She poured another glass.

Barbara raised her eyebrows, noticing Polly's method of drowning out work. This time she managed to keep her doubts to herself.

'Hi! How many years is it?' For once Anthony intervened:

'Go get a c-cup of tea now, Pol,' he said gently… 'or water.'

*

'I'm sure I can help Mags,' Barbara said, on her last evening after supper. The four of them were relaxing in easy chairs after a sunny day out. Anthony smiled.

'Thank you. Thank you very much. C-can we t-talk again on the phone?'

Barbara became suddenly animated.

'There might be wedding bells fairly soon, by the way.'

'Max?' they questioned with one voice.

'Yes, Max and Mags.'

Polly and Piers asked for more detail while Anthony sat quietly listening. Barbara then turned to him:

'That business of your going to Spain. Why do you think you won't be able to go?' Polly was suspicious. *Why is she so keen?*

'I suppose it would just take too much energy,' said Piers. 'We wouldn't feel we could risk it.'

Polly reached out to Anthony. 'You get around alright, but you get exhausted easily, don't you?'

'I rang Michael,' Barbara said. They wondered what was coming. 'You know how our readers have followed the Arches news over the years?' They agreed, curious.

'We think they'd like news of you, and – it's a big *if* – but if you were willing, we would like to offer a small support team to escort you and help with the admin and so on. I'd come myself, of course, and write up your journey. The team would be delighted to do it.'

'Ummm. That's s-sounds attractive. B… b-but I don't know,' said Anthony. He was apprehensive. They all considered the idea which seemed complicated.

Piers frowned: 'I don't know either…' He squinted doubtfully at Barbara and then at Polly who was staring at Barbara. 'We'll have to talk it over… But thanks for the thought.' He was still frowning.

'Yes,' said Polly thoughtfully but made no further contribution.

'B-but thank you.' Anthony was hopeful.

'Who's Michael?' asked Polly thinking back to Barbara's frequent references to him on their walk. Barbara looked sheepishly at the floor before replying with scant detail.

'My boss.' Her red cheeks gave her away. *Polly's guessed. Damn and blast.*

Polly broke the awkwardness by saying her goodbyes.

'I've got an early start tomorrow, so I'll turn in now.' She went over to Barbara and kissed her. 'I'll say goodbye. I might be gone before you get up.'

Barbara smiled weakly. 'Don't overdo things, Polly.' At breakfast, she remarked, 'I still have a feeling Polly doesn't like me.'

'She's a very principled person and doesn't often take a dislike to anyone,' Piers reassured her. 'She needs time and space to adjust to…' He gave Tony a questioning stare.

'L-life,' Anthony said. 'A d-different s-sort of life.'
'As an alcoholic?' asked Barbara and immediately berated herself.

CHAPTER 37

'What a relief,' Polly commented as she felt his grip relax. Piers was wringing out a flannel. Anthony's breathing was no longer laboured. The Nurse examined the syringe driver.

'It'll need renewing in a couple of hours. His breathing is still noisy but don't worry, he's comfortable. Can I get you anything?' They shook their heads, sadly gazing at their dear friend.

'No thanks.'

'How about going home tonight and swapping with me in the morning, Pol?' asked Piers. *So tired*. For six months they had seen Anthony deteriorate horribly, at home most of the time and unable to talk coherently for a month. They'd coped with violent outbursts and restless episodes when he kept throwing the bedclothes off, pulling out his drip and trying to get out of bed. To see him like this now was an enormous relief. Meanwhile they'd had the dreadful experience of losing Tiffany to heart disease; still too sad to talk about.

She poured a drink as soon as she got home, and phoned Vic.

'Polly!' The voice was uncharacteristically downbeat. 'What's the latest?'

'It's been gruelling, Vic. I'm so upset. He changed. We lost our dear Anthony a few weeks ago, but at last he is more relaxed.' She couldn't hold back the tears.

'I'll get Nina.'

'Polly! We were wondering about you.' Polly could hear her sympathy.

'I'm sorry, Nina.' She gasped through the sobs. 'I wanted to ring and tell you – he's peaceful at last. I don't think he's got much longer… His local priest visited and administered the last rites this morning.'

Nina sympathised and tried to be positive. 'Did he get things done?'

Thinking of happier times helped Polly pull herself together. 'Mostly, thank God.' She hesitated as she noticed what she had just said.

Nina ignored it. 'Spain?'

'Yes, with loads of help. Barbara organised it. I can't bring myself to like her. I think she was more interested in publicity for her precious paper than anything else. But Anthony achieved his goal.'

'He enjoyed revisiting Dali?'

'Mixed feelings, I think.'

'Mixed?'

'It reminded him of his own early paintings. When he was obsessed with the disjointed body. As a young boy he felt disassociated in himself and for him Dali expressed how he felt. He'd longed to see his old work but he couldn't. I'll explain another time.'

'Poor Anthony. It must have been awful to go through all that.'

'Yes, but he had the satisfaction of knowing he had come to terms with himself. I can't really understand what it meant. It's all quite outside my experience.'

'Oh… no… of course.' Nina let Polly get things off her chest.

'Then there was the Catholic side of things – he bought a replica of Dali's "Christ of St John of the Cross" and hung it in the hall here, in a similar position to the crucifix at The Elms. I think he saw Christ without thorns and nails and applied the symbolism to himself.' Polly puffed out her cheeks, exhaling loudly.

'It must have meant something special for him to hang it in the hall.'

'Yes, it's nothing like the traditional crucifixion picture. Light shines down on Christ from above, the cross is suspended above a touch of brightness, and somehow Dali gives the dreadful scene a beauty.'

'If it hadn't been for Barbara he wouldn't have found that.'

'True, but she made the most of it in an article she wrote afterwards.' Polly was torn.

'But why not? I guess it's a win-win situation.'

'She's a typical journalist. Very pushy. Grrrr…'

'But that's her job.'

'They sometimes forget they're writing about real people though.' *Change the subject.* 'How's Nicola?'

They talked about family things for twenty minutes, and Polly felt better after Nina invited her to stay with them for a few days later in the month.

A few days later Piers and Polly were warned Anthony could die at any time, Polly wondered about telling Gus.

'Do we have to? Would Anthony want him barging in at this point?'

'No, but he *is* family, and poor Henry has lost his memory completely. He can't use the 'phone.'

A decision wasn't made because Anthony's breathing changed to a gasp every now and then. Piers held his hand. 'I'm here, chook. I'm here, my love. And I'll be with you again one day. See you there, Tony.' His tears were flowing, shoulders rising and falling as Anthony gasped his last few shallow breaths.

Polly's hand rested on Piers as she fought to keep her emotions in check, trying to be strong for him.

'I'll never stop loving you, Tony. Not ever.'

How wonderful to have a love like theirs. Polly yearned for a love she had never had.

All was quiet, still, white, and empty. Just Piers' sobs. Polly passed him more tissues, until eventually he eased himself from Anthony. 'First Simon, now Tony.' Both crying together. They rang the bell. The nurse put her hand in front of Anthony's month, felt for a pulse, put a stethoscope to his heart.

'I'll tell the doctor,' she said gently. 'You take your time.'

They sat by Anthony for half an hour as it got dark. The air was still. The curtains gently and briefly fluttered. Polly gazed out of the open window. 'Some nurses think that it is the spirit leaving the room. It's full moon,' she said looking upwards. 'Thank God he's at rest.'

'With God?' picked up Piers. 'Do you think he's with God?'

'We won't know till we find out for ourselves, will we?' Polly replied. 'But we *do* know he isn't suffering.'

'I want to be with him again,' said Piers.

'And Simon?' asked Polly, immediately condemning her own stupidity at such a sensitive time. Piers turned away.

'Sorry, Piers. I'm such an ass.'

'Polly!' he said wearily. They held hands as they were led into a quiet room where a nurse brought them a drink, and Piers repeated and repeated his lover's name.

'What shall I do now, Pol?'

But Polly remained silent. *What do I think happens to the soul now?*

*

'There's so much to do, and I don't want to do any of it,' said Piers, after they'd been given the paperwork and collected the belongings the next day.

'It is one thing to tell patients' relatives what to do, and a different matter to have to do it yourself,' agreed Polly.

'Let's go outside. We could do food, water and eggs – then talk.' Polly brought drinks to the table. The place felt empty.

'He's not coming back,' Piers told the chickens as he scattered the feed. 'You'll have to make do with us.'

This bought a wan smile to Polly's lips. 'You're one of us now, Piers.'

They sat quietly.

'The last thing Tony said before his mind blurred was: "Bury me amongst the needy in London."' Piers continued between sobs. 'He never needed for worldly goods, but he was truly needy for love until we met. And needy for purpose, until Mags bumped into him. That morning, when he said, "God bless you my child", he had no idea what it would mean to her. It seems God was involved in a mysterious way. Her life started to change fundamentally from that moment.'

'Yes, I suppose it does seem a bit like that, but couldn't it be coincidence?' She mulled over her recent thoughts but let the matter rest. *Maybe there is an omniscient mind out there.*

'He wanted Father Dominic to bury him because he accepted him as he was. He never tried to get him to change in any way.'

Polly reached out to hug Piers. 'What shall we do first? Shall I contact Father Dominic?'

'Let's ask him to arrange the whole service. He probably knows better than I do the sort of music Anthony would like.'

Polly brightened up. 'Good idea. It would be a relief to have that load off our shoulders, and having the funeral in London would be easier for everyone… except us.'

'Yes, except us. He didn't know many people here. Just having a plan helps.'

CHAPTER 38

'Thank you for leading such a comforting service.' Piers was talking to Father Dominic as they talked in the hall after Anthony's funeral. 'Tony would have appreciated that.'

'He was a special person.'

'Yes. Not many people really *knew* him.'

'I've never met anyone so humble, so sincere, as he,' Dominic replied.

Polly joined them, putting her arm though Father Dominic's whilst balancing a plate of food in the other. 'This is *just* what Anthony would have wanted. To be surrounded by people who understand what it means to get on with life bravely however unfair it seems.'

'I need to take over where he left off,' mused Piers, much to the surprise of Polly and Dominic. He scanned the mixed assembly: homeless people of every age and type, clergy, Salvation Army, monks, journalists, family members too – Gus, Vic and Nina were all there. Barbara's colleagues, Michael and Penny were talking to Reginald, Mags, Max, even Maisie and her sister. Everyone was chatting. All because of Anthony. Even though the occasion was sad there were occasional outbursts of laughter. Gus was engaged in conversation with an older over-demonstrative woman wearing chunky jewellery.

Father Dominic regarded Piers keenly: 'Yes?' he questioned closely. 'Are you sure?'

Piers was thoughtful. 'I might just do it. Tony would like that – and I think I would too.'

Polly was stunned. 'You've always thought of this as Anthony's job,' she said. *Are you leaving me? Alone?* But she was agitated. *We've been here long enough. Time to go to the pub and have a stiff drink.*

'What are your plans for this evening, Pol?' asked Vic, coming over with Nina.

'Oh, I don't know. There's not much to do now. I'll have a quiet pub drink I suppose. Don't know what Piers has planned.'

'Let's take you out for a meal around the corner.'

'Come to supper with us this evening,' said Father Dominic to Piers.

Piers checked with Polly who smiled back, 'Vic and Nina just asked me the same thing.'

Piers and Polly had reserved hotel rooms for three nights. 'Meet back to the hotel?' She put aside her urge to escape and started collecting plates. 'But we should help clear up first.'

Barbara and Michael came over to say goodbye. 'What a service!' said Barbara. 'I can't explain what I felt.' She was holding Michael's hand, but Polly noticed he looked uncomfortable.

'I should get back,' he said. 'Family duties!' Barbara's smile faded. 'Bye.' He pulled his hand away and dashed off leaving Barbara to her own devices.

'I'm going with Vic and Nina in a moment, said Polly. And Piers is eating with Father Dominic.'

'Join us!' Nina called over.

'Thanks!' Barbara gulped as she searched earnestly for her purse. 'Where do you live?' she whispered, her mind reeling.

*

'We couldn't have wished for a nicer service and wake, could we?' asked Polly when she and Piers met that evening in the hotel lobby.'

'Let's go to my room,' he suggested. 'I'm relieved it's all over. But it feels so final – and empty.' They walked upstairs to the second floor, it felt more open than the lift.

'I'm numb. Don't know what I feel but yes, it was good, really.'

'Father Dominic was so *exactly right* though.' Piers was thoughtful.

'He was. And all those Arches People, and volunteers too. I didn't realise so many people knew Anthony. Mags was quiet, but she's still adjusting to a totally different life. She's never lived in an immovable house!'

'That Barbara! She wants to attend the reading of the will.'

'Huh, she would. But she isn't invited. Let's not think about her now.'

They selected gins and tonics from the mini-fridge, and Piers sat on the bed whilst Polly slumped in the easy chair.

'Anthony used to keep himself to himself; but he was so interesting when he got going. He knew such a lot,' said Polly, taking in the boring picture on the wall.

'I admired him, the way he gained confidence while we were together.'

'That was because of you! I could see what you meant to him after I'd been at Belle View a while. I only knew him slightly from Elm Close days, and then from his letters.'

'He reminded me often of Simon. Simon was quiet and unsure of himself but didn't have a stutter. On occasion I forgot it was Tony I was with!'

Polly smiled. 'We used to write letters about faith – our different faiths. It kept me going at the time; thoughts of my own salvation, and a desire that everyone should believe *my* way. And Anthony was equally convinced I should believe *his* way.'

'Funny how so many people of different faiths are so sure they *know*.'

'Well, obviously people like to think they are right. But did I tell you about his dream?'

'Which one was that?' Piers smiled. 'We had some very unusual talks some mornings, wondering whatever his dreams meant! I never remember my dreams.'

Polly smiled weakly. 'Before he lost his reason he told me how Vincent had interpreted a dream in which he and I cared for different breeds of chickens separated by our garden wall. Vincent saw that one day we would find the wall had disappeared. Our differences wouldn't matter any longer because we'd realise that basically we were both doing the same thing. It would be alright.' Then he took my hand saying, 'We built our wall ourselves, didn't we? It's gone—'

The emotional toll of Anthony's death combined with emotive reminders of the struggle which in some ways continued within her, were too much for Polly. She couldn't continue.

Piers was in no fit state to console her. He managed a 'Shusssh' which was enough.

'What time did the solicitor say tomorrow?' asked Polly at last.

'Not until two o'clock.'

'I must go to bed,' said Polly, standing up unsteadily. 'See you at breakfast?' That night she dreamed she was surrounded by bottles of alcohol. All sorts, shapes and colours.

Barbara was at her shoulder: 'Which would you like next, Polly dear? Your choice. Your choice…'

*

At the appointed time Piers, Polly, Mags with Father Dominic, and Gus assembled for the reading of the will. The solicitor looked over the top of his glasses.

'Good afternoon everybody.' He opened a large folder. 'The last will and testament of Anthony David Wheeler.' After a lengthy preamble he came to the division of the estate:

Mr Piers LeTissier: 50% of the property named Belle Vue, Guernsey, together with pictures and art paraphernalia; plus £50,000.

Miss Polly West: 50% of Belle Vue, Guernsey, together with its goods and chattels; plus £50,000.

Miss Mags McGee: £20,000 to be spent on learning to read and write, and setting up a home.

Mr Gustavus Wheeler: To collect an item from a named carpenter (address supplied). To arrange delivery to Mr Henry Wheeler's nursing home, the costs of which are covered and £500.00 for expenses. The solicitor to ensure the task is completed. If satisfied, £5,000 will be entered in an account for upkeep of said item, plus expenses. If not, it will go to Father Dominic.

St Mark's Project for the Homeless under the direction of Father Dominic: All remaining monies.

This will be an unknown sum until tax and expenses are deducted, but I estimate it to be over £200,000.

The 'item' was to remain a mystery until Gus put the plan into action. As Henry had enough savings for his care and was not of firm mind, a bequest would mean nothing to him.

The solicitor scanned the company: 'Copies of this will and more detail can be obtained from my office.'

'Is that *it*?' asked Gus, red in the face and hardly able to talk.

'That is all that concerns you, sir.'

He studied his notes: 'It will take several months for the money to be released, but I will be in contact in due course.'

Polly and Piers glanced from Gus to the solicitor, to each other. Father Dominic studied his shoes. He too was a little red of face. Delighted. Mags turned to the priest. Completely out of her depth.

The door slammed and Polly jumped. Gus had gone. As he stormed out of the front door as fast as his limp allowed, a stranger intercepted him: '*Shorewell News*. Did Anthony leave you anything Mr Wheeler? Is the house yours?' She followed him to the corner of the street repeating her questions, but he said nothing.

Then turning the corner, he conceded, 'I'll ring you.'

He's not a happy man. Not happy at all. She saw her bus and ran for it. *Can't wait – I just can't wait.*

The rest of the group were chatting, preparing to leave. 'You've been a good friend to Anthony for many years, Polly,' said Father Dominic. 'And as for you, Mr LeTissier, Anthony told me you were his rock and stability.' He turned to Mags, 'I'll see you home, my dear.'

Piers had tears flooding down his cheeks again. 'End of an era, isn't it?' he spluttered. 'I'd love to take over where Anthony left off. It's the only thing that I want to do.'

Polly put her hand in his, studying his face. 'Anthony would *love* that'.

Dominic continued in measured tones: 'Life will be different for me too. The Lord gives, and the Lord takes away. But this time it seems that the Lord has taken away and given at the same time.' His expression conveyed the idea he was seeking the face of God. 'Given in abundance, I would say. We must be faithful stewards of His bountiful provision.' He clasped his hands together as though he was concluding a service, 'May Anthony's soul rest in peace, and God bless us all.' He made the sign of the cross over nothing in particular.

*

Hardly a word was exchanged on the journey back to *Belle Vue*. 'Anthony will never sit with us in the kitchen again,' Polly said, taking the top off the gin bottle. She raised the bottle towards Piers. 'You?' He answered in the negative and moved towards the kettle.

'I'll have a hot drink.' And without filling the kettle, he turned on the switch, sat down again. 'Anthony!' he said, under his breath.

'Water!' Polly dived for the kettle and grabbed it as it hissed and steamed. She gave Piers his mug, and felt better after quaffing her gin. After the second she was more talkative. 'Fancy, though, Piers. I felt so awkward about Gus. Quite a shock.'

'We haven't heard the end of that. Poor Tony couldn't forgive him for selling his work and beloved

Canaletto,' he replied. 'I think if he'd had longer to come to terms with it... I don't know.' He paused. Then, determined, 'I don't want to stay here. I must get out. I've got no Simon, no Anthony and no Tiffany.'

'Drink.' Polly knew he was distraught.

'Why don't you stay here, Pol?'

'What all by myself? I can't think. We're still dazed.'

She put her glass down. 'I needn't work!' she said, almost shouting. The sadness had temporarily passed; the drink was taking over.

Piers was staring at the door to the hallway.

'He's never going to come through that door, is he?' Polly followed his gaze.

'We're supposed to move on now, Piers. Move on.' Unsteadily, she put her arm round his shoulders. 'Sorry,' she said softly, 'I'm not sinking state.'

Piers linked her arm to support her. 'Fresh air?'

*

'Who did you say?' It was late and the office was empty apart from Barbara. It was a bad line and the caller sounded drunk. She pressed the receiver closer to her ear.

'Gus Wheeler here. W-H-E-E-L-E-R. You pestered me yesterday! So, for your information, I got nothing. NOTHING.'

'What do you mean? Who got the money?'

'Polly and Piers got the whole bloody lot.'

'I'm so sorry to hear that. Speak up please, Mr Wheeler. I saw Father Dominic there. Why was he there?'

'Absolutely zilch for me. *His cousin.* Bloody damned cousin. Only sane relative too.' He slammed the phone down.

'Mr Wheeler?' Barbara was frustrated and shouted into the mouthpiece. The line was dead. She picked up her pen. But her mind was still reeling from Michael's rebuttal. *Michael, I thought you loved me. I can't stop thinking about you. You made a public show of humiliating me. Now this. And Piers and Polly got all that money.* In a fit of pique, she typed furiously.

GAY PARTNER AND EX-MISSIONARY INHERIT
FORMER MONK'S ESTATE
Only Relative Fuming

An unconfirmed report indicates that the estate of Anthony Wheeler, ex-monk turned Arches Outreach Worker, includes nothing for his only surviving relative. It is understood he was very wealthy, owning a house in Guernsey inherited from his businessman uncle.

His gay partner has reportedly been left a considerable legacy, as has his ex-missionary friend.

Mr Gustavus Wheeler, his cousin, enraged, reported he has inherited nothing. Mr Henry Wheeler, an elderly and sick uncle is also bequeathed nothing, despite giving considerable help to Anthony Wheeler in the past.

Angrily, and ignoring usual protocol, she authorised printing.

CHAPTER 39

Seven months later Penny met Barbara for the first time since the *hullabaloo* caused by the article. It was sunny and they'd agreed to have sandwiches in the park. Penny was still offended by Barbara's behaviour. She frowned as they walked towards each other. There was no small talk.

'I thought we were meant to be friends and why on earth didn't you check the facts?' For once it was Penny speaking impulsively. Barbara took a sharp intake of breath but Penny continued. 'Whatever happened? Michael was so angry. He was beside himself.' They sat down on opposite sides of a picnic table. Barbara looked around more concerned about who was looking.

'You sure Michael won't see me?' She looked miserable.

'He's on holiday.'

'*So?*'

'But he threw me. Just like that.' She flicked her thumb and middle finger with a loud click.

'And that's your excuse? For letting us all down…ignoring my calls…' Barbara broke in, 'I just flipped. I was devastated, in a flat spin, upset. I had to get my own back at him.'

'You're blaming Michael then that you lost it. Didn't you even imagine the consequences?'

'Mmmm.'

'You were holding hands at the funeral?'

'Exactly. That was my big mistake. It made him realise he didn't want to be seen in public with me.'

'Aha,' Penny nodded. 'He left you, your world collapsed, you wrote that article, left him to sort out the mess and it's his fault.'

'You could put it that way… but I was shocked. He'd said, no, he'd *promised* me he'd leave his wife. Then Gus rang – angry about the will and—'

Penny saw the light. 'You were angry Anthony left you nothing too?'

Barbara's hackles were up. She said crossly and loudly: 'He did ask me to help him – which was a darned cheek.'

'Hmmm. But you wrote it all up. About the Dali exhibition and Anthony's choice of picture and the symbolism – those lovely pictures. That was lapped up. It was good for the paper. *Work*. Then your bombshell ruined the whole thing. It was devastating. And as for Michael, well, I warned you, didn't I?'

'I was so sure of him.'

'Be that as it may,' Penny was trying to calm down but kept going, 'you believed what Gus said even though the line was bad, he was angry and out to make trouble – probably drunk – or high.'

'He said those two got everything. I thought the story would sell.'

'But why trust him?'

'I know, I know. I got it all wrong and didn't check. I'm the angry one now, and damned miserable.'

'What's done can't be undone.' Penny had made her point and could tell Barbara was paying the price for her reckless behaviour.

'The times I've wished I'd kept control of myself.'

'You should have heard Michael effing and blinding when he had to deal with the spin-off, though. It damaged our reputation you know. Father Dominic was publicly embarrassed, and Mags doubted she was in the will for a while.'

'I was in such a state, I lost track of the truth. I still feel *terrible*. One thing's sorted though. I never want to see Michael again.'

'We found a temp to cover for you. She was fine. But I was hurt too. Your aunt just kept repeating you weren't available.'

'I'm not proud of myself. Sorry.'

'Father Dominic was diplomatic, and the Salvation Army tried to explain what they knew, puzzled why the *News* ignored the gift to the church. Mags is used to people lying. And in the end, she was probably the most helpful in smoothing the path ahead. Michael published a correction, of course, when he established the facts.'

'Don't tell me. I can't process it.' She threw her sandwiches to the birds.

'What are you going to do?' Penny was still miffed. She checked her watch and folded her paper bag. She offered Barbara a biscuit which she accepted.

'I've learnt my lesson.'

'Are you sure?' Barbara nodded.

'I won't forget this. When are you due back?'

'Half an hour.'

'Thanks for coming – I've got to get away.'

'A trip to the sun would do you good.'

'Yes, a budget package in Majorca, or Greece, maybe.'

Penny dropped her grudge. 'Find a nice man, who's free to be a proper partner!' She worried Barbara would over-react, but her fears were unfounded.

'At sixty-five?' She smiled wryly. 'Maybe I'm not quite past it…'

'Of course you're not!'

'In a few months. I'll have to find a job first. Must start earning again.'

They paused at the park gate. Barbara arched her eyebrows. 'Do you ever go back to Maisie's Cuppa?'

'Yes, with your "replacement". She isn't so much fun as you were. And Max is happy, but not so friendly as before. He's invited us to his church though! It's *their* church really now 'cos Mags goes too… and Reginald. The Pentecostal one. There are several Jamaicans in the congregation and they have welcomed them with open arms. Mags just loves the gospel singing.'

Barbara sighed. 'I never got round to helping Mags either.'

'Nope, that was the other thing. Father Dominic found a tutor for both Mags and Reggie. They still live with Max but family in Jamaica have sent Reggie money to move to his own place after the wedding.'

'*Wedding?* Have they set a date?'

'Apparently the invites are going out soon!'

'Works out all right for the chosen few, doesn't it?' Barbara pouted.

'You'll manage if you face up to facts and move on.'

'I should apologise to Father Dominic.'

'And Michael?'

'Couldn't possibly. He should be the one to be sorry.'

Penny bit her tongue. 'Your call.'

They parted. Barbara thought about visiting Father Dominic but switched to dreaming about a Greek-god boyfriend. That cheered her up, until she realised they didn't grow on trees.

CHAPTER 40

'Who's there?' Polly heard the front door of Belle Vue open and waited for Piers to find her.

'On the bottle again, then?' asked Piers, walking onto the patio into the watery sunshine. It was early spring but cloudy. Just about warm enough to sit outside.

Polly stood up and flung herself at him, giving him a hug.

'I didn't expect you! What a lovely surprise. You're looking good. How long can you stay?'

'I'm not going yet!' he joked.

'Of course not, I wouldn't let you. And it's lonely… this great big house with only Yolanda to talk to twice a week.'

'I'm never bored now. It's really helped me – thinking about other people's problems instead of my own. And Father Dominic is quite jolly when he's relaxing. In fact, he's interesting too. He's into art, mainly classical. And woodwork; he's got a little workshop outside his mother's old house. He's taken me there a few times. I love it.' Piers was far more talkative than before.

Polly saw him measuring up the almost empty bottle on the table. 'I'm still sober though!' she said, laughing loudly.

Piers said nothing.

'But I'll put the kettle on and have a cuppa with you if you like!'

'And the chooks?'

'They're fine. Omelettes for supper?'

'Then walk to the beach?'

'With next door's dog?'

'Don't remind me of Tiff. No,' Piers said sensitively.

Mistake. Again.

'Big Anthony gap, big Tiff empty space.' He slumped in a kitchen chair but pulled himself together. 'I'm better outside.' He got his coat on again.

'I suppose we need to talk,' started Polly, as they sauntered along the beach, tide low.

Piers breathed in deeply. 'This is the hard part. Another hard part. But we must.'

'You are hardly at home, and what's the point of my being in a house like this alone? I've been working a lot, and done quite a few nights, so it doesn't make sense anymore.'

They sat on a rock. 'It's not as though he'd been at Beau Vue all his life,' Piers deliberated. 'Simon enjoyed the luxury. Tony wasn't materialistic at all. Apart from art works.' He smiled then pursed his lips as he came to terms with reality. 'I'm sure he wouldn't want the building to become a burden on us.'

Polly agreed. 'But what about you?'

'I'd rather be near St Mark's now. My family have room for me to stay if I want to visit.' He raised his eyebrows. 'Would you choose to live on Guernsey?'

They faced each other. Polly shook her head slowly. Reluctantly. 'Sell?'

'Sell,' said Piers decisively. 'How else can we divide the property between us?'

'Unless one of us buys the other out,' said Polly. 'But I can't afford to.'

'Nope. Ditto.' It felt a significant moment to them both. 'Can you find out how to set about it, Pol?'

'I'll get advice. Anthony's solicitor might have contacts. Oh dear, the thought of having to decide where all Anthony's things will go.'

'He owned almost nothing when he came. The furniture, pictures and so on were Simon's, remember, and nothing was left from The Elms after Gus helped himself. It is basically the pictures he purchased including the Dali. That will mean the most to me.'

Polly was thoughtful.

'I'm glad.' After a while she said, 'Can you use the furniture, Piers? I don't need much.' Piers was cautious.

'I don't know. You'll need a few items of furniture surely; chairs, table, bed? It feels as though the sand is shifting beneath my feet. It's all change.'

Polly said. 'Yes, I'll think a bit more. You're right. We'll see what the solicitor says first and take it from there.' They walked home and saw the postman turning away from the front door.

'What exciting news has he dropped on the mat?' asked Piers, glad they both seemed to think along roughly the same lines.

'Probably bumph,' said Polly, taking off her coat. Her expression changed to delight: 'It's a wedding invitation – to both of us!' The card was hand-made, decorated with silver stick-on bells and 'GLORY BE TO GOD!' across the front.

'Mags and Max, at Shorewell Pentecostal Church!' said Polly pouring a glass of wine.

'That'll be a cheerful affair!' Piers had brightened up.

'But,' she grimaced, 'teetotal.'

They clinked their glasses, smiling: 'To Mags and Max!'

CHAPTER 41
1990s

'They are so happy and Mags looks stunning.' Piers turned and studied Polly's bright flowery dress with sky-blue jacket. 'And you look lovely too!'

Polly was enjoying the occasion: 'Thank you! I thought I'd make an effort for a change.' She leant towards Piers as they filed out of the church, 'It's the first time I've spent money on proper clothes and I rather like them!'

'You've certainly got it right. But Mags, what a transformation! Can't believe that's the person who bumped into Tony because she was hungry.' Piers became solemn. 'Tony would have loved this. Our church services are so different... even weddings. You'd never think we both worshipped the same God.'

'It's those walls in Anthony's dream. We don't realise we've built them ourselves. We're all so small-minded and sure we're right. I see it now.' But Polly's eyes were scanning the refreshments.

'Only fruit juice!' Piers teased.

'Shame,' said Polly. 'Juice or tea!' They ate buffet style then the rising *shush* and a spoon being knocked on a glass brought the gospel band to a stop and the chatter subsided.

The pastor stood with a wide smile on his face. 'PRAISE THE LORD!'

'Praise the Lord!' echoed the guests. The drummer performed a drum-roll with flourish. Everyone clapped Mags and Max, the centre of attention.

After the speeches, Polly and Piers spied Father Dominic and wandered over to join the group around him.

'Piers! Just the person I was looking for! Come and meet a friend of mine.' Polly scanned the room for Vic and Nina but was shocked to see Barbara making her way over. *Don't argue*. They hadn't been in contact since the 'article'.

Polly remained straight-faced waiting for Barbara to speak first. 'I was hoping to see you, Polly,' she said.

Despite her attempt at self-control, Polly pulled a face. Without hesitation, she blurted: 'Why did you do *that*? WHY?' She turned away, cross with her own reaction.

'Hands up. I'm kicking myself. I don't know what got into me. You have no idea how sorry I am.' Tears were welling up in Barbara's eyes.

'Oh?' Polly was surprised.

Then they were distracted by a roar of laughter from the end of the hall where the newly-weds were surrounded by cheering church members.

Both Barbara and Polly were reminded they were deeply affected by the atmosphere in the church and the happiness of the gathering. The friendliness was infectious. Polly was also recalling the pastor's message to the newly-weds. Emphasising each word, he'd said: 'There will be times when you disagree: I want you to remember that we *all* sin,' he settled his eyes on Mags and Max, 'and if we don't forgive even the *unforgiveable*... how can we expect our Heavenly Father to forgive us?'

'Forgive' resonated in Polly's mind, as she stood there faced by a penitent Barbara.

'You probably don't want to talk to me,' said Barbara, tears still brimming although her cheeks were dry. 'I'll understand if you'd rather not... but I'd suffered a terrible blow. I was bereft – and I went mad. Totally mad.' At this, the tears ran down her cheeks and she turned away from the crowd.

Oh dear, not now. In spite of herself Polly also turned away and gently guided Barbara to a door that, luckily, led outside to a little courtyard. 'It caused such an upset, and nothing made sense. Nothing.'

'I know.'

'But you must have *known* Michael... well... Anthony said a long time ago your boyfriend was married and had family.'

'But I was so sure he'd leave them for me.' Barbara fished a hanky from her sleeve and blew her nose.

Polly remembered her feelings when Darren left her. She sighed. 'Go on.'

The courtyard was small and untidy with nowhere to sit or hide. The door opened: '*There* you are!' Piers registered an immediate signal from Polly, and his smile faded when he saw the state Barbara was in.

'I mustn't spoil the wedding, on top of everything else.'

'Did Mags invite you?' asked Piers.

'Never mind about that now,' cautioned Polly.

'I must go,' said Barbara.

'Should you have been here in the first place?' insisted Piers.

'Piers!' Polly just wanted to calm things down.

'Please give me a chance to explain... another time. Can we meet up, Polly? Please.'

'Give me a ring next week, then.'

Barbara sighed and wiped her eyes. 'Thanks.' She made for the door, smiled weakly at Piers, and left the two friends standing there.

'What's going on?'

'Yes, I was angry when she came over, but the pastor's message echoed up here somewhere.' She tapped her head.

'And?'

'Forgiveness is still a powerful force, even if you don't have faith.'

'But did she explain?'

'Not exactly, but she was devastated because she'd written the article in a fit of pique.'

'That's no excuse.'

'Sometimes things just happen. No rhyme or reason. She might ring next week. She wants to talk.'

'I don't think she should ever have been here.'

They re-entered the rejoicing crowd and found Reginald, smile fixed from ear to ear. He happily introduced his equally elated family from Jamaica.

*

'…olly-stalking.'

'Is that you Polly?'

It was Barbara's voice, but Polly was in no mood to speak. She wanted to put the phone down but the voice was urgent. *Concentrate.*

'Is it too late? We must talk. I've done a lot of thinking since the wedding. We both need help, don't we?'

Polly gave a start, staggered over to the tap and gulped down a glass of water.

'Polly. We can sort something out… please, talk to me.'

Polly could only giggle. 'Huh-h-help? Ring's back ins- smorning.' She put the phone down, bashing it twice in the wrong place before cutting off the call. 'Ring's back,' she giggled again to herself. 'Help?' she puzzled. 'H-h-h-*help?*' She clambered upstairs, sat on the edge of the bed, and slid off.

After a strong black coffee for breakfast the phone rang again. 'Polly, how are you now?'

Polly had forgotten last night's conversation.

'Yes, hello Barbara. Did you ring recently?'

This time, they had a long conversation and agreed to meet.

'You could keep me company for two or three days if you like,' Polly suggested. They arranged a time. *Uh-ho! How will we get on?*

*

Polly arrived home in the pouring rain and in a bad mood to find Barbara waiting outside umbrella up, dripping wet. She was reminded how Barbara pushed herself into their home back in Elm Close, and her heart sank. 'I wasn't expecting you yet,' she shouted.

'Sorry, I *know*,' Barbara excused herself. 'My mistake *again*.'

'What a morning; a complaint about me and two deaths. Let me get the key in then!' Barbara moved out of the way and Polly struggled with the key.

'That's better.' They stared at each other. 'Yolanda's probably upstairs and wouldn't have heard you knock. If you go up she'll show you the bathroom. I'll take the umbrella.' Polly needed a drink badly but thought better of it and put the kettle on. She was exhausted having been on a late duty the evening before and up early that morning.

Barbara came downstairs refreshed. 'What a house,' she said, 'and wonderful views!'

'Yes, it's lovely.' Polly poured tea. 'I'm not going to be much good until I've had an early night. Will you be happy with a pub meal this evening?'

They settled down in easy chairs and assessed each other. The awkward tension in the room made chatting stilted and eventually Barbara's convictions came to the fore. 'You certainly give the impression of being the worse for wear. You know what I think? You've never got to know yourself.' *Will I never learn?* She kicked herself for blurting out her opinion so quickly.

'Gee thanks,' retorted Polly. *What a nerve. Not a good start.*

'Sorry, I know I'm a blunderbuss. But that's me.' She seemed cross with herself but ploughed on. 'Now I've started I might as well finish. I meant it when I said we *both* need help.'

Polly glanced up sharply. 'I really don't want to get into all this now. Let's just finish this tea and get ready to go.'

She'd made up her mind to survive the evening without losing her temper.

'Do you think you're alright to drive?'

'I can manage.'

By the time they reached the pub the sun was shining. They sat at a table with a view out over the sea. Barbara perused the menu.

'This reminds me of Maisie's Cuppa,' she said.

'Isn't Maisie's Cuppa a café in a busy London street?'

'Yes, but it's small and friendly, and you feel at home.' She looked up. 'But now I see out of the window,' she smiled weakly, 'Mmmm, see what you mean.'

'The sea, the sea, the shining sea!' Polly spoke quietly, remembering how Anthony loved those words. She was thinking how contemplating the sea, the far horizon, helped to put things into perspective. She decided it was time to swallow her annoyance.

'I'll be sociable tomorrow, promise,' she said with a slight smile.

'Have you got chickens here?' A nice neutral subject to talk about.

'Yes' said Polly. 'For the time being anyway.'

'What's wrong?'

'Could we discuss it tomorrow, please.' Polly thought she should have had that drink earlier because her dark mood was back. The depression deepened as they tackled their food, and Barbara began to feel a rising sense of panic.

She blurted out, 'What's wrong, Polly? What's going on for you? Come out with it!'

'So, you write all about the ex-missionary who's inherited the ex-monk's riches and conclude she doesn't know herself?'

'NO! It's not like that. I've come here to suggest you stay with *me* for a time – while you're unsettled.'

Polly was taken aback at the unexpected suggestion. 'And do you *honestly* think that would *work*?'

'I don't work for the *News* anymore.'

'Oh! You're as lost as I am. And two lost people are not going to be much help to each other, are they?'

Barbara sighed, resigned to the fact that her good intentions were going nowhere. 'Oh well if that's all you can say…' She resumed her meal.

'I've tried to explain!' Polly realised she was talking too loudly and lowered her voice. The people at the adjacent table were glancing over and whispering to each other. She thought she recognised one of her ex-patients.

'I wasn't expecting you tonight, I'm tired, and I'll be better tomorrow.'

In the morning it was Barbara who was dishevelled but Polly was refreshed: 'Did you sleep?' she asked her guest. 'I'm sorry about yesterday.'

'I think I'll go today.'

'Oh, I see.' Polly picked up the cereal. 'You sure?'

Barbara was feeling low after a restless night and Polly was resigned to dealing with her visitor rather more gently, whatever her mood. She tentatively put her arm around Barbara's shoulder. 'What would you like to drink?'

'Coffee. I can see it won't work.' Barbara blew her nose, and pulled her chair up to the table, her eyes still closed. 'I thought we could work through our problems together.'

'Stay a couple of days now you're here. We'll talk.'

They managed to calm down as they went into St Peter Port for Barbara to buy beach wear then drove to the shore. The following day they even enjoyed a long walk.

Finally, Barbara was saying goodbye. Polly was relieved but felt the depression and anxiety returning. As they parted Barbara recalled a question which had been on her mind: 'By the way, didn't you think it was odd that Anthony ignored his uncle's side of the family at the end?'

Polly was glad of the opportunity to enlighten her. 'No. There was only Henry and Gus. Henry had all he needed and had advanced Alzheimer's. Anthony suffered badly from Gus's bullying in childhood, and distressing theft later.'

Barbara sighed. 'That makes me feel even worse—'

Polly cut in. 'The past is over and done with.' Then she looked thoughtful: 'Oh yes. When Father Dominic visited Henry in his Nursing Home, Matron showed him an inscription on an oak garden bench which said: 'To Uncle Henry in memory of your brother Ris, my father. Thank you for the lesson in laughter. Anthony.'

Barbara's eyebrows shot up. 'Hahhhhh, Gus's task! A *garden bench!*' She exploded in mirth. They laughed together and it felt a good conclusion, though neither understood exactly why. Nobody would guess Anthony's secret or know how important it was to him: when the old bench collapsed not only did he discover laughter for the first time – but more importantly – he felt the presence of his father joining in.

As for Polly and Barbara, the amusement helped them to part on good terms. After their farewells, Polly drove to the cliffs. She carried her water-bottle down the steps to a favourite spot. A gentle breeze blew her hair away from her face, clearing her mind. The significance of the bench came back to her: Piers had decided to visit Henry's nursing home himself. Alone, he sat down and stroked one of the oak arms sensually. Anthony's presence came flooding back. He was reassured the discombobulations in Tony's life had been totally resolved. All was well.

Drawing strength from her reflections, Polly unscrewed the black top of her water-bottle and drank. *Get a grip. Decision time. Water!* She studied the bottle then the sea. Disconnected phrases blew through her mind as successive waves broke on the beach.

Find myself.

Missionary with no money and plenty of faith now ex-missionary with no faith and plenty of money.
Lost.
Space. It's all space. She watched the choppy sea and horizon for a long time. Gulls drifting on the breeze, wings outspread.
What about the comfort Anthony got from his father's presence?
Piers... and the bench?
What is it all about?

She remembered Anthony telling her something about the dear monk he helped in the garden: 'For all the religion and dogma of the Roman Catholic Church, Vincent was content to be gathered up under the mother hen's wing. A tiny chick finding love and protection in the end.'

She smiled an inner smile. *Yes, Anthony. Yes!* She walked back to the car filled with fresh determination. Once home, she put a sheet of paper in the typewriter and made a list.

```
1. Solicitor - ask advice
2. Tell Piers
3. Vic and Nina - keep in the
   loop
4. Get valuation
5. Don't keep procrastinating.
   Just do it!
```

She took the paper out of the typewriter and found her broad-nibbed pen. She thought of Anthony's calligraphy and tried to make the sixth point stand out:

Number 6: ~ *Know my real self.* ~

She completed her tasks in the garden, then had to do something she couldn't put in words. *Do it. Straight away.* She removed two bottles of gin from the cupboard, unscrewed the tops, hesitated near the sink. *Come on Pol, free yourself: close your eyes; upturn bottle.* She poured it, all, every drop… down the drain.

CHAPTER 42

'Don't you think it's a bit cold for a picnic?' Barbara and Penny were smothered in winter coats, hats and scarfs, their gloves on a bench. Christmas and New Year over, they were by the Thames eating sandwiches. Barbara was looking forward to her adventures. 'Only a week and I'll be basking in the sun!' She hooted.

'So, you're taking the plunge... you absolutely sure?'

'No turning back now. And I'll book a hotel for both of us in Greece next Easter. I'll need a break by then.' She felt more optimistic than she could remember since childhood.

'Well, good luck then.' Penny patted Barbara's arm, then dropped crumbs on the ground. She cast around, 'Come on birds,' she called, 'lunch time!'

'Thanks.'

'What sort of work are you going to do?'

'They say there's always something on the big cruisers, so I'll try those. But my main occupation will be travel writing. Apparently, several editors are interested in the difference terrorism is making to the tourist industry. I mean, things like: "Tourists to America choose different destinations out of fear." Oh, that's no good – but you know.'

'So how do *you* feel about that? I mean your own safety?'

'Not thinking about it!' Barbara became over-animated. 'I'm going to concentrate on finding my dream man: fit, young, strong, solvent, single...'

'Whoa-a! Listen to yourself.' Penny joined in the fun but was dubious about her friend's future direction. 'You just mind you don't get drugs planted in your rucksack… or have all your worldly wealth nicked!'

'I'll be all right. Of course, I will.' She grew serious. 'I know… I'm not a Polly or Anthony… more a Mags underneath, aren't I?' And thank God I didn't land up with Michael and all his baggage.' She didn't pinpoint exactly why she'd reached that conclusion.

When it was time to go, Penny cautioned Barbara again. 'Now you take care of yourself.' She smiled.

'You're too cautious! And jolly well don't change your mind about the Greek Island.'

'I might bring *my* man with me,' Penny warned. Barbara tended to forget her friend had a partner. She rarely mentioned him.

'And don't forget God has pointed his finger at you!'

Barbara was reminded of significant questions that came to mind after Max announced his prayers had been answered. 'I don't think that will happen twice – but you never know!' *Maybe Rome?*

'That *was* an especially remarkable episode, I have to say.' They were both thinking of Barbara's time involved with Anthony, Dominic, and Mags. 'Maybe you'll come back with religion rather than a handsome hunk!' Penny quipped.

'Watch this space!'

They kissed goodbye and went their different ways.

Barbara turned and called to Penny, 'Vatican, here I come!'

CHAPTER 43

'Hi Polly.' It was Nina. 'How are you getting on? Much more to do?'

'Nina!' Polly was tired but pleased to hear her sister-in-law: 'Not too bad. Fairly organised.'

'Will you be finished by Christmas?'

'Not really. The contract won't be signed until the New Year. But the sale is going through and I've given in my notice. December 15th, my last shift.'

'We were hoping you might be able to join us this year, but it sounds as though you'll be too busy.'

'Piers told Father Dominic that he'll come and help me over the holiday. There're so many last-minute jobs. I'll have to play it by ear, but I'm aiming to see you for Nicola's birthday in February.'

'Next year, then.'

'In my new diary!'

'But there's interesting news.'

'Oh? Can't wait!'

'Two things… one I think you'll be pleased about, and the other I'm not so sure.'

'Do I need to sit down?'

'Maybe. Beth is trying to contact you!'

'No, really? Beth *Johnson*? Urrr, as was Johnson?'

'She wants to meet you, not phone. Face to face!'

'Tell her she's welcome to come as soon as she can. I won't be here much longer. How odd. Did she give you any hints?'

'She was very cagey… couldn't make her out.'

'Is she embarrassed or what?'

'I just don't know. I presume it's alright to give her your address?'

'Of course, and thanks! What's the other thing?'

'Darling,' Nina cleared her throat, 'be prepared…'

'What?'

'After all this time, Darren is rebuilding number 14. He and Dot are going to live there.' She was right to wonder how Polly would react to this news, and whether she still had feelings for him.

She *did* need to sit down, bewildered, legs outstretched. *No, Polly, no gin.*

*

A week later Polly was back at the airport, this time in curious anticipation. *Will I even recognise her? Why the sudden contact?* A confusion of questions tumbled through her mind.

There was no mistaking Beth. Still fair hair, upright figure, dainty hands. O*lder – of course*. But now tired, drawn and what was lurking in her eyes – fright? Soon they were hugging like old times. 'Pol,' she exclaimed in haunted tones. 'Pol, I'm a wreak. And I've been a dreadful friend.' Polly detected a slight Irish twang.

'Come on, we'll relax at home. It's not far.' Polly, surprisingly, felt motherly towards her long-lost friend. 'You're upset. Are you ill?'

Beth was tense: 'I'm not ill, just very tired, devastated and unhappy. Pol, I made a big, big mistake.'

'Flynn?'

Polly was concentrating on the road so didn't see Beth nod her head, but she sensed her quiet agreement.

'I let you down, badly,' she insisted.

'You're still my friend.' Polly sort of chuckled. 'You're the oldest friend I've got. I mean our friendship goes right back... Nothing will alter that.'

'But I wasn't a proper friend once I met Flynn. That's why I feel guilty.' Beth talked wistfully, with insight now.

'Beth – where's Judith? Is she all right?'

'Judith's with Flynn. She can't do anything wrong in his sight. She goes along with everything he says.'

They had reached *Belle Vue*.

'This is beautiful!' Beth came to life. 'Polly, is this really yours?'

'Half of it! You'll probably meet Piers before you leave.'

'Piers?'

'No relationship. I told you Anthony had a partner. You have no idea what's been going on with me...' Beth was stunned, and incredulous. 'So, this is how God rewards people who give up everything for His sake – the irony!'

Polly didn't comment. She parked the car crookedly in the drive and unloaded her friend's bags. 'Come in and make yourself at home!'

Once through the door, the tension eased, but it felt odd to be together after such a gap. Polly stopped trying to work out what 'the irony' was.

'Come here!' Polly put her arms around Beth and kissed her cheek. 'Hello! A proper hello.'

'Aren't you going to tell me off?'

They went into the kitchen, where Polly had been baking. 'Have a piece of fruit cake!'

'I'm so wound up.'

'Come to the sitting room.'

'I can't get over this place'. She was eyeing the décor, enjoying the space, and talking with her mouth full. 'There's so much to say and I don't know where to start.'

Polly held back from questions and waited for Beth to unload in her own time.

'It's chilly, but I'll show you the beach later if you like. We often escape there. Or we could just go down the garden and – you know what!'

'No! You're still obsessed with poultry?' Beth managed a smile.

'Absolutely! And we'll be eating their eggs. You can help me clean them out too.' Polly assessed Beth's clothing. *Good quality*. 'I'll lend you some old clothes.'

Beth studied herself and said with a hint of sarcasm 'Only the best for Flynn.'

They went to the beach and sat until they got cold. Beth stretched her limbs. 'Just what I need. *Just* this.' Polly explained what had happened to Anthony.

'We're still getting used to not having him around.'

Beth linked into Polly's arm, as they walked home talking about Anthony, both avoiding the touchy subject of homosexuality.

The casserole only needed heating up and there was practically no washing-up. It made Beth remember how Polly used to complain about all the saucepans and dishes Vera expected her to do.

'I haven't done much washing-up since I married.'

'Was it so different from life in Halebridge?'

'Utterly. In every way.' Beth froze. Before blurting out, 'I've left Flynn, Pol.'

'*Left* him...?' Her eyebrows shot up sharply, and her neck strained forward.

'Yes. Everything's gone so wrong. He says I'm not keeping my wedding vows, so I've been cast out like a leper.' She burst into anguished tears, and sobbed uncontrollably. After a while she stammered, 'I want to go to church, Pol. Would you let me come with you, please?'

'To my church?'

'Would they let me partake?'

'You mean break bread?'

Beth was eager for Polly to understand. 'You don't know what it was like when I had to go back to Mum.'

'Beth!' Polly hugged her. 'Beth! My ole Beth. Listen carefully to me.' They ambled into the garden, hardly noticing the cold. 'I've got a sort of confession too. Although it isn't one I feel guilty about. In fact, I'm relieved. My burden to save the world has gone.' Polly was breathing deeply, anticipating the impact of her news.

Beth was intrigued. 'Not an affair?'

At this Polly smiled to herself. 'Oh, much worse than that! I've *left the church.*'

It was Beth's turn to be stunned, and she raised her voice for the first time. 'You've LEFT the church?' The shock seemed to have stopped her tears. 'But the Lord called you. You were so dedicated. You gave up *everything* for Him.' She was astonished.

'I know, everything I had went into the Lord's work. I was completely committed.'

'Then why?'

'I'll tell you, but it's a long story. Anthony's circumstances didn't fit into my beliefs somehow.' She hesitated. 'Then people arguing over the Bible… judgements made over funding. I studied. Prayed. I'll go into detail later. But all sorts of things merged and led me to where I am now.'

'Aren't you scared?'

'Scared? What of?'

'But, Hebrews ten, verse twenty-nine: You are trampling the Son of God underfoot.' Beth was dead serious. Neither said a word for couple of minutes. Polly letting her announcement hang in the air.

'I won't be preaching at you for leaving Flynn. We've both made mistakes, haven't we? But we mustn't—'

'—argue,' Beth finished.

Polly slapped her forehead: 'It's dark and you know what I've forgotten?'

'I'll come with you.' Beth followed Polly into the darkness.

The chickens were roosting. As torchlight shone round the shed they took notice and looked as though they were asking who the intruder was.

'I'll come and see you in the morning.' Polly told them. 'You're not starving.' She topped up their water. 'You can collect our supper.' She gave Beth a small bowl and shone her torch to the right.

Beth lifted the lid and felt inside. 'Takes me back,' she said.

'To Elm Close?'

'To home. When things were simpler. We were children. Life was so simple.'

'We argued about everything then!' said Polly. 'Even though we were totally ignorant about life, and the stuff it throws at you.'

Beth became preachy. 'I've been tempted to doubt my faith, but I overcame. You must have forgotten your armour, Pol. Remember the whole armour of God?'

Polly was quiet. 'Let's wait until tomorrow.' She led the way through the dark garden and back to the house.

'Do you mind if we have an early night?' They were both tired.

'What about a word of prayer?' asked Beth.

'We'll just commit everything in our own ways.' Polly was determined not to argue.

'Okey dokey,' Beth smiled. 'I'll pray for you anyway.'

They hugged goodnight, and as Polly drifted off she remembered how she worried for Beth when Flynn flared up. Next thing, she and Beth were in the old apple tree where they played as children. They were higher in the tree than usual. Looking down, around, and into the distance Polly could vaguely see Croften, Darren, Flynn, Elaine and several others coming and going. She tried to see what Darren was doing more clearly, but the branch taking her weight started to give way. Falling… falling.

*

Polly was down the garden first thing in the morning. 'Hello everybody!' The hens were agitating for food and fell over each other as she put it in the trough, gobbling it down as fast as they could. 'Enjoy, girls!' None of them were listening. It was cold and Polly was wearing her jumble-sale boots, plus a chunky duffle coat. She rubbed her hands together. 'We're happy, aren't we, chooks?' She stood there watching, chattering on: 'I don't think Beth is though, do you?'

A couple of the birds seemed aware of her from time to time, whilst getting as much food down as they could. 'I don't think you're *really* interested but I need to tell you: Darren is moving in opposite my brother. What about that? And I've just got to try and be myself. No pretending…'

'You going mad?' Polly hadn't noticed Beth creep up on her, like she did when they tried to make each other jump.

'I'm talking to my friends. They don't try to convince me I'm wrong.'

'So, tell me what you aren't going to pretend?'

She hasn't grown up at all. 'We used to be good at pretending, didn't we? I was dreaming we were in the apple tree last night. But all that's behind me, Beth. I've changed how I see things, and for the first time in my life I'm discovering myself. But let's get back inside; it's cold.' They turned to the house.

'Did you sleep all right?' Polly asked, observing how unkempt Beth looked when they were in the warmth of the kitchen.

Beth ignored her. She was obsessed with Polly's change of heart. 'So, why did you give it up?'

'Do you remember that missionary doctor who wrote those books on being honest about her life serving God?'

'Published about your first year in India? I read the first… real page-turner but Flynn said it could lead people astray.'

'But she told the truth. No pretending everything in the garden is lovely because you're born again.'

'Suppose…'

'I managed to meet her. I didn't realise she's now a qualified counsellor, but she listened to my story and didn't charge.'

'Did that help?'

'She told me I was like a canary in a cage and needed to be set free.'

'Ohhhh... but fly out of *what*?'

Polly sighed and started to lay the table. *Will she ever understand?*

'Change of subject: Do you want to ring Judith, or anybody?'

'I rang Mum last night, after you went to bed, and she was all right. But Judith, I miss her so much, Polly. She insisted on staying with Flynn.' Beth rubbed her forehead. 'I think he's all right with her... I *think*.' She frowned. 'But he's more and more controlling with me, and if I disagree with him... he won't stand for it. He—'

Polly stopped concentrating on the omelettes.

'He *what*?'

'I haven't told anyone, even Mum...'

'What?'

Beth rubbed her eyes and, in the absence of make-up, Polly was shocked to see the remnants of bruising.

Then it all poured out. Over breakfast she disclosed details about her home life with Flynn and the church in Ireland. The longer Beth confided in her the more Polly saw the mistaken virtues of blind belief in the scripture. *How naive we were.*

She felt humbled. 'You've done the right thing, Beth. I'm sure you need get away if you want to keep your sanity.'

'Mum doesn't think so, but she only knows the half. Oh, Pol, thank you. You've changed so much, and I don't know what to think. But…' She stretched out her arm to Polly. 'I desperately needed to tell somebody.'

'We'll find a way – between us,' Polly sympathised.

The telephone rang. 'Piers is coming back in three days, and I need to pack up linen – this is such an enormous house and...'

'I'll give you a hand.'

They went upstairs and spent a quiet hour together, packing linen in trunks.

'But don't you miss the Fellowship?' asked Beth eventually.

'Dreadfully. A large chunk of my social life has gone.' She moved her hands, palms down, swiftly away from each other as though clearing the air.

'Then, did you just fly out of the cage, whatever that was… was it the church?'

'No! There was a lot more to it than that. I'd cherry-picked Bible passages which fitted with Mrs Holland's teaching but now I know you can prove anything that way. I prayerfully worked through different books of the Bible over several years, looking at the overall picture.'

'But it's the pastor's job to do that.' Beth was open-mouthed. They'd both stopped packing. 'I've trusted the Pastor or Flynn to know best, or even Mum – and the Fellowship too.'

'Don't you feel like a hypocrite singing and saying things you don't really believe?'

'Not really, but you always take things so seriously. I'm – umm – I'm different.'

'Whatever.' Polly nodded. 'But Beth, as I asked more questions it suddenly came to me. A voice clearly spoke in my head: "*The Bible is written by men.*" It was as definite as my conversion. Gears shifted inside me.

The world turned upside down.' Beth took a deep breath in to speak, but Polly continued. 'Then I thought, *Hell's gone*! And that was just the start. So many ideas shifted around in my thinking. My burden to convert the world fell off.'

'Whatever would Flynn say?'

'Sorry Beth, but no-one can change my mind. *No*body.'

'So what next?' Beth sat and waited for an answer.

'I just don't know. I'm still working it all out. Several Christian friends don't know what's happened yet. I'm still finding my real self. I'll have money when it comes through. But the question is, where shall I go? There's nothing to keep me on Guernsey.'

'Vic and Nina?'

'I couldn't... not for more than a few weeks anyway.'

'I have been wondering,' Beth spaced out her words, hesitated, then blurted it out: 'I wonder if you might think of coming to help me with Mum?'

'Has she got a problem?'

Beth's face fell. 'Didn't you hear about the crash? She was in a car accident almost three years ago now. Her back was broken, legs paralysed and now she's in a wheelchair. My brother and his wife cared for her a while but they're tired out. Now I'm home, I don't blame them, Mum can be difficult.'

'Oh no! Poor Nessa.'

'Yes, it's hard. And I hate doing personal stuff – I'm rubbish at it, but needs must. A nurse comes in three times a week, but that's not much. It's tough and she gets so impatient.'

Polly was taken by surprise. 'Cor...'

'You don't want to come, do you?'

'Well,' Polly tried to be positive. 'I'll think about it.'

'So, you will think about it?'

'Don't you think we would argue all the time? Whatever you say I'm not going back to church and I need space to sort myself out.'

'I'd be happier having you with me and occasional disagreements, than a stranger.'

'We don't really know each other these days!'

'We could try to get to know each other again.'

'Let's finish this for now, and go for a trip around the island.'

They talked non-stop as they drove, Polly telling Beth more about her quest for 'the truth', and her 'sort of Pilgrim's progress in reverse' experience. And Beth relating stories about Judith, the nightmares with Flynn, and her mother's difficulties.'

By evening they were exhausted, but Beth was fired up and still needed to talk.

'When you said you heard that voice saying how the Bible is written by men, I wondered if you were right.'

Polly was pleased Beth was thinking for herself. 'I suppose calling it a '*deconversion*' might be a good description.'

'You seem peaceful in a way you never were before you went abroad. But this life is so short, and isn't the point of it – treasure in heaven?'

'There's so much I haven't worked out.'

'I go to Mum's church but they don't know what's going on. I do my best to fit in,' Beth said wistfully. 'But it's certainly all or nothing with you, isn't it? Aren't you throwing out the baby with the bathwater?'

CHAPTER 44

'Welcome back to Halebridge!' Nessa was wheeling her wheelchair laboriously down the hallway. Polly stooped to kiss her on both cheeks. She scanned her surroundings.

'Much water under the bridge, Nessa.' Polly tried light-hearted conversation.

'Circumstances have changed a great deal,' said Nessa. There was an understandable air of bitterness in her curt response.

'We're talking at least twenty years.'

'So, you never found anyone else after Darren?' *Blow below the belt*. Polly tittered half-heartedly but was lost for words. Nessa carried on, 'It was just as well. I always thought Darren's faith was only half-hearted.'

Beth changed the subject. 'Come and see your room, Pol.' She threw a withering stare at Nessa. 'Mum, can you make it into the sitting room while I take Polly upstairs?' Nessa groaned with the effort of turning the chair so Beth helped manoeuvre her into position.

'Sorry about that, Pol,' she apologised when they were out of earshot.

Polly was nonplussed: 'If this is how your mother intends…'

'Be firm with her. Don't take any nonsense. We're adults. I've been given the treatment too.'

'I'll have to tell her about my faith situation somehow.'

'Just fudge it to start with. She'll settle down.'

I doubt it.

They closed the door on Polly's bedroom. 'Not very spacious, I'm afraid,' said Beth worried it might not suit. 'Not exactly Belle Vue. It was a huge adjustment for me coming home. I had to put most of my clothes in the loft.'

'You've got lovely clothes. The only quality togs I've got were for a recent wedding.'

'You haven't adapted to your new life-style. These old things,' Beth took hold of Polly's skirt and shook it, 'are still missionary hand-outs.'

'I haven't been too bothered, actually. And when you wear uniform at work you don't need much.'

'Oh, I don't see it like that.'

'I don't even know what style would suit me. As a kid it was Mum's choice, then hand-me-downs. But looks didn't matter in the Lord's work.'

'Oh, but they do!' Beth loved fashion. 'Our lives…' She bit her bottom lip. 'Never mind. Come downstairs when you're ready. Mum can doze and we'll chat in the kitchen.'

'When do I start work?' Polly grinned. She was keen to nurse again. *Although… Nessa might be trickier than I imagined.*

'You tell me when you're ready. I'll care for Mum tonight and tomorrow.'

'Just tell me what she needs: what you do, and what she can do for herself.'

'Do you want to ring Vic and Nina – or anyone else?'

'I'd love to visit them as soon as possible.'

When Polly went up to bed that night she was daunted by the challenge. *It's not going to be easy. But I'll plough on and after a few weeks I can always tell*

Beth it's not working. She went to sleep wondering – then worrying – how long would she manage to put up with Nessa, and vice versa?

*

She rang Piers. 'Belle Vue is all settled and I'm installed in Beth's mum's place.'

'I thought it would never happen after the sale fell through.'

'Second time round – it's sorted. Can we meet up?'

'Shall I come to you?'

'Best not... what about Max's café?'

They arranged a date and arrived at the same time. 'Wel-come, my friends,' cried Max, with his signature grin. 'It's great to see you. Come and sit down.' He showed them to the 'press' table. He looked round the busy shop, and excused himself to attend to another customer. 'Lunch on the house!' he said in a stage whisper as he dashed away.

'I couldn't invite you to Beth's,' Polly explained to Piers. 'Nessa's in a bad way and stuck in the past. She disapproves of anything that's unbiblical in her view.'

'Does she know you've left church?' he asked.

'I'll work round to it slowly. I can't upset her too much. Beth's much more understanding now, with all she's been through. She's talking more openly about life's ups and downs. But Nessa is, to put it mildly, difficult. Does Father Dominic preach at you?'

Piers laughed. 'Far from it. We tend to concentrate on things practical – fire-fighting problems most of the time. In our free time he's interesting to be with and avoids topics we might argue over. He's great!'

Max placed two aromatic plates of pepper-pot stew before them and they caught up on news, the remaining business and chat.

'Things tricky with Nessa and Beth then?'

'Yes, but so far I'm handling it, and it is early days. I've got nowhere else to go at present.'

'But you've got money.'

'Oh yes, but I'll take my time, and Beth does need help. Her brother needs a rest and I feel she's landed with such an arduous task. It's hard being separated from her daughter too. You?'

'I'm happy and made myself useful at St Mark's. I'm even enjoying the prayer sessions. It takes me back to childhood. I'll think more seriously about that side of things now. I compromise a little, but then most of the others do too.'

'Don't get too serious on me! And no theology, thank you,' Polly grimaced, before she realised her differences with the Roman Catholic Church didn't matter anymore.

'Thank you for getting Belle Vue sorted, Pol.'

'It worked out well. Yolanda's husband helped with the heavy packing. Everything's in order.'

By the time they'd finished the café was quiet and Polly caught Max's eye: 'You're happy, Max.'

'I am. Couldn't be better. Dad and Mags fill up the house and life is… it's wonderful!'

'Has she started her lessons?'

'She got down to that as soon as she could. She's bright – and a beautiful singer too.'

'Does she sing at the church?'

'She sings at the church and in the bath! They all love her, and she's settled in fine. Plays my guitar something heavenly.' He raised his eyes upwards. 'Just so happy to have the life the good Lord has sent us. Praise the Lord!' he whispered.

Piers and Polly smiled with him. *Isn't life funny?* Polly pondered about the way the church suited Mags and wondered how much she'd questioned it. *She's bright, yes. Maybe she was just led by emotion? It'll probably work out better for her than it did for me. I'm pleased for her.*

Max chatted until they were ready to go. 'You come again one day.'

Piers and Polly prepared to part: 'OK, And don't you stay with Nessa if she doesn't behave herself.'

'I'll come running if I need to off-load! Suddenly losing control is an enormous challenge. Poor Anthony changed, didn't he?'

They agreed, and the thought subdued them. 'Still raw,' said Piers, 'but in time I'll go back to Guernsey for a visit. I'm not exactly homesick, but I miss it.'

Polly agreed. I expect I'll be over there for a holiday in a couple of years or so. *Piers is like family to me.*

'Bye for now, darling.'

*

Polly went straight upstairs for a rest after walking in the front door. She reversed her steps when she heard Nessa call sounding more upbeat than usual.

'Something exciting happened?'

'Have you heard the news? About the charismatic movement that's been sweeping the country?' Polly was somewhat alarmed. 'No, not the latest.'

'I'm going to be healed!' This was the last thing Polly was expecting. She was thrown. 'Healed?'

Nessa was laughing with joy. 'Brother Johan is over from America and Pastor Ingrams says he's coming to Cotsford in the new year.'

'You mustn't get your hopes…'

'POLLY! *Have faith.* Mark eleven, verse twenty-four: "*Whatever you ask for in prayer, believe that you have received it, and it will be yours.*" We *must* believe.'

Polly was tired. *I should've been honest with Nessa about my faith before. How will I handle this one?* 'Nessa,' this called for diplomacy, 'could you tell me all about it in the morning? Do you want a hot drink before bed?' Nessa's evening care, getting her into bed and comfortable usually lasted at least forty-five minutes.

'Beth gave me a drink, but I do need the toilet.' They dealt with the practical issues of undressing, but once in bed Nessa confided, 'It's a direct answer to my prayer… at least stay with me and thank the Lord that He has heard me!'

This idea is not going to go away. 'I'm pleased for you, but let's think it through in the morning.'

'You never seem to want to talk about the Lord these days… you've changed.'

'I've learnt a lot about myself – and other people too.' *I can't deal with this.* 'Nessa, I'll tell you in the morning.' She gave Nessa her sleeping tablet.

'That's a fine way out, isn't it? But make sure you do. You've got a lot of explaining to do.'

Polly was sympathetic and, for once, kissed her on the cheek. 'You're tired too, Nessa, with all this excitement. It will be much easier when we're both fresh.'

They said goodnight, but Polly was fully aware there might be more to do before the morning. It was her 'night on'.

She got a drink and went upstairs, relieved she had escaped for now. However, her pleasure was short-lived. Passing Beth's open bedroom door she heard her sobbing quietly.

'Pol! *Oh Pol.*'

'Whatever is it?'

'I've had the most dreadful letter from Flynn. He's *inhuman*. Read this.'

Resigned to a late night, Polly took the paper from Beth's trembling hand.

> *Belfast.*
> *Beth,*
> *I would like to remind you of some facts that should help you clarify your aberrant position.*
>
> *You became my wife in a ceremony witnessed by family and fellowship in which we vowed to love and remain faithful to each other. You promised to respect and obey me.*
>
> *We have lived happily as committed Christians, and have a child whom we both love. We travelled, and I bought an excellent house due to my hard work at the bank which has supplied a good salary. You have wanted for nothing.*
>
> *But despite having help with Judith and everything you need you have gradually become more and more unresponsive to me. I did what I could to provide for you,*

and supported you when you lost our second child, but you have chosen to please yourself and have become what I can only describe as rebellious and disobedient.

You have broken our holy vows and deserted both your husband and your daughter.

I suggest it is high time that you choose prayerfully between the following options:
1. *Come home to your family and fulfil your responsibilities.*
2. *Stay in England, which would inevitably give grounds for divorce.*
3. *Stay in England and, as a godly family, we remain married.*

The option of divorce will make things problematic for both of us with the Fellowship. As you know, we believed our vows were for life and in the sight of God. If, however, I convince them I have sufficient complaint against you, I stand a good chance of continuing to partake in the Lord's Supper. As for you, it will depend on the attitude of whatever fellowship you belong to in England. It will not be my concern unless they choose to write and ask my side of the picture.

My preferred option would be for us to come together in prayer and resume the happy life we had at the start of our marriage.

I will wait to hear from you at the earliest moment.

Your husband, in Christ,

> *Flynn*
> *P.S. Judith naturally finds it hard to understand what is happening. But she is full of her own life and friends, and Nanny is still here to retain a female presence in the house. So, it doesn't bother her that much. Flynn.*

'He was only ever happy if I did what he wanted all the time,' sobbed Beth. 'He was so controlling. Didn't even want me to visit family.'

'Oh dear,' Polly tried to comfort her friend. She linked arms and said gently, 'I'd forgotten you were expecting a second,' she said, heart in boots. Beth steadied herself. 'He blamed me – no sympathy at all. I couldn't write or talk about it at the time. I still don't really want to.' She blew her nose and forced herself to continue: 'But it makes me realise how judgemental Christians can be.'

'That's true, we all can be.' *Beth has so much emotional baggage.*

'Life doesn't always work out how you imagine it will, even if you pray about everything.'

'No.'

'But how could I stop believing in Jesus. What would Mum say, for one thing?'

'We've got to trust our own convictions in the end, Beth.'

'What shall I do? Nothing's right. I don't know how to make it better – and that letter is just vindictive. This is the only place I can turn to, with my sick, querulous mother! What shall I do?' she asked desperately.

'We're tired, Beth. Maybe a path will be clearer in the morning.'

'I don't want Mum to know about this letter.'

'I'll sleep in here tonight if you like. Then you can wake me if you want to talk.'

They arranged bedding on the floor and Beth, knowing her friend was close by, fell asleep as soon as her head touched the pillow. Polly tossed and turned before her breathing deepened and she became aware of being held securely under the wings of a loving creature. Mountain tops were all around her and in the wind she could hear a voice reminiscent of a church bell: "Ding, dong. Ding dong, be-lieve, be-lieve!" Then, over there, a huge stone starting to roll downhill. It picked up momentum as it fell, bouncing off rocks on the way getting smaller and smaller until…

She awoke with a start. Nessa's bell was ringing. She wanted the toilet.

CHAPTER 45

'Oh no. I don't believe this. Well, yes I suppose I do.' Beth was in the sitting room reading a Christian newspaper.

'What?' asked Polly, glancing up to identify the paper. 'Another survey on sexual habits of Christians or similar?'

'No... yes, not exactly.' Polly was only half listening, being deeply engrossed in a novel.

'Do you remember that doctor person; the amazing preacher; the one the Lord used to call you to the mission field?'

'That doctor. What's-his-name. Yes! Goodness, what about him?'

'Hedges. He's on trial for wife-beating.'

Polly was all ears. 'No! And I thought he was filled with the Holy Ghost.'

'Yes, not only you. We were all convinced God spoke through him.'

'Ummm. Then I thought I was refusing God's call to give up everything so I gave in because I felt so guilty.'

Beth was not listening. 'So, Flynn isn't the only one, then.' Her brain was working over-time, it was comforting to know others had been abused by a Christian husband. 'I haven't answered Flynn's letter yet.'

Polly was gentle. 'I'll come with you to see a solicitor if you like.'

Beth responded with horror. 'Pol! You are the only person who knows…' She shuddered. 'I *couldn't* and that's it. Full stop.'

'POLLY!' Nessa's summons ended the conversation.

'Coming!' She noticed tears in Beth's eyes and the tremor in her voice. 'Speak this evening when your mum has settled down,' she whispered.

'What do you fancy for tea this evening, Nessa?'

'What is there?' Polly helped her onto the commode. 'If only I could just nip down to the shops, have a chat, and buy what I fancy.'

'It must be really frustrating.' Polly had no idea how often their conversation covered the same subjects. She tried to be sympathetic. Then came the most challenging topic for Polly:

'Of course, when I'm *completely* healed…' Nessa became animated and her anxiety frown segued into a smile. 'Then I will! You wait!'

Despite the discomfort, Polly was thankful she had a heavy cold on the day of the healing service: coughing, sneezing, nose and eyes running. Nessa didn't want to be anywhere near her. 'Beth and I will manage, thank you!' she said dismissively. 'I don't want your germs! It's a shame you'll miss all the miracles. You need to be reminded that God is on His throne. But there we are. And that's it.'

The next day Nessa's condition seemed unchanged. 'It was inspirational,' she shouted to Polly who was ordered to keep her distance, 'people were being filled with the Spirit – and I was given the gift of tongues! A complete stranger knew my problem and prophesied my healing. She told me I need to keep faith *season in, season out*.'

*

Polly eventually learnt how to deal with Nessa. 'Are your legs any stronger today?' she would ask.

'Yes! A little touch. Just a *little* touch. The Lord has given me a verse: *They who wait on the Lord shall renew their strength; they shall mount up as on eagle's wings*. Praise our loving Lord! – I'll have cheese on toast for tea.'

'So be it. Brown or white bread?' They all had the same with a side salad. Beth put the television on. Nobody spoke.

At bedtime Beth wanted to chat. 'I'm not getting anywhere. I know I've got to be positive but I can't function properly. Every time I try to get sorted, I feel paralysed like Mum.'

'You can't keep sitting on the fence,' said Polly. 'Try and keep it practical. You don't have to go into details about his behaviour. Just consider the facts. Put yourself in the place of my preacher chap's wife – what do you think she should do?'

'I sent a note to Flynn telling him more about Mum, and told him I need more time.'

'And has he replied?'

'*Has* he! No sympathy at all. Demands a decision.'

'So, the preacher's wife leaves preacher and he writes saying it will ruin his career if she divorces him, but she must make up her mind: Return, live apart (which would be impossible to conceal from his congregation), or divorce.'

'What's her name?'

'Call her *Faith*.'

Beth smiled.

Good start. 'What would you advise Faith to do first?'

'Decide she is not going back. Speak to her GP. Visit a solicitor.'

'Will she write and tell him?'

'She needs to tell the GP what happened and get help to deal with it, and ask the solicitor to write and tell the preacher her decision. Then go on from there.'

Polly touched Beth gently on her arm. 'So, shall we make a GP appointment?'

Beth nodded uncertainly. Then relief poured through her. She felt stronger in both mind and body. 'I'm not going to the GP. I'll go straight to a solicitor and ask them to write a formal letter to Flynn telling him I can't live with him anymore.

'Good! Hang on to that plan.'

'Then I'll have to tell Mum. I think I dread that more than anything else.'

*

Beth started her task straight after breakfast. *I'll answer his letter in the same tone as he wrote to me.*

> *Halebridge.*
> *Flynn,*
>
> *I was quite aware of the 'facts' of our marriage before you enumerated them in your undated letter.*
>
> *Yes, I promised to obey you but in turn you promised to love and honour me. How could you expect me to continue loving you when all you did was control more and more of my life. You have no idea how*

blaming me for the death of our tiny son made me feel. You threw yourself into working towards promotion as though nothing had changed.

I left you because I couldn't bear to be with you any longer. I was afraid of your 'punishments'.

I have chosen your second option and whatever the consequences I will not change. I want a divorce and I'll live in England.

I do not want the publicity of accusing you of anything (you know what I'm talking about) so you can file for desertion after an agreed time.

I would love Judith to visit me. I will write to her again. I don't know what she thinks.

I will not be coming back.
Beth

She sealed the letter and went straight to the post-box.

At the same time a letter arrived for Polly. It was from the Fotheringills telling her Veena had been saved. *One thing after another.*

'...The family are making life unbearable for her now she's joined our church and refuses to worship their idols. We must pray for her as we think it would be better if she moved away from home. She needs to get to know Christian men, too, or they'll force her to be unequally yoked to

an unbeliever. And we all know what a drastic mistake that can be.'

Polly was in her bedroom, pondering the plight of the new convert. *Torn from her family to serve a God they don't understand. At least mine weren't Hindu. She'll be intoxicated with happiness now, like I was – full of the Spirit. But will she regret rejecting her family, and how much will they suffer?* She massaged her temples firmly. *I felt guilty leaving the poor heathens to hell. Now I feel guilty for dragging them away from their own culture. Am I taking it too seriously? No! Deal with the guilt. Move on. We're all responsible for our own lives.*

She read Elaine's letter again. *What am I going to say?* She lay back against her pillow… *what will I dream tonight?*

CHAPTER 46

September 11th 2001 onwards

'It's eight whole years since I bought my dear little flat.' Polly and Nina were sitting in the kitchen of number 16, sipping coffee.

'Not that long, surely?' asked Nina.

'Getting away from Nessa and buying that flat was the most sensible thing I've done in my life!'

'You were smothered, weren't you? We were so pleased you managed to free yourself.'

Polly was in full agreement. 'Totally tied to apron-strings,' she smiled, 'not that she ever wore an apron. The worst thing was trying not to upset her and being true to myself at the same time. Humouring her in her belief she was healed…' Polly focused back on the present: 'anyway, yes *eight*. And I think it's time we celebrated! Just you and Vic, Walter and me.'

Nina leant forward, eyes bright, 'That's an idea. Walter is such fun.' But their expressions changed to alarm when they heard desperate thumping of fists on the back door. Nina dashed to open it.

'Turn on the telly! Turn it on!' Darren, shouting, red faced, wide eyes, frantic, dashed to the living room and turned on the TV himself.

'Whatever's wrong? What is it? You're *shaking*!'

Shocking, totally devastating news flashing from America. They stood rooted to the spot, aghast, till Darren, suddenly weak at the knees, collapsed into an armchair, horror-struck. The pictures showed New York, live. One of the Twin Towers in flames. Nina's brain changed gear when she remembered Darren's wife and boy were there. Her hand went to her mouth. Darren uttered 'Dot's there!' and with growing realisation. '*AND ROY! NO!*' his eyes were glued to the screen, and there, compounding the awfulness, another plane heading for the second tower. More flames and wreckage. Darren ran his hands through his hair, murmuring over and over, '*Dot and Roy.*'

So hard to believe. *Unreal.*

'Wait…' said Polly, thinking there must be some credible explanation. It was impossible to put two and two together.

No such hesitation for Nina or Darren.

'You *don't know* they're anywhere near there, Das. No one knows,' she said quietly, sitting on the arm of his chair and stroking his arm. Polly felt weak, incredulous. *It must be real*. She went to find a stiff drink and found a brandy. When she came back Nina was holding his hand – very tightly. He took the brandy absently, still shaking. Nina guided the glass to his mouth. The screen showed surreal scenes as if from science fiction. People on the upper floors realising there was no way to escape. Darren became increasingly distressed; one minute staring, another covering his face, getting up, sitting down. They were all horror struck.

His house was bombed, now this. Poor, poor Darren, thought Polly. *He couldn't be destined to suffer this torment too, surely.* Darren paced, then walked in a circle. 'I've got to get out there. I've got to go.' And he circled round again.

Nina lifted the handset and dialled Vic. Her hand unsteady, she dialled a wrong number. 'Damn it, Vic. Vic, where are you?'

It was mid-afternoon by the time Vic managed to get home: his colleagues all knew what was happening. They would soon find out more. Darren couldn't eat, only wanted to make plans. Between them they helped him pack and sort the house. The shock clouded their thinking. Vic wondered if Darren should wait until definite news came through. 'Mate, the airport might be closed.' But nothing could change Darren's determination. 'There might even be a problem getting into America,' said Vic, focused and serious.

'Then I'll go to Canada.' They saw him off early in the morning and promised to keep an eye on the house. It was a year before they saw him again.

CHAPTER 47

'It's time you got a computer,' said Vic as they were watching a new puppy roll around on the floor playing with a cardboard box and some old pyjamas.

'She is just so cute,' said Polly entranced – but what would I use it for?

'Write letters, keep information,' Nina said, 'you can store all sorts of files on it and…'

'Computers are the future,' Vic continued. 'They've got a lot more functions than a calculator.' He spoke to Walter, 'You'd find one useful for the theatre, too – bookings and so on.'

Polly thought her typewriter was sufficient: 'Do you know anything about them, Walt?' She nudged him.

'We're getting a supply at work, but they say it's easy to lose stuff and most people are tempted to throw them out of the window when they first get going. As for the theatre… those old biddies at the ticket desk?' He guffawed.

'You're meant to be on my side,' laughed Vic. Having Walter around encouraged him to be even more flippant than usual. He went to answer the hall telephone, still laughing.

'Hey! Darren's back next week,' he announced casually. Polly froze.

'Friend of yours?' questioned Walter.

*

There was only one person Polly could talk to about Darren: Piers. She went to St Mark's, mid-morning, and found him in the food store.

'Now let me get this straight: you thought you were over Darren, something terrible happened to him, you're upset, you don't want to hurt Walter.' He'd never seen Polly in such turmoil. He knew how, years ago Darren couldn't go along with her religious call and how unbending she'd been. He thought of the way she'd changed since he'd known her. *At least twenty years? She must be in her sixties.*

'Come here and calm down.' He held out his arms and kissed her gently. She felt grounded and exhaled noisily.

'I never expected this.' She couldn't articulate her reaction to Darren's situation. 'I'm all mixed up now. At *my* age, for God's sake. And *Darren – what he's been through.*'

'What difference does age make? You deserve a special person in your life after all your giving up this and that. Put yourself first for a change. Have you still got feelings for Darren then?'

'Yes – no. Not really, well maybe.' *I don't know.*

Piers studied her carefully. 'Do you know what sort of state he is in?'

'I haven't seen him. Vic and Nina say he needs distracting all the time. He can't even bring himself to go back to his old home yet.'

Piers heaved a box of tinned fruit into the bottom cupboard: 'They were lost, presumed dead?' Polly nodded silently.

'After Tony passed, I…' He was still too upset to put it into words… 'But in those circumstances… so much worse.' They were both silent, unmoving, contemplating.

'Dominic is an enormous support… he's not intrusive, helps me build up confidence. I still need help. I imagine Darren's going to need very gentle, tiny nudges – only when he's ready. Or nothing. I had time to prepare, but the sudden shock of *that*. I can't imagine. Far worse.'

Polly agreed. 'He's had support from other grieving relatives, and from professionals in New York. Now he's staying with a footy mate. Apparently, he kicks a football around on the playing field with one or two close friends; and that helps him to take his mind off things. But not for long.'

'He needs to find a way out of himself one way or another.'

'But you see, for me Walter,' she hesitated, 'you see, Walter—'

'—has muddied the waters.' Piers finished her sentence.

'Well, sort of – yes. But I'll…'

Piers said 'Just be there for Darren. Don't plan anything. Just *be*.'

She closed her eyes: 'No decisions. No pleading with God to work things out or trying to think out a solution. Stop thinking. Just be.'

*

A few weeks later Darren was sitting in Polly's flat. They were alone for the first time since their teens.

'Pol!' Darren was rubbing his fingers over his scalp agitated as though trying to be rid of something. Polly was doing her best to 'just be' and take her lead from him.

'Pol,' he started again. 'Could you ever imagine… *ever* imagine this happening?'

She shook her head but what could she say? She felt completely inadequate.

'No.'

'People try to be helpful,' he rambled. 'I'm still a mess… I can't even *think straight*.'

Polly felt close to tears herself. 'It's still early days, Das. Such early days.' She faded into reverie and they stopped talking while Darren kept moving around.

He walked to the window, full of indignation: 'Why did they do it?' he burst out loudly, repeating himself over and over in a whisper. He was hanging on to the curtain and twisting it round his neck. 'Why, Polly? You know all about God. Why, why?' It wasn't the first time he had asked the question. 'Polly, what makes people do such drastic things? So damnable. I still see those people driven to throwing themselves out of windows. I don't even know if Dot and Roy… I'll never know.' He banged his fists on the window frame, but fought back the tears and wouldn't let them flow. 'The thought… those people falling… it's never going to leave me, is it?'

Polly scratched her head, bewildered. She spontaneously came out with: 'There are people who feel guilty if they stand on a certain person's toe but...' She intended to add a comparison but caught Darren's eye, and they shared memories of her first attempt at dancing in high heels. For the first time since their long separation, they smiled slightly, both remembering the same instance. Shared youthful humour shot like an arrow into the gloom.

But seconds later: '*You* told me you were willing to die for God, you know.'

Is he accusing me or questioning? 'I felt that – at the time when I was trying to obey the Bible. And the nuns drummed the lives of the saints into us as if we all had to strive towards sainthood, to be unconditionally faithful, even if that meant being willing to die a terrible death.'

Darren was appalled, as if she understood nothing of his torment. But she ploughed on: 'One nun, I remember her making us live through the death of St Catherine. We had to visualise her arms outstretched circling around on the Catherine Wheel. Mother described the fire; the licking flames, burning skin, the pain, smell, smoke. We thought it was real. You could hear a pin drop. We must be ready to suffer like Catherine and I dedicated myself right then. '*Fidelis ad mortem* Faithful unto death.' I learnt that as a child. It was fixed. Never deny God however much I suffer.

She regretted describing the Catherine wheel so vividly after Darren's experience, but his mind was diverted.

'We were watching the cock chase the hens once and you said, "When the cock crows, remember Peter!" I thought of a chap in my class and asked you why on earth?'

Polly was staggered to think Darren still remembered that conversation. 'Silly me. I assumed you knew the story about the cock crowing like I did. I was trying to say you'd regret it later if you denied Jesus now. I so wanted you to be saved like me.'

Darren smiled wryly: 'You know I never had any truck with that. I thought religion was a girly thing, or for weak boys.'

Polly made a noise somewhere between a groan and a pig's snort.

Darren was calmer. He untangled himself from the curtain and studied the street. 'But you were a brick wall. Nothing I said made any difference. You were adamant. No dancing, beer, cards. It wasn't much fun, Pol.'

Polly reached out to his arm: 'Darren… I can see that now. I do know.'

But he pulled away, angry again.

'Those terrorists are just the same! They're obsessed with Allah and their own afterlife. It's just *Allah be praised* the same as you were bloody saved! They've got to please Allah and torturing infidels is part of the process.' He tore himself from the window, wiping the sweat from his face and slumping back in a chair, still holding most of his anger in. 'Every time I look at the sky… is there a plane coming?' Polly placed her back to the window, subconsciously trying to block the view. *I still have nightmares about those enormous bombers coming low over the house too… Shall I touch him? What shall I do?*

'I wasn't as bad as *that*… was I?' she asked, meekly. Darren rubbed his eyes. 'But, I suppose, in a way…' She didn't know how to put it.

'It's called indoctrination, Pol.' Darren shook as he spoke. 'I watched every stage of it happening to you, and can imagine what happened to them.'

'You're saying you're my victim, as well as theirs?'

He nodded grimly. 'We're both victims, I suppose. Polly, they blew my boy, my darling wife to smithereens!' And this time he was inconsolable, dissolving into heaving sobs, mouth drooling, eyes and nose freely running. After a while he rallied. 'They were stolen by the same GOD, just wearing a different costume! And there was Mum, my dog, my home. My dear loving mother – killed by the Nazis.' He spluttered between the sobs: 'All these convictions, addictions, ideologies, whatever… they grab a person's attention; start to satisfy inner cravings; it's only their own hobby horse, but it grows and then gets big. Really BIG. People get consumed by one notion. It's contagious, crowds are sucked in convinced nothing else matters.' He couldn't stop.

No words fitted the heart-wrenching pit he was in. Polly, sat on the arm of the chair, put her arm around him and drew him close. This time he didn't pull away. They wept together.

CHAPTER 48

Polly walked up the drive to The Elms Nursing Home soon after the episode with Darren, her thoughts occupied with trying to make sense of what happened. James was comfortably settled in a downstairs bedroom overlooking the back garden. He was sitting by the French doors, Zimmer nearby, and happy to see his daughter.

'Hello, Dad. How are you today?'

'All the better for seeing you!' His voice was shaky and legs swollen.

'He needs to get back to bed soon,' a nurse called in the door.

Polly drew a chair up so she could hold his hand: 'Dad, it's such a lovely day, and you look good!'

'I love watching the birds from here. There's quite a few finches today; more than usual.'

'They knew I was coming!' said Polly.

'Now why didn't I think of that?' He leant back in his chair.

Polly tightened her grip of his hand. 'Dad, I want to ask a question.'

'Anything to do with Darren, pet?'

Polly liked his calling her *pet*.

'In a way, but I doubt…'

'So, you're not getting married before your old Pop pops off?'

'Dad! Don't be daft!'

'It won't be long now you know, my dear.'

'Oh, Dad,' she grasped his hand with both of hers. It was no use arguing, she knew he was probably right. They just kept holding hands for a while.

'What were you going to ask, then?'

'Well, Dad, you know how I let Darren down all those years ago?'

'I don't know if letting him down is the right way of putting it, but I enjoyed thinking of him as my son-in-law,' mused James.

'I never thought of that.' She paused, thinking for the first time how it must have seemed from her father's point of view. 'Aww, Dad... yes sorry.'

'Water under the bridge, isn't it?' He smiled. 'We can't exactly do anything about that now.'

'No. But... well, this might sound a bit extreme...'

His reactions were slow but he spoke with certainty: 'I'm used to extreme. Tell me...'

'When I was so wrapped up in the Church and so sure I was right, was I behaving like the terrorists who killed Dot and Roy?'

James jolted his eyes wide: 'Of course not, Polly! What on earth made you think that?'

'Darren made a comment. He sort of indicated I was like them and...'

'Arrrr. Darren is still deeply affected by the unspeakable atrocities that have wiped out his family. He's angry and mourning. He'll regret it later.'

'I know, Dad. But that really hit home. It hurt terribly, although I'm deeply sorry for him.'

'Of course you are. Those people leave their families, even young babies, to go and fight... even put on a suicide jacket for the sake of their religion.'

'And I left you, Mum, Vic, and tiny Nicola – home.'

'Your poor mum, I couldn't help her.'

'Yes, Mum. I was a heartless daughter.'

'But at least you didn't go around killing infidels.'

'But I was genuinely willing to die for God.'

'I knew you were a good person underneath, Pol. And looking back I understand you tried your best to do the right thing.'

'But was Mum like that because of me?'

'You were young and headstrong. We couldn't understand what was happening to you. And your mother—'

'She just wanted me to stay at home although she was cranky all the time. I didn't know what was going on for her but I couldn't stand it. I had to get away.' Polly was getting tense.

'After the last time you visited she never asked for you again. But she never made much sense after that, and then when she faded away we knew you couldn't get home.'

Polly closed her eyes and sat still for a while. Then said in small voice: 'Sorry, Dad.'

'I can't say you had nothing to do with your mum's problem, but, Pol, it wasn't your fault she was like that.' James nodded slowly. 'You never knew your grandmother, did you?' he asked. 'She died when you were about two.'

Polly's attention was captured. She'd never learnt anything about her grandmother.

'She expected Vera to be at her beck and call until the day she died. Mum never knew any other way. Never had any freedom as a teenager – not even after we were married. Ma lived with us you know.'

'Really? How did you two meet up then?'

'We were at school together! I kept my eye on her, and eventually we managed to sneak time together.'

'Poor Mum. So that was her only life.'

'But, unlike me or your mother, you had strong religious inclinations. When we let you go to Sunday school we just thought it would keep you busy on Sunday afternoons. That backfired on us.'

James was giving her new food for thought; information she couldn't process immediately.

'Dad!' She kissed his frail hand. 'I wish I'd known.'

'We can't change the past. In some ways you reminded me of my own regrets. I should've enlisted in the army, but I was adamant it was wrong to kill. But enough. Let's talk about more cheerful things, pet. Don't berate yourself. You're a chip off the old block and I'm proud of you, the way you stuck to your principles.'

'Thank you, Dad.'

He let his head droop. But then looked up at her quizzically, 'Nina says you've changed your mind about religion and so on. Tell me, pet... what about the Bible these days?'

'It's a good book, Dad,, but I don't think... well, I mean, I can see now you can prove anything from it if you choose your verses. I don't know the answers any longer.'

'I've been waiting a long time to hear you say that. A long, long time.'

Polly sucked in her lips thoughtfully: 'Oh, Dad. It's great to say "I don't know" without feeling guilty.' She looked out of the window and then back at James. 'You've no idea what a relief that is.' He was nearly asleep but she knew he was listening. She sat while he had a little nap.

Then he continued to quietly describe his thoughts to his daughter. Only a fly on the wall could see how much the conversation meant to them.

When he'd had enough, Polly stood up. 'The theatre club is such fun, Dad, and Walter has us in fits of laughter.'

His tired eyes sparkled: 'Next time you come, share a few of the laughs with me!' He nodded off again.

'I'll bring Walter next time and we'll have you splitting your sides, Dad. You just wait.' She kissed him, as it transpired, for the last time.

CHAPTER 49

In my wildest dreams
I never thought I'd love God and go to church...
Me, Mags! Yes, Me.
The rebel.
Angry, because I had nothing and had to beg and steal.
Now, bloomin' amazing. I love singing HYMNS!
Yes! I have a wild side, but I've got a good man.
Max is top drawer and I love my two boys.
They read and write and love me.
What would I have done without Nick? (Reg doesn't suit him).
Dead now, bless him. Still looking out for me like under the arch.
And I see him in Max. Wonderful Max.
One day just followed another on the streets until
The BIG THING happened. The 'Creeper' in the market.
'Fag,' I said to myself. 'Rip him off.' He looked easy prey.
Bulky shopping bag. 'Food,' I thought. I was hungry.
His clean crisp shirt! All new. He must have money! I wondered often about having money.
Then – I bumped into him. He thought it was his fault.
This really hard thing hit me in the face and I was shocked to see it was a CRUCIFIX!
I didn't think twice. Went for him, swearing, spitting, and angry.

But what did he say?

Of all things he said, 'Pardon me!'

Pardon me!

No! I'd never heard that said before. Never. And certainly not to me.

What did he mean? He was staring at the ground. Pardon me?

He wasn't angry like everyone else.

I had to get the bag! I got close to his face and held his eye. I held his wavering eye and saw bewildered care.

'God bless you, my child,' he whispered.

*What? WHAT the **** (trying not to swear now).*

'Quick. Grab the bag and Go,' I told myself. 'Run!'

That moment was the turning point. BIG CHANGE started.

Whatever it was, I don't know, but something awoke in me.

I think it was the Crucifix! It must have been the crucifix. Jesus kissed me!

Now I know love. I know Creeper's prayer came true. Mr Anthony loved me; I think (rest his soul). Such a special person.

And God loves me. God has definitely blessed me!

CHAPTER 50

'Dad would have a fit if he were still alive!' Vic aimed the sledgehammer at the wall between the dining room and kitchen.

'My muscles!' He collapsed onto the floor and leant against a remaining wall, holding the hammer out to Darren. *Crash! Crash.* Darren replied, but the words were lost in the noise of falling masonry. Dust flew all over the house. Vic stretched and flexed his arms.

'SHUT the bloody door to the hall, VICTOR!' Nina pushed the vacuum cleaner viciously around the landing. *Chump! He's got no idea how much work he's making for me.* Vic's retirement project was turning into more than they'd bargained for. The banging stopped. 'You got any idea what the time is?' Nina yelled downstairs.

A muffled, 'Good God!' followed by a sneeze could just be made out, then discussing takeaways. She went downstairs and shouted through the door: 'See you round the back.' She made her way through the front door and down the side passage. '*Look at you two*!' She burst into laughter. 'Just keep away from me!'

Darren and Vic flopped on the grass worn out. The late afternoon sun was warm and soporific. Nina brought out three cold beers. 'We must be mad,' said Darren, yawning.

'Yes,' answered Vic slowly. 'Could have been lazing around in the sun.'

'*You* sunbathing?' Nina mocked. 'That'll be the day.' After a while she lifted herself onto one elbow. 'Polly's asked if we want to go round to her place this evening. She and Walter are explaining the drama club ticketing system to Beth. She's trying a spot of volunteering at the theatre now she has some spare time.'

'Decent grub?' asked Vic, more interested in his stomach than dramatics, or being sociable.

'Chinese.'

'Okay, suits me. You, Das?'

Darren rolled over onto his side picking blades of grass absentmindedly. 'I'm in food-wise, but I don't go a bundle on Walter.'

'What d'you mean?'

'Can't quite make him out,' Vic and Nina stared at him. 'Nor Polly, these days, come to think of it.'

'Walter's lovely,' said Nina. 'So good for Polly, and they probably aren't quite sure what to make of you either.' Darren rolled over with exaggerated effort and looked at Vic with a questioning frown.

'Mate,' said Victor, 'you know me. I don't go in for this soft stuff, but I *know* you and I wonder—'

'—what's going on with me?' Darren finished Vic's sentence. He thumped the ground with his fist. Vic spotted the warning sign and stood up. *Be positive or Das'll spiral down into himself.* He bent over and pulled Darren up by the arm.

'Take the bull by the horns, mate. Get a shower, and we'll all go out. Let's not get into psyche stuff now, Das, just think about the food.' Nina loved the way her husband knew exactly how to deal with Darren. *Funny really, considering he doesn't do personal.*

*

An hour later they pricked up their ears at the sound of raucous laughter as Nina rang the bell of Polly's flat. A flushed Polly opened the door and wiped her eyes, 'Come and enjoy the show,' she laughed.

'What's going on?' asked Vic, always ready for fun.

'Walter's a hoot when he gets going! He's describing a scene they're rehearsing for *The Lady Killers*. I don't know how he ever keeps a straight face on stage.'

'Are you going on stage too, Polly?' Darren asked.

Polly felt that glimmer of the warmth they'd shared in days gone by as she went for the drinks. 'Joke!' she called back from the kitchen. 'Oh yes, very funny. Just costumes for me!'

They settled in the sitting room where Walter was sitting on a stool, legs akimbo round the upright vacuum cleaner, feather duster in left hand. He looked up. 'Ready for action?' He rested the feather duster on the cleaner with the aplomb of a cello-player in the Albert Hall. Darren, taken unawares by the change of mood from builder's mate and introspection to the group camaraderie and clowning he'd been dragged into, spat out his drink as his mouth exploded with uncontrolled mirth. He wiped his face and grinned at Walter's farcical rendition of classical music. Polly was singing along then stopped and doubled up laughing as the duster and cleaner were tossed hastily away and Walter grabbed a spare mop cover, putting it on his head. Then he impersonated a smart little old lady. With posh, clipped, falsetto voice 'she' asked, 'And what did you say that was?' As he grabbed the mop cover off and recovered his cello-playing role, he revelled in the delight of his audience. Used to controlling his humour, his mouth twitched, but he managed to announce seriously, with deliberately unposh pronunciation: 'Luigi Boccherini's *Minuetto*!' before giving in to humour and joining in the laughter of the other five.

'That'll be the neighbours complaining!' said Polly getting up to answer the door.

'Or wanting to join in,' said Vic. They all had their own take on the motive of the caller, and were all wrong. It was the takeaway. Beth sorted the food while Polly poured wine, and ginger beer for herself.

'Just what the doctor ordered,' said Vic, as they sat eating on their laps, second helpings on the coffee table.

'So, you're going to do the tickets, Beth?' Darren was trying hard to be at ease in the group of friends. They all stared at Beth waiting for an answer.

'Hmmm,' said Polly.

'That's a leading question!' chuckled Walter. 'Ain't it, gal?' He had a way of lightening the atmosphere at awkward moments.

Darren grimaced. 'What?' He picked up his drink. 'I thought…' They waited with bated breath for the pregnant silence to end. Even the chewing ceased.

'Okay. I'll do it!' She smiled at Walter who missed his mouth and spilt satay down his front.

This time it was Polly who jumped into the awkward moment, 'So how's the retirement project doing? Wearing yourselves out?'

Vic twisted his mouth to one side, slightly dubious. I… we…' He waited for Darren's opinion.

'Rather wish we hadn't started?' Darren echoed Vic's thoughts exactly.

'WHAT?' Polly and Nina were both aghast.

'You said it wouldn't take long when I agreed to it,' Nina accused.

'Yes, well…'

'Thank goodness you agreed to help,' said Nina to Darren.

'I'm enjoying myself actually. Realised that after I got going with the hammer. Just what I needed. It is rather a mess though.'

Walter picked up the feather duster and tickled Polly's neck: 'Music while you work then?' Beth giggled.

Polly smiled and pushed the duster back into Walter's face, spreading the sweet and sour further afield. She addressed Darren: 'When he gets in the mood, he's an awful tease!'

'Yes,' said Nina finding it impossible not to laugh at Walter with sweet and sour around his face and down his shirt, 'he gets in the zone, then that's it!'

'Anybody would think you were a load of teenagers,' said Vic surveying the scene.

'And why not?' retorted Walter, wiping the feather duster with his not so clean handkerchief. 'We're not pensioners *yet*.'

Polly studied each head of hair for signs of grey. 'No, not quite.'

It did them all good to forget work, and pain, and lose themselves in the mood of the moment. No further mention was made of the wall, or of Darren's state of being. They all topped up their glasses and chatted about the theatre club and the coming production of *The Lady Killers*.

'I might join the club myself,' Darren said uncertainly, stealing a glance at Walter who didn't appear to consider him a threat in any way.

'Yes, why not!' said Polly putting her hand on his knee. 'Don't you think that's a brilliant idea?' She scanned the group.

Walter threw the feather duster in the air and flung his arms wide. 'Yippee!' he yelled. 'Another member!'

'Walter!' Polly scolded. 'That's got sauce all over it!' but she was smiling. It didn't really seem to matter.

*

'It's my bedtime!' announced Nina. 'Are you staying with your footy pal tonight, Darren? You know you're welcome to come to us, don't you?'

'You can sleep in the kitchen!' joked Vic, and they all laughed again.

'I don't know what I'd do without you. But yes thanks, I'm going to Jake's.'

They stood up. 'Want to stay over, Walter?' asked Polly. He hesitated. 'You're welcome.'

He gave in. 'Oh, might be a good idea, thanks.' Darren was surprised that no one batted an eyelid when Polly and Walter waved them goodbye.

'That did me good,' said Nina as the group walked down the hill together.'

'And me,' said Beth. 'I hadn't realised what a character Walter is!'

'You'll get to know him better at the club,' said Vic. Then, on second thoughts. 'And you would too, Das. You *must* join.'

'You think it would be all right?'

'Of course!' Walter was over the moon at recruiting *two* new members.

Beth linked Darren's arm. 'Come on, it'll be fun, won't it?'

Darren still sounded doubtful. He spoke quietly into Beth's ear: 'Does Walter know our past history, Polly and me?'

'There isn't much Walter hasn't wheedled out of Polly!' Beth chuckled, then light dawned. She looked at Vic then lifted her arm to Darren's shoulder, pulling him towards her. 'Walt is like another Anthony to Polly – only far way less serious – just what Polly needs. He's done her the world of good. You *do* know he's gay, don't you?' His shoulders dropped. Beth sensed relief.

*

Darren and Vic were transferring rubble to the front garden. 'You going to the theatre club, then Das… see what you think?'

Darren hesitated. 'I've been thinking… but what could I do there?'

Nina overheard, and called from the window, 'I'll come with you if you like! I quite fancy seeing what they get up to backstage.'

'If you really think it's a good idea, I'll come along with you. Thanks! What time?'

They rang Polly, and discovered she would be working on costumes Monday evening for a performance later in the year. She'd show them round for an hour after she'd finished and then they could nip round to the chippy.

'Sounds like a plan,' said Darren, feeling lighter than he had since 9/11.

'Eight p.m. Monday. We'll have to meet there,' said Nina. 'I'll be helping out with the Stroke Club till seven thirty. That all right then?'

Darren arrived on the dot of eight and as he couldn't see Nina, he went to find Polly. She was hanging elaborate clothes on a rail. They were not the sort he expected. 'These aren't for *The Lady Killers* surely?'

Polly sniggered. 'No, no, no! They'll be wearing their own gear for that. Just everyday things. This lot is for a period drama in the autumn. We always work way ahead. But clothes aren't your strong point really, are they?' She thought back to their school days. 'Remember that dress I made for the ball? It was horrible – and you didn't mind at all!'

'Didn't I?'

'No, see! You don't even remember it. I'll never forget it, but at the time I felt quite proud of myself!'

'That's the point,' said Darren, seemingly remembering more of how he felt back then. 'You were always so positive and made the most of everything. I expect I liked it because you made it yourself and you were wearing it! You were such good fun.'

'But then things changed,' filled in Polly, wistfully, before hastily changing the subject. 'Anyway, let's see if we can find Walter, or anyone working on props. That might be more your department.' It was. Besides showing Darren the workroom and tools, he demonstrated lighting and sound.

Darren was fascinated. 'You need your wits about you to operate all this…'

Walter nodded. 'We aim for a smooth run…'

'We can definitely say that it is our aim,' said Polly, grinning at Walter who burst into laughter.

'We could tell you some cracking stories!'

'Do you want to entertain us over at the chippy then?' asked Polly.

'I promised Mum I'd help her with the television after this…' He addressed Darren, joking: 'Will have to leave you in suspense until next time, muscleman.' Polly feigned disappointment but Darren suddenly blinked and searched the room.

'Where's Nina? She hasn't turned up.' He looked at Polly.

'Oh, I forgot to pass her message on.'

'Something wrong?' Darren reacted with alarm. Polly stroked his arm.

'It's alright. I forgot. One of the Stroke Club folks needed an ambulance and she was the only one who could go with her. She'll come another week. She said to say sorry to you.'

'I wouldn't have come by myself you know.' Darren wasn't sure where to put himself.

'Save me a chip!' Walter winked at Darren who hesitated then took the plunge carefully assessing Polly's response. 'Just us, then?'

It was Walter who replied full of his usual bonhomie, 'I think you'll manage alright by yourselves. Give me a ring if you get lost or what-not!'

Polly, slightly flushed, gave Walter a quick kiss on the cheek, then replied: 'We will. Thanks, Walt.'

Turning to Darren, she said, 'Just us!'

*

They sat opposite each other, in the furthest corner of the fish shop away from the deep fryer and counter where people queued for takeaways.

'This has bought back memories now, Pol,' they shared a rare moment of contemplation.

'I'm not sure if we want to go there, but I really want to apologise to you. I'm sorry I became so one-track-minded after I found the baptist church and my supposed calling. I only thought of myself, and I was so sure I was right.' She put a hand on top of Darren's hands clasped on the table. She looked straight at him, 'It's late now. But I'm so, so, sorry.'

He gave the impression of having understood what Polly was saying. 'In a way it was good for me. I learnt so much about myself. Learning engineering at Uni was a great experience. It was absolutely the right thing for me and I've done such interesting work – well, technically, still do – I'm not properly retired even though I've been off since...you know.'

'I know.'

'I can't seem to get back.'

His mood blackened and between gritted teeth. Throwing Polly's hand off and thumping his fist on the table, he said, 'I can't get myself back to consulting, and I still can't live in my house.' He turned red and angry, 'My home, my dammed home! I don't even know why I built on that site with such dreadful memories.' He moaned, 'Oh... Pol what shall I do?'

They sat in silence. Eventually Polly said quietly: 'I don't really like thinking about number 14 either. I still only see it as a bombsite. S'pose 'cos that's all I grew up with.'

Darren calmed and looked up. He shook his head as though ridding himself of the past, then rested his chin in his hands, elbows on the table, and stared at her with determination. 'Well then. We'll have to say good-bye to that place and find somewhere cosy that suits us, won't we?' His mood had changed. Polly did a double take. Swallowed.

We? Us?

The food arrived. Polly sprinkled salt over the chips and the table, mind in a whirl. She said nothing, but handed Darren the salt. He studied her, then picked up a chip and offered it to her lips.

ACKNOWLEDGEMENTS

A big thank you to all who have helped me to write my story.

Thanks to Cannongate Books Ltd, Palantine Books and Bernard Cornwell for permission to use quotations.

And thanks to New Generation Publishing for all their help.

Milton Keynes UK
Ingram Content Group UK Ltd.
UKHW040015191024
449863UK00004B/53

9 781800 310476